PRAISE FOR CHRISTINE NOLFI

"[*Sweet Lake*] has such a charming small-town vibe and endearing characters that readers will find themselves falling in love with quirky Sweet Lake and hoping for a series."

—*Booklist*

"In this uplifting and charming story, each room of the inn is filled with friendship, forgiveness, and love."

—*Kirkus Reviews*

"Craving a literary trifecta of romance, small-town drama, and soul searching? That's exactly what you'll find in Linnie Wayfair's life as she tries to restore an inn in Sweet Lake, Ohio, to glory—all while navigating affairs of the heart. This is the literary answer to *Gilmore Girls* withdrawals, and we don't give that compliment lightly."

—Marina Kendrick, YourTango.com

"In her endearing style, Nolfi delivers a cast of quirky characters and a suspense-filled plot in a story you won't want to end!"

—Patricia Sands, author of the Love in Provence series

"Nolfi's characters are believable, fun, and easy to love. You'll want to visit the town of Sweet Lake time and again. Highly recommended."

—Bette Lee Crosby, *USA Today* bestselling author

Second Chance

"Nolfi writes with a richnes̶   ng."

̶ *Fetish*

"An emotionally moving contemporary novel about the power that relationships have to transform lives."

—Susan Bethany, *The Midwest Book Review*

The Tree of Everlasting Knowledge

"Poignant and powerful, *The Tree of Everlasting Knowledge* is as much a saga of learning how to survive, heal, and forgive as it is a chilling crime story, unforgettable to the very end."

—Margaret Lane, *The Midwest Book Review*

The Comfort of Secrets

ALSO BY CHRISTINE NOLFI

The Sweet Lake Series

Sweet Lake (Book 1)

The Comfort of Secrets (Book 2)

The Liberty Series

Second Chance Grill (Book 1)

Treasure Me (Book 2)

The Impossible Wish (Book 3)

Four Wishes (Book 4)

The Tree of Everlasting Knowledge (Book 5)

The Dream You Make

Heavenscribe: Part One

Heavenscribe: Part Two

Heavenscribe: Part Three

The Shell Keeper (Kindle Worlds Novella)

The Shell Seeker (Kindle Worlds Novella)

The Comfort of Secrets

A Sweet Lake Novel

CHRISTINE NOLFI

LAKE UNION
PUBLISHING

Text copyright © 2017 Christine Nolfi
All rights reserved.

Published by Lake Union Publishing, Seattle

www.apub.com

Amazon, the Amazon logo, and Lake Union Publishing are trademarks of Amazon.com, Inc., or its affiliates.

ISBN-13: 9781542045711
ISBN-10: 1542045711

Cover design by Rachel Adam Rogers

Printed in the United States of America

For Alan and Ruth
I am honored to know the former,
and I wish I had met the latter

Chapter 1

The poster wagged before her nose: SAGE ADVICE: THYME TO DISCOVER NATURE'S MEDICINE—RIGHT IN YOUR SPICE RACK!

Speechless, Cat Mendoza shrank back in her chair.

"These are merely rough ideas." Behind thick eyeglasses, the elderly Penelope Riddle beamed. She shook the homemade poster. "Your new ad agency should design the posters to hang around the Wayfair."

The urge to duck beneath the desk proved tempting. At half past eight in the morning, Cat didn't relish dealing with a group of excitable women. She'd arrived to find several of the Sweet Lake Sirens lurking outside her office like merry vultures.

"You're proposing a talk on the medicinal properties of herbs? Interesting," she murmured, thinking, *Not.*

"We have oodles of great ideas."

"You do?"

"The Sirens will host different talks each season for the Wayfair's guests. We'll fill out your whole event calendar."

A sensation of doom sidled toward Cat. Ideas from the Sirens spelled disaster.

The activities under her current consideration ran along the lines of wine tastings for couples or family boating excursions on Sweet Lake. A stroll through the forest with a local naturalist, or an afternoon cooking class with the Wayfair's chef. An event calendar hijacked by the town's most eccentric women would hurt the inn's marketing efforts before they began.

Three of the Sirens hemmed in her desk. Politely she asked them, "You're proposing these talks year-round?" Nix the idea before the presentation ended, and they'd never leave.

The diminutive Tilda Lyons stepped forward. "We have more than enough ideas. Want to hear my favorite?"

"Do I have a choice?"

Evidently not, since the perky Realtor held up her poster. Another homemade job, this one done with purple Magic Marker and orange glitter. Handing the posters off to Adworks, as if the ideas held merit, didn't appeal. In despair, Cat read the pitch.

Then she gasped.

STILL ANGRY? REACH LOVED ONES IN THE AFTERLIFE AND HAVE THE LAST WORD.

Tilda gave the poster a shake. "Don't you love it?"

"It's spooky." The sensation of doom threatened to swallow Cat whole.

"You'd feel differently if you were peeved at someone who'd crossed over." The Siren turned to her comrades, adding, "I have a friend in Columbus who found out her husband was a cheater after he kicked. Talk about unfinished business."

The disclosure rounded Penelope's eyes. "Your poor friend. How many women?"

"Nine on speed dial. One was an exotic dancer. She does an act with a snake and red tassels—I checked out her website." Tilda shook her head with disgust, sending her cinnamon-colored locks swishing across her cheeks. "How's any wife supposed to compete with a python?"

"She can't!" Penelope cried.

"Which is why my friend deserves the last word. Frankly, she deserves a sit-down with Saint Peter." Tilda's eyes flashed. "Her cheating husband has earned a ticket to hell."

Tilda's previously hidden dark side gave Cat pause. "Let's put a hold on your idea," she said carefully. "Mostly because lots of families booking rooms have young children." *And it'll creep out the guests.*

A defeat, but the Realtor stood her ground like an avenging fairy prepared to send unfaithful husbands straight to hell.

"We won't hold séances or do anything to scare kids," Tilda assured her. "We were thinking about training in dream interpretation for adults."

"I don't understand."

"People who've entered the next world make contact through dreams. Once you learn the basics of interpretation, you direct your subconscious to give them a piece of your mind."

Dish out a verbal smackdown while snoozing? Probably not the best way to get into deep REM sleep. Astonished by her own curiosity, Cat asked, "What about the people you're not mad at?"

"Oh, that's different. You can use the dreaming hours to catch up with loved ones you haven't seen in a while. Like sitting around the kitchen table with your favorite people, only you're asleep."

Teatime with the dead. Still too spooky for Cat's taste. She fished around for a way to shoo the women out.

As if on cue, her smartphone buzzed.

Before she could pick up, the striking Norah Webb—by far more intimidating than the avenging fairy—shot her a black look. Letting the phone go silent, Cat dropped her hands into her lap.

Why did the women choose today of all days to barge into her makeshift office? *Makeshift* being the operative word. Until recently, the cramped space had served as an extra storage room for the kitchen staff.

The pinewood shelving was now gone, the trails of sugar and flour swept from the floor. A pleasing citrus fragrance still clung to the air— from lemons or oranges, or a delectable combination of both. The air also contained thuds, bangs, and the occasional shouted command.

The kitchen lay on the other side of the wall, and breakfast service was in full swing.

Compared to the women herding around the desk, knocking elbows and jostling to talk over one another, the noise marking the inn's breakfast rush was subdued.

Only Ruth Kenefsky hung back. She leaned against the doorjamb, her oddly girlish braids framing her leathery face. The retired police dispatcher seemed content to guard the door while the others pitched ideas sure to derail Cat's marketing plans. With her thumbs hitched inside the pockets of her unfashionable jeans, Ruth looked like she was gearing up for the shootout at the OK Corral.

What goofy suggestions would they pose next? As the daughter of a Sweet Lake Siren, Cat didn't relish ousting the women without a fair hearing. The group, whose members were mostly middle-aged or older, was as integral to Sweet Lake, Ohio, as the historic inn where she found herself trapped.

Penelope looked to her expectantly. "Well? What do you think so far?"

"About hosting seminars?" Cat produced a manufactured smile. "Gosh, I don't know. We're just getting the inn back on its feet. We aren't ready to consider activities for the guests." A lie, but a better way to spare Penelope's feelings didn't come to mind.

Norah said, "Getting the Wayfair back to healthy profits affects us all. Think of the businesses that'll reopen. A fresh start for the town— you'd do well to thank us for helping with the effort."

"And your help is appreciated . . . later. I have a big meeting tomorrow—lots to prepare beforehand. May I get back to you?"

"No, you may not. We've spent days working out the kinks for each talk." Norah produced a notepad from her oversize purse, a leather number artfully decorated with tiny gold beads. "We'll finish this now."

Heart sinking, Cat stole a glance out the window. Trees danced in the gusting September breeze. Farther off, men crawled across the roof of the south wing, the hammers in their tool belts glinting in the sun.

"We shouldn't discuss this without Linnie," she said of the inn's manager and majority stockholder. "She's busy overseeing the renovations and doesn't have time to spare. Perhaps we can all get together later, like in November?"

Norah peered down her hawkish nose. "Weren't you recently promoted?"

True enough. With Linnie's blessing, she'd taken charge of a generous advertising budget with the freedom to steer the inn's long-term marketing plan. Cat's good fortune still felt surreal. Given the foolish mistakes she'd made in the past, the do over was an undeserved gift, an opportunity to spread good karma.

She refused to waste the chance.

"I'm still the hospitality manager," she said. "Same old, same old. I can't make decisions without Linnie's go-ahead."

"You're also now the events director, in charge of the on-site promotions Linnie plans to implement. You don't need her approval to make a decision."

Caught beneath the heavy-lidded stare, Cat understood why children in town believed her adversary kept a broom at the ready. In her early sixties, Norah gave her flowing silver hair added beauty with distinctive plum streaks. It was a new look for the formerly raven- haired Siren. A runway model in her youth, she had buried four husbands. Her personal tragedy led to wild gossip about the danger to any man charmed by her arresting grey eyes.

For today's surprise attack she wore hip-hugging black jeans, a silk T-shirt, and a gorgeous hand-knitted vest of plum and azure. Long fringe hung from the vest. The shells wagging on the ends of the fringe clicked furiously around her knees.

Cat swallowed. "Okay, you've got me," she confessed. "I'm in charge. Linnie's too busy to hang over my shoulder. She's having new carpeting laid in some of the guest rooms this week, and the painters are wrapping up in the lobby."

"Then make a decision."

"We're still in the planning stages. Might be months before we host activities for the guests." She licked her parched lips. "Years, maybe."

Penelope, a more agreeable adversary, wrenched the notepad from Norah's grasp. The owner of Gift of Garb, the consignment shop in town, adjusted her eyeglasses.

"Norah, stop scaring her." Penelope's rheumy gaze scanned the notes.

"I'm not trying to scare her. I *would* like to knock some sense into her. She's being obstinate."

"She hasn't asked us to leave, has she?"

"I haven't," Cat agreed. Norah wasn't violent, but her tongue could eviscerate the mightiest opponent. Remaining on her good side was a smart plan.

In a lively tone, Penelope said, "Here's a perfect idea for women of a certain age. 'Helpful Hot Flashes: Sweating Your Way to a Thinner You.'" Delight shivered across her double chin. "A chat on the benefits of menopause will help lots of women avoid fear of the aging process."

Cat's smile froze in place. If this was the best idea, she dreaded hearing the worst.

She didn't have long to wait.

"I have another. We'll host this one for older couples." Penelope gazed at her with fizzy excitement. "Ready?"

"No."

"Oh, you'll love this—promise! 'Sex in the Twilight Years: Myth or Magic?'"

Drumming up a response wasn't necessary. By the door, Ruth unleashed her gravelly voice. "A myth, if you ask me," she growled.

"Haven't seen a man in my bed since the turn of the century. If one's hiding beneath the covers, I would've found him by now."

Norah threw an impatient glance her way. "You can't possibly believe sex is reserved only for young adults like Cat. Why, if the right man came along, I'd want to enjoy him in every way." Her disapproving regard took a stroll across Ruth's high-waisted jeans before stalling at her plaid, mannish shirt. "If you're looking for romance, retire your Western wear. This isn't Texas. There are no rodeos scheduled."

"Meaning I should dress like a filly half my age?" Ruth examined her nails, which were as blunt as her personality. "I'll let you in on a secret, Norah. Designer duds won't land you a fifth husband."

"I'm not looking for a fifth husband."

"Paint me surprised. With all the cash you spend on glam, I assumed you had an itch you wanted some poor bastard to scratch."

The shells on Norah's vest clacked madly as she swiveled toward her opponent. "Must you resort to vulgar language? I dress to please myself and no one else."

"Suit yourself. Just keep in mind every bachelor in town believes you're deadlier than a black widow."

Norah's expression evolved from irritated to thunderous. Trouble on the horizon.

"If I choose to find love again, I won't waste my time rooting beneath the covers in hopes of finding a warm body," she announced. "Wishing isn't necessary with the proper attitude. The perfect man is sure to arrive if my heart beckons. It only takes time."

The remark drew a sigh from Cat. For years she'd searched for the right man. Fate wasn't listening, or didn't care—the men dropped in her path possessed the charm of garden snails, or they stuck her with the check on dinner dates. The rest played around, like the cheater Tilda would bar from the pearly gates. All she had to show for her efforts was the blow-up man received as a joke gift from Linnie.

Beefcake Bill valiantly guarded Cat's suite in the south wing, but he wasn't much company on lonely nights.

The argument between the Sirens escalated, and Tilda planted herself between them. Her pacifist tendencies, though admirable, didn't make her trustworthy. The fortyish Siren had a deplorable habit of texting the latest gossip the moment it pinged her smartphone.

"Ladies, please! Let's not waste time on petty arguments." The Realtor tapped a manicured finger on the notepad in Penelope's fist. "You have the floor, Penelope. Tell Cat the next idea."

"Go for it," Cat said, thinking, *I should kill my agreeable nature with black widow venom.*

Faking interest, she tamped down her growing impatience. Tomorrow her old college roommate would arrive. Although they were no longer close, Miri Blum, the owner of Adworks, had been offering guidance and expertise for over a month now. Would the new marketing campaign put the Wayfair back on the map of great travel destinations in the Midwest?

A monumental task, and Cat dreaded failing.

❧

"*¡Mi florecita!*" At the stove, Marco Mendoza opened his arms wide.

Cat grinned at the apron covering his barrel chest and the small potbelly he'd grown since retirement. **I Cook. You Clean.** No doubt he'd found the apron in Penelope's consignment shop. An understandable purchase, since the war over dish duty often raged in her parents' household. They viewed this as a real problem since they enjoyed cooking lavish meals together and neither liked cleanup.

He wrapped her in a bear hug, then held her at arm's length. "How is my little flower today?"

"I'm tired, Papa." She peered at the top of his head, which was bald as an egg and covered with angry red blotches. Tufts of salt-and-pepper hair surrounded the sunburned skin. "Were you gardening without a hat again?" His culinary abilities were matched only by his green thumb.

"The little kisses from the sun? I hardly feel them."

"You're getting as silly as Mami." Cat was forever dropping off bottles of suntan lotion her mother rarely used. "If you're spending the afternoon outdoors, wear a hat."

"Ah, you worry too much." He flicked the colorful earring swinging from her ear.

"Is Val coming for dinner?" Cat's older sister, Valentina, was the social studies teacher at Sweet Lake High. In a lucky coincidence, she'd applied for the position the year Marco decided forty years of teaching social studies was long enough.

"Val's busy. Waiting for a furniture delivery."

"She bought that new couch for her apartment?" Val had been mulling over the purchase for weeks.

"And a coffee table—made a snap decision." Marco peeked inside the oven. "Never thought my oldest child would do something impulsive like *mi florecita.*"

Not exactly high praise. With the exception of Cat, the Mendozas rarely made snap decisions that went awry—not her parents, Val, or her younger brother, Alberto. Too often Cat's impulsive streak brought trouble or unintended consequences. Even the failure of her event-planning business seven years ago was due mostly to a desire to sprint off without first questioning if she'd run straight into a wall.

After Grandma Maria died, all three of the Mendoza children received money they were unaware their grandparents had squirreled away. Val promptly used her inheritance to pay off the last of her college loans. Alberto tucked his away into a retirement account.

Cat, newly graduated from Ohio U, where she'd majored in dating and having a good time, struck upon the perfect career. Since she'd always possessed a romantic streak, why not organize weddings?

Helping brides select flowers, vendors, and music for the special day seemed the perfect career.

Naturally her parents advised against the hasty plan. Her nonexistent organizational skills, combined with a lack of business acumen, sank Dream Weddings & Events in one year flat.

Brushing away the humiliating memory, she told her father, "I'm glad Val did something impulsive. She ought to loosen up."

The testy comment drew Marco's attention. "You seem down. Bad day at work?"

"Several of the Sirens stopped by first thing."

"I heard. Your mother would've gone with them if she'd had the time."

"Why didn't she?"

"Too busy helping Frances with this year's tokens." Frances Dufour was her mother's closest friend. "They're taking the stuff to the cemetery tomorrow." Ruefully Marco shook his head. "I'll never get why Frances makes such a big deal over a dead pet. If she went overboard memorializing Archie's death date, it would make more sense."

Cat went to the sink and looked out the window. "You're assuming Frances's September ritual is for Demeter." Two goldfinches swooped between the trees, sending flashes of yellow across the yard. "She's been making those special trinkets for a whole lot longer than Demeter's been gone. There must be another reason."

"We'll never know, will we? Your mother and Frances have enough secrets to fill a treasure chest."

They also shared a treasure trove of ideas about the sacred feminine power and ideals worthy enough to guide a woman's life. Kindness. Self-confidence. A respect for nature, and a nurturing love for family, friends, and the greater world. Cat admired their high-minded thinking, even if she wasn't yet a master of the Sweet Lake Sirens' code. Self-confidence in particular was difficult to attain. Most days found her mired in self-doubt.

Her father removed a casserole from the oven, and she asked, "What's for dinner?"

"Enchiladas with green sauce."

One of her favorites. "Should I set the table?"

"Your mother took care of it. We're eating in the dining room."

Cat accepted the news with sinking spirits. Eating in the dining room was reserved for special occasions—or times when her parents felt the need to intervene in their children's lives. The advice they bestowed always came with affection. But after the long day preparing for Miri's visit tomorrow, she wasn't in the mood for even a gentle interrogation.

"Where is Mami?"

He pointed a wooden spoon due south. "In the sunroom. Why don't you tell her dinner's ready in ten?"

Rising nerves accompanied Cat out of the kitchen. She wandered through the living room, decorated in vibrant yellow and terra-cotta hues, to the equally bright sunroom. In a nod to the Sirens' meetings often held there, three walls featured built-in benches. The seat cushions wore a rainbow of colors. They matched the runner trailing down the middle of the long oak table that dominated the center of the room.

Working intently, her mother threaded twine through pretty stones hollowed out with a jewelry drill bit. The stones glimmered with a variety of blue paint colors.

Silvia paused in her work. "Cat!"

She took a seat, leaned in for a kiss. "They're pretty. You're making them for Frances?"

"You just missed her. We've been working since I left the office. Put in a good two hours on our little craft project."

Cat fingered the tiny pile of azure feathers placed beside the stones. "You're going to the cemetery tomorrow?"

"Might as well. Frances is as ready as she'll ever be."

The temptation to ask for details nearly drove Cat to pry, but she shrugged it off. Her father was correct—the secrets her mother and Frances shared were guarded vigilantly.

Instead she got straight to the point. "Why are we having my favorite meal in the dining room? I'd guess you're buttering me up, but I get the feeling you're not."

Her mother finished threading the stones, then set them aside. "Wouldn't you rather wait for the three of us to talk?" She punctuated the question by smoothing a hand down Cat's flowing brown hair.

"Not really."

"Fine." Her mother didn't have much in the way of patience and appeared happy to explain. "I want to help you put together the marketing budget for the Wayfair. I'm a CPA, and you don't have much love for numbers. I'd ask if you've learned how to balance your checkbook, but I can't bear the truth. Linnie's given you control of more money than you're used to handling. You need my input to ensure every dime is well spent."

The suggestion seemed overdue. Since receiving the promotion, Cat had been waiting for her mother to drop a hint, or—more in keeping with her bold personality—draw up a typewritten list of reasons why her involvement was necessary. At least she wasn't offering a home-cooked meal to chat about the Sirens' goofy ideas for seminars at the inn, a conversation Cat would gladly put off until forever.

"Well?" Her mother smiled encouragingly. "Will you accept my help?"

The question stirred the doubts Cat never fully escaped. "Mami, I appreciate the offer—I really do. But I want to do this on my own. I've been researching other inns to see how they bring in business. I've put together everything for the concert we're holding on the beach in October without once asking Linnie or Jada for help. I've also met with Miri in Cincinnati to discuss options for the fall and spring ad campaigns."

"You drove to Adworks?"

"Twice. If I run into problems, she'll help."

"Just because you roomed together back in college doesn't mean she's willing to spend hours on the Wayfair's marketing budget. She's done enough already. Isn't Miri giving you a discount on her services?"

"She is—and she'll have more than enough time to help. She's coming to stay for a week."

Silvia patted her cheek with the pained, motherly affection that indicated Cat was missing something obvious. "Miri may wish to help, but don't send your expectations to the sky. A woman juggling pregnancy and thirty employees doesn't have the energy to give extended lessons in marketing."

"She said she's willing to help, and I believe her." The idea of wading through spreadsheets without Miri lending advice was an intimidating prospect. Not that relying on parental guidance appealed either. "Besides, if I get in over my head, I'll ask Jada to check the numbers. I won't drop thousands of dollars on radio ads or new brochures without a second set of eyes looking over my decisions."

"You'll foist this on Jada? Her responsibilities have increased, just like yours. Isn't she now splitting management duties with Linnie?"

"You know Linnie promoted us on the same day."

"Then you see how relying on Jada is an imposition."

"Mami, I don't want your help. This time is different. Linnie's put me in charge of the marketing, and I want to prove to her—and myself—that I can do a great job on my own." The hurt in her mother's eyes hastened Cat to add, "Don't get me wrong. I love how you and Papa look out for me. Lots of people grow up without loving parents. I've never taken your protection for granted."

"We had to protect you, dearest heart."

The catch in her mother's voice made Cat's eyes dampen. *Florecita*, the little flower her parents nearly lost. It was a miracle her brother and sister didn't view her as spoiled, but they too understood. They'd sheltered Cat with equal vigilance, long after the monthly visits to the pediatrician had ended. When a child has a difficult start to life, those struggles change the fabric of a family.

From the dining room, her father called them in to dinner.

"If I run into problems, I won't hesitate to ask for your help," she said to soothe her mother's bruised ego.

The familiar heat filtered through Silvia's features. "This isn't like the last time when you rushed in too fast and lost a business you'd opened," she warned. "Linnie has worked long and hard to keep the Wayfair from failing. The inn has been part of her family legacy for generations. Don't rush ahead blindly, Cat. If you do, you'll risk her one good chance to succeed."

Chapter 2

"Heard a rumor you were ambushed yesterday."

From the doorway of Cat's office, Linnie Wayfair made no effort to hide her amusement. Shorter than Cat and with a pleasingly curvy figure, she wore brown tights and a thigh-length sweater of burnt orange. Her thick tawny hair tumbled around her shoulders.

From the looks of the plaster dusting her clothes, she'd been trooping around the premises with the construction crew. By early October, the squadron of workers would finish the simpler renovations in the main inn: refinishing floors in some of the rooms, repainting others, and making minor improvements in the lobby area. Come November, the crews would begin tackling the bigger issues plaguing the south wing, where Cat and Jada Brooks—the inn's baker and the third member of the Wayfair's management team—each kept a personal suite. Cat wasn't looking forward to moving out at the end of October and losing the free digs she'd enjoyed for the last seven years.

She pushed the keyboard away. "Ask about the Sirens later," she said. "I have tons of work to finish before Miri arrives."

"She's driving in from Cincinnati?"

"And staying for a week in your old suite." Last summer Linnie had moved out of the south wing and into her boyfriend's house in town. "I've told you about Miri's visit a dozen times."

An apology flashed through Linnie's hazel eyes. "I forgot."

"She's interviewing staff members for the new brochure and steering me on ad buys for the fall and next spring. Plus she's getting a feel for the inn. Where and what to photograph, the best time of day to capture the Wayfair in its prime—she'll send a photographer and videographer for the concert in October. We'll post some of the material on the new website, use other images for print and digital."

"And you thought you didn't have the chops to handle our advertising."

Cat still wasn't optimistic—even less so after her mother's warning last night. "I can't do this without Miri's help," she admitted. Given all the decisions required, overseeing the marketing was a more intimidating task than she had first envisioned when Linnie handed over the reins.

"Nice how she gave us a discount on her services."

"Adworks usually handles big corporate accounts. She said this job'll be a breeze."

"I'm looking forward to thanking her in person."

"Guess she's running late." It bothered her that Miri hadn't returned her calls. Running the agency kept her old acquaintance in constant motion.

Still, how much trouble was it to send a text from the road?

"If she's late, you have time to spare." Linnie shut the door. "Tell me about the preparations for the concert."

"I've still got a ton of work."

"One month and counting."

"I wish I had longer to finish the preparations. Unfortunately I've hit a few speed bumps."

The Sweet Lake Fall Concert, slated for the second weekend in October, was to be the first event for the general public held by the Wayfair in a decade. Contrary to her mother's doubts, Cat was sweating the tiniest details. Even if she didn't have natural management skills, she planned to leave nothing to chance.

With Linnie's blessing, she'd hired a specialty events company, a lighting professional, and a boy band with a large following in Ohio. She'd even worked with Jada and the kitchen staff on a Sunday buffet to draw back people who'd attend the Saturday night concert but weren't able to secure rooms at the inn. Thanks to advance marketing, the Wayfair was booked solid for the weekend of the concert.

Linnie dropped into the old tapestry chair Cat had commandeered from the relics stored in the Wayfair's basement. "There's a problem with the arrangements?" she asked.

"Splendid Events reneged on the dance floor. An investment firm has their employee picnic the same day. They tried to talk me into a smaller floor." Cat wanted ample space on the beach for guests to get their groove on. "So I fired them. I found another company. They have two smaller floors we'll bolt together."

"Don't let them set up too close to the water. We don't need drunken revelers falling in."

"We'll put the dance floor twenty feet from the lake." She'd already mapped out the section of the beach to use, although she'd misplaced the notes on her paper-strewn desk.

"What about Midnight Boyz? Still giving you headaches?"

The popular Cleveland band, whose oldest member looked too young to vote, had bombarded Cat with demands she'd had no choice but to grant. A corner suite for two days prior to the performance. Use of the ballroom each afternoon for practice. A detailed menu for the lead vocalist, who avoided gluten, and another for the drummer, whose carnivorous tendencies were sure to blow out his arteries one day. The curly-haired brat demanded porterhouse steaks with every meal.

"I'd love to fire them too." The option wasn't realistic, given the constraints of her budget and the band's rising star in the Ohio music scene. "Success and puberty at the same time does *not* bring out the best in people. It's a miracle they didn't ask for a masseuse, or a private chef on call 24/7."

"They did win a competition in Cleveland. They're worth the trouble."

"Two competitions, actually. There's a rumor they'll sign a recording deal before Christmas. We're lucky to get the brats before they hit the big time."

Letting the topic go, Linnie asked, "So how many of the Sirens showed up yesterday?"

"Four of their more insistent members. And before you ask, my mother didn't lead the charge." Silvia shared co-leadership with the elegant Frances Dufour.

"What about Frances?" Since gaining majority control of the inn last summer, Linnie had struck up a friendship with the Sirens' oldest member.

"Also MIA. They're out at Walnut Grove this morning—a secret vigil they hold every September." Her mother didn't usually traipse off with Frances during business hours, but she did make exceptions. "Papa thinks they're holding a memorial for Demeter."

"They're holding a memorial for a Greek goddess?"

She laughed. "Don't you remember the huge cat Frances used to walk on a leash? Must've weighed twenty pounds."

"The Persian masquerading as a dog—how could I forget?" Linnie cocked her head to the side. "Should I touch base with Frances to make sure she's okay?"

"Don't worry. They battle constantly, but my mother always has her back."

"Seeing how you share everything with your mother, I'm sure you'll get to the bottom of it."

An exaggeration, but Cat did cherish their special bond. "I don't share *everything* with her."

"Yeah. Right. If you were deep in a romance, you'd serve up the juicy tidbits to your mother before throwing a bone to me or Jada."

"Guess I'll keep her on a diet, since there's nothing juicy to share." Though she was loath to admit it, she harbored the teeniest bit of jealousy about Linnie's dry streak ending. Her relationship with Daniel Kettering was sure to lead to marriage, assuming Sweet Lake's only attorney got the careful Linnie to the altar. "Between marketing tasks and work for the concert, I don't have time to date."

"Do I detect a hint of pessimism from my favorite optimist? When you least expect it, the right guy will come along."

The comment gave Cat a boost. "I believe you. Mostly because I *am* an optimist."

"One of your best qualities." Linnie twirled a finger through her hair. "So, what did the Sirens want?"

"To hold weekly talks for our guests." Cat sent a jaundiced eye over the handmade posters stacked on her desk. Tossing them into the garbage can was tempting. She didn't dare. "As much as I hate disappointing the Sirens, it's up to *you* to kill the idea without angering them. We're building an image as the perfect family destination, not a pit stop for spooky spiritual excursions."

"This isn't my problem. You're the one who believes in channeling energy and the mystical qualities of feminine power. Use your vibes to influence them."

"You're making fun of me."

"Only because you're Silvia's daughter. Can't you restrain her troops?" Linnie knit her fingers behind her head, the amusement in her eyes increasing. "When you finish work, ask Beefcake Bill for advice on how to let them down. I've got nothing."

The reference to the blow-up doll in her suite put a twinge of anxiety in Cat's belly. Did Linnie mean she wouldn't deal with the Sirens? A dismissal of their silly ideas was sure to make Penelope mourn in dignified silence. Tilda? She'd throw a tantrum for all of ten seconds.

Norah and Ruth were another matter. They'd find devious ways to make Cat's life hell. Or they'd ask Silvia to intervene. Cat adored her mother, but a volcanic eruption she could do without.

"Linnie, I can't stand up to them. They're like weird fairy godmothers hovering around the edges of my life. There isn't a woman in the bunch I haven't known forever. Would you want to disappoint a quirky great-aunt who never forgot a grudge?"

"You're acting like they'll drag you behind the woodshed for twenty lashes."

Frustration welled in Cat. Naturally Linnie believed she was overreacting. Until Linnie's friendship with Frances, she'd rarely given the Sirens a second thought. Nor did she have knowledge of their more memorable feuds.

"When it comes to getting even, they're inspired," Cat said. "Trust me. I know what I'm talking about."

"Yeah?" Linnie noticed the plaster dust on her sweater and brushed it away. "Enlighten me."

"Here's a fascinating tidbit. When you and I were in our early twenties, Tilda spread gossip about Norah getting breast implants."

"Breast implants at her age? Impressive."

Norah didn't have the most agreeable personality, but it was impossible not to admire her glamour. "In Manhattan," Cat supplied. "From what I heard, she took a flight one evening and didn't return to Sweet Lake for three days."

"I wonder if she got a discount, like a senior coupon day from her favorite plastic surgeon. Maybe AARP runs deals."

The conversation was veering off track, and Cat shushed her. "Anyway, the day after Tilda texted around town about Norah's boobs, all the watermelons and every last tomato went missing from her garden. She thought raccoons had invaded, but there wasn't any mess in the garden rows." She paused for emphasis. "Then Tilda noticed a feather token hanging from one of the naked tomato plants."

"Like this one?"

From her pocket Linnie produced a feather. Blue like the ocean, the feather clung to a length of twine. Last summer Frances had given her the token, to provide strength and protection, or a virtue like fortitude, which most people rarely mustered.

For the oldest Siren, the color held special significance. Cat recalled times during childhood when she snuck into the backyard to find her mother whispering soothing words to her closest friend as they prepared the tiny objects. On those nights, when grief unaccountably consumed Frances, the tokens were crafted with blue feathers only. Even the stones and the shells were painted a vivid blue like the Pacific Ocean.

Cat said, "The token in Tilda's garden had red feathers, not blue. Pretty ominous."

"What happened to the stuff poached from her garden?"

"She got a nasty surprise after driving into work. The fruit was heaped on the doorstep of Lyons Realty with a sign impaled through the mess."

"What was on the sign?"

"'Got something to say? Grow a pair.'"

Linnie chuckled. "Guess that stopped her twitchy texting finger."

"Yeah, and imagine what they'll do if I nix their ideas. Do me a solid. Just this once."

"Pass."

"Pretty please?"

"No, but I totally understand if you need to check the odds of survival." With ill-concealed mirth, she strolled around the desk and pulled open a drawer. She withdrew the Magic 8 Ball. "Go on. I know you want to."

No one sensible believed a children's toy foretold the future, but Cat *did* resort to the Magic 8 Ball in times of stress.

In times of crisis? Prayer was always a good bet. She also wore enough Siren tokens and amulets to send dark energy fleeing across state lines. Success was never guaranteed, but she liked the notion of feminine protection increasing the odds on a spiritual level.

She gave the ball a furious shake. "Will the Sirens forgive me?" she asked aloud.

The answer pulled a groan from her. **Don't count on it.**

Ditching the mirth, Linnie patted her back. "Two for two?"

Another shake, and Cat asked, "Will anything else go wrong today?"

The answer sent her worry into the stratosphere.

Better not tell you now.

Birdsong drifted across Walnut Grove Memorial Gardens.

The acres of tree-dotted grounds served many of the towns in the area, and Frances approached her husband's grave with pride quickening her strides. Before his unfortunate passing, her beloved Archibald was the owner of Sweet Lake's only construction company. His success had allowed her to secure a plot on the cemetery's central hill.

Silvia, less impressed by grand gestures, plunked down the mason jar of black-eyed Susans they'd brought. "Hello, Archibald." She appraised the unmarred grass on either side of his grave. "I see you're still lonely up on your perch. What's that? No one else in these parts can afford to join you?"

"He has Demeter to keep him company," Frances pointed out. Her sweet Persian had trotted off to heaven one short year after the dreadful loss of Archibald.

"We're *not* discussing your deceased pet."

"I'm curious. Why did you give your younger daughter a feline name if you despise the glorious creatures?"

The remark put disgust on Silvia's face. "There's nothing glorious about an animal shedding fur like a chemo patient. As for my daughter, Catalina is a family name. There's no connection to felines whatsoever."

"Don't get snippy. We've just arrived." Twigs and papery leaves deposited by the breeze were scattered on the headstone's gleaming top. Brushing them away, Frances bent slightly as if to engage a child. She wasn't sure why the posture brought the conviction Archibald heard her words from wherever he resided in the afterlife. "Now, let's see. News. Quite a bit has happened since we last dropped by."

"Are we back to your kooky conversations with the dead? No wonder Tilda got it into her head to develop a seminar about the afterlife. No doubt she caught you chatting with the family portraits in your den. You're one lousy role model."

The remark was a senseless provocation. "Silvia, *you* believe in the afterlife. You've burnt enough incense to honor your ancestors to fill a temple in Jerusalem."

"Not the same as holding a conversation with a headstone in the deluded belief anyone's listening."

"Stop acting like you're an expert on my late husband's conversational preferences. I'm sure Archibald looks forward to these chats." She offered his grave a beatific smile before landing her deadly regard on her friend. "You're in such a terrible mood, I can only assume Marco is on sabbatical from the sexual arena. Any other woman would hang party streamers from the rafters to have a man his age with a strong libido. Can't you let him rest once in a while? If he's not putting out, don't zap me with your negative energy."

"My only frustration is your kooky behavior."

Pure poppycock, but Frances held her tongue. Shrugging off her comrade's bad mood, she told her late husband, "This will tickle you pink. The Wayfair now has three talented leaders. Jada is now co-manager, and Cat's also been promoted. She's handling all of the inn's marketing."

Silvia gave a mulish look. "He knows. You told him the last time we visited."

Undeterred, Frances gave the headstone her full attention. "Archie, did I mention the south wing?" It was just like Silvia to get peevish because she was still fuming over the cat. "Linnie has a crew putting on a new roof. Once they've finished, they'll overhaul the interior. New heating and cooling, replastering—the works. Soon every room at the Wayfair will be open to guests."

"He knows."

Frances gripped the handle of her sun parasol. "Sweetheart, do you remember the autumn dance?" The notion of whacking Silvia was an awful lure, and she despised violence. "Linnie is reinstating the custom. Not in the ballroom, at least not this year. She's bringing in a band and hosting the gala on the beach. They're expecting several hundred people."

"Now, there's something he didn't know."

"Zip it. I'm communing with my husband."

"No, you're stalling." Silvia patted the headstone. "Archie, they aren't bringing in a big-band ensemble like you remember, or asking people to dress up. My daughter's hired a band of youngsters from Cleveland. Blue jeans and rock and roll. There'll be couples doing the nasty in the forest."

"Ignore her sass, dear. She's chewing sour grapes over Demeter."

Sparks lit in Silvia's dark eyes. "Bingo." She poked Frances in the chest. "I still haven't forgiven you."

An old complaint, and Frances swiveled away. Calmly she went about rebuilding the tiny memorial for the feline's grave. "Demeter, Silvia says hello." The groundskeepers never failed to mow right over, sending the stones flying every which way.

"I'll put up with these nutty conversations with your late husband because he mixed a mojito nearly as well as I do. I am *not* offering salutations to a dead cat."

"Hush, now. Demeter will hear you."

"Frances, someone pulled the aces from your deck."

"You're tossing around insults in a cemetery? Better watch out. You'll create enough bad energy to chase your hide for weeks."

Seeming to catch herself, Silvia regarded the marble headstone. "I'm sorry, Archie. I'd give your wife my last pint of blood if she needed it. She wasn't this off-center when you were alive. Since you've gone, she's flakier than a Christmas blizzard."

From the grass Frances retrieved the last stone, a heart-shaped beauty of silver granite. "I'd give you my last drop of blood." Rising, she sent a baleful glance. "But only if you were bleeding to death."

"Sneaking in here to bury a cat—I should've put *you* six feet under."

"What did you want me to do, toss her out by the lilacs?"

"She could've fertilized your lilacs for three years straight. Small dogs were afraid of your massive Persian."

The part about small dogs was beyond dispute, but comparing Demeter to compost was deplorable. Frances angled her chin. "You aren't a cat person, Silvia. You don't understand."

"I should thank my lucky stars you aren't a dog person. How would we have hauled a Great Dane over? I nearly broke my hip vaulting onto the grounds."

"We didn't vault." They'd brought a ladder for the midnight excursion, climbing gingerly over Walnut Grove's iron gate. Silvia had taken a bit of a tumble going over, but she did more harm to her festive capris than her bones. In Frances's estimation, if she traded a burrito for a salad occasionally, she'd remain more nimble.

The sun burst out from behind a cloud, urging Frances to snap open her parasol. In contrast, Silvia risked melanoma and grass stains by reclining on the turf. Her eyes drifting shut, she tipped her bronzed face toward the sky. Even in the autumn she never missed an opportunity to work on her tan.

Christine Nolfi

Frances slipped off her pumps. "Did you bring sunscreen?" The grass felt soft beneath her toes, as if Mother Earth thrummed energy through the soles of her welcoming feet. "Skin cancer is a serious matter."

"It's September, not July."

"UV rays are present year-round."

"I'll take my chances. The sun isn't hot."

"You're insane. I'm sweating like a moose."

"Do moose sweat?"

Frances tugged lightly at the collar of her dress. "Visit Toronto. Ask a Canadian."

Opening an eye, her drowsing friend regarded her with interest. "Tell me when you'd like to begin." Sinking deeper into the grass, she ran slow fingers through her thick black hair, fanning the tresses out around her head. A dye job to cover the grey, but there was no faulting the stylist's technique. "I cleared the morning schedule. Meeting with my first client this afternoon to organize P&L statements. Working on payroll for the Wayfair afterward. Take all the time you need."

"I'm not ready yet."

"I don't care about the stalling. Use every delaying tactic at your disposal, just shut up about the cat—and the sun. I'm tanning."

"And working your way to cancer." Reluctantly Frances retrieved the tin from her purse. Placing her purse on the headstone, she inhaled deeply.

Silvia eyed the tin. "You did a nice job this year."

The compliment provided a needed balm for her ravaged emotions. "I think so too," Frances murmured. She'd chosen cobalt blue and azure for the feathers and stones, and baby blue for the connecting twine.

Sadness coasted through her. Time didn't soften the grief, which lay inside her like a pockmarked stone scraping against the memories, sharpening the regrets. Like a heart-stone, painful and malignant.

The breeze caught the ruffle on the plunging neckline of Silvia's blouse. "Do you think Archie minds?" She smoothed the ruffle back into place. "We could do your remembering just as easily by the lake. Our own small act of love."

"No act of love is small." Frances looked over the rolling hills. "We have privacy here. Besides, a cemetery is naturally imbued with the sacred. The energy of Walnut Grove feels right."

"I hate the plastic."

"What?"

Rising on one elbow, Silvia appraised the vast expanse of emerald hills dotted with headstones. "Plastic flowers," she clarified. "Most people don't visit often, and the fake stuff bothers me. If you love someone, you should bring a real bouquet."

A point of decorum upon which they both agreed. At dawn Frances had filled the jar to ensure the black-eyed Susans remained fresh. "My husband appreciates our thoughtfulness."

During their marriage he'd brightened many a dreary winter day by surprising her with fresh roses, tulips—whatever struck his fancy. Their marriage had celebrated an eternal spring in no small part because of Archibald's thoughtfulness.

A memory Silvia dulled by remarking, "He *would* appreciate the gesture if you'd intended the bouquet for him."

"Oh, do be still."

"We should've asked Penelope for roses. The ones in your garden are nearly dormant."

"Her yellow roses are still blooming profusely."

"Wonder how she fared at the inn. Four of our members went up to see Cat yesterday."

The change of topic put Frances on alert. "About the talks for the inn's guests? I thought we agreed to wait until after the October concert. Why are they bothering your daughter now?"

"Penelope and the others were eager to pitch their ideas."

"How did it go?"

"I didn't ask Cat when she came for dinner last night. We had other matters to discuss." Silvia's head lolled to the left, her nostrils flaring to inhale the carpet of greenery. "She'll come around. Hosting talks by the Sirens will give the inn prestige. I'd like to see her promote them in the ads she's developing."

A fool's dream, but Frances hid the opinion. Cat's devotion to her mother was strong, yet she had other duties now. Along with the new responsibilities, the hardworking girl carried too much guilt for the mistakes of the past. The Mendozas guarded their middle daughter with admirable tenacity, but they seemed unaware of the scars of self-doubt festering in her.

"We shouldn't expect her to consider the seminars until after settling into her new responsibilities. For heaven's sake, she's still unpacking her office."

Silvia plucked a blade of grass, held it up to the light. "She'll never finish unpacking her office. I adore my daughter, but she's a procrastinator."

"Let's wait a few weeks."

"Are you deaf? Penelope and the others have already talked to her."

"Then let me follow up. Cat has such a strong desire to please you. I don't want her to feel pressured."

"I won't pressure my daughter."

Frances twirled her parasol in hopes of dispelling the tension jangling through her. "You're like a mad bull when you're intent on getting your way," she said, risking the firestorm. "If I speak with her, she won't skirt the truth. We have no idea if she likes the idea or not."

"Now you're implying my daughter will lie to me?" The suggestion pulled Silvia from her sleepy repose. She struggled to her feet. "Not one of my children would ever lie to me. They love me too much to dishonor our relationship with falsehoods. How can you think otherwise?"

"Calm down, will you?"

Silvia's hands sliced through the air. "I'll do nothing of the sort. You're implying my middle child, *mi angelito*, is more apt to speak truthfully to you than her beloved mami. Forget what I said about a pint of blood. I wouldn't give you a drop of my precious—"

Tiring of the rant, Frances snapped her parasol shut and took aim. She struck once, on the crown of Silvia's head.

The assault, coming unexpectedly, produced the intended result. Silvia's hands stopped flailing. The rant ended.

Then her more bullish impulses shuddered across her face.

Frances was ready. She swooped the parasol downward lest her friend take this too far.

En garde!

Fifty years since her last fencing class, she still recalled the basics.

Chapter 3

Partially hidden behind the drapes, his mother watched the street like a general in spandex.

Knotting his tie, Ryan D'Angelo paused between the piano she no longer played and the couch, where she spent too much time watching movies. She still favored sappy flicks glazed with undying love, the type of fare with absurdly soulful guys named Stefan or Colt. Why didn't she prefer movies about vengeance-seeking heroines besting evil men?

On the plus side, a love affair with aerobics got her out of the house on a regular basis. He needed to find the right moment to suggest adding a mild weight-lifting regimen. It worried him that she looked like a ten-pound chicken in neon athletic wear. Add some padding to her bones, and she'd stop resembling undernourished poultry.

The drapes swished. The pink tennis shoes beneath tiptoed sideways. A school bus rolled past, the kids inside jumping up and down. Swinging the binoculars in a slow arc, Julia D'Angelo followed the bus until it disappeared into the morning glow. A high-pitched yip, yip, yip caught her notice. Opening the drapes wider, she peered in the direction of the white ranch house next door.

On the sidewalk before the house, an old man with a goatee studied the dazzling pinks and blues streaking the morning sky. Unaware of the surveillance, he scratched himself in unspeakable places. His miniature schnauzer stopped barking at the cars rolling past, choosing instead to curl onto its haunches to drop a stink bomb.

Breaking the silence, Ryan said, "If the guy doesn't bag the turd, arrest him. Twenty days in the county lockup."

The comment threw his mother against the picture window with a thud. Outside, the vigilant schnauzer began yipping with gusto. The drapes fluttered as Julia pushed off the glass.

Righting herself, she spun around. "Ryan, what's wrong with you?" Her mossy-green gaze landed on him with a brew of affection and irritation.

"Sorry. Didn't mean to scare you."

She rubbed her elbow, and he winced with sympathy pains.

"Well, you did. Don't creep up on me."

"Tall men don't creep. Mostly because we move with the grace of water buffalo." He hesitated. "Mind explaining what you're doing?"

Sandy-brown curls mixed with silver fell around her troubled eyes. "That must be a rhetorical question since you know what I'm doing." She gave the curls a hasty swipe, pushing them off her forehead.

"I'd like to haul you away from the window. What are my odds?"

"Not good."

"C'mon, have breakfast with me."

"You don't eat breakfast, although you should. Most important meal of the day." She returned to her inspection of the street. "Go to work. Miri's about to give birth at her desk. She can't run the place without you."

He wasn't headed to Adworks, a fact not worth mentioning given his mother's behavior. "Miri's fine. She has another three months before her due date." He pulled on his sport coat. "Pity she isn't having twins. She's made a run through every baby store in Cincinnati."

"Good for her."

Against his better judgment he asked, "Where'd you get the binoculars?"

"Amazon—where else? They were delivered yesterday." She nodded at the wall clock above the TV. "Are you planning to be late?"

There was more than enough time for the road trip, another salient fact not worth mentioning. With his mother acting like an edgy watchman, he felt less comfortable about starting his day. Purchasing binoculars without his knowledge sure didn't fill him with optimism. She hadn't displayed this level of paranoia since his bashful teens—a lifetime ago, and he wasn't prepared for a replay of those dark years.

Ryan suffered a dose of self-recrimination. When the reporter had called, he should've turned down the interview. The boost to his career—not to mention the benefit of national exposure for Adworks—had been a selfish consideration. He should've factored in the impact on his mother.

From the kitchen, the scent of coffee bloomed. He hungered for a quick jolt. The SOS from Miri still hadn't sunk in, and he chafed at the notion of an hour-plus drive into the boondocks. An account he didn't want, and a client sure to dislike him taking over.

An unpleasant day ahead. Still, he couldn't deal with the problems until he talked his mother off a ledge.

Treading carefully, he said, "There's no one outside. Well, other than the old fart and his schnauzer."

Beneath the green tank top, her back stiffened. "There's nothing wrong with checking to make sure."

"You're mixing up the days. The feature is in the newspaper tomorrow."

Distress flickered across her face. "You're certain?"

"No, I'm taking a guess. Tossing a dart blindly, hoping to hit a target."

"Don't be glib." Clearly he'd struck a nerve with that last comment; her voice was testy. "A half-page spread in the Money section of *USA Today* with big photos of your smiling face—why don't *you* see the problem?"

"Because there isn't one. The world will see a successful ad executive, nothing more."

"What about your father?"

They hadn't discussed George Hunt in years. "If you're genuinely frightened, I'll do my best to locate him. I assume he's still in Idaho, or he's drifted back out to California." Hunt, a mechanic, was a ghost in cyberspace. The odds of finding anything new on him were remote in the extreme. "Keep in mind I don't give a damn where he is. If it'll make you feel better, I'll pay someone to find him and keep tabs."

The suggestion planted fear in his mother's eyes. "I don't want you anywhere near him. Go poking around in his life, and he'll find out."

"Then let this go," he suggested, refusing to debate.

She set her mouth in a stubborn line. "I can't."

"At least promise you won't spend the day staring out the window. You're dressed for the gym, so go. There's nothing coming our way I can't handle." He glanced longingly toward the kitchen. "Need coffee? I'll pour you a cup. Might help with the senility."

The light mockery brought her chin up. "Senility doesn't run in our family."

The comment unleashed the frustration he'd learned to suppress. "Now, there's an insight. How would I know what runs in our family?" Her life before she'd spirited them to safety remained a taboo subject.

"Ryan, please. Let's not do this. I don't expect you to understand . . ."

Sorrow overtook her features as she traced the moon-shaped scar beneath her right eye. An unconscious habit, an echo from a past still playing beneath their normal lives like background music. The evidence of brutality never failed to hollow out his heart. In a gruesome coincidence, he bore a nearly perfect replica beneath his left eye, the marred skin a reminder of all they'd endured.

Only fragments of that fateful day remained. Ryan carried a dim memory of waist-high grass tickling his arms, and the dappled shade of the forest sending tendrils of darkness toward the glaring sunlight.

At the forest's edge, a man shouted. His rage became a startling complement to the discomfort Ryan struggled against, the hard press of his mother's fingers digging into his shoulder in a failed attempt to push him to safety. A bottle swooping through the air. A crack of sound as the lower half met a tree's knotty trunk. In a perilous moment of wonder, he escaped his mother's hold. Shards of glass exploded skyward like stars bursting to life in the lonely field.

His fascination came at a cost. Ryan didn't see the bottle's jagged upper half become a weapon.

Running from the memory, he came across the living room. Softly he said, "Mom, how long has it been since you used binoculars? There's nothing to gain by reviving old habits. The feature in *USA Today* won't change anything. We're safe." He rested his palm on the narrow bone of her shoulder. "We've been safe for years."

"Only because I've kept us hidden," she reminded him.

Love for her rolled over him in an inexpressible wave. "You did a good job."

"Not at first. What about Twin Falls?"

Another memory from his unhappy childhood, more unsettling than the forest, accosted him. "We survived," he said, pushing it away.

"Barely. You act as if your father can't find us again. Have you stopped to consider if you're taking the news coverage too lightly?"

A remote possibility, and he searched for the right words to offer reassurance. A difficult prospect—she carried other, equally dark memories he couldn't guess at. Couldn't bear to guess at, if he was honest with himself. Given the injury to her psyche, it was blessing enough that she'd managed to live a relatively normal life.

He did his best to drum up a reassuring smile. "I'm sure he's somewhere on the other side of the country. He probably remarried, found someone else to abuse. After all this time, he's forgotten about us."

"A naive assumption."

"No, a realistic conclusion. You're blowing this out of proportion."

"A man doesn't forget when his son is taken from him. We were lucky in Idaho. It doesn't mean your father has given up." She followed up the disturbing comment by adding, "What about the family resemblance? You can't erase genetics."

The observation made Ryan flinch. Although the topic remained off-limits, she knew about his unfortunate discovery.

Last spring, after breaking off another casual romance, he'd stumbled across the truth. While cleaning the garage to work off his gloom, Ryan found the photo album high on a shelf behind a box of forgotten Christmas decorations. In an era when digital images were parked in the cloud, the evidence of his mother's former life gave a quaint, if dark, answer to the questions he'd stopped posing long ago.

Plumes of dust curled through the air as he flipped from one page to the next—his mother during childhood standing in a group with other kids at a carnival or an amusement park. A much later photograph of her striding toward a jewelry store in a suit of the palest pink, the San Francisco skyline shimmering in the background. Several pages with the photos torn out, the gaping rectangles edged with grime that had seeped in from the dusty perch where she'd hidden the album. Next a flurry of images depicting a red-cheeked toddler born into a treacherous world his mother finally abandoned to save them both.

He was returning the album to its hiding place when three photos dropped out.

Tendrils of mounting paper stuck to the back of each. The photographs depicted a man in his prime—standing on a wharf, inside a car dealership beside a Mercedes, seated at a restaurant sipping a glass of wine.

Bringing the last image close, Ryan's hand shook.

The uncanny resemblance sent dread rolling through him. Raven hair and eyes greener than California's foxtail pine. The strong, angular features and the rangy, muscular build. The images jolted Ryan to his core.

Five months later, the awareness he'd grown into his father's carbon copy haunted him still.

Dismissing the memory, he drew his mother from the window. The wish, so familiar he wore it like a second skin, caught him unawares.

On their first day in Ohio, why hadn't she destroyed the photos?

Chapter 4

Yellow streaks formed ghoulish spatter art on the Beemer's windshield.

Thirty minutes outside the city, Ryan made the mistake of opening the window for three unnerving seconds. Enough crap flew inside to make him wish he'd tossed insect repellant in his briefcase.

The sheer volume of airborne creatures swarming the countryside disgusted him. Mosquitos, gnats, bumblebees as big as his thumb, and a prehistoric monster that dive-bombed his head while he swatted vainly, risking a collision with a truck as his car veered dangerously out of the lane. A bucket of sudsy water wouldn't have removed the jellied corpse from the passenger seat.

He reached his destination with the windows rolled up and the AC blasting. Indian summer in Ohio was in full swing; with grudging respect, he regarded the autumn colors painting the trees. He drove around Sweet Lake Circle with its center green filled with picnic tables sitting lonely in the leafy shade. Half of the buildings enclosing the circle lay vacant, the brick structures growing moss. Rechecking the GPS, he took a boulevard that wound ever higher. At the top, the golden sandstone mansion perched near the glittering lake.

He estimated that the walk from the inn to the lake was an easy stroll for guests staying at the Wayfair. According to Miri, the town derived its name from the honeysuckle growing in abundance around

Sweet Lake. The beach appeared empty with the exception of a couple strolling in the surf.

The Wayfair's parking lot was about one-third full. Not bad for a country inn past the peak tourist months. Cutting the engine, he hoped Miri would remember to transmit her notes. They'd chatted during most of his drive to familiarize him with an account he didn't want. On a nasty wave of retching, she'd hung up abruptly.

Morning sickness. Not a fun price to pay for motherhood.

Gravel crunched beneath his feet. He paused to survey the long, sloping lawn and the workers farther off, clustered around the foundation of what he presumed was the south wing.

"No solicitations, buster. Whatever you're selling, they aren't buying."

The old geezer's warning came from behind.

Turning, Ryan blinked. A wrinkled individual of indiscriminate sex marched across the lot. Plaid shirt with nothing beneath to provide a clue, until he took note of the unruly white braids snapping across her shoulders.

"Good morning," he said. The woman scowled, and he hastened to add, "I'm not selling anything."

"You're not a guest, with your fancy briefcase and no luggage." Hostility simmered on her features. "This is private property."

He wondered if Sweet Lake had an overly zealous neighborhood watch. "Ma'am, I have an appointment with Cat Mendoza."

"Why?"

None of her business, but he wasn't usually rude to the elderly. "I'm with Adworks, the agency she hired."

Her brow collapsed in a webwork of scrutiny. "You're not a woman."

"Not today."

"Cat hired a woman, some hotshot she whored around with at Ohio University. College," she muttered, emphasizing her distaste by spitting. Repulsed, he took a step back. "Parents spending thousands of dollars just so their children can make whoopee with strangers. What brainiac dreamt up coed dorms? When I was young, you finished high school and got your butt into the workforce."

"A nobler era," he remarked dryly.

Evidently she'd been alive when Sinatra ruled the airwaves. Or earlier, like the colonial era.

"What would you know about noble eras?"

"Not much, I suppose." He held out his hand. "Ryan D'Angelo."

The peace offering was ignored. "Ruth Kenefsky." She hitched her thumbs in the pockets of her oversize jeans. "You pushed Cat's BFF aside to horn in on the job?"

"No need to horn in. Miri's puking in a garbage can." He'd had enough of the woman's sass.

Ruth grunted. "Heavy drinker?"

"Pregnant."

"Gave you the account fair and square?"

"I'm in charge."

"Tell Cat the Sweet Lake Sirens want an answer by sundown. We can't practice our speeches until we get this wrapped up."

Requesting clarification was a chancy move. Finding his gambling spirit, he asked, "You're one of the Sirens?"

"Are you stupid?"

Apparently, since he hadn't walked away. "You're speaking at the inn?" A plan he'd derail at his earliest convenience.

"We're hosting talks for the guests."

"Why?"

She gave a look implying he'd left the functioning half of his brain in the car. "As a perk for staying at the inn, why else?"

"Ah, I see." He held up his briefcase. "Hold off on the rehearsals. I have a number of projects to discuss with Ms. Mendoza."

"Get in line, pal. We've already got an appointment for our beauty shots." She swiveled her head to lend a profile view. "Can't decide which is my better side. If you've got an opinion, let's hear it."

"Outside my area of expertise, I'm afraid." Her profile gave an unsavory impression of the FBI's most wanted.

His distaste went unnoticed. "I'll ask Tilda," she said, kicking gravel with her sturdy boots. "She found the photographer. Nice boy over in Fairfield. We'll get the photos to you once they're ready."

The implication being she expected publicity. *Not a chance.* His boss had accepted the Wayfair account out of misplaced loyalty. Miri didn't like saying no to anyone. While Ryan was agreeable to helping out in a fix, he refused to flame out by promoting Ruth and her friends.

"Ma'am, your desire to help is laudable," he said, loading his voice with deference. "From what I've seen, the Wayfair is the only draw in Sweet Lake. Why wouldn't you want to pitch in?"

"You're telling me to push off?"

"No, ma'am. Merely assuring you that I'll take it from here."

A threatening silence bloomed between them. Scouring his face with disdain, she tilted slightly forward.

Then she reached behind her back.

Ohio was an open-carry state. Ryan wasn't into hunting; he didn't see the point in harming Bambi, and he detested any place not lathered with concrete and shadowed by skyscrapers. But this was the country, the red-blooded backbone of the US of A. Presumably folks propped their rifles by the door and kept a pistol handy for target practice. What if Ruth toasted his ass with a Saturday night special? It would serve him right for shooting down her ideas.

From her back pocket, she whipped out a dried gourd on a stick. The apology froze on his lips. Her weapon of choice looked like an oversize baby rattle. Swirly African designs covered the gourd's knobby flesh.

His shoulders sagged.

Violently she rattled the gourd, extinguishing his relief. The strange form of aggression started his heart racing.

On a wave of muttered threats, she marched off.

Mouth agape, he regarded the puffs of dust kicked up by her strides. The aftereffects of fear zinged through his system, forcing him to work to regulate his breathing. When he was sufficiently calm, he climbed the steps to the veranda with delayed bolts of amusement zipping through him. If she'd delivered a hex with her rattling gourd, he'd take his lumps.

Working an account in the boondocks didn't thrill, but menacing fruit he could handle.

In the lobby, a middle-aged couple studied a map of the area. To the right, he spotted a short corridor with a ballroom at the end. The sightseers brushed past, and he approached the reception desk. A man of Japanese descent with a perky disposition gave directions to Cat's office.

The air held the tang of fresh paint. The interior of the inn looked classier than anticipated with ornate crown molding and a nice seating area by the lobby that gave the impression of a cozy living room. Toward the back of the inn, the large restaurant featured a wall of glass that displayed the autumn colors and the lake beyond. Several diners were finishing breakfast.

Down a second, shorter corridor, he found a door partially ajar. Behind the desk, a woman with a waterfall of dark hair sat with her face tilted into the rosy light streaming through the window. Lost in thought, she ran her fingers down her glossy mane with the sensuous repose of a woman assured of her privacy. The sensation of catching her during an intimate moment gripped Ryan.

He cleared his throat, and the chair wheeled around. "May I help you?" she asked.

Her desk was crammed near the window. A whimsical butterfly constructed of colorful wire hung on the adjacent wall. Boxes waiting to be sorted hugged a file cabinet with rust creeping up the sides.

She peered around a computer that should've been retired during the Bush presidency. "Did you hear me?"

Everything was second rate, except the woman behind the desk.

"I'm Ryan, your eleven o'clock." Her pretty brows lowered with confusion, and he asked, "Didn't Miri explain?"

"I've been trying to reach her all morning. She's not answering."

He'd seen Cat only from a distance, chatting with Miri in the Adworks conference room. This close, her allure struck like strong current. Yet another inconvenience on an unusual day.

Sheepishly he grinned. "My fault, I'm afraid. I kept her on the phone most of the drive. She promised to fill you in after we hung up."

Disappointment flitted through fetching brown eyes. "Miri's not coming?" Again her fingers coasted through her hair, drawing his attention.

He'd always had a weakness for women with long hair. Cat's heavy tresses flowed invitingly past her shoulders, and he imagined bunching the locks in his hands. Her outfit was another matter. Given the plunging neckline, the floral-patterned dress was too sexy for office wear.

An inspired choice.

"Hello? I asked if Miri's coming."

The impatience sparking her voice lifted the hairs on the back of his neck. With the thrilling sensation came an equally rousing thought: she resembled a dark-haired version of Botticelli's Venus. It wasn't the most constructive observation for a business meeting.

He didn't care. He'd take Cat naked on the half shell any day.

The fully clothed version of Venus was quickly losing her patience. "Are you listening to me?"

"Miri's not feeling well," he rapped out, yanking his attention to her hairline. He wasn't in the habit of objectifying women. This wasn't a good time to start.

The effort to thwart a sudden and thoroughly regrettable attraction sent the wrong impression. She glanced over her shoulder, then back at him. The look she gave reduced his ego to three inches in height.

"What are you staring at?" she demanded.

"Nothing."

"You're staring at my forehead."

The perplexity in her wide-set eyes gave his ego an inexplicable boost. "You have a nice forehead," he heard himself say.

Her mouth quirking, she tapped a long finger on her temple. "Here. Focus on my eyes. It's what polite people do."

A challenge, and he hit her full on with the intensity of his stare. A tricky game, this, and he won when the heat of his attraction singed away the last of her impatience. Her eyes widened.

"You're very beautiful," he offered, as if her physical appearance explained his unprofessional behavior. From a male viewpoint, it did.

She nearly looked away, leaving him impressed when she managed to hang tight. Women often dodged a direct challenge, but Cat seemed exceptionally comfortable in her own skin.

"Are you flirting with me?" Grudging pleasure flitted across her lips.

"I'm trying to stop."

"I wish you would," she said, and the flush rising beneath her golden skin tasted like glory. "Miri really isn't coming? I was looking forward to her short vacation."

"What vacation?"

"She planned to stay in Linnie's suite in the south wing."

"Where would Linnie have stayed?"

"Oh, she doesn't live on the grounds. She moved in with her boyfriend. He owns a house in Sweet Lake."

"I'm sure Miri would've loved the break from routine."

Worry shifted across Cat's features. "What's wrong with her?"

He explained about the morning sickness and added, "I got the marching orders first thing this morning."

A blunder, and her worry switched to irritation. "What are you, an unwilling conscript? Thanks a lot."

"Not what I meant." But it was, and he tried not to breathe. Her perfume contained a bewitching mix of spicy and sweet notes.

"You're happy Miri gave you the account?" She laughed shortly. "I don't believe you."

"No reason you should." If beauty was a knockout punch, he was going down fast. "Let's start over."

"Great idea, Einstein." Her cell phone rang. "Hold on."

Having blown the opening pleasantries, he was grateful for the opportunity to locate his missing composure. How to start over was a distinct problem.

She swiveled toward the window, her throaty voice dropping an octave. "Norah, slow down. She did? No, I haven't made a decision . . ."

A ratty chair hugged the front of her desk. Ryan took the liberty of seating himself. For a woman so polished, Cat's desk resembled tornado alley. Travel magazines, spreadsheets, scrawled notes on loose sheets—if any of the employees in his office worked in such a crap fest, they'd get the boot.

A stack of posters snagged his attention. A drawing contest for kids staying at the inn, he guessed. Not the worst idea he'd ever heard from a client. At least Cat was experimenting with themes he could build on.

Relieved by the opportunity to get down to business, he slid a poster from the pile.

Immediately Ryan wished he'd put a damper on his curiosity.

SEX IN THE TWILIGHT YEARS: MYTH OR MAGIC? Definitely not a child's art project. Why a young woman lush and sensual like Cat wondered about sex among the elderly was impossible to comprehend.

The inconvenient thought plastered a grin on his face. Maybe the Wayfair's hot Latina manager was giving pointers to the madwoman who'd menaced him with the fruit in the parking lot. A waste of time, really.

At that precise moment, the sheer silliness of the women inhabiting his world conspired against Ryan. His mother, surveilling the street with binoculars, and Miri, running him through an account long distance while heaving into a garbage can. The hex delivered by the unsavory Ruth. And topping them all, the knockout punch of an unexpected attraction to the client who'd cut him off to argue on the phone.

Now this: the poster's spicy title, coming on the heels of his spectacularly bad opening remarks.

Breaking protocol, Ryan laughed.

Chapter 5

Inappropriate laughter spun Cat around.

Being ditched by Miri was bad enough. Now her raven-haired replacement was grinning from ear to ear.

Glitter from one of the Sirens' posters trailed across the desk. **SEX IN THE TWILIGHT YEARS: MYTH OR MAGIC.** With rising embarrassment, she followed the trail to him.

In her ear, Norah continued the rant. Cringing beneath the assault, Cat gestured wildly at Ryan as she mouthed, *Put it down.*

A responsible adult would follow the request.

Ryan held up the poster.

Magic, I hope, he mouthed back. He pointed to the others. *May I look?*

Cat's gaze threw daggers. Better yet, machetes—big ones intended to cut the prankster down to size.

No.

Did he think she'd allow him to sift through the other wacky ideas? Granted, the Sirens *were* nuts. Whether they were lightly roasted or heavily salted, they were her kind of nuts, women she admired and protected and sometimes just tolerated.

The air crackled as he reached for the stack. Or her ears did, since Norah was still shouting on the phone.

Furious, Cat leapt from her chair.

Her opponent was faster. Launching forward, he nabbed the stack and sat back down. With a mock shiver, he read the poster about hot flashes. She lunged across the desk. Ryan leaned out of reach, his eyes skipping across Tilda's poster, the one about talking to the dead. A chortle burst from him.

She cut Norah off midrant. "I'll call you back." Hanging up, she tossed down her phone.

She remained standing with the sole intention of wresting the tactical advantage. Ryan owed her an apology. A *big* one, with maraschino cherries on top and a dollop of whipped cream on the side. Who admitted they didn't want an account, then followed up by rooting through the stuff on your desk? He leveled his green-eyed gaze on her with a mix of defiance and blunt flirtation that nearly made her order him out.

A course of action she quickly dismissed. She needed this gorgeous man's help.

Men often flirted, but Ryan wasn't your garden-variety ogler. The cuff links glinting beneath the sleeves of his sport coat were elegant, a carefully chosen accessory. A fierce intellect glowed on his face. The crow's feet fanning out from his eyes were pronounced, as if he worried a lot. Beneath his left eye, a pale indentation drew her attention.

A scar from a childhood accident?

He said, "Want to fill me in on the Sweet Lake Sirens?" Begging forgiveness wasn't high on his agenda, obviously. "I'm curious, because one of them put a hex on me in the parking lot."

"Ruth, and she didn't cast a spell. If she put bad vibes around you, don't expect me to fix it." Snatching the posters back, she nodded toward the phone. "That was another one of the Sirens calling. You're building a real fan club in Sweet Lake."

"Will the fans continue to threaten me with gourds?"

"They have other means of showing their displeasure."

"First time I've been accosted by someone wielding fruit on a stick." His regard took a leisurely stroll across her lips. Then he jolted her with a yummy sensation when his gaze captured hers. "What are they, a batty women's group?"

"They aren't batty," she replied, distinctly aware of the warmth spilling all the way to her toes. She remained perfectly still, yet the predatory atmosphere he'd brought into the room made her feel like she was sprinting.

He was closing in on her.

A provocative thought she pushed away, saying, "The Sirens are more like town matriarchs, if you can imagine a town with too many wise women. They want you fired."

"You can't fire me."

"Says who?"

A grin played at the corners of his mouth.

His arrogance really was annoying. "Are you always this full of yourself?"

"Not usually," he said, and the grin overtook his mouth. "I'm not sure why you're bringing out the worst in me." He motioned to her chair. "Why don't you sit down? You're trembling."

The comment made her blush. She *was* trembling. The tiny fissure in her composure seemed a declaration of weakness. Barely visible, but he'd noticed.

There was apparently little Ryan missed.

Complying, she returned to her chair. Shoulders squared, she knit her fingers together.

In a more congenial tone, he said, "You had every right to call me out. I don't want this account."

"Perfect. Tell Miri I'll wait until she's feeling better."

"Plan for a long wait. She always takes on more than she can handle. Don't worry about it. I'm the best in the business."

"Then we have a problem." The temperature rising between them made her desperate for escape. She managed a look of disinterest. The attempt only made her more aware of the effect of his regard—like a magnet pulling her in. "I can't work with you."

"Miri is willing to waste my talents on a country inn." The merriment eased from his features. "I suggest we make the best of it."

"You're not much for sugarcoating the facts."

"Why waste your time or mine? Under normal circumstances you couldn't afford my services."

Silently she agreed. Even if another agency were brought in on such short notice, how to pay the exorbitant fees? Without the discount Miri offered, there would be no choice but to navigate the marketing alone.

Defeated, she asked, "Where do we start?"

"I need somewhere quiet to read. Miri has hopefully loaded my e-mail with notes. After I familiarize myself with the Wayfair, we'll get started."

"You'll need to print out her notes?"

"All of them."

Considering, she rolled a pen beneath her fingertips. A delayed case of nervous tension jangled through her. The reaction provided a distressing complement to the jarring thrum of her pulse. Drag a second desk into her tiny office? She was still deciding the wisdom of working in close proximity when Ryan spoke again.

"I can't work here—you're too much of a distraction. I'll stop flirting and get my head screwed on straight, but I need several hours and a quiet place to work." A supreme confidence was evident on his face as he rose to his feet. "We can agree I'm having the same effect on you."

The tray in Jada's grasp smacked down on the center island. "You aren't picking up Linnie's bad habits, are you?" She blocked Cat from nearing. "Go away. I don't have sweets to spare."

Although the bubbling apple pies wafted the delicious aroma of cinnamon and brown sugar, Cat was too upset to imagine sampling them. At the opposite end of the long, rectangular kitchen, the prep staff chopped vegetables for the upcoming lunch rush. Thankfully they were out of earshot.

"Your pies are safe." Cat pressed her hand to her belly. "I'm just looking for an out-of-the-way corner to have an anxiety attack. I have a million butterflies winging around in my stomach."

Jada gave her the once-over. "You don't get anxiety attacks. That's more Linnie's thing."

"First time for everything."

"Is this about the Sirens storming the gates? Listen, if Tilda wants to send hate mail to the great beyond, tell her to do it on her own time. She's not hosting a seminar here."

Given Ryan's bold entry into her life, she'd momentarily forgotten about the Sirens. "Thanks for the reminder. As if I need more to stress about."

Jada angled her hip against the counter. "Don't let them push you around. They act like you're under a special obligation to kowtow to them because you're Silvia's daughter. Stand your ground."

"They aren't the reason I'm having heart palpitations."

"What's wrong?"

"I've just had the strangest meeting of my life. Do I look okay? Maybe this isn't anxiety. Might be a heart attack."

"Unlikely at your age." The reasonable conclusion didn't stop Jada's caramel-colored skin from taking on an ashen hue.

The bottle of Jack, used to infuse the syrup Jada drizzled on her famous bread pudding, nestled in a cupboard behind spice jars. Cat took it down. "Talk about a guy with a big head," she blurted, slamming the cupboard shut. "What sort of man points out your attraction to him? Okay, so I didn't call him on it. It's hard to ogle and think at the same time. Doesn't make his behavior any less obnoxious."

The finer points of the outburst flew past Jada. "What are you doing with my Jack Daniel's?" Her territorial streak extended to the kitchen domain.

"Drinking." Cat found a glass, poured two fingers. She downed the whiskey in one gulp.

She flinched, the firewater scorching her throat.

Jada pulled out her cell phone and sent a text. When she'd finished, she said, "You're now part of management. This means you don't get drunk right before the lunch rush. It sends the wrong message to the staff."

"Try to stop me."

The irritated baker snatched the bottle, then stopped a waiter walking by. "Don't let anyone near my pies," she instructed. "I don't have time to make another dessert for today's menu."

Latching on to Cat's wrist, she led her past the curious staff. They took the corridor abutting the ballroom out to the lawn unfurling behind the inn. Avoiding the lobby got Cat's vote. Before dashing into the kitchen, she'd stopped at the front desk to ask Mr. Uchida to print out whatever Ryan needed. Then she'd abandoned the ad executive in the seating area with his MacBook Air and a briefcase chock-full of neatly arranged files. Even the sticky notes were aligned with geometric purity, the cursive beautifully formed.

Who still used cursive? Her own scrawl resembled hieroglyphs.

By the time Ryan had arranged the contents of his briefcase on the coffee table, he'd dispensed with the flirtatious remarks and smoky glances. Which would've been helpful if he hadn't already knocked Cat off her axis.

She was still searching for her inner balance as Jada slid the bandana off her ebony curls and halted beneath a maple tree. "Start talking." To punctuate the command, she took Cat by the shoulders and propped her against the tree.

Grateful, Cat sank against the trunk. "My friend from college is dealing with morning sickness. She sent a replacement."

"Ryan D'Angelo," Jada supplied. "Some of the women in housekeeping saw him talking to Mr. Uchida. They said he was hot."

"Like he's Photoshopped."

"So you get to enjoy eye candy while putting together our ad campaigns. Not much of a hardship."

"It *is* a hardship."

"Yeah? How?"

Making sense of the interlude in her office proved difficult. "He put the moves on me," Cat said. The memory blistered her cheeks. "Only he didn't."

Jada shook her head, the tight curls framing her face dancing with her impatience. "Girl, you're making *no* sense."

"You had to be there. He walked in, and the air shivered. If he'd pointed a laser, he couldn't have turned my insides to marshmallow faster. I mean, we've all been hit by sudden attraction, but this was attraction squared. Attraction thrown at you from the top of a roller coaster and the tracks lead off a cliff."

"Is this you talking or the booze?"

She felt miserable and exhilarated, a combustible mix that made her even more miserable. "He's so *intense*. Plus he's unleashed this primal energy between us. Like I need hot thoughts mucking up my brain the same month I'm trying to master Excel." She glanced wistfully at the inn. "Maybe I should get drunk. Sneak back to the south wing and pretend none of this is happening."

Linnie came across the grass, no doubt alerted by Jada's text. "What's the problem?" She cradled a slice of apple pie wrapped burrito style in a napkin. Upon noticing the simmer rising off Jada, she added sweetly, "Now, don't get peeved. You said there was an emergency. I don't do emergencies without self-medicating first."

"Consider yourself invited to a five-alarm fire." Jada broke off a chunk of the pie's flaky crust, popped it into her mouth. "Little Miss Nitwit has a crush."

"I do not!"

With relish, Linnie bit into her burrito pie. "The guy from Adworks?" She chewed thoughtfully. "Daisy in housekeeping wants to have his babies."

Jada grunted. "I'll hold the baby shower." To Cat, she said, "Put your hormones in lockdown. You aren't having a fling for all the obvious reasons. We don't have money to spare, and you need help with publicity. None of us has experience with ad buys or purchasing airtime."

"Or how to write ad copy, design the new website, or target potential customers," Cat threw in. "I get it."

When she'd opened her events-planning company in her early twenties, wasn't this exactly how she sashayed into disaster? Putting her attentions on dating in the hopes of finding the right guy, and letting her small business flounder? A repeat performance was *not* happening.

This time around, the stakes were much higher. Without a series of well-targeted promotions, they'd never return the inn to full occupancy. The ad budget allocated by Linnie was generous, but if Cat squandered the money?

The answer gave her pause. Allow the inn to slide back toward ruin, and the town of Sweet Lake would go down too.

Linnie read her expression with misgiving. "You have a crush?"

"Ryan told me I'm beautiful." The confession brought a disconcerting wave of euphoria. Ignoring the emotion, Cat plunged on. "We had a stupid battle over the posters the Sirens left on my desk—it really got out of hand—then he said he couldn't work in my office because I was too much of a distraction. He was so matter-of-fact, but the way he looked at me . . . like it was perfectly normal to tell a woman you're bowled over by her and need alone time to screw your head on straight."

"Whoa." Linnie nearly dropped the burrito pie. "He said all that?"

"Most of it was inference, but I caught the drift."

Jada said, "Guess I'll cancel Daisy's baby shower." She plucked at the clingy waistline of Cat's dress. "Tone down the sexy outfits. Nothing wrong with taking pride in how you look, but for the time being dress more like Linnie. The bag-lady style will hide your more provocative attributes."

Linnie nearly choked on her pie. "I don't dress like the homeless!"

"You come close. Whatever Daniel sees in you has nothing to do with your fashion sense." Jada wrinkled her nose. "Or lack thereof."

Cat put in, "You dress to hide your figure, but you shouldn't. You have nice curves." The familiar squabble brought a welcome sense of normalcy after the surreal events in her office. "Daniel wouldn't like you half as much if you were skinny."

They both moved in toward Linnie, to offer reassurance and steal a bite of the pie. Slapping them away, she looked to Cat. "What's the plan?"

The pragmatic Jada added, "We totally get how you'd like to find the perfect guy. I would too. But I'd never go looking on the job."

"I'm not looking on the job."

"Face it, Cat. You never have to look too hard. And no falling for the compliments. I admire your romantic streak, the way you're so damn hopeful about men, but you need to cultivate a healthy dose of cynicism. A guy who puts the moves on this fast is only after one thing."

"You're probably right," Cat agreed.

"Don't let him use you—use him. We're getting top-notch marketing expertise at a discount. The countdown to the concert is only the beginning. You're supposed to have the spring ad campaign nailed down soon."

Cat bobbed her head. "Right." She began walking away.

"Don't forget the other problem," Linnie said. "Much as I'd like to do you a solid, you're on your own."

Cat's self-confidence veered off the tracks. *Norah.*

She'd hung up on the fuming Siren.

Chapter 6

Julia padded across the kitchen, then removed the tightly wrapped plate from the refrigerator. "You're awfully late." She went to the microwave.

Ryan decided against reminding his mother about the three times he'd called to check in on her. The muscles from his neck to the base of his spine burnt with exhaustion. Strange how digging through paperwork took more endurance than sweating through a workout at the gym. After plowing through Miri's notes in the Wayfair's lobby, he'd spent most of the afternoon alone on the veranda mapping out ad proposals. Tomorrow he'd present his recommendations to Cat.

"Did I forget to tell you about the commute?" he asked, finessing the situation. This morning, he'd purposely avoided mention of the drive to Sweet Lake because he despised worrying her. "I spent the day with a new client."

The microwave pinged, and the aroma of lasagna brought a rumble from his stomach. He'd skipped Cat's stilted invitation to join her for lunch in the Sunshine Room. They were both uncomfortably aware of the need to limit their interactions until they got their lust under control. Tomorrow would be easier. They were both professionals. An ill-timed attraction wouldn't disrupt their working relationship.

"What sort of account?" Julia asked.

"A country inn."

"You're working out of town?"

The anxiety in her voice made him drum up a reassurance. "It's not a big deal. I'll handle the work from the office," he said, uncomfortable with the lie. If he explained about commuting to Sweet Lake over the next few weeks, she'd remain in a state of hypervigilance.

"This doesn't sound like your usual sort of account. You prefer large companies."

"This one's a favor for Miri." He peered out the sliding glass door at the backyard, ablaze in light. As was the front of the house—another bad sign in a day rife with bleak omens.

Setting the plate before him, his mother took note of his scowl. She switched off the patio lights.

"Don't start." Frowning, she cinched the belt of her bathrobe. "There's nothing wrong with being vigilant."

The defiance crowding her features increased his exhaustion. The usual reassurances were in order, starting with the state-of-the-art burglar alarm and the unlikelihood of anyone breaking in, least of all the abusive husband she'd escaped years ago. Reciting the litany required more strength than Ryan had on tap. The memory of Cat's waterfall of hair latched on to his senses, filling him with a miserable longing.

His mother rested her palm on his brow. "Would you like a glass of wine with your dinner?"

"Make it a big glass."

"Would you like something stronger? I'll join you."

"Dewar's, and please douse the lights out front." He never should've agreed to add spots on the roofline or replace the dim bulb in the lamppost with 150 watts. "You've got the place lit like a state penitentiary. I almost ducked down and drove past. If any of the neighbors complain, you'd better have a good excuse."

"Stop complaining. It's just past nine o'clock."

He pushed a chunk of lasagna across the plate, his appetite receding. "On a school night."

"I'll turn out the lights." She marched into the living room.

On the way back she made a detour to the wet bar, the pleasant tinkling of glass reaching his ears. He gladly accepted the glass of scotch neat. She'd poured herself the same and thoughtfully brought along the bottle.

"I can't recall ever seeing you drink on a weeknight." She regarded him with concern. "My diligent son. What's wrong?"

"Nothing's wrong. I'm just tired."

"You look like someone knocked you off your pedestal. What happened?"

"I met a woman." A sappy opener, but nothing better came to mind.

"You meet women all the time."

"Not like this one."

He nearly added, *She's beautiful.* During the long drive home, the holes in this rudimentary explanation had become glaringly obvious. He knew any number of attractive women. They didn't punch through his composure—not ever. Something more elemental drew him to Cat. The inability to ferret out the reason bothered him more than the attraction itself.

"Will you ask her out?"

He took a long pull on his drink. "She's the client." He yanked off his tie.

"Awful when love hits like a thunderbolt."

The conclusion was ludicrous. "That's it. I'm cancelling Netflix." She looked genuinely upset. "We've got to wean you off the romance flicks."

"Make light of this if you must. I'm not fooled. You look utterly thrown."

Having made the assessment, she rested her chin on the steep hills of her knuckles. An old woman's hand, knotted with arthritis, and yet his chest constricted when he met her gaze. Her interest put a girlish sparkle in her eyes. She was keen on gaining his trust, waiting patiently while he sifted through his thoughts.

An opening, and he walked through. "I wasn't expecting this."

"No one ever does." They clinked glasses and she said, "Tell me about her."

"She's earthy, warm—and funny. I'd swear I saw one of those Magic 8 Balls under the crap on her desk. Who checks their fortune in a kid's toy?"

"And she likes you?"

He took a long pull on his drink.

"I take it from the moody silence you'd rather not share."

"She's not like any woman I've ever met." He searched his mother's face for judgment, experiencing relief when he found none. "Listen, I don't buy into the concept of soul mates or finding the woman of your dreams. There's no love at first sight to guarantee you'll make it five years, let alone longer. Bullshit in a bottle." He looked up quickly. "Sorry." He drained his glass.

His mother laughed. "Some relationships do more than survive."

"Name one."

"The Brownes next door. Happy as campers with their three boys."

"Jim Browne works more hours than I do, and Jenny has a wandering eye. They spend most of their time avoiding each other. It won't surprise me if they call a divorce attorney before the boys reach junior high."

"What about Miri?"

"Too early to tell. Second marriage for them both. Not the best track record."

"Ryan, your pessimism is showing." Sobering, Julia looked at a point past his shoulder. Her voice thinning, she added, "I nearly didn't survive George, but I *did* feel as you do. Struck by a thunderbolt from the very first moment. Nothing was the same afterward."

The revelation put a buzzing in Ryan's ears. He set his glass down, unsure if he'd heard right. The moments when she found the stamina to discuss the past were more rare than tanzanite. He tried to recall the last time he'd broached the subject. During the rebellious years of his early twenties, he guessed. Now she was divulging the deepest mysteries of her life without prodding.

On autopilot, he reached for the Dewar's and refilled their glasses. After she'd taken a sip, he asked, "You met at Lux Jewels, right?"

"George came in to have his watch fixed. Working for a Mercedes dealership at the time, making good money as a mechanic. He was younger than you are today, and just as handsome. It was flattering to have a man so much younger take an interest. Disconcerting too."

"Why did you marry so quickly?"

"Will you think I'm foolish if I admit I was swept off my feet? I had a full life, with many friends in the art community—I'd stopped hoping for marriage. I was paid generously to manage the store, and the owner had become a close friend. Plus I'd done well enough designing jewelry on the side, which Lux Jewels carried exclusively."

She'd forsaken jewelry design to lead a life of anonymity. After arriving in Cincinnati, she'd managed the art department at Saint Justin's, one of the finest private high schools in Cincinnati, until her retirement. With a start, Ryan stumbled across the connection: the wire butterfly hanging in Cat's office had reminded him of the whimsical designs crusted with gems his mother had once wrought in platinum and gold.

They'd reached the nexus of her secrets. "After you finally left your marriage, why didn't you reunite with your family?" Dispatching George Hunt to the past never brought any qualms. Ryan felt differently about the relatives she'd seen fit to expunge from his life. "I guess I assumed you'd reconnect at some point."

Plainly the more difficult question. Considering, she allowed memories he couldn't guess at to flood her deep-set eyes. "We ended on such bad terms." Her shoulders curved inward. "Your aunt came to visit the summer you were three. I shouldn't have let her come. You don't remember, but we used to take you to see my family once a year. That year, she insisted on visiting us in San Francisco quite unexpectedly."

Ryan knew not to ask for his aunt's name, or for identifying details about the extended family he didn't remember. His mother had always guarded the details of the past as if they posed a danger to his well-being. It was yet another example of the damage George Hunt continued to exert on her psyche.

He asked, "Why didn't you want your sister to visit us in San Francisco?"

"George never treated me badly when we flew back East. Never when we spent time with my family."

Back East. Ryan filed away the nugget of information. Lots of geography hidden behind the cryptic words. She could've grown up in Bangor, Maine, or New York City.

"George treated you badly only when no one was around to stop him?" Anger followed the question.

"He behaved appropriately when we were with others."

"But your sister wasn't fooled?"

"Not for a minute. She had a terrible argument with George. Naturally he denied everything. He swore I got the bruises from a fall down the steps."

"Why didn't you leave with her?" Ryan wanted to follow up with the more gut-wrenching question: Why had she readily forgiven, time and again, the man who'd abused her repeatedly?

"Sweetheart, you can't understand. I know that sounds like an excuse. It's not."

The lasagna had grown cold. He dug a forkful from the plate.

He finished half of the meal before asking, "Why can't I understand?"

"You've never been in love."

"Debatable."

"Oh, Ryan. You've never felt anything near the irrational, all-consuming love I felt for your father. The emotion can lift you up. It can also blind you. I wanted to believe your father would change. I needed to believe."

"It's all right," he murmured.

"I never meant to put you in danger."

"What happened after his argument with your sister?"

"George left for work, and she called our parents. Afterward, she relayed their ultimatum—leave my husband, or they'd disown me." Julia laughed, a tinny sound bitter with regret. "A bluff, really. They would've braved fire or worse to keep their daughters happy and safe. I'm sure they assumed I'd come to my senses if they made clear how frightened they were for my welfare—and yours."

Putting together the rest was painfully easy. "The following year, you left George for the first time, moved us to a new apartment in San Francisco. After the camping trip, when he . . ." Ryan found himself unable to fill in the rest. The memory of a forest's draping shade, and a jagged bottle slicing across his face. The sheer, shocking pain ripping through the placid surface of his life. Trying again, he added, "You did leave."

"I only left your father for six months when we moved to the new apartment in San Francisco." She hesitated. "Then I forgave George, and brought you back to a life I knew was dangerous for us both."

"Yeah, but you finally wised up, moved us to Salt Lake."

"And reconciled again."

Not for long, that last time, and the memory put acid in Ryan's stomach. How his father showed up one day at the apartment in Salt Lake and moved right in. How George waited a full week before punishing Ryan's mother for disappearing from San Francisco five years earlier.

Changing tack, he said, "I still don't see why you didn't patch things up with your family eventually."

"Sweetheart, I can't tell you how many times I nearly picked up the phone. Especially those first years, and always on your birthday. Thank goodness I didn't. I'm sure we both have guardian angels."

"That's a leap." Given all they'd endured it seemed more likely a malevolent spirit had dogged their heels until they reached the sanctuary of Ohio.

"Believe what you will. I thank our guardian angels for stopping me from reaching out to my family. George hated them and probably would have tried to hurt them too. He definitely would have hurt me for contacting them. When we reconciled in Salt Lake, I promised him I'd never let my family meddle again."

The comment nudged another memory buried deep inside Ryan. He recalled George camped out in front of the TV with a six-pack, and his mother shut inside her bedroom in the Salt Lake apartment, saying a tearful goodbye on the phone. Whether she'd been talking to her sister or her parents, he doubted he'd ever learn. For days afterward, she barely spoke at all.

"Why *did* you keep taking George back?"

The question hung between them for a painful moment. When Julia spoke again, her voice carried a dull resignation.

"I took our marital vows seriously. I loved your father even when I felt I had no choice but to leave him again. For five years after we left him behind in Salt Lake, I grieved. And I still loved him. Then, of course, he found us in Idaho. Do you remember that day in Twin Falls?" Her fingers skated across her brow. "What a stupid question. You were in high school by then. Of course you remember."

Ryan shut his eyes tightly. Memories he'd done his best to never examine crowded in. Even now, there were giant holes in his recollections, moments from childhood he'd entirely blocked out.

A secret he continued to keep as his mother said, "After your father found us that last time, I knew it would never end. I had to change our identities and get as far away as possible."

A sensation like suffocation bore down on Ryan. The final day in Idaho represented the blackest hours of his life. Trooping in from high school to find a man he barely recognized drunk on the couch, his unfocused gaze failing to track Julia staggering across the room, blood streaming down her face.

Within minutes, they were on the road.

Ryan pushed to his feet, then went to the sink to wash and dry his plate. He rattled the dishes in the cupboard while putting his away. He took his time filling the coffeepot and setting the timer, giving his mother room to compose herself. The conversation had taken a toll on her.

The squeak of a chair announced her imminent departure. Coming across the room, he clasped her wrist gently and turned her into his arms. For long minutes, he rocked her.

They each cherished a predictable routine, and went their separate ways to ready for bed. A long hallway divided their bedrooms, with two guest bedrooms in between. The house wasn't lavish but it was orderly—another trait they shared, a gift from the chaotic past. Ryan checked his laptop for mail from the office. Finding none, he crawled into bed.

Before dawn, he woke with a dream of Cat lingering in his senses. He had hours before he needed to don a suit and make the drive out to Sweet Lake. Restless, he pulled on jeans and quietly slipped out of the house. He drove through the darkness with his thoughts turning to the sad details his mother had shared.

On Springdale Road, the bluish lights of the gas station fell across the street. Behind the counter, a kid with dreadlocks played games on his smartphone. Beside the cash register, the morning's copies of *USA Today* sat in a stack.

He walked outside, leafing through the pages with urgency. Sure enough, the feature took up most of the front page of the Money section. The photographs, larger than he would've preferred, depicted an executive content in his success, a man who'd willingly traded anonymity for news coverage.

Ryan tossed the paper on the passenger seat. Across the parking lot, the first traces of sunlight bled into the shadows.

Chapter 7

Toweling her hair dry, Cat stepped from the bathroom and frowned at her unexpected visitor. On the side of her bed, Jada rustled through a newspaper.

A soft thumping carried across the ceiling. The men tasked with repairing the roof were already clambering across the opposite end of the south wing. In a nod to the two women still living inside, they avoided the portion closest to the Wayfair's main structure until after 9:00 a.m.

Cat shook out her damp hair. "Shouldn't you be in the kitchen?" At eight o'clock, Jada was usually baking.

"I thought you should see this." She handed over the Money section of *USA Today*.

The headline read "The Unsung Hero of Corporate Giving." The article detailed Ryan's efforts to bundle corporate ad campaigns with worthy charities. The piece took up most of the page, with three photos of him interspersed with the copy—leaning against the desk in his spacious office at Adworks, meeting with the manager of an organization that assisted battered women and their children in the tristate area, chatting with an executive in the boardroom of an Ohio aerospace company.

When Ryan had stated he was the best in his field, she'd written the comment off as false bravado. Obviously the wrong conclusion.

Overwhelmed, Cat sank onto the side of the bed. "I finally reached Miri last night. Why didn't she mention this?"

"I'm sure she thought Ryan would bring it up."

"He didn't." She hadn't given him the opportunity. She'd spent most of yesterday avoiding him. "I had no idea Miri sent her top employee to make up for bowing out."

"Have you seen the commercial on TV, the one with Buckeye Steel employees working on Habitat for Humanity projects? I love that commercial."

"It plays on TV constantly."

"Ryan's behind it."

"I've seen the ads by Freidman Investments for WomanCare," Cat murmured, skimming the article. "The theme's called Investing in the Safety of Families."

"Ryan's done some incredible work."

Cat's heart shifted. "He has."

According to *USA Today*, his ability to integrate charities with the campaigns of regional corporations reaped millions in donations for good works—and a sharp rise in customer satisfaction for the companies involved. Thanks to his efforts, Annette Givens-Coyne, president of WomanCare, expected another four percent increase in giving this year. Farther down in the article, representatives from a Cleveland charity for children with autism and the president of the Make-a-Wish Foundation also sang Ryan's praises.

Jada said, "Forget what I told you yesterday. Ryan's not the type with only one thing on his mind. You can't date him, but he's obviously a good man."

"Stop worrying. With all my new responsibilities, I don't have time to date." Rising, Cat went to the dresser and began applying makeup. "This is the first time I've felt like my actions make a real difference. With the right marketing mix, the Wayfair will become a jobs engine for Sweet Lake, just like when we were younger."

"We'll get there."

She finished applying mascara, then hesitated. "Yesterday I ran into LaTasha Peale coming in to work second shift in the Sunshine Room," she said, referring to the inn's restaurant.

"Tough raising two kids on your own."

"Not that you'd know it."

"She *has* received help from the Sirens. I overheard Frances talking to Linnie."

Cat knew about the clothing purchased for LaTasha's girls and the trips to the grocery store, which her mother and Frances orchestrated. "Sure, but she's been getting by on part-time work since losing her job at the Wayfair years ago. I've never seen LaTasha complain, and her daughters always look happy. When I ran into her, she thanked me for the job. Second time she's done that."

"Yeah, she's thanked me too." Jada smiled. "We did the right thing."

She meant the decision, made together with Linnie, to quietly draw up a list of past employees and decide whom to reinstate first. LaTasha's name had topped the list. An obvious choice, given her work ethic. What Cat hadn't expected was LaTasha's gratitude—she'd earned the reinstatement, and the inn belonged to Linnie, after all.

Dating, even someone like Ryan, came in a poor second to the chance to make a difference in people's lives.

Sheepishly she took in the large suite she'd called home since the Wayfair fell on hard times. Her own life needed improvement. The chairs by the window lay buried beneath clothes she'd forgotten to put away. Beefcake Bill leaned against the wall, his cartoonish face peering toward the dresser with its jumble of cosmetics, jewelry, and odd receipts. Her office looked no better. It was a wonder that Ryan hadn't walked in, taken a quick look, and walked right back out.

Cat scooped up a handful of receipts and pitched them into the garbage can. "I'm an idiot. Next to the other work Ryan's done, dealing with the Wayfair must feel like a demotion. Do I owe him an apology?"

"I wouldn't dump him in the lobby again. He can't help us if you're constantly ditching him." Jada stalked to the closet. "Wear this today." She pulled out a knit dress with a high collar and three-quarter sleeves.

"My funeral dress? Get real." She hadn't worn it since her grandmother's service. "Pick something else."

"Nope, this is the one. You'll put the kibosh on Ryan's libido if you give off a funereal air."

"But I don't want to look like death!"

"And no jewelry. I'm not blaming you for leading on our hot new ad exec, but you *can* send the right signals."

The inference wounded her pride. "You act like I sent the wrong signals yesterday."

"Cat, your femininity's been on steroids since you were twelve. Stop drawing attention to your attributes, and he'll lay on fewer compliments."

Her pulse jumped. "What if he doesn't?" She'd spent the better part of a sleepless night coming to grips with the facts. She'd felt the same instant attraction.

Jada pushed her toward the bathroom. "Like you said, you're too busy to date. If he throws steamy glances, ignore them. If he makes another comment about your looks, pretend you've lost hearing in *both* ears." She glanced at her watch. "I've got to go. Another hour of baking, then I'm doing the walk-through with the heating and cooling guys."

"Ask them to work on the heating first." The unit in the south wing was shot.

"Already done." She brushed a damp strand of hair from Cat's eyes. "You'll be all right? If there's a problem, drum up an excuse to drag me into the meeting."

"I'm sure he'll behave." Cat picked up the newspaper they'd left on the bed. "Look at the work he's done. I should've treated him better yesterday. I thought he was bragging. Who knew he was understating his accomplishments?"

"He's not the only one I'm worried about." Jada paused in the doorway. "Stay on your best behavior."

The door clicked shut.

Heeding the advice, Cat shimmied the dress over her head then grabbed the blow dryer. The butterflies returned to her stomach, as if she were readying for an important date. Quashing the thought, she bundled her hair into a loose ponytail and slipped on her ugly beige flats. She couldn't recall the last time she'd left her suite without earrings, or at least a few bracelets. Resisting the urge to add a touch of glam, she went downstairs.

She breezed into her office and immediately skidded to a halt. Ryan had beaten her to work. Only he'd done more than show up early.

He'd literally rolled up his shirtsleeves to get started. Not on the marketing campaign—he was riffling through the boxes surrounding her filing cabinet.

With a nervous smile, he straightened. "Good morning." His attention leapt from the clump of papers in his fist to the clock on the wall. "I got in early. Mr. Uchida told me to wait in your office. Thought I'd pitch in."

A fan of hanging files sat atop the cabinet. She spotted his neat penmanship. "You're unpacking my stuff?"

"Do you mind?"

"I'm not sure." There were few tasks she despised more than organizing paperwork. "I guess not."

He opened the next box, studied the contents. "You'll have room to walk around in here once the filing cabinet's filled."

"Where should I begin?"

He slid a box toward her feet. "Guest receipts dating back to 1974."

She stifled a groan. "Must we keep them all?"

The desperation lacing the query seemed to ease his nervousness. Which proved startling—she wasn't the only one suffering from anxiety.

"Keep the last ten years, and ask Linnie to put the rest in storage. After we nail down the fall ad buys, I'll help you input the names and addresses in a spreadsheet. I have some ideas on simple mailers to reach out to past customers."

"Ryan, I can't ask you to help with secretarial work. Your time is too valuable."

"Think of it as my gift to the inn's new marketing manager."

Evidently the remark didn't come across as matter-of-fact as intended, and embarrassment flickered across his features. Turning away, he opened the last box. The arrogance he'd displayed yesterday was nowhere in evidence as he began filling the cabinet.

Unspoken tension clung to the air, but Cat saw the wisdom of following his lead. Feigning immunity to the crackling awareness bounding between them, she got to work. She wanted to mention the *USA Today* feature, but his single-minded focus warded off potential compliments.

In less than an hour, the filing cabinet groaned with paperwork. Together they deposited the last boxes in the corridor.

"Mind if we wait until this afternoon for the grand tour of the inn?" Sorting through the paperwork had subdued her nervousness over working with a man she liked far too much. "We should walk down to the lake while it's still early."

"Wouldn't you rather go over the ad budget first?" Ryan adjusted his tie, a beautiful green silk that matched his eyes. "I've put together the proposal."

"Let's go over the numbers when we get back. There aren't many guests booked this week, but the sunbathers will be out in force once the Sunshine Room finishes serving breakfast."

Relenting, he followed her out to the veranda. When they started down the steps, she caught the odd tightening of his lips.

"You have something against the great outdoors?" Out of habit, she stretched out her arms to capture the September warmth. A flawless day, without a cloud in the sky. "Loosen up, Ryan. A brisk walk is better than coffee to start the day."

"For some." A bee zipped past, and he swatted it away. "I'm not crazy about the great outdoors."

"Allergies?"

"No."

Who preferred four walls to fresh air and sunshine? If dragging her desk to the front lawn wouldn't inconvenience the guests, she'd work outside in all but the winter months.

"I can take small parks in cities. Baseball fields, backyard cookouts in suburbia with the neighbors leering over the fence and police cruisers squealing in the distance." He surveyed the untamed vista, the dense emerald band of the forest, and the leaping waves of the lake glittering in the distance. "I'm not really an outdoor guy."

An odd revelation, and she wondered if he suffered from some sort of phobia. "Jada hates enclosed spaces. If the Wayfair had an elevator, she'd still take the stairs."

He cast a quick glance. "You've always lived in Sweet Lake?" Apparently a discussion regarding his aversion to nature was off the table.

"Born and bred. I can't imagine living anywhere else." She led him down the stone path toward the lake. "What about you? Always been in Cincinnati?"

He appeared to weigh the question with a strange misgiving. "I was born in San Francisco." He paused to look behind. Three blue vans were disgorging construction workers in the parking lot. "Linnie's hired a big crew. When did the renovations begin?"

"In August." Evidently his background was another topic he'd prefer off the table, but she found his evasions annoying. There was no harm in getting better acquainted. "You grew up in San Francisco?"

"No."

She'd had enough. "Don't take this wrong way, but has anyone mentioned you're weirdly unpredictable? Hot and cold. First you do this nice thing, and help organize my office. Now you're acting like someone in the witness protection program." She made a half-hearted attempt to stanch the impatience in her voice. "I'm asking about your childhood, Ryan. It's called an ice breaker."

The direct approach nearly put amusement on his lips. It seemed a great loss when the crow's feet framing his eyes deepened.

"I didn't grow up in one place like you did. My mother took us to Utah, then Idaho." A long pause, his strides quickening as he added, "We left Idaho when I was sixteen."

She hurried to catch up. No mention of a father, and she sensed the conversation gave him no pleasure. "I'm sorry."

He stopped abruptly, and they nearly collided. "Why are you sorry?"

The intensity returned to his features, but she detected the sorrow underneath. "I'm getting the impression they weren't happy moves." He looked uncomfortable, the muscles in his jaw growing taut. "What came after Idaho?"

"Cincinnati. Been there ever since."

"Why Ohio?"

Another sharp glance, but this one carried amusement. "You sure ask a lot of questions."

"The habits of Curious Cat. That was my nickname growing up. Feel free to mock me if the prying goes overboard."

"I'd never mock you, and I'm not sure why we chose Ohio. I guess my mother needed the Continental Divide between herself and the past. I know I did." They reached the last, steepest hill, where the lawn met the golden sands of the beach. Helping her down, he added, "We have a house in the burbs. I bought it exactly one year after landing the job with Miri. We lived in a condo before then."

"We?"

"I live with my mother."

Best guess, she and Ryan were about the same age. Which made her wonder why a successful man in his thirties chose to live with his mother. The answer came immediately.

He didn't live with her; *she* lived with him. There was a gravity surrounding Ryan that hinted at pressing responsibilities, greater obligations than most adults carried.

"She's retired now," he added. "She taught art at a private high school near our home in Cincinnati."

"Interesting. My dad taught at Sweet Lake High. Social studies. My sister got the post when he retired. Not that he's slowed down much. My mom's a CPA in town, and he runs the house, gardens—he loves to cook, and they're always holding parties in their backyard."

"I wish my mother were as sociable. Change is really hard for her, so she keeps a strict routine. She's turning into a recluse. I'm working on springing her from a self-imposed prison."

"Good works for charities, and you look out for your mother." With a laugh, Cat made the connection that should've dawned when Jada handed her the newspaper this morning. "Your name is a perfect fit."

"D'Angelo?" Devilry glimmered in his eyes, tripping her pulse. "Cat, I'm no angel. I got so many speeding tickets in college, the cops took away my license—twice. Call it a late adolescence, with me acting out because I wasn't successful at processing the worst parts of my childhood." They approached the lake, and though his features grew somber, he seemed carried away by his loosening tongue. "When Miri hired me? I blew my first two accounts by showing up late more often than not. Too much drinking in my twenties, too many women—I didn't get my act together until recently. One of those shock-and-awe moments that blast you into normalcy."

"I'm not sure I've ever had one of those."

"Mine came while cleaning out the garage, of all things."

Again he came to a standstill to take in the melody of the waves and the sands cradling the lake. He appraised his oxfords with ill-concealed disgust.

Cat slipped off her pumps. "Take yours off," she advised, wishing he'd finish the story. What was the shock and awe that brought him to his senses? In a garage, of all places. "The sand will destroy them if you don't."

He did, hooking his expensive shoes on one hand and stuffing his navy socks in his blazer pockets. The breeze tufted his raven locks. He quickly gave up on smoothing his hair into place.

Veering from the surf, she made a line in the sand with her toe. "This is where we'll put the dance floor for the music."

"You're holding the concert the second weekend in October, correct?"

"The second Saturday."

"Where will you put the band?"

"We'll set up the dais over here." She pointed to the area. "We'll put folding chairs in rows, leave the sides open for people to sit on the sand. I'm also bringing in a bar to serve drinks and a line of tables for munchies."

"Plans for Sunday?"

"Jada's putting together a brunch service in the ballroom. We don't have enough rooms for everyone who'll come to the concert. We're hoping to lure some of them back."

"We should put together a trifold brochure to have visible during brunch, with spring and summer discounts if people book early. You've got a captive audience—don't let them leave without pitching future bookings at the inn."

She liked the idea. "I'll talk to Linnie about rate discounts if people book early."

"Who's playing Saturday night?"

"Midnight Boyz, from Cleveland."

"They're an unholy pain."

"You've worked with them?"

"Pulled my client out in the nick of time. We needed ambient noise for a commercial." Head bowed, Ryan followed the line she'd made in the sand. "They e-mailed a crazy list of demands. I told the client I'd find another band."

"Porterhouse steaks, that sort of thing?"

"I would've agreed to a year of free meals at Sizzler. The client owns sporting goods stores in Ohio and Pennsylvania. Midnight Boyz wanted free rock climbing equipment and an all-expenses-paid trip to Joshua Tree."

He continued trailing behind, too close, and she picked up the pace. "Talk about chutzpah," she said, moving nearer to the forest's shade, where she planned to set up the tables for snacks.

"Chutzpah," he repeated, chuckling softly. "There's a word I didn't expect to hear from the hot Latina client. Who taught you Yiddish?"

She sensed his attention weaving across her back. "My brother's girlfriend. They live in Columbus." Heat spiraled across her shoulder blades, the pleasure it brought unwelcome. "And don't call me hot."

"A woman with an aversion to compliments. Must be a first."

"Ryan, we agreed not to flirt."

"Did we?"

Hesitating, she dug her toes into the sand. They'd almost reached the edge of the forest. Ryan, honed in on her with his usual intensity, didn't seem to notice.

On an intake of breath, she found the courage to face him. "It was implied."

"I suppose." He gave an appraising glance. "I'll admit to a strong desire to ask you out, if only to get the lowdown on the Magic 8 Ball. Do you also read tarot cards?"

"Hardly. The Magic 8 Ball is more like a nervous tic." He waggled his brows, prodding her on, and she added, "Don't you have any silly superstitions? Stuff you do for no logical reason?"

"Like step over cracks in the sidewalk? Sorry to disappoint you."

"What do you do for fun?"

"Big Cav's fan, and I'll never stop rooting for the Browns. I don't care how many times they tank in the second half. I also like to dance. I don't get much chance to lately, with all the work." The devilish gleam was back in his eyes. "Do you like to dance?"

"Let's wrap up the beach tour. Did I show you where I'll set up the buffet?" She loved to dance, but imagining the pleasure of his embrace would upend the professional relationship they'd only started to build. He grinned, no doubt aware of her discomfort, and she added bluntly, "Whatever this is that we're doing to each other, we have to stop."

"You first." He suddenly looked feverish, his Adam's apple convulsing. "Stop doing that thing with your dress."

She stared at him blankly.

Embarrassment followed. While kicking up sand, she'd bunched her stretchy skirt in big handfuls. Add in a daydream about dancing with him beneath dim club lighting, and she'd managed to hoist the fabric halfway up her thighs. Speaking around her frozen larynx proved impossible.

The unconsciously sensual act sent her thoughts into free fall.

Did he think she was deliberately taunting him? He'd displayed more than common courtesy by arriving early today, taking the initiative of sorting through the mess in her office. Without his encouragement, she would've let the boxes grow dust until Christmas.

"Ryan, I'm a nitwit. I didn't mean to—"

With bewilderment, she broke off.

The passion sank from his features like the moon dipping beneath dark waters. It disappeared so quickly, the air stuttered in her lungs. He no longer seared her with a hungry stare. His pupils constricting, he no longer seemed aware of her at all. Transfixed, he locked his attention on whatever he glimpsed beyond her shoulder.

The trees.

For reasons beyond comprehension, the forest terrified him.

Cat knew she wasn't the most practical woman. She wasted too much time daydreaming, too much time primping instead of deciding what to accomplish in any given day. But her protective streak was bred to the bone.

Taking Ryan by the arm, she forcibly walked him out of the shade. She led him all the way to the water, her palm pressed firmly to his back. His shirt was damp; perspiration beaded on his brow.

Without seeking permission, she slung her arm around his waist. He was a good four inches taller and fifty pounds heavier, but he leaned into her like a child caught in a nightmare.

A waking nightmare, triggered by the forest.

Helplessly, she searched his face. "What is it?" A shudder convulsed his back, and she held on tight. "I feel awful—I had no idea. You weren't kidding about hating the great outdoors."

"No worries. Just give me a sec." He shrugged off her embrace. He stood apart with his eyes fixed on the waves rolling toward shore. "It's been a long time since I've had one of these attacks. Doesn't usually hit this hard. Hell, I should've noticed where we were walking. I hate forests."

"Should I get help?"

"Relax. I'm not diabetic or anything like that." He scraped a lock of hair from his brow. "So much for booze on a work night and too much conversation."

"With your mother?"

"Last night."

"What did you talk about?" she prodded, and her stomach fell at the blankness on his face.

With the methodical rhythm of an ingrained habit, he traced the scar beneath his left eye. An old injury, a mark left from childhood no doubt, but one so deep, he'd carry it for a lifetime.

He stopped tracing the scar, his expression closing. "Let's get going on the budget proposal." He retrieved his socks from his blazer and pulled them on quickly. "It's extensive, with lots of options. You'll need time to digest it all."

He didn't wait for her response. He tugged on his shoes and walked off the beach.

For the remainder of the day, Cat hid her natural effervescence behind polite questions about his suggestions for the inn's marketing. In the late afternoon, and again throughout the week, Ryan searched for a way to apologize.

He'd upset her on the beach with his ill-advised flirtations, not to mention the panic attack—his first with anyone nearby. She made no more offers to take him outside. She meant well, but her thoughtfulness scraped against his pride. He didn't like appearing weak.

There was something of the natural healer in Cat's personality. In the afternoons, she slipped off alone to take in the unusually warm weather and the autumn colors. She returned with short branches of crimson and gold leaves she stuffed into vases, and handfuls of acorns she left in tiny mounds on her desk. If he couldn't enjoy the riches of the countryside, she seemed intent on bringing the natural world to him.

The sweet tactic brought the unintended result of increasing the attraction he was doing his best to cool. Try as he might to view Cat as merely a warm and engaging colleague, his feelings for her grew deeper and more complex.

On Friday, needing a break from the supercharged air in her office, he invented an afternoon meeting at Adworks and left the inn at two o'clock. In Sweet Lake Circle, a trio of young mothers shared conversation while their children raced between the picnic tables. Taking care not to disturb them, Ryan chose a picnic table at the opposite end to sit with his thoughts in private.

A boy in the group of children broke off his play with the others. Trailing laughter, he began spinning in a circle. Faster and faster he went, his arms flying out from his sides and his face beaming. Then he lost his dance with gravity and flopped to the ground.

The laughter he sent out, the wild, uncontained joy, gripped Ryan with glum fascination.

Turning away, he trudged back to his car.

Chapter 8

The doorbell chimed twenty minutes too soon. Guiltily, Frances weighed the option of pretending she wasn't home.

A quick peek through the living room drapes sent the notion into the trash. On the front stoop, Ruth swayed from foot to foot with spicy impatience. Ignore the bell, and the retired police dispatcher would stomp around back. Once she found the silver Audi coupe in the garage, she'd pound on the back door.

"Coming!" Frances donned her most gracious, if manufactured, smile. "Ruth, did we have an appointment? Forgive me. We must reschedule. I have another engagement."

"I only need a minute." She stalked into the foyer.

"Fine. A minute." Frances studied the familiar MacBook Air with its lime-green cover. "What are you doing with Tilda's laptop?"

"Borrowing it. She got a new one in August. Doubt she cares if this one takes a vacation."

"For a woman with a background in law enforcement, you have sticky fingers."

"I'm enterprising." Ruth made a beeline for the living room.

Frances nearly pressed her to remove her dirt-encrusted boots. She loved all the Sirens, her sister warriors in the pursuit of the highest feminine ideals. Unfortunately some of her comrades held little appreciation for the sort of attire one should wear for a social visit—or for planning said visit in advance.

The beautifully appointed colonial was a source of great pride for Frances: antiques handed down in her family attractively combined with newer pieces in a pastel color scheme, brightened with carefully selected art. If her unexpected guest left clumps of mud across the Aubusson carpet, there was no sense in being upset. She'd simply call the cleaning service a day early.

"Can we please make this quick?" It wouldn't do to have Ruth hovering nearby when the others arrived. For days now, Frances had been searching for the perfect excuse to get them together at her house. Whether they'd appreciate her effort to intervene, she'd discover soon enough. "I do wish I had more time."

The polite dismissal raised her comrade's antennae. "What's the hurry?"

"I was about to go out back to deadhead my roses."

"You're gardening this late in the afternoon?"

"About to start."

Ad-libbing at random proved disastrous, and Ruth arched what was left of her brows. "You're gardening in a dress and fancy heels? Not like you to risk grass stains on your daywear." It was strange how the aging process had taken most of her facial hair, while leaving the glaringly white braids dangling from her head.

"Exactly why I'll change first."

"Need help? I don't have plans for the rest of the day."

"Did I say deadheading roses? Why, I finished the roses yesterday. I meant I'm pulling up poison ivy." Ruth's allergy to poison ivy was so severe, she steered clear of any clump she came across. "It's invading my petunia bed."

"Guess I'll pass." Ruth flipped open the laptop, patted the seat beside her on the couch. "Show me how to set up an Airbnb account and I'll be on my way."

"Why are you interested in Airbnb?"

"I might as well make some cash in October like everyone else," she said when Frances joined her. "I hear the Wayfair is expecting a full house for the concert."

"You're renting your spare bedroom to strangers during the weekend of the concert? I can't say I approve."

"Color me surprised."

"Ruth, there are dangerous men in the world." There were men capable of inflicting great harm. "What if you end up with the wrong sort under your roof?"

"Are you suggesting I can't protect my hide? Any tough guy who tangles with me better come packin'."

"Ruth!"

"Relax. Tilda says we'll mostly draw in young couples. Doubt your typical ax murderer will roll into town just to hear a boy band from Cleveland."

"There's no such thing as being too careful. On the off chance an ax murderer *is* clicking around on Airbnb, I'd hate to find you chopped up in little pieces, all because you were determined to make a buck."

Ruth glowered. "You got a corset on under your dress? Your adventurous spirit is laced up so tight, it's just about suffocated."

"For your information, corsets went out of fashion during the Edwardian era." Shrugging off the insult was advisable—Cat and Silvia were due any moment. "Airbnb, of all things. Who put this silly idea in your head?"

"The idea's not silly. Half of the Sirens are renting out rooms. Cat's got a new ad running on the radio. I hear she's expecting hundreds of people. Why shouldn't we cash in on the crowds?"

The doorbell rang. Answering wasn't necessary—Norah barged right in.

"Has Frances shown you how to put up your profile page?" She plunked her laptop on the coffee table beside the one lifted from Tilda's house. "If this works, we should open our homes whenever the Wayfair runs big events. I heard the handsome young man who's helping Cat with marketing has suggested events for every warm-weather month. Imagine how much we'll earn renting out rooms."

"I hope we get a chance to meet him," Frances said. "From what Linnie has told me, he's giving Cat wonderful ideas to boost the Wayfair's visibility. They're on their way to rebuilding Sweet Lake's reputation as a tourist town."

A noise between a grunt and a snarl emitted from Ruth. "I met Ryan D'Angelo on the day he took the account. Full of himself, if you ask me."

"Must you remind us about your one-woman welcoming committee?" Frances replied with a sigh. Ruth was the only Siren to have met Ryan, and she certainly hadn't rolled out the welcome mat. "Rattling a gourd in his face—if he'd jumped into his car and raced back to Cincinnati, the inn would've lost out on his expertise."

"Stop defending him. He acted like he'd have the final decision on whether the Sirens conduct seminars or not."

No, Frances thought, *he won't have the final say.*

She would.

Soon, in fact, assuming she wrapped up the unscheduled visit before Cat and Silvia arrived. She reached for Norah's laptop. "Let's make this quick. All right, here's the site."

Airbnb popped onto the screen.

Norah pursed her maroon-tinted lips. "According to the rules, we can decide who stays, and when." An unbecoming and rather predatory glee lit her features.

Ruth's antennae went back up. "Norah, it's your happy day. Tell the site you only want single men, any age, the hornier the better."

"Must you resort to vulgar allusions?"

"With all the ammo you're doling out? Yes."

"You sexless old biddy. Someone amputated your libido before the Berlin Wall fell. If I only prefer single men in my home, how is that any of your concern?"

"If you're playing hostess in a negligee and there's money changing hands, I'll draw any conclusion I damn well please."

Furious, Norah smacked her adversary's jean-clad knee. Ruth poked her right back, igniting a squabble. Once more the doorbell rang. Frances struggled out from between them. She'd barely escaped the living room when Sylvia let herself in.

Pausing in the foyer, Silvia regarded the yelping women. "Airbnb? I told them I'd set up their listings after I got off work."

"Then why are they hounding me?"

"Greed, mostly. They're eager to get their profiles built and find customers. If this keeps up, the inn will have competition in the hospitality trade."

The noise in the living room rose to a fractious pitch. Ruth latched on to Norah's flowing scarf. She yanked her sideways like a horse she was determined to break. What Ruth lacked in size she made up for in sheer aggression. Flailing wildly, her statuesque opponent rolled off the couch.

Frances pressed a hand to her heart. "Stop them, will you?"

"Frances, I wish you'd grow a backbone. We're supposed to be co-leaders of the Sirens. You always leave me with the dirty work."

"Silvia, please. I'll never get the blood out of my upholstery."

"A tragedy, I'm sure." Silvia cupped her hands around her mouth. "Who wants ice cream?"

It was the sort of summons sure to break up a brawl between schoolboys. Norah, a New York model in her youth, was immune to the bait. However, Ruth never missed an opportunity to sample the Häagen-Dazs Frances stowed in the freezer.

Silvia was scooping a bowl for her when the doorbell chimed once more, and Frances hurriedly opened the door.

On the stoop, Cat scanned the cars in the drive with ill-concealed trepidation. "Frances, is this a stealth move by the Sirens? I'm out of here."

⤳

Frances ensnared her wrist, propelling her forward with an impressive show of force. The pearls around the elderly Siren's neck bounced. Teetering on her pumps, she hauled her quarry up and into the house.

The Waterford lamp on the foyer table joggled.

Righting it, Cat shot her a look of pure exasperation. "Geez, Frances. Planning to knock me out cold if I refused to enter?" Perking her ears, she zeroed in on the lively conversation in the kitchen. "Oh no you don't. I'd expect my mother to form a lynch mob to hunt me down. Coming from you, this is a real shock."

"There's no lynch mob." Frances straightened the belt on her stylish dress. "I apologize for inviting you here under false pretenses."

"Did you feed Mami the same line about needing advice on rearranging your den?" A crafty stratagem, since they both loved to help with the never-ending decorating of the spacious colonial. Lowering her voice, Cat added, "I don't care how many Sirens are lurking in your kitchen. I can't let them hold seminars. I've resorted to having Mr. Uchida send text alerts whenever the Sirens show up at the inn. I'm tired of making business calls in the ladies' restroom. The place echoes."

"Relax, dear. I'm on your side."

Cat was taken aback. "You are?"

"Of course I am. The seminars are an imposition you don't need."

Shrugging off her irritation, Cat checked her appearance in the foyer's gilded mirror. She'd grown tired of the dull grey and taupe dresses Jada insisted she wear and had switched it up today. If she donned sackcloth, would it matter? For a week now, she'd been dodging Jada in the mornings and trading soulful looks with Ryan for the remainder of each day.

From the kitchen, her mother appeared. "Where have you been? Your father's invited you to dinner twice this week, and you've canceled both times."

With an angry shimmy, Cat repositioned her breasts in her bra. "Leave Papa out of this. I'm sure he's blameless." Her skin-hugging dress had also shifted halfway around her hips, thanks to Frances's manhandling. "If I had come over, were you planning to feed me in the kitchen or the dining room?" She wasn't remotely interested in one of her mother's advice-laden meals in the dining room.

"Now, hold on. *I'm* the one asking questions."

"Ask someone else. And don't flare your nostrils at me. Frances is right. You look like a mad bull when you're upset."

Frances blanched. "Leave me out of this, please. You're both upset, and I'm part Dutch. My genetic makeup doesn't allow me to handle turbulent emotions."

The comment skimmed past Silvia. "I'm not flaring my nostrils!" She squared off before Cat. "Avoiding my calls and your father's meals— he spent hours making pineapple barbecue sauce just for you. This is the thanks we get? I'm angry like a wasp."

"Like that's news. The seminars are still *out*."

Ruth came into the foyer with a bowl of ice cream and Norah tracking her heels.

"What did you say?" Norah snapped.

Silvia whipped around. "Back off, Norah. Arm wrestle Ruth all you'd like, but I expect you to use a civil tone with my daughter."

"I am using a civil tone. Considering how many of my calls she's ignored, I'm being damn polite."

Frances patted her salt-and-pepper hair. "Would anyone like a drink?" she asked in a shaky voice. Evidently this much excitement was playing havoc with her central nervous system.

The suggestion went unheard by Silvia. Index finger raised, she made jabbing motions in Norah's direction. "I don't care if my daughter deleted your number and never calls back. Butt out of my family business."

"Wake up, Silvia. The seminars are Siren business. If you can't pull your daughter into line, someone else will."

Frances smiled with the manic gaiety of a woman on the edge. "I'm having a sherry. Anyone care to join me?"

Ruth eased past the battling women. Crossing the living room, she headed to the built-in bar nestled beside the fireplace. Dumping her ice cream into a glass, she added Bacardi.

"Let's vote." Her gravelly voice silenced the others. "Who agrees Cat should cut us loose to get the talks going for the Wayfair's guests?"

Silvia's and Norah's hands shot up.

Squaring her narrow shoulders, Frances walked to the bar. "We're not voting." She took down a bottle of sherry, her sympathetic gaze finding Cat. "I'm tabling the idea indefinitely."

Cat winced as her mother stomped her foot. "Who put you in charge of this matter?" Silvia demanded. Her bond with Frances never stopped her from battling for the upper hand.

"Zip it, Silvia. We're not climbing Mount Everest, and I'm not vying for first rights to the summit." Frances drained her glass of sherry, then refilled. She looked to the others. "The inn has three capable women sharing the helm. We mustn't stand in their way. How can we pretend to uphold the finest ideals of womanhood if we're intent on sabotaging the works of our younger peers? Are we meddling old fools, or are we Sirens?"

Norah scowled. "I'm not old, and I never meddle." She threw an icy glance at Ruth, who was slurping her ice cream and rum. "You must be referring to someone else."

"Norah, be still! We're all equally guilty, equally to blame for butting in when our help isn't needed. What right do we have to devise plans to entertain the Wayfair's guests without inquiring if our help is wanted? 'Hear the Siren's call and give kindness in secret.' Isn't that our guiding principle? Isn't that the noble ideal we seek? If we strong-arm Cat or visit her office uninvited, we're neither kind nor acting in secret."

Cat nodded in vigorous agreement. Assuming the eloquent Siren finished her sermon before pouring another sherry, there was a good chance she'd sway the others.

The lofty speech evaporated the cloud of anger surrounding her mother. "Let's hope she finishes the speech before the sherry," Silvia murmured, echoing Cat's thoughts. She chuckled softly. "Get too much booze in her, and she'll stop making sense."

Cat released a pent-up breath. "I'd better lend a hand." Relief over her mother's improving mood gave her the courage to join Frances. "She's right. I can't let any of you host seminars."

At her unusual show of guts, her mother and Frances nodded approvingly.

Buoyed up by their tacit approval, she added, "I haven't made any final decisions because we're nearing the date for the concert on the beach. There are a thousand other tasks to deal with. However, my associate from Adworks is putting together an event schedule to carry us through next year."

Ruth made a face. "Ryan D'Angelo," she muttered. "I should've popped him on the head with my gourd."

An impossible feat given Ruth's petite stature. "I'm glad you didn't," Cat replied. "He's been an incredible help."

"Why can't you add our ideas to the mix?"

Silvia, never one to shy from battle, took up the gauntlet. "Ruth, you read the *USA Today* article just like the rest of us," she said. "You saw how many accounts Ryan has managed for big companies. Cat has a true professional guiding her decisions, and he's working at a discount. With all the fine work he's done tying charities into marketing for Ohio corporations, he's better at drumming up business than all the Sirens combined."

Cat added, "I need to use Ryan's expertise while it's available. We won't have him for much longer." The admission leached something vital from her. "After the concert, he's handing off the Wayfair to a secondary team at his firm. The feature in *USA Today* is a bigger boost to his career than anyone expected. He's fielding offers to work for companies across the state."

At the strain in her voice, her mother and Frances looked up. A knowing glance passed between them, the secret communication that was the hallmark of their friendship.

Silvia dumped the last of Ruth's ice cream drink in the wet bar's sink, drawing a muttered complaint. "We're done here. Ladies, if you don't mind, I have a private matter to discuss with my daughter."

From the coffee table, Norah scooped up her laptop. "What about Airbnb? We haven't set up our accounts."

"Stop by my house after dinner. Ruth, you too."

They left. Silvia returned to the living room with her bronzed features brewing another storm. "Cat, why do you care if Miri's golden boy leaves and someone else takes over? You haven't sounded this sad since the Clemson kid moved to Chicago for the insurance job."

Her mother was referring to Tory Clemson, whom she'd dated for nearly a year. "Mami, I was sad because Tory conveniently forgot to return my iPad before he left." He was one of the nicer men she'd dated. "I wouldn't put him in a league with Ryan."

"Am I getting this straight? Something's going on between you and the boy from Adworks?"

Impatience flashed through Frances's eyes. "Silvia, you act as if anyone under the age of forty is still battling acne and low self-esteem. Ryan D'Angelo isn't a boy." She regarded Cat. "Are you and Ryan dating?"

"We're not."

"Is he thinking about asking you out?"

"Look, it's hard to know what Ryan thinks about anything. He's warm and funny for hours. Then he's aloof." Although he tried to stay upbeat whenever she was nearby, the sadness in his eyes hinted at something from the past that still haunted him. He was moodier whenever he received a flurry of calls from his mother.

She recalled the day of his unexplained panic attack on the beach. *I guess my mother needed the Continental Divide between herself and the past. I know I did.* The moon-shaped blemish beneath his eye wasn't the only scar he carried. Some event from his life made him wary of intimacy.

Breaking into her thoughts, Frances asked, "You're saying he's not interested in dating you?"

"I wouldn't go that far. We're caught up in this ritual where we behave professionally for an hour. Then I find an excuse to touch him, or he bumps into me when we're crossing the room, and we're back to trading glances hot enough to leave blisters."

Three bar stools were stationed before the wet bar. Silvia slid onto one. "You *are* smitten." Her tone felt carefully neutral.

"I passed *smitten* ten laps ago."

"I'm not sure that's happy news."

"It's not. Ryan is already spending more time than needed in Sweet Lake, and I feel guilty about taking his mind off his other accounts. Not that I'm giving the right signals to send him away. I can't wait to see him. When he finishes work each day and climbs into his car, I spend the night missing him." She shrugged. "But what does it matter? He's got a great career in Cincinnati, and I love my job. Linnie's put her trust in me. I'll screw up a dozen times along the way, but I want to succeed in my new post. For her, and because it'll make a difference to the employees we'll rehire once the advertising kicks in."

The explanation didn't sit well with her mother. "Ambition is fine, but we're talking about your happiness. What does your heart tell you? Is there a chance our talented Mr. D'Angelo is the one? I don't need to remind you that your favorite childhood game was staging your own wedding—and stealing my best lingerie for your costume. You've been waiting to meet your life mate since you were a little girl."

Despite her misery, Cat chuckled. "I'm long past the pretend weddings." Back then, she'd destroyed her mother's nicest slips. Hitching each one up like a wedding dress, she'd waltzed down an aisle designed with rocks snatched from the flower beds, then concluded the pretend nuptials by tromping through the flowers with her imaginary groom. "Ryan is everything I'd hoped to find. Kind, generous—scary smart, but also patient. None of which matters because this won't go anywhere."

"Real love doesn't come around often. It requires sacrifice—on both sides. If Ryan does get up the nerve to ask you out, don't make assumptions. He might choose to live in Sweet Lake because you're more important than his career."

"Mami, there's more than Adworks keeping Ryan in Cincinnati." His obligations to his mother, for one, and the mystery behind the Continental Divide. Whatever the event they'd shared, it had marked both mother and son in a profound way.

"Well, I don't want you involved with a man who'll ask you to leave Sweet Lake."

"As if I'm cut out for the city. All the people crammed under the bright lights, and no stars overhead. Every time I take a road trip with Linnie and Jada, I'm always the first to get homesick. Some people wander endlessly, searching for the place where they belong. Can you imagine me living anywhere but here?"

"I can't. Frankly, I couldn't live without you." Silvia grew thoughtful. "My suggestion? Keep things light with Ryan. Don't get in over your head."

"Too late. I'm already in deep."

"Then swim your way to shore. If there's no future, protect your heart."

"I will," Cat assured her. "I've never been this happy—or miserable." Pain knotted in her throat. "Ryan won't stay in my life, but at least he showed up."

Chapter 9

Behind the mountain of yellowed guest receipts, Cat picked at her chipped nail polish. Punching names and addresses into a spreadsheet wasn't difficult. Ryan shook his head ruefully. Thirty minutes at a pop taxed her concentration.

Today she'd worn another slinky dress. The outfit was purple, with a band of silver fabric drawing his eager gaze to the plunging neckline. On the side of her face, the heavy locks of hair were drawn into a barrette with jewel-colored rhinestones. A pendant of matching stones nestled enticingly between her breasts. Another ensemble more suitable for dinner and drinks, but he'd come to love her utter disdain for professional wear.

Unable to ward off the desire, he came around the side of the desk. "Are you typing or daydreaming? Honestly, Cat—you have the attention span of a newt." Pretending interest in the numbers glowing on the screen, he breathed in her floral scent. She changed perfumes often, from blends with rich amber notes to lighter fragrances like the rose-infused concoction she wore today. He had yet to come across one that didn't stir his senses. "We should've finished building the data on Monday."

"Don't nag. I'm working on it."

He poked through the stack of papers by her elbow. "You aren't hiding nail polish in here, are you? Fooling around with your Magic 8 Ball, anything like that?"

"I am not." Dutifully she lowered her hands to the keyboard and resumed typing. "I'm nearing the halfway mark."

"Want me to take over?"

"Ryan, you've typed in most of the pages already."

"Stop keeping score. This isn't a competition."

"Says you. This feels like a footrace, and I didn't hear the starting gun. Staring at all these numbers is melting my brain." Finishing a receipt, she flung it toward the pile scattered on the floor behind her desk. "How did it go with Mr. Uchida?"

The interviews for the brochure were going well. "Got everything I needed, and more. Lots of quotable material on the inn's history. He took me down to the basement afterward. Like being on a scavenger hunt."

"What did you find?"

"There's a steamer trunk loaded with memorabilia dating back to the 1920s. Menus, photographs, clippings detailing the construction of the south wing—Mr. Uchida promised to check if there's anything else hidden beneath the sands of time."

"Count on it. Linnie's ancestors built the main portion of the Wayfair in the eighteen hundreds. She comes from a long line of pack rats. Instruct Mr. Uchida to keep searching. More items will turn up."

"Will Linnie mind if I take some of the relics back to Adworks? I'd like the art department to sift through, see if they can make digitals for future use."

"She won't care. Just return whatever you take."

Ryan's cell phone vibrated. Another text, the fifth one this morning. He typed a reply, wondering if he ought to call instead.

With uncanny precision, Cat read his thoughts. "Do you need privacy? I have a few items to run by Linnie. I can go now."

Although the subject never came up, Cat was increasingly aware he never stayed out of touch for long. The number of times she found him on the veranda in muffled conversation was a particular embarrassment.

"I'll call back later."

"If you need to touch base—"

"It's not an emergency. My mother is just having one of her more anxious days." At this slim revelation, Cat's soft gaze followed him to the chair before her desk. The compassion she sent emboldened him to add, "Lately she's really on edge."

They were entering territory he'd marked off-limits with a dozen cryptic remarks. Guilt nicked his heart. The past was a topic he never explored with outsiders, but Cat wasn't a stranger. In the last weeks, she'd woven through his emotions with the sturdy threads of her easy companionship, and the earthy glances she sent whenever she presumed he was too busy to notice. The impulse to let her in equaled his dread at what she'd find once he did.

"What's bothering her?"

"She insists someone's been in the backyard. Most likely the neighbor kids, chasing stray baseballs." Opening up, even in a small way, felt good. Which gave him the confidence to add, "She's been messaging nonstop since the feature in *USA Today*."

He searched without success for a way to continue. Discussing why a newspaper article caused so much grief meant bringing up George Hunt. His emotions shifting, Ryan appraised the photo of the Mendoza family propped on the windowsill. A handsome family, dressed ridiculously in matching red-and-green sweaters for a holiday shot. Cat didn't mention her older sister very often, but she chatted regularly with her brother in Columbus and her parents. The short calls were punctuated with laughter.

They were nothing like the tension-filled exchanges he shared with his mother.

Rescuing him, she said, "Do you need pointers on how to calm down an emotional parent? I'm an expert."

"Yeah? What's your most winning strategy?"

"Hugs. They work wonders. And brownies."

He liked the way she became earnest in a flash, as if a confection might vanquish the ghosts his mother faced. "I'm not sure brownies will do the trick, but you never know."

"I'm glad my parents aren't big on texting. I'd never get them out of my hair."

"And you have incredible hair."

She shrugged off the compliment. He couldn't decide if he was relieved or disappointed. If they delved too deeply into a discussion of their torrid attraction, he'd attempt to lure her into his arms. For days now, he'd been battling the temptation.

Instead, he confided, "The news coverage frightened her more than I expected. She's been watching the street with binoculars."

"What's she looking for?"

"My father. She's afraid he reads *USA Today*. I'll wager there's a better chance he's too busy drinking or picking up women to read a newspaper, but my mother isn't convinced."

"Why does it matter if your father saw the article? Are your parents divorced?"

"Long time ago."

"You aren't in contact with him?"

"No way."

"I'm sorry your mother is upset. Ryan, it was a great feature. All the good work you've done for charities is fantastic."

The encouragement she offered vaulted past his aversion to sharing the details of his complicated life. "I should've declined the interview. She's afraid my five minutes of fame have destroyed our safe obscurity. The feature came out more than two weeks ago—she should've calmed down by now." Although the facts might lead Cat to view him in a less than positive light, he refused to gloss over his shortcomings, adding, "She's aware I've taken on an out-of-town account. I've led her to believe I'm handling the work from the office. Not exactly a winning move, but I don't want her frantic because I'm outside the city limits."

This was the closest he'd come to confessing the true reason he chose to commute an absurd amount of time. On the rare days at the office, he spent most of the time brooding over Cat, torturing himself with what-ifs they would never have the opportunity to explore. Even if he could imagine uprooting her from her country paradise—and the idea made no sense whatsoever—he refused to contemplate sharing the responsibility for his mother.

A relationship with a third person hovering on the sidelines didn't have much chance of success.

"Ryan, why don't you go back to Cincinnati? I'll need your help leading into the concert, but we're still two weeks out. We *can* handle most of the tasks remotely."

"I'm not done interviewing employees."

"You're not obligated to talk to the entire staff."

"I'd like a few more. We'll archive most of the interviews, rotate them on the updated website."

Anguish filled her eyes. Quickly she blotted it out. "Do the interviews over the phone."

Her resistance made him more intent on forging ahead. "There are other tasks on the agenda, including Penny Higbee," he said, aware he was drumming up excuses to hang out with Cat. "She's our top photographer. I've asked her to drive down tomorrow. She'll shoot the interior of the inn, get a few shots of the staff."

"We're shooting the day of the concert. Why make her come twice?"

They were perilously close to discussing their predicament. He wasn't prepared for a conversation sure to conclude with disappointment. Ryan prided himself on his practical nature. Yet his feelings for Cat flew in the face of every pragmatic instinct he harbored.

Ridiculously he clung to the belief he'd find a solution, a way yet undiscovered, to grant their relationship a future.

On impulse, he rose. "I need some fresh air," he announced, mimicking one of her oft-used phrases. He never accompanied her on the short breaks to "breathe in the sunshine," another colorful phrase in her vernacular he liked.

"You're inviting me outside? Ryan, you don't like the great outdoors, except parks inside the city walls, or stadiums with blue sky above and a crush of screaming humanity around you."

"Cities don't have walls," he offered dryly. "Or moats."

"All the same, want to reconsider?"

When he'd agreed to take the Wayfair account, he'd given no thought to working outdoors. Now he knew that on the Saturday of the concert, he'd spend both the day and the evening traipsing between the inn and the lake with Penny, and overseeing the videographer filming the event. Better to overcome the panic attacks now than in front of his associates—or the concertgoers queued up to hear Midnight Boyz play.

"If I start to feel anxious, we'll turn around. Head back to four walls and a roof, where I'll nurse my ego in shame."

"You're too hard on yourself."

"Sometimes."

"Let's stay by the lake. I'd rather not take you anywhere near the forest. No reason you must conquer all your fears in one day."

Her protective tone nicked his ego. It also moved him deeply. "Sounds like a plan."

Tomorrow was the first of October, and Ohio's temperate autumn remained glorious. Clouds banked on the horizon in a slowly drifting parade of white. The recently mowed grass was fragrant, the calming scent punctuated by the distant activity of the construction crew, their pneumatic tools buzzing and hammers pounding. Overhead, the afternoon sun beat down on Ryan's shoulders, making him glad he'd left his sport coat inside.

Cat lofted open palms toward the heavens. "Want to hear a fun fact?"

"Sure." A first glimpse of the lake rose up, a sparkling blue necklace tucked behind the green hills.

"Trees talk to each other. Not like people, obviously, but they do communicate."

The forest lay to the left, a dark swath of shadows. Grimly, Ryan became aware of the muscles in his back tensing.

He swung his attention to her. "How do trees communicate?" he asked.

"Through their roots, one tree to the next. They aren't really separate life forms."

"Life forms? Paging Spock."

"These are fun facts of the natural world, not *Star Trek*." Grinning, she pushed against his shoulder. "Root systems intertwine from one tree to the next like a great net. Isn't that a beautiful image, a net finer than spun gold hidden beneath the earth? They use chemical interactions to talk through their roots. If a portion of a forest is under attack from insects, it'll send a signal to the healthy trees. Then the healthy trees make defense enzymes to ward off the invasion."

He liked how she became freer the moment she tasted fresh air, her gestures more fluid, more animated. Cat was endowed with a voluptuous body with strong athleticism added in. No doubt she'd spent a happy childhood climbing trees and swimming in the lake. The notion soothed him for the briefest interlude. She'd never witnessed violence, or hidden inside a closet in the hope she'd disappear.

"They use enzymes to warn each other?" He wished to prolong the conversation for the simple joy of listening to her voice. "You aren't making this up as you go along, are you?"

"Don't believe me? Ask Siri."

"Guess I'll believe you. Mostly because the story's too kooky, even for your imagination."

"There's no harm in a well-developed imagination. We can't improve our lives without the vision to imagine a better way."

"And a Magic 8 Ball to check the odds."

"Back to teasing me?"

"A desperate strategy. Keeps me from thinking about kissing you." It also kept his attention from being drawn to the trees looming up behind his back.

The declaration, unplanned, put heat in Cat's gaze. "Stop, okay? We agreed not to flirt."

"Right." His pulse hammered at his temples, a reminder they were outdoors for a less pleasurable reason than a heavy necking session. With a forced level of calm, he returned to safer topics. "If what you say is true, I'll realign my thinking about trees and forests in general. Pretty cool if they have the ability to ward off invaders."

"Animals within a species do the same thing. Nothing in nature survives by going solo. It's all about sharing."

A fierce and unanticipated gratitude knotted his throat. In her chipper voice, she meant to switch his apprehension regarding forests to appreciation.

She meant to teach other lessons too.

He flicked the hair bounding across her back. "Let me guess. You're a tree hugger? Remind me to make a donation to your favorite environmental group."

"The next time you're hired to do ads for a corporation, put the environment on your to-do list." The beach rose into view. She slowed her pace, giving him time to compose himself. "I do hug trees. The spirit inhabiting the earth nurtures and protects us. It's a mother spirit, replenishing us. I showed Linnie and Jada the best way to hug a tree when we were kids."

"Who showed you?"

"The Sirens, of course. My mother and Frances started the group. Frances is miles more dignified than Mami but, that year, she misplaced her usual decorum. She'd cry for no apparent reason. Pretty unnerving, the way she'd be overcome."

"How old were you?"

"Awfully small. Around three, I guess. Frances crying for no apparent reason is one of my earliest memories."

"How long did this go on?"

"Months, I think. Mr. Dufour was still alive. He'd sit on the patio drinking mojitos with Papa while my mother took Frances into the yard to console her. The way she grieved, I guess someone she loved had died." Cat's delicate brows puckered. "I'm not sure which one of them got it into her head to make a ritual out of Frances's grief, walking in circles beneath the moon, calling up the energy of Mother Earth to ease her pain."

"Lessons from the baby boom generation. They exited the psychedelic sixties with more than a penchant for tie-dye clothing. They came away with an expanded view of spirituality."

"If you're talking about my mother and Frances, they sure did."

"So the Sweet Lake Sirens were founded to help Frances with her grief." He knew the group held special importance in the town.

"They founded the group right in my backyard over the rim of a tasty mojito."

"How did the other women get involved?"

She laughed. "You really want to hear this?"

"You bet." Listening to the story was preferable to focusing on his crawling skin. They were in open space now, with the hot sands before them, and the lake a blinding field of blue. She'd wisely chosen a path away from the forest, although snatches of dense green were visible far to the left. "I haven't seen Ruth lately, thank God. I'll wager she pushed her way into the Sirens. She doesn't strike me as the sort to need much encouragement."

"Sorry to disappoint you. Penelope joined next. Her father died, and she was inconsolable. They brought Ruth in later."

"Why did they let her in at all?" Given her abrasive personality, he was unable to mask his distaste. It was hard to fathom Ruth enjoying *any* friendships.

"Give her a break." Leaving him stranded on the beach, Cat walked toward the surf. "Ruth has a tough hide, but she's a good person. Best marksman in the county, and a real help to the PTA during the holiday food drive. She lives in a shoebox, but manages to donate more canned goods than just about anyone."

"Guess I'll revise my opinion."

The apology snuffed out the reprimand flashing in Cat's eyes. She appeared to gather energy from the gentle flow, her arms opening wide. Eyes drifting shut, she tilted her face toward the sun.

The desire to join her nearly sent him forward. He'd already become aware of the queasy waves of fear invading his blood. The compulsion to return indoors growing, he kept his mind trained on the story Cat seemed eager to share.

"Before she retired, Ruth was a police dispatcher in town. Sweet Lake doesn't see much violent crime, not like a city the size of Cincinnati . . . my mother and Frances asked her to join the Sweet Lake Sirens after Tamron Pereira's father was murdered."

"The young woman who owns the greenhouse?" Tamron supplied the inn with flower arrangements; he'd met her briefly. The Wayfair didn't have the budget for elaborate displays, but her designs were attractive.

"The murder shook everyone in town, Ruth especially. She was close with Tamron's dad. He was an officer on the Sweet Lake PD."

"Why didn't Ruth join the force? Why settle for a job manning a desk?"

"I've never asked. There weren't many female officers back then. Anyway, the murder hit her hard. She became a Siren soon after."

The melancholy turn of conversation didn't seem what Cat intended, and she dropped the subject. From over her shoulder, she gave an appraising look. "Will you take off your shoes?"

Fear shot through Ryan. She wanted him to join her in the surf.

"I don't do water," he said.

"Ryan, there are precious few pastimes more lovely than the feel of the surf rushing over your toes. I swear I won't point out how pathetic it is for a grown man to sweat on the sands when he has the perfect opportunity to cool off. I certainly won't mention my heartbreak at the thought you went through childhood without once floating around on a rubber raft. Did you go through adolescence without skinny-dipping? Let's not discuss all the boobs you *didn't* see on the sly."

"Are you teasing me?"

Her eyes threw sparks he'd gladly dance in. "Keeps me from thinking about kissing you."

The declaration stole something from her, and he watched helplessly as regret sifted across her face. Evidently he wasn't the only one who'd concluded their feelings for each other wouldn't lead to a promising future. The reality squeezed his heart. It was miracle enough that their lives had intersected at all.

But she rallied, and held out her hand. "C'mon. You can do this."

After he tossed his shoes and socks in a heap, he rolled his pants halfway up his calves. Pulling a chicken-shit routine in front of a woman he liked more than was reasonable didn't appeal, and he came forward quickly. The water was still warm from the long summer, the sand beneath the bubbling surf incredibly soft. He hooked his fingers through Cat's, like lovers on holiday, and got his bearings.

A difficult proposition once the surf rolled out. It came rushing forward with a splash. He was significantly larger than Cat, and the wet sand beneath his feet gave way, sinking him to his ankles. With a startled laugh, he threw his arms out. He grappled for balance.

"You could've warned me about the suction," he said.

"And ruined the fun? Not on your life."

"Tell me that I won't sink down to my knees."

"Not likely."

A boat drifted across the center of the lake. It was too far out to see clearly. Ryan admired the sail snapping in the breeze. The anxiety drumming through him eased off. A nearly hypnotic serenity flowed through him.

He could get used to this.

Cat appraised the tension melting from his features. She asked, "Have you ever talked about your father with a friend or a colleague?"

He studied her with growing admiration. She didn't have a mind for spreadsheets or numbers, but her emotional instincts were infinitely more valuable. Luring him into the soothing waters to unlock his dark secrets was a masterstroke.

"Cat, I've spent most of my life trying *not* to think about my father. I have discussed him with my mother, briefly. We've tiptoed around the subject a few times."

"What happened in the forest? Something made you frightened about being outdoors."

"Near the forest," he corrected, hating the apprehension furrowing her brow. "The panic attacks are worse this time of year, but not because of what happened that day."

"Why are the panic attacks worse in the autumn?"

"It has to do with an argument I overhead when I was ten." Frustrated by his inability to explain in an orderly way, he gathered his thoughts. "Maybe it's not accurate to characterize it as an argument, although there were several heated exchanges during the phone call. It was more like a heartbreaking goodbye. I overheard the conversation when we lived in Salt Lake City."

"You overheard your parents fighting?"

"No, my mother was on the phone with her parents or her sister. I'm not sure which. She made the call in yet another misguided attempt to placate my father. She was cutting off all contact with her family." He laughed bitterly, adding, "My parents never argued. My mother wouldn't have taken the chance of setting George off."

"Let's talk about Salt Lake some other time. Tell me what happened near the forest," she urged. "You won't escape the pain until you do."

Marshaling his thoughts, he let the pregnant silence draw out. Cat didn't live a surface life. Whatever he found the stamina to discuss, she'd feel down to her bones.

The surf rolled back in, the swirling waters calming him. "I only remember snatches of the day. Fairly typical for a kid so young. We went camping outside San Francisco, in a state park, I suppose."

Bile rose in his throat. He swallowed it down. Cat was right—he needed to get this out. He needed to let go, even at the risk of burdening her. He'd never shake the memories if he didn't release at least a small portion of them from his heart into hers for safekeeping.

"My father got pretty drunk. He smashed a bottle against a tree. Beer bottle, wine bottle—my mother won't talk about it. He came at me first." Ryan tapped the scar beneath his eye. "George would've cut me again, but my mother pushed me out of the way. Which is when he cut her."

"Oh, God. How old were you?"

"Four years old."

"What if you'd lost your eyesight? Your father could've blinded you."

A sickening thought he'd mulled over for years. "I was lucky."

In an automatic gesture of self-protection, she wrapped her arms around her waist. "Where is your father now?"

"Presumably out West."

"When did you last see him?"

Fear curled across his shoulders. "During my teens." He had no intention of discussing those last months in Salt Lake, or the harrowing events in Twin Falls. "I had nightmares clear into high school about a forest and a man coming at me, which is why my mother finally gave a limited explanation. George got us both—clean sweeps, right across our faces. Hers is under her right eye. Another thing we have in common, like our aversion to clutter and love of Italian food."

"I'm glad you trust me with the story."

"You're easy to trust." Impulsively he hooked a lock of Cat's thick hair behind her ear. But he didn't retreat, as common sense advised. "Thanks for listening."

Her expression thoughtful, she seemed unaware he hadn't moved off. "Geez, my office must give you the willies. No wonder you were fired up about organizing my file cabinet the day after we met. I thought I'd hired a maid service, not the best marketing guru in Ohio. Why does clutter bother you?"

"Don't worry. Your sketchy organizational skills aren't a big deal." When she began to offer another apology, he brushed his lips across hers. He didn't stop to weigh the wisdom of breaching the line of professional conduct they'd worked so hard to maintain. She tasted warm and inviting, and it took all his resolve not to pull her into his arms. "Cat, I can deal with your office. The only thing that makes me anxious when we're squirreled away together is the work I'm *not* thinking about when I'm fantasizing about you."

"You fantasize about me?" she asked breathlessly. The husky tenor of her voice sent heat racing from his scalp to his spine. "Even with all the clutter underfoot?"

"Oh, yeah."

He kissed her then, partially because she appeared ready to make a resolution impossible to keep, like the impulsive resolutions people made on New Year's to lose weight or quit smoking. Her ability to give herself over to the moment, to drink him in without equivocation, filled him with something good.

When they drew apart, panting and grinning, she bit nervously at the corner of her lips. "Was that a good idea?"

"Probably not."

"It won't make working together easier."

"No, it won't." She looked dizzy and slightly perplexed, and he couldn't resist adding, "Especially since I'd like to do it again."

A smile overtook her lips. "We should get back." She kicked absently at the surf, then glanced at him. "I've been meaning to give you something. This feels like the right time."

Her hand dipped beneath the neckline of her dress. She withdrew a delicate chain.

"I always wear a token first, before giving it away—to fill it with positive energy." She pulled the necklace over her head.

A series of unusual trinkets dangled on the chain. With care, she slid off the length of feathers, tiny stones, and even smaller shells. The trinkets were threaded together with simple twine.

He wasn't sure what to make of the arts and crafts project. "Is this a gift?"

"Protection. This is a Siren token." Her fingers coasted across the two feathers. "The gold feather will give you courage."

"And the silver?" he asked, his heart thumping. A memory from long ago, stubbornly lodged in his mind, refused his efforts to ferry it to consciousness. "Looks like you decorated the thing with metallic paint."

"Sure left a mess on my mother's table. She'll be scraping up droplets for weeks." She patted his cheek. "Silver is for happiness. Because, you know, you need to loosen up."

"What about the stones and the shells?"

"The stones will ground you. The shells will give you the ability to hear your heart's desire."

The last of her explanation barely reached his ears as he tried to answer the question rising inside him. With wonder, he examined the delicate string of objects. The memory, teasing at the corners of his mind, refused to appear. Which struck him as immaterial since he'd already reached a startling conclusion.

He'd seen this token before.

∽♋∽

The cop slid the release papers through the window's slot. "Sign here."

George flipped through the sheets and scrawled his name across the last page.

The officer, a clean-shaven youth with strangely mismatched pupils, took back the paperwork. "Do yourself a favor," he said. "Don't do anything that'll send you back here."

"I shouldn't have been here at all." A week at the Hamilton County Justice Center for nonpayment of fines on missed court appearances—it was a shitty break. "I'm a law-abiding citizen. I didn't deserve this."

The officer gave him a jaundiced look. "You got a ride home?"

"What home?"

After his last woman convinced the authorities to charge him with battery, she'd kicked him out. He spent more than a month roaming through halfway houses in Cincinnati. Nearly six weeks, in fact, before the cops picked him up at his grease monkey job and took him in. With the week in lockup finished, George doubted his job at Dalton Car Care was waiting for him.

A map came through the slot. "Catch the bus one block up. It's not a far walk. Here are the directions." A plastic bag of his belongings followed. Cell phone, wallet, lottery tickets—the forty bucks in his wallet wouldn't last long.

George took his stuff and strode through the cavernous lobby. First order of business? Pick up his wheels, parked behind Dalton's. Next? Finding a job would take time, but he needed cash now.

He'd gone through rough times in the past. This felt like the bottom of the gravel pit.

Which left him with only one choice. The time for another visit to Sweet Lake was long overdue.

Chapter 10

"We're having a slumber party? Sorry, ladies. I'm not in the mood."

Leaning against the doorjamb, Cat regarded her friends with exasperation. She didn't have the emotional reserves for girl talk or much of anything else, with the exception of a hot bath and a depressingly early bedtime for a Friday night. Watching Ryan drive away at 6:00 p.m. with the awareness she wouldn't see him again until Monday was certainly a hardship. After the disturbing story he'd shared this afternoon, she'd hated to see him go at all.

On the queen-size bed, Linnie and Jada reclined with Beefcake Bill stuffed between them. They'd arranged the inflatable man in a sitting position. The savvy move allowed Bill to hold the chips and the bowl of salsa they'd brought along for the unsanctioned hangout.

Linnie dunked a chip in the salsa. "I'd stay for a slumber party, but Daniel would miss me. This is your standard-issue rescue operation." She popped the chip into her mouth.

Cat tossed her purse on the dresser. "You're rescuing me? From what?"

"Ryan. You're back to wearing sexy outfits, and we've both noticed the door to your office is closed an awful lot lately."

"There's nothing going on." A half-truth, but she wasn't sure how she felt about the kiss they'd shared on the beach. Giddy, confused—elated.

"Hey, I don't care if you have a fling. Just don't let it get in the way of your duties." Linnie peered past Beefcake Bill. "Someone else has a different opinion. She wanted to check your lingerie drawer, see if you've made any new purchases."

Jada, stuffing her mouth, spit the chip back out. "I did *not* say I'd check her lingerie drawer. I was only curious if she'd made any recent online purchases. She has an addiction. We both know it."

"Like it's our business if she buys naughty lace."

Cat pulled the knit dress over her head. "I haven't made any purchases." She grabbed the fluffy robe from the clothing heaped on the chair by the window.

The prospect of two days without Ryan already had her dreading the slow weekend. Plus her emotions were bubbling too close to the surface, a consequence of everything they'd discussed on the beach.

"Change the subject. I've already been over the Ryan issue with my mother and Frances."

"So there *is* an issue," Jada remarked, her voice refreshingly free of censure.

"I like him a great deal."

"I'm getting the impression you more than like him."

"If you're worried my emotions will get in the way of my duties, they won't. Actually I'm getting more done, faster, thanks to him. If we're sneaking in too many long glances while writing copy for ads—and while building a database that's easily the most boring job I've ever done—well, then, so what? Granted, making out on the beach was *not* an inspired decision, but shit happens."

Linnie, dipping her hand into the chips, froze like a burglar caught in the act. "Ryan kissed you on the beach?"

"Yes, Linnie. He hit me with a hot, mind-blowing kiss that had me more revved up than a pubescent boy."

"How long has the romance been going on?"

"Since this afternoon." Cat shrugged her shoulders, flopping her arms to her sides. "Don't tell me it's a stupid move—I know. Now I'm torn between wanting to protect him because he's been through so much, and wanting to seduce him."

The statement, delivered with more high-pitched angst than intended, layered the suite with a heavy stillness. Linnie removed the munchies from Beefcake Bill's lap and set them on the nightstand. Jada, her jaw hanging loose, tossed the inflatable off the bed, sending Bill rolling toward the closet. She steered Cat into the space he'd vacated.

She said, "Be honest, girl. Are you thinking Ryan is . . . ?"

"The one?" A heaviness centered inside Cat. "Feeling this sure when I've known him for less than a month has *flameout* written all over it. There's a lot about his life I don't understand—might never understand. I've always assumed I'd find someone with a similar background, and an equally stable life. Our pasts are so different. But I *am* sure. He's everything I'd hope to find in a man."

The remark drew a quizzical glance from Linnie. "Slow down, Miss Optimistic. Get to know him before you make any life-altering decisions."

"Like it matters what I do. After next week's concert, Ryan hands over our account to lesser talents at Adworks. I'll never see him again."

"He lives in Cincinnati, not Tokyo. Why not date from a distance? Take turns with the commute."

An option she'd considered and immediately discarded. His responsibilities to his mother were heavier than she'd assumed. They included a Continental Divide, with an ex-husband Julia D'Angelo still feared. Although Ryan had given only a rough sketch of his formative years, Cat had gleaned enough to conclude his obligations trumped his attraction to her.

"He can't leave the city. I doubt he has much time for dating, let alone a girlfriend."

"*Now* you're a pessimist?"

Cat let the remark linger for an agonizing moment. Reflecting on Ryan's past, she wavered between spilling her worries and protecting a confidence. Unlike in the conversation with her mother and Frances, when she was unaware of the brutality he'd experienced during childhood, she now understood. The gravity of that knowledge seeded her thoughts with fear.

There was danger here, more than Ryan credited. The intuition compelled her to say, "This isn't a matter of discussing where to live if our relationship grows. Ryan can't move. His mother lives with him, and he needs to look out for her."

"So he brings her along. You all live happily ever after in Sweet Lake."

"Linnie, you don't get it. Julia is emotionally fragile. She feels safe in Cincinnati. Change frightens her."

Jada took her hand. Threading their fingers together, she asked, "Why does she fear change?"

"Ryan's father abused them both. He's a monster. Julia has been hiding from him for a long time."

A chilling disclosure, and Linnie rubbed her arms. "Why do I have the sensation you're not exaggerating?"

A sharp pain bolted through Cat. *Heartbreak*, she thought. *This is what heartbreak feels like when someone you care about has been brutalized.*

Jada squeezed her hand. "Tell us."

"I don't know much. Ryan hates discussing his past." She gave a stilted accounting of how he received the scar beneath his eye. Summing up, she added, "I didn't have the heart to ask why Julia kept reconciling with George. I have the impression she didn't finally get away from him until Ryan was a teenager."

Linnie's eyes grew large with alarm. "Ryan's entire childhood was a nightmare?"

"I guess so. Now his mother watches the street with binoculars."

"She's upset about the *USA Today* feature," Jada guessed. "She's scared because they're no longer invisible."

"Ryan thinks she's overreacting."

"He's no lightweight, Cat. If his father shows up after all this time, Ryan will protect himself and Julia."

"Which is the point. Watching out for his mother occupies much of his time. You wouldn't believe how many texts she sends while he's working. He wasn't even comfortable telling her that he'd taken an account outside the city. Can you imagine how she'd react if he tried long-distance dating?"

Linnie sighed, her expression softening. "In my opinion, Julia D'Angelo's reaction is secondary. Is Ryan also falling hard?"

Despite her low mood, Cat nodded in the affirmative.

"Then don't bail out. At least not yet."

"I'm not bailing. I'm choosing not to get involved. There's a difference."

Linnie chuckled. "Sometimes your optimism is hard to take, but I've got to tell you: your new gloomy streak is worse." The amusement fading from her features, she muttered under her breath. "Oh, heck. I forgot to tell you about the call from Midnight Boyz."

"Why are they bothering you? They're supposed to direct all calls to me."

"Like the brats know how to follow directions. They're playing in Cincinnati tonight. Since they're in the general vicinity, they're dropping by tomorrow to scope out the venue for the concert next weekend."

"What time are they coming?"

"Late afternoon." Linnie grinned. "I got the impression they contacted me because they've worn through your last nerve."

"With all the demands for special meals and the best rooms at the Wayfair, that's putting it mildly." She pushed the frightening thoughts of Ryan's past, and his father, from her mind. "I'm glad they're coming.

Dealing with the brats is a better use of my time than worrying about matters beyond my control."

⌒9

By the time George took three buses to pick up his wheels at Dalton's Car Care, the sun burnt orange fire across the Cincinnati skyline.

The engine of his Mustang snarling, he peeled out of the lot with his last paycheck. He was itching to make the drive to Sweet Lake over the weekend. Next Monday, when he met with his parole officer, she was sure to hand over a list of garages she expected him to check for work. Spending days going from one car shop to the next interviewing for a grease monkey job wouldn't end his money woes—it never did. He needed a bigger score to get his life back on track, but he still hadn't figured out a plan sure to dupe his ex-sister-in-law.

Wheedling cash out of the high-and-mighty Dufours had been easier before the old man died. Archie Dufour had treated his snooty wife like she was in the running for sainthood, gladly palming greenbacks into George's hand to get him to push off. Since his death, the she-devil who hung around Frances got in the way. The last time George paid a visit, Silvia Mendoza flew out of the house screaming at him to get off the premises.

Like she had a right to stick her nose in family business.

The memory ate at him as he swerved into the lot of Kip's Tavern. Wrenching the key from the ignition, he strode into the bar. Cheap booze, even cheaper women—he surveyed the pickings with an eye to finding somewhere to crash tonight and pad his wallet in the bargain. Sex was the best option to keep his mind off his troubles. Once he worked out a scheme to get Frances to hand over a wad of cash, the bad times were over.

Sliding onto a bar stool, he ordered a whiskey. Across the room, pool balls clacked at the three tables sitting in a row. Men crowded near the tables, with babes roaming the perimeter in clingy tops, sipping fruit drinks in tall glasses. Checking out the women, he searched for one that looked like she had a good job. He'd spend the night at her place, clean out her wallet before sunup, and slip out.

The bartender was setting down his second whiskey when George noticed a heavily made-up woman in too-tight jeans. Listing against the wall, she nursed a drink alone. Early forties, trying to look ten years younger—she had nice hair and an even nicer purse falling open on her shoulder. From the looks of it, she'd already drunk too much.

George kept up the steady gaze until she finally caught on. She did a double take. Pushing her bangs off her brow, she seemed unsure if the come-on was meant for her. Another drink or two, and she'd swear George Clooney's twin was escorting her home for the night.

Which suited him fine.

Chapter 11

Pulling into the lot, Ryan wondered if he'd left his more pragmatic sensibilities at home.

With dawn an hour off, the air held a chill that had him scrubbing at the sleeves of the lightweight polo shirt he'd donned before slipping out of the house. Lights blazed from the Wayfair's lobby, the shafts of gold barely denting the darkness. Plodding through the shadows, he skirted cars to the stone walkway. At the top of the veranda's steps, indecision gripped him.

Go inside, or wait until a respectable hour before making his presence known?

The choices narrowed to one as the brunette at the front desk spotted him. Lowering her magazine, she gave a cautious wave.

With a sheepish grin, he went inside.

"Mr. D'Angelo, hi." She gave the clock a cursory glance. "You're here to see Cat?"

"I am, but I'm early." Embarrassed, he started over. "Not early, precisely. I *am* here to see her."

"For a meeting?"

"More like a social visit."

She reached for the phone. "Let me call up."

"Don't wake her." He nodded toward the veranda, conscious of the jitters barreling into his chest. "I'll take in the sunrise. Mind if I wait outside?"

"She might sleep in."

"Does she usually sleep late on Saturday?"

"Sometimes."

A tough break, especially since he needed a strong cup of coffee. "Then I'll continue to wait." He should've packed a thermos before hitting the road.

He slipped outside with the full extent of his impetuous behavior notching up his adrenaline. To hell with the coffee. Packing a flask of scotch would've made more sense.

He was mulling over the wisdom of sneaking into the Sunshine Room's bar when the door creaked open. Contrary to his request, the girl had followed her own judgment.

Cat tiptoed onto the veranda, cinching her robe. "Ryan, what are you doing here?"

She caught him leaning over the railing in a vain attempt to decipher the sounds drifting from the vicinity of the lake. "Interesting question," he remarked, feeling foolish. "Will you give me a sec? I don't have a reason yet." He couldn't decide if the sounds were animal or human.

"This is a spur-of-the-moment visit?"

"Essentially." Her hair was charmingly mussed, her features still glowing from sleep. "Forget the glam looks. You'll never beat this one."

"You're crazy. I look awful."

"You look sexy. Warm, approachable—what's under the robe? Mind allowing a peek?"

"And disappoint you? I'm wearing boring pj's, nothing exotic." She stifled a yawn.

"Nothing boring about pj's on a sexy woman."

He took hold of the robe's sash with the intention of drawing her near. Her lips parted in sweet anticipation. Then her eyes cleared. She shook off the last vestiges of sleep.

She stepped back, and the rejection struck him hard. It was no more than his due. From the day they'd first met, he'd been sending mixed signals.

"Ryan, seriously. What are you doing here on the weekend?"

"Couldn't sleep."

"So you jumped in your car? Other people try meditation, or sleeping pills."

He was a novice at sharing his emotions, but he tried now. "I couldn't sleep because of you. I figured I might as well stop by."

Eyes lowered, she smoothed her hands down her thighs. At last she stepped closer to feather light fingertips across his jaw. "What about your mother? She's been awfully worried lately. Doesn't she deserve to spend Saturday with her son? It's not like she sees much of you during the week, with all the time you've been spending in Sweet Lake."

"I'd planned to spend the day with her. Turns out she's got a full agenda." Cat's tentative caresses seemed an invitation. He inclined his head slightly to rub his nose across the smooth skin of her brow. She shivered, her response thrilling. "You're not wearing perfume." It was a first.

"Who wears perfume to bed?"

"Hey, I love the stuff you wear. Merely pointing out your natural scent's better."

The compliment barely dented her stern regard. "You were explaining about your mother."

"Every year, she goes on a sewing binge in October."

"Sewing her fall wardrobe? Some of the Sirens make quilts. I've never met a woman with the time or the talent to sew her own clothes."

"She's not that ambitious." He fondled the heavy locks of Cat's hair, arranging the gleaming lengths around her shoulders. He toyed with the idea of stealing a kiss.

The idea was dismissed as she lowered her hand from his jaw. "Your mother has been anxious for weeks. She's all right by herself on a Saturday?"

"Not by herself, and happier than I've seen her in a long time. She's spending the day sewing Halloween costumes." He shoved his hands into the pockets of his jeans to ward off the temptation of drawing Cat near. "There are lots of families on our street, and she loves helping the mothers sew costumes for their kids. I'd planned to take her out today, catch a sappy movie at the theater—she loves sappy movies—then grab dinner at a restaurant afterward. Last night I got home to find the living room buried in stacks of fabric, and my mother organizing patterns on the dining room table."

"It's nearly daybreak. What'll she do when she wakes up to an empty house?"

"I left a note, said I'd gone to see a girl."

The simple truth crowded her features with doubt. "We're spending the day together?"

He didn't like the worry collecting in her eyes. An understandable reaction, since he'd repeatedly battled the same doubts: Why risk deepening their attraction unless they found a way to have a future together?

Yet he'd followed his heart to Sweet Lake regardless.

Taking a gamble, he said, "We're probably thinking the same thing. Not much sense in starting a relationship unless there's a chance of building something together. I don't have an easy solution; I don't have any of the answers, not yet. I can tell you this: I've spent most of my life feeling like there's a wound inside me, one I'll never heal. Being with you makes me feel whole. How can I give you up without giving this my best shot?"

The hastily composed speech was too much, too soon. Ryan saw her expression change, felt her withdraw slightly. "I'm not pushing you," he said, desperate to ensure he wasn't pushing her away. "Just being honest."

"I'm not sure what to say," Cat admitted.

"I didn't mean to come on so strong."

"You didn't, Ryan. I appreciate your honesty."

He was intent on pressing his case when the murmur of voices rolled across the lawn. Above the forest, the first traces of sunlight revealed the bold autumn foliage.

"Who's down by the lake?" Curious, he looked out over the railing. "You don't have guests on the beach, do you? Too chilly for camping out."

The question seemed to rescue her from the emotional pressure he'd put her under. "Tell you what," she said, taking him by the hand and leading him inside the inn. "Grab something for us in the kitchen while I run upstairs to dress. You can raid Ellis's larder before he comes in with the morning staff."

"Who's Ellis?" The Wayfair employed fifty people, and the name wasn't familiar.

"The day cook." Nodding at the girl stationed behind the front desk, she started down the corridor near the ballroom. From over her shoulder, she added, "According to the women in housekeeping, Ellis is our resident hot body. Since you've been showing up, he has competition."

The remark quelled a portion of his anxiety. "I'm a hot body?" Not the worst nickname, especially if Cat agreed.

"As if you don't know." Leading him into the kitchen, she flicked on the lights. "Check the counter over there for pastries. There's fruit in the fridge." She opened a drawer, handed him a bag.

"We're going on a picnic?"

She smiled, and it was a relief when the last of the worry left her features. "If we don't lie low during this little excursion, we're in trouble."

He began asking for clarification, but she'd already darted out. In record time, she reappeared in jeans and a light sweater deliciously molded to her curves. They went out back and rounded the side of the inn.

"Why are we staying out of sight?" He followed her through the parking lot. "Are we spying on someone?"

"You'll see."

He stumbled on a rock hidden in the gloom. "Can I get a few more specifics?"

She chuckled. "Geez, you're a worrywart. Let the moment unfold in its own sweet time. You'll get a kick out of this, promise."

Clearing the parking lot, she went across the lawn. The sun peered out from above the tree line. Dew glistened on the grass like raindrops, suspended on a million emerald blades. The moment held a magical quality, like something out of a dream. Ryan focused on appreciating the surroundings as the familiar panic jolted him.

From the bag he'd packed, Cat withdrew a Danish pastry. She took a quick bite. At a clump of bushes forming a barrier between the lawn and the beach, she drew him to a standstill. The noise grew in strength, a repetitive hum reminiscent of singing.

"Stay low." She stuffed the pastry back into the bag. "If they see us, I'll never get out of hot water." She jogged left, to a larger clump of shrubs.

Ten paces from the surf, a group of women stood in shadows the advancing day was quickly flinging away. Eyes shut, they clasped hands. The Sirens, presumably, and Ryan scanned the group with interest. He spotted Ruth, her wrinkled face scrunched with concentration. Finding Cat's mother was a simple task. She possessed the same arresting features as her daughter, with a softly rounded build.

He arched a brow. "What's with the headgear?" Like the others, Silvia Mendoza wore an elaborate headband festooned with feathers in vibrant pinks, greens, and yellows.

"The Sirens make ceremonial garb for their rituals."

"What are they doing?" He counted eighteen women.

"Gathering positive energy from the new day. They do this once or twice a week. Not in the dead of winter, though. In January, they hold most of their rituals in Sweet Lake Circle. The temps get pretty nippy by the lake."

"They're all Sweet Lake Sirens?"

"Every last one." Cat ducked lower, pulled him down beside her. Together they peered through the bushes. "This isn't the whole group."

"Where's the rest of their merry band?"

"Sleeping in, getting ready for work—how should I know? They show up if they have time."

A ticklish sensation darted up Ryan's spine. The feathers on the headbands were twined with small stones and tiny shells that fell around the women's heads like a sprinkling of pearls. The overall design reminded him of the gift Cat had given him.

Retrieving the keepsake from his pocket, he held it out. "Your mother taught you how to make these?"

"Way back in childhood. My older sister, Val, never had much interest in learning about the Sirens' practices, but I was always fascinated with the idea that the natural world is inherently feminine, and women have the ability to connect into that nurturing spirit. I began helping Frances and my mother forage in the woods for the right stones, and scavenging the beach for the prettiest shells to use in their tokens, before I entered kindergarten. The feathers were the hardest to find, especially in the autumn once many of the birds had flown south." She regarded him with satisfaction. "I'm glad you keep the token with you."

"Cat, I've seen something like this before. The feathers weren't silver and gold. Purple, maybe, or blue." The inability to remember had plagued him since she'd presented the gift. The keepsake was important, a mystery he needed to solve. "How long has your mother been making these?"

"Since she founded the Sirens with Frances. I'm sure the design is original, something they came up with together. They also came up with all of the Sirens' rituals together, mostly from their opinions regarding feminine wisdom and the like. You're sure you've seen a token before? I can't imagine how you came across one."

"I'm positive."

On the beach the women's humming grew louder, and Cat and Ryan brought their hushed conversation to a close. The women's locked hands lifted into the air. The soft drone of mingled voices calmed the drumbeat of Ryan's heart. His eyelids grew heavy.

A rustling at his side snapped him out of his doze. Before Cat could take another bite, he swiped the Danish and wolfed it down.

"Sorry," he mumbled. "Hungry."

"I hope you packed more than one pastry."

"Two Danish, plus an apple and an orange." He forced his attention due west, to the forest.

She found the apple, studied him appraisingly. "How are you doing? Should we turn back?"

The sun broke free of the horizon, sending purplish ribbons of light across the beach. "I'm fine." The panic darting through his chest was manageable. His legs were another matter, the muscles burning from hunkering down to remain hidden. "The great outdoors isn't the real problem. I associate open spaces with my father."

"If we keep talking about your past, you'll get past your nerves," Cat said, her voice laced with hope. "I mean, I know it's hard. But you can try."

"I want to."

"Whenever you're ready, I'm here for you."

"Yesterday was a good start." He took in a lungful of the pine-scented air, frowned. A trace of worry returned to Cat's brow, and he didn't relish the prospect of being coddled. "Want to test a theory, see if I survive?"

He posed the question lightly, in part because the sight of grown women in feathered headbands tickled him, but also because the dawn cresting above the treetops was breathtaking, nearly as soul stirring as the woman regarding him with wary suspicion.

"I'm afraid to ask." Cat dropped the apple back into the bag. "What's your theory?"

A path edging the beach led into the forest. If they kept low, they'd avoid detection by the Sirens. He started down it.

"Hold on," she hissed from behind. "We should test your theory on a lab rat first."

Following a band of sunlight into the trees, he winked at her. "No guts, no glory."

At a steady pace he entered the forest, assessing his emotions along the way. Fear, nausea, and the predictable instinct to flee—nothing a red-blooded male couldn't handle.

Cat tossed their bag of goodies beneath a tree. Catching up, she pulled him to a halt. "You're sweating." She took a concerned swipe at his cheek.

"I have goose bumps."

"I'll reserve the ghost stories for a later date."

Catching the mirth in her eyes, he flicked her nose. "I knew I could count on you." He walked past. "Come on."

"You want to keep going?"

"Sure." He took three steps before stopping in astonishment. "My God. I had no idea."

Missing entirely was the deep, empty stillness he associated with a forest. In the leaves rustling far above their heads, a melodious chorus from unseen birds rained down. Bright calls and sharp chirps, sweet warbling and low trills—the birds sang with a vibrancy that was exhilarating.

Cat followed his attention skyward. "Cool, huh?"

"How long will this last?"

"A while yet. They sing like this every morning. They're welcoming the day, just like the Sirens."

"This is better than listening to the orchestra at the Taft in Cincinnati." He still felt panicky, but the birdsong spinning around him lessened his tension.

"Want to see something else? Less magnificent, but good."

He nodded, and she ducked onto a secondary path, hurrying past a ravine with gurgling waters rising from the dense shade. Moss blanketed the ground, the emerald carpet cushioning his long strides. They entered a small clearing.

Shafts of sunlight banded across a magnificent oak tree with a trunk thicker than three men. One ponderous limb grew at a nearly perfect ninety-degree angle. A charming tree house nestled in the nook where the limb met the sturdy trunk. Impressed, Ryan noted the fresh coat of pale-yellow paint on the structure and a rope ladder dangling from the doorway. Evidently the owner cared enough about the tree to avoid nailing the ladder into the trunk.

He studied her with interest. "Is this yours?" Given her nature-girl tendencies, keeping a tree house into adulthood wasn't surprising.

"Don't I wish. I do steal a few minutes out here, whenever I get the chance." Approaching, she smoothed her fingers across the knotty bark. "Linnie has an older brother. Freddie owns a film studio in California, Bad Seed Productions. B movies with bizarre plots. This place is his."

"Freddie built the tree house?"

"When he was a kid. You can see the place got a recent upgrade."

"Why fix up the tree house if he lives in California?"

"Linnie practically rebuilt it for him last summer. A peace offering."

"What were they fighting about?"

"The Wayfair. Their parents retired to Florida with the assumption they'd hand over the reins to their son."

"Freddie worked here? Neat trick, what with the film career."

Cat expelled a breath. "No, Freddie did *not* work here. Jada and I would've killed him before letting him womanize his way through a job at the inn, and drive Linnie nuts in the bargain."

Her reaction started him grinning. "What happened?" He loved her animation, the way her hands danced through the air to emphasize her words.

"When he tried to stake his claim last summer, Linnie threatened to walk out."

"She would've quit the inn?"

"With the staff also threatening to go if Freddie wouldn't back down." Cat flicked at the rope ladder, which obligingly swung across the craggy trunk. "Everything worked out in the end. Linnie got majority control of the inn, and Sweet Lake's original bad boy opened his wallet. All the renovations, and the money to ramp up the advertising? Freddie's bankrolling us."

Us, as if she and Jada held the same commitment as the inn's majority stakeholder. Maybe they did, Ryan mused. From what he'd witnessed since taking the account, the three women were lifelong friends dedicated to steering the Wayfair to prosperity.

"You like working for Linnie?" he asked, sadly aware he'd stumbled on another reason why she'd never leave Sweet Lake.

"More than expected." Considering, she leaned against the tree. "Seven years ago, Freddie cleaned out the Wayfair's accounts. Nearly bankrupted the inn. Lots of businesses in town closed, including my place and the bakery Jada owned. Losing those tourism dollars really hurt the town. That's when Linnie asked us to work for her. She was already living in the south wing, so we moved in too." Cat looked up quickly. "Between you and me, I didn't go out of business because tourism dropped."

"What *was* your line of work?"

"Event planning."

"What happened?" he asked, conscious she was sharing a painful secret.

She looked away. Making the revelation clearly came at a cost, and he suspected she was stalling. A guess proven accurate when she angled toward the ladder.

"Want to see inside?"

"Will you mock me if I admit I've never climbed a tree?" He took a gander at the rope, calculated the odds of anything so flimsy supporting his weight. Bad odds.

"Ryan, did you spend your entire childhood indoors?"

"Not all of it."

"You're not climbing a tree. You're climbing *into* a tree house. Perfectly safe."

"Got the building specs on this contraption? Let me check if everything's up to code."

"Don't chicken out on me."

"I'm a grown man. Stop hitting below the belt."

"Yeah, scaredy-cat? Prove it." Planting her foot on the first rung, she hoisted herself up. Her long hair, swishing past her shoulders, banished all thought of building codes. He didn't follow immediately, choosing instead to appreciate the soul-stirring sight of her long legs and the suggestive movement of her hips as she ascended.

At the top, she threw a mischievous glance. "Planning to stand there grinning at my ass, or join me?"

All the incentive required. Grabbing hold, Ryan swiftly climbed up.

Thankfully the small structure boasted a sturdy plywood floor. White paint covered the interior walls. The conscientious Linnie had even added throw pillows sensibly protected from the elements in a jumbo-size plastic bag. The only problem was standing up—Ryan was six feet tall in his socks. The walls weren't more than five feet in height.

"Cozy," he murmured.

"I love it here."

Dumping the pillows from the bag, she handed two over. Following her lead, he sat against the wall. Being this close, hidden together in the woods, hitched up his pulse. A vision of heady lovemaking with birdsong for background music poured heat through his veins. With effort he shook off the image. She'd invited him inside to share a secret, not for an hour of hot sex.

He let his gaze linger on her for as long as he dared. "You were saying . . . ?"

"Well, everyone thinks my business went under like all the others, because the inn went through hard times. Truth is, I was going broke before Freddie cleaned out the Wayfair's accounts."

"You would've gone under regardless?"

"Within months—something I should've noticed sooner, but I was too busy dating a series of losers." Lost in the memory, she made lazy circles across her jean-clad legs, the gesture unconscious and utterly sensuous. "I didn't care about learning *how* to run a business. Accounts receivable and accounts payable, the major migraines of keeping track of money—I spent more time dating than wondering if I was bleeding cash. I made a humiliating number of mistakes."

"Guys came first, eh?" He made the comment lightly, astonished by the accompanying dart of jealousy.

"Years dating all the wrong guys. I was such a nitwit, waiting for a dreamy man on a white steed."

"My middle name's Lancelot."

"Funny, Ryan."

Ditching the jokes, he took her hand and planted it on his thigh. "Why did you choose event planning?" She began doodling across his jeans, igniting tiny fires he did his best to ignore. "I'd have pegged you as going for something in fashion."

"No way. I loved planning weddings for other women, picking out flowers and venues, looking at gowns. Trying on gowns if the bride was busy checking out shoes or veils. We get only a few perfect days in our life. I've always known my wedding will be a day I'll always cherish, even when I'm too old and senile to remember my name." She paused abruptly, searched his face. "I've only told my parents the true reason my place went under. Not even Linnie and Jada know."

"Loose lips sink ships." He offered his most engaging smile. "I won't tell a soul."

She did a double take, laughed. "World War II, right? I've only heard one other person use that phrase."

"I'm parroting my mother. One of the things she says when swearing me to secrecy."

"Weird. Frances Dufour uses it too." She stopped doodling, released a sigh. "Thanks for keeping my secret."

"An honor, my lady."

She found him worthy enough to share a humiliating memory. Her trust moved him.

Then he found himself clinging to another, more thrilling fact. "You took up event planning because you were dreaming about your own wedding?"

Given his general pessimism about the lasting power of relationships, the irony wasn't lost on him.

She bumped against his shoulder with engaging sobriety. "Yes, Ryan. I was totally hooked on the idea."

"When did you catch the bug?"

"Are you kidding? I was one of those frilly girls playing dress-up all the time. Pretending I was getting married was my biggest fantasy. There was a period between kindergarten and third grade when my parents stopped planting *any* pink flowers in the garden. I'd pluck whole impatiens plants to weave through my hair. Cut my fingers on thorns while nabbing roses, raided the pink geraniums—let's not go into what I did to my mother's best slips."

"Made them into wedding gowns?"

"Thank God I didn't think to use scissors. I'd steal twine from Mami's craft supplies to rig up pretend gowns. You'll never meet a girl who wasted more time dreaming about Mr. Perfect."

"Do you still?" he asked.

The merriment faded from her features.

For an excruciating moment, he hung suspended in confusion. She studied their legs flung out side by side, seeming to weigh her response. He wanted to recall the question, another clumsy move.

When she finally looked at him, emotion tumbled through her eyes in a mesmerizing display.

"No, Ryan," she said evenly, "I stopped dreaming in September when I found him."

Chapter 12

Was candor the wrong move? Unsure, Cat waited for the pronouncement to sink in.

Pain, relief, anxiety, delight—the emotions scuttling across Ryan's features were breathtaking in their variety, distressing in their potency. Taking in her declaration, he appeared beyond speech. His Adam's apple convulsed in his throat. Apparently his thoughts were shuttling forward too quickly for him to catch.

Abandoning the pursuit, he bent his head to hers.

He kissed her with a slow, thorough urgency that telegraphed his response to the core of her being. When she returned his passion with equal fervor, he steered her down on the floor.

A groan erupted from his throat, a hungry sound that rippled pleasure through her. He rolled on top of her, the claim he took of her senses firing the motion of his hands, molding and caressing her flesh. Shuddering beneath him, Cat let her eyes drift shut to better experience the sensation of his lovemaking, the hot press of his mouth as he dragged his lips across her neck, the tantalizing impression of his teeth nipping and teasing her sensitized skin. Then he took her mouth again, his kiss harder, nearly taunting, driving her higher with the sheer force of his desire.

He kissed her until she was breathless. He kissed her as if he adored her. In that heady, faultless moment, she believed he did.

When he finally broke off, he left her dizzy and ravenous for more.

Ragged breaths shuddered his rib cage. "I'm not making love to you in a tree house." Sitting up, he raked his hand through his hair. "Cat, I'm crazy about you, but I'm not into quickies."

She stared at him, the comment finally getting past the fog of sensation he'd put her under. Curling her knees to her chest, she let the doubts flood in. They were moving too fast. Their sexual compatibility came with an unnerving number of hazards, including its ability to burn past their common sense. She needed answers about his past, and his obligations, before getting in too deep.

Sparing her the opener, he said, "I can't ask you to take this further until we work some things out. Don't misunderstand—I want to take this further. A lot further." He slid a sidelong glance rife with passion her way. "But I don't want to hurt you. I'll never forgive myself if I do."

"We need to discuss your mother." They'd barely touched on the subject.

"Cat, she's not selfish. Clinging to a routine helps her ward off depression. She's tried meds in the past, and they've helped, but she doesn't want to spend the rest of her life relying on pills to feel normal. I don't want her to either. Some people can't manage without antidepressants. She does fine if her routine is stable."

"You haven't seen your father since you were a teenager, right? She stayed with him until then?"

"On and off."

"How did you deal with it?"

"Not well." His shoulders sagged. "Three times she resolved to leave him. The first time, she moved us to a new apartment in San Francisco. God only knows why she stayed until then. I hardly remember the move to Salt Lake, but those years were good."

"How long did you live in Utah?" she asked, greedy for a fuller accounting of his life.

"Until I was ten. George found us when I was nine, tracked us using the jewelry store where she'd worked in San Francisco. The owner of Lux Jewels had family in Salt Lake. Turns out the jeweler was born in Twin Falls, Idaho." Ryan glanced at her ruefully. "I didn't get all of this from my mother—I pieced together some of the facts through online searches. Anyway, my father found us in Salt Lake, and they stayed together for about a year. She cut off all contact with her family, and toed the line as best she could." A black despair formed around him so quickly, Cat tasted the bitterness. "It didn't stop the beatings."

George. My father. Ryan's emotional disconnect was disorienting. Careful to keep her voice even, she asked, "Yesterday, you said he's somewhere out West. You don't know where he lives?"

"I haven't seen him since he found us in Twin Falls."

Another move, another story she doubted she wanted to hear. "He didn't follow you to Ohio?"

"He couldn't."

"Why not?" The question sent his attention skittering across his shoes. Emptiness overtook his features. It seemed best to save the question for another day.

Changing tack, she said brightly, "If we're dating, I don't mind taking turns on the commute. Your place in Cincinnati, is there a guest bedroom?"

"A nice one." He took her hand, brushed kisses across her knuckles. "Commuting short term is no big deal. Doubt it'll satisfy me for very long."

"Ryan, I won't leave Sweet Lake. I love my job, and my parents live here. Don't ask me to give them up, or find a new career in Cincinnati."

"I won't." He leaned heavily against the wall. "Assuming everything works out, I need to find a way to make my mother understand."

The explanation squeezed her heart. "You really care about her well-being."

"I care about yours too. And mine, which is pretty much taken care of, assuming you're in my life."

"I want to stay in your life. There's nothing I want more."

They were getting ahead of themselves, wildly so. Yet the idea took shape, a perfect solution to give Julia a taste of country living. "You're in Sweet Lake all of next week helping me gear up for the concert and finish next spring's marketing plan. Instead of commuting, why not bring Julia and stay until Sunday?"

"Where would we stay? In case you've forgotten, the inn is booked solid."

"Not all of it. Linnie's old suite in the south wing is vacant. I'll bunk in Jada's room, and you'll take my suite. Linnie's is larger, so we'll give it to your mother."

Weighing the suggestion, Ryan drummed his fingers on the floor. "No harm in asking, right?"

"All your mother can do is refuse. Hopefully she'll agree."

He rubbed his chin, clearly taken with the idea. "A week in the country might stop her from obsessing about George tracking us down. She's still lighting up the house like a state penitentiary every night, and surveilling the street with binoculars. Once she gets going like this . . ."

"It's just a phase."

"She'll grow out of?" He chuckled. "You realize we're discussing her like she's a child."

Rising, he helped her up. After they'd climbed down from the tree house, he said, "I'll ask her to come."

They neared the forest's edge and the lilting murmur of the surf. "Just don't pressure her, okay? Say we've become good friends, and I thought you'd both enjoy a stay at the Wayfair."

"She won't buy the *friends* explanation, Cat. Not once she hears me creeping into your bedroom at night."

"Dream on. You're staying in my room, and I'm bunking with Jada," she reminded him.

"Doesn't Linnie stay at her boyfriend's place in town? Ask them to put Jada up next week."

She blocked his path. "Put the thought of late-night rendezvous out of your head. I've never met your mother. I'm not giving her the wrong impression."

Passion darkened his eyes, and delight. "You're pretty when you're upset." He reached for her. "Should I fire you up more often? There might be benefits."

She darted out of range. Allow him to kiss her senseless, and she'd never establish the ground rules. "Don't embarrass me in front of Julia. I want her to like me. No midnight visits, okay? Later, if we get serious about each other—"

"We *are* serious about each other," he cut in, his expression growing flirtatious. She swatted at him, but he easily captured her. "You aren't backing out already, are you? We've only been a thing for ten minutes, tops."

Giggling, she evaded the kisses he seemed determined to give. "Ryan, this is important. First impressions count."

"No worries. You've already made an incredible impression—on me, anyway." Driving the point home, he kissed her urgently. When he finished, he said, "Will you relax? She'll think you're fantastic."

"Good."

With puzzlement, he looked past her. "Heads up. We have company."

The warning jolted Cat. Ryan let her go.

At the edge of the forest, Silvia shielded her eyes for a better view into the dense stand of trees. Most of the Sirens were gone, but Tilda, Ruth, and Norah stood nearby. Ruth hadn't removed her headdress. The drooping feathers fluttered around her scowl of disapproval.

She pointed directly at them.

Cat got a nasty image of public disgrace and scarlet letters. "We're doomed."

"Unlikely. I survived Ruth's hex, didn't I?"

"Ruth is the least of your worries—and mine."

Immediately he caught her drift. "This isn't exactly how I'd hoped to meet your mother. We'll manage. Who's with her?"

"The pretty elf with the cinnamon-colored hair? Don't let Tilda's tiny stature fool you. She has an outsize ability for gossip. Half of Sweet Lake will hear I was fooling around with a man in the woods before you can say *scandal* three times."

"And the tall woman?"

"Norah will flirt, but she's essentially harmless. She's buried four husbands, which put a real kink in her eHarmony bio. Know any older gents with sturdy constitutions? She'll be less bitchy toward the rest of us if someone asks her out."

Ryan plastered on a nervous grin. "Four husbands, eh? When a woman has that sort of track record, I don't play matchmaker."

"Well, then, you might as well meet my mother. She plans to keep my father indefinitely." Scooping up the bag of goodies they'd left under a tree, she gave Ryan the once-over. She reached up to fix his mussed hair precisely as he began smoothing down hers. "We could make a run for the hills, but Mami's pretty fast. Tilda's even faster."

"Stop stalling. They're watching us." He gave her a second take. With a look of apology, he gingerly touched her neck. "This is not good. Nope. Not good at all."

Mortified, she patted her neck. "What is it?" Her skin felt warm to the touch.

"I left a hickey on your neck."

"Gee, thanks. Does my hair conceal the evidence? I feel like this is high school all over again."

"Sort of."

Not the best reassurance, and Cat breezed forward with the moisture in her mouth evaporating. Tilda waved merrily, no doubt elated to begin the weekend with grade A gossip.

Ruth favored Ryan with a glittering stare while Norah, her long, highlighted tresses dancing in the air like plum-colored snakes, folded her arms with a harrumph of disapproval.

Silvia lobbed Cat a questioning look before planting her startled attention on Ryan.

With her brain entering deep freeze, Cat searched for a suitable opener. The Arctic at dawn, with her neurons crystallizing. How to explain trooping out of the forest with a man loping on her heels? Her lips were love bruised from so much kissing, and the hickey now felt tingly hot. It took all her self-control not to clamp a hand over the evidence.

Miraculously Ryan strode past her with an air of self-possession stronger than his yummy cologne.

"Mrs. Mendoza, hello." Taking her hand, he shook heartily. "Ryan D'Angelo. A pleasure to meet you."

Cat imagined Norah's sexual radar blinking on as the older woman asked, "Did you enjoy your romp in the forest? Cat certainly looks like she did."

"Ah, well, she showed me the tree house."

"Freddie's tree house? I imagine you put the cozy abode to good use."

To his merit, Ryan kept his cool. "We only stayed for a few minutes."

"Some events only *need* a few minutes, young man. Care to explain yourself?"

Silvia stared her into silence. "I'm wondering the same thing," she growled.

Ruth said, "Are you both stupid? There's a love bite on Cat's neck."

Tilda clapped her hands. "So there is!" She shimmied her dainty shoulders, a voyeur thrilled with the peep show. "Oh, look. There's another one beneath her ear!"

Cat's stomach dropped to the vicinity of her ankles. "Mosquito bites," she blurted. "Big swarm in the forest—weird for October. Must be the heat wave. Who needs July with an Indian summer like this one?"

Jangly embarrassment pinged through her. She angled toward Ryan with the quixotic belief he'd perform a second rescue operation. He opened and closed his mouth, his language skills presumably AWOL. She pitied him. He looked like a guppy hurled from a fishbowl.

Her mother came forward. "Ladies, Ryan, if you'll excuse us." She dragged Cat toward the shoreline. Once they were out of earshot, she let go and flapped her arms. "You were in Freddie's tree house making whoopee? You do realize I'll have to arm wrestle Tilda before she gets into her car. She won't surrender her cell phone without a fight. A strong breeze could blow her to next Tuesday, but her upper-body strength is nothing to mess with. Just what I need to start my Saturday."

"We were only talking in the tree house." Kissing too, but that was miles away from making whoopee.

"Give me a break. You're covered in hickeys and your lips are puffy. I wonder why I *don't* believe you?"

"Because you're too angry to listen," Cat pointed out. "It's not easy talking to you when you get like this."

"Don't even try to turn the tables on me. I can't believe you're being this reckless. Didn't you say at Frances's house you couldn't make sacrifices for love? When you said you'd enjoy your time with Ryan for as long as it lasts, I assumed you meant dinners out. A man can be intimate without risking his heart."

"I hope Papa never hears you talking like this. Aren't you selling men short?"

"I'm not talking about your father. Maturity teaches a man to shape the fires of youth. At Ryan's age, desire is a wild flame."

She'd heard enough. "Stop jumping to conclusions," she snapped. "You don't know the first thing about Ryan."

"Cat, listen to me. Why set yourself up for heartbreak when he's leaving after the concert?"

"He's not leaving me—only the Wayfair account, although it's a safe bet he's reconsidering the decision." Fighting for patience, she added, "He came this morning to talk. We've decided to begin seeing each other."

The news elicited a barrage of unintelligible complaints. When she'd finished, Silvia added new combustion to her tone. "You said he couldn't leave Cincinnati under any circumstance."

"Only because of Julia," Cat blurted. "He takes care of his mother—she lives with him. Julia really likes their home in Cincinnati, and she doesn't go in much for change."

"You're assuming if things work out, she'll agree to move here?"

The incredulity in her mother's voice made Cat defensive. "Why wouldn't she? I mean, if Ryan is on board with the idea?"

"Are you nuts? People my age don't change." Silvia thumped her chest. "Our personalities become brittle like our bones."

"You're wrong. We're capable of change at any age."

"My foolish little dreamer. Julia D'Angelo may come to love you nearly as much as I do—but she'll have expectations, and *you'll* toe the line." Silvia inhaled sharply, her bosom shuddering with the full brunt of her imagined suffering. "How can you leave me and your father? Who'll keep us company when we're old, or drive us to the doctor? I'm not spending my golden years in a retirement home if you run off to the city. Those poor souls live on canned tuna and trust their pedicures to strangers."

The guilt trip, on top of a remarkable morning, galled her. "Alberto moved to Columbus," she said of her younger brother. Her parents even threw him a going-away party. "You didn't freak out when he left."

"Yes, I did. I wept for days."

An exaggeration. "You erupted like Mount Vesuvius, and Papa wept for days. You drive him bananas when you get frothy."

"I can't believe you're arguing with me." Her mother splayed her hands across her generous bosom. "I'd expect this type of sass from your older sister. Not you. Not my sweet Catalina."

"I'm not leaving Sweet Lake. Val won't either. You'll always have both of your daughters within shouting distance." She hesitated. "We'd prefer you shout *at* us less often."

Not the best stab at a peace offering. Luckily the tart comment went unnoticed.

Looking toward the forest, Silvia heaved a sigh. "Now what does she want?"

Norah, whose fear of her volatile leader bordered on nonexistent, prowled across the sands with the avidity of a lion scenting a meal. She'd left Ryan fending off questions from Tilda and Ruth.

"Cat, why have you been hiding Ryan from us? You should've made the introductions weeks ago. He's glorious." With dreamy abandon, Norah swished her feather crown through the air. "How long have you been seeing our fabulous Mr. D'Angelo?"

"Oh, for about twenty minutes."

"My, you *are* eager. Sex on the first date. In a tree house, no less." The fashionable Siren regarded her with newfound respect. "Intrepid."

Silvia whacked her, drawing a yelp. The pain she inflicted seemed to satisfy her, but only for a moment.

She returned her disenchanted regard to Cat. "Is Ryan spending the weekend? I won't waste my time lecturing you on the dangers of mixing business with pleasure since he's already put his teeth in your neck."

"No, he's not spending the weekend." Cat allowed her fingers to move her hair more advantageously. She stood hiding the evidence in an awkward pose. "He might spend next week."

"The entire week?"

"If he does, he's bringing Julia. They'll stay in the south wing. He wants her to see Sweet Lake."

The implication wasn't lost on her mother. "He's confident she'll agree to a visit?"

Cat shrugged.

Dismissing the ambiguous reply, her mother pivoted away. She paced across the shoreline, bobbing her finger to keep time with her thoughts. "All right," she said, "take Monday night to yourselves. We'll have the three of you over for dinner on Tuesday."

An evening of "meet the family"? Given Julia's introversion, she'd never survive a night of nonstop questions. Better to let her acclimate to Sweet Lake and leave the social visits for a later date.

"Mami, don't fill up my social calendar just yet. Let me talk to Ryan first." Hopefully he'd nix the idea, putting her in the clear.

"Talk? What talk? I'm not packing my daughter off to Cincinnati without a fight."

Norah peered down her hawkish nose. "You're leaving Sweet Lake, child? How traitorous."

Cat wanted to supply the meddling Siren with a second whack. Recalling Norah's boob job and her subsequent punishment of the gossipy Tilda, she thwarted the urge.

"On Wednesday, let's all dine in the Sunshine Room," her mother continued, undeterred. "On Thursday we'll have a small barbecue, just a few friends. Easier to get Julia D'Angelo alone and make my opinions clear if we have privacy."

"I'll bring my shrimp casserole," Norah told her. "A cooling complement to the Mexican hellfire you'll undoubtedly serve."

"Watch it—"

"I'm merely stating fact. Your intestines were forged with titanium, but I wouldn't presume Mrs. D'Angelo has a solid constitution. If Marco serves his spicy watermelon salsa, have him tone down the serrano peppers. You can't wage war effectively if the enemy spends the evening in the toilet."

Cat stepped between them. "Both of you, stop gearing up for war. Julia is a sweet old lady." Pure conjecture since they'd never met, but it was a safe assumption. "Well, maybe she's not old, but she's not the enemy."

Norah flared her nostrils. "We'll see about that."

"Norah, I'm not inviting you," Silvia decided. "Five minutes into the festivities, you'll start grilling Ryan about the sex he's enjoying with my daughter. I can't have Julia keeling over in shock. Not before I put her lights out."

"Will you both stop? We weren't doing the nasty, and no one is declaring war!" The retort drifted across the lake, unheard.

Norah looked to Silvia, aghast. "What do you mean I'm not invited?"

"You heard me."

"Fine, Silvia. Party on without me."

"I will, thanks."

Norah spun off, her feather crown fluttering in her fist.

Glad for the privacy, Cat said, "I mean it—don't make any plans for us. I'm not committing without clearing this with Ryan first."

"He's already telling you what to do? Tell *him* you're dining at your parents' house, and Julia's coming too."

The opportunity for another squabble disappeared. Down the beach, someone shouted.

Jada raced toward them, waving madly. She wasn't in the habit of running around in long johns and the silly zebra slippers Linnie had given her as a joke gift last Christmas. Only trouble of the first order would send her racing outside in her pj's.

Cat left her simmering mother and dashed off.

"What's happened?"

Wheezing, Jada bent over to suck in deep breaths. "Mr. Uchida called up to my room," she got out between gasps. "The boy demons . . . raining chaos on the inn."

"Midnight Boyz are here? They aren't due to arrive until this afternoon!"

"Have to stop them . . . destroying the ballroom."

"*What?*"

At last Jada regulated her breathing. She felt around for pockets in her long johns, frowning at the stretchy fabric. "Monkeybums. I left my phone on the nightstand."

"You haven't notified Linnie of trouble in paradise?" Meaning she was still blissfully asleep at Daniel's house, unaware of the chaos.

"Do you have your cell? We need her to send Daniel over to beat the crap out of the little monsters. I'd ask Ellis to do the honors, but the kitchen crew hasn't come in yet." Ryan jogged up, and Jada latched on to the collar of his shirt. "Never mind—you'll do, big guy. C'mon."

Behind the front desk, Mr. Uchida was stationed for the day shift. Cat was certain he wished he'd stayed home. As a screech resounded from the ballroom, he flung himself against the wall. Then a boing, boing, boing reverberated through the lobby, the odd sound combining with the squeal of wheels rolling fast. Something crashed, and Mr. Uchida fled toward the safety of the kitchen.

Ryan charged to the ballroom. Pushing Jada forward, Cat followed.

A split second later, Ryan's voice boomed out. "What the *hell* are you doing?"

Feet planted wide apart, he inconveniently halted two paces inside the ballroom. Cat and Jada were unable to stop in time, ramming full on into his back. Ryan was solid muscle, and the impact hardly budged him. He righted Cat before her feet disappeared from beneath her.

Jada wasn't as lucky. She tumbled backward, landing on her butt. One of her zebra slippers flipped skyward in a crazy arc.

In the center of the ballroom, Midnight Boyz had rigged up an electric skateboard with ten feet of bungee cord. All four of the band members wore knee pads; most of Davy Keen's face was hidden behind large swim goggles. Evidently the lead singer was the most recent thrill seeker—his sandy-brown hair stuck out in all directions.

"Hey, Cat!" The loose-limbed youth ambled forward, presumably to wrap her in an unwanted hug.

The demon was barely in his twenties, but a waltz with fame in the regional market of midwestern rock bands had made him unusually hands-y. If the band reached national stardom, no rear end would be safe.

From behind the goggles, he winked at her. "I'll bet you've missed us. How are you?"

She eyed the other band members and the bungee cord. "I've been better."

"Why've you been holding out about the playground? This place is cool. We had no idea the ballroom was so big!" Davy opened his arms wide.

Ryan let him get within striking distance before lifting his palm like a traffic cop. "Touch her, and you'll be picking your teeth up off the floor."

Davy's eyes rounded. Weighing the threat, he tapped anxious fingers across his chompers. He had nice teeth.

He also reeked of pot, a circumstance that Ryan also appeared to pick up on.

Ryan's voice lowered to dangerous levels. "What. The hell. Are you lunatics doing?"

"Geez, man. We're not doing nothing."

"Anything."

"What?"

"Speak properly. You were raised in Pepper Pike, not the Badlands."

"What are you, one of those stalker fans? How do you know where I grew up?"

The remark brewed storm clouds around Ryan. A typhoon in the making, and the lead vocalist slowly pulled off the goggles. Recognition hit his dizzy skull like a brick.

"Mr. D'Angelo?"

"The one and only."

"What are you doing in Sweet Lake?"

"At the moment? Reading you the riot act."

Cat recalled that Midnight Boyz had lost out on a lucrative commercial deal by adding a list of ridiculous demands. Ryan had pulled his sporting goods client out of the negotiations.

Apparently Davy, licking his lips and searching for an expression in the vicinity of contrite, remembered too.

The singer dredged up a smile. "Running into you at the Wayfair—talk about handy. When we wrapped up last night's concert? Man, we drove right by Adworks. We were wondering why we haven't heard from you. After Cat shows us where we're playing next weekend, can we have a sit-down about the commercial? The one for the sporting goods stores?"

"Not on your life. In fact, if you pull any more stunts, I'll advise Cat to fire you. Losing out on the commercial will be the least of your worries."

"You're handling the Wayfair?"

Ryan gave a stiff nod.

"Hey, we're looking forward to playing on the beach. There won't be any problems." Davy raised his hand, a repentant Boy Scout swearing an oath. Ryan merely grunted, and the singer strapped on the charm sure to make him a favorite pinup for adolescent girls across America. "About the commercial. We weren't serious about the all-expenses to Joshua Tree. Throw in the free rock-climbing equipment, and we're ready to sign."

From the floor, Jada said, "Someone hold him. I get the first shot at wiping the stupid grin off his face."

"Save your strength," Ryan said. "Why don't you go upstairs, get dressed? I'll handle this."

The suggestion brought Jada to her feet. With a salute, she went out.

Cat's second-least favorite member of Midnight Boyz sauntered up. The carnivorous drummer had demanded porterhouse steaks with every meal during the band's stay at the inn. The sticking point had put Cat at odds with the kitchen staff and their tight-fisted budgeting. Heavyset, with curly blond hair framing a moon-shaped face, Nathan Dukowski gave her a look that was one shade from lecherous.

"Good to see you, Cat." He scratched the beginnings of a beer belly. "Kitchen open yet? We couldn't find a diner on the road."

"Sorry, Nathan. The kitchen doesn't open for another hour." She studied him warily as he began rooting around in the book bag slung across his beefy shoulder. "What are you doing?" If he pulled out Silly String, she'd kill him.

"I write the blog posts for our website." Taking note of the anger still brewing around Ryan, he kept a respectful distance. When he spoke again, the genuine contrition layering his words came as a surprise. "Mr. D'Angelo, the bit about putting Joshua Tree in the contract was Davy's idea. I swear, I didn't go for it. The other guys didn't either. I told him Adworks is a big agency, and it'll help our careers to get one of our songs in a commercial."

"Tell you what. Give a stellar performance on the beach, and I'll keep Midnight Boyz in mind the next time."

"Sure thing, Mr. D'Angelo."

"You'll use the ballroom for rehearsals, not play. Understand?"

The drummer removed a laptop from his book bag. "You got it." Sitting Indian style on the floor, he shot a disgruntled look at his bandmate. "The electric skateboard? I'm not the one who packed it when we took off from Cleveland for the concert in Cincinnati."

He began typing as Ryan put his sights back on Davy. "This was your idea? You could've caused serious damage."

His air of defiance fading, Davy rocked on the balls of his feet. He seemed unwilling or unable to formulate a reliable defense. At the opposite end of the room, the two other band members began collecting the bungee cord and the skateboard with skittish movements. They looked like teenage boys caught skipping school.

Nathan paused in his typing. "Mr. D'Angelo, may I mention Adworks in the blog post?"

"Call me Ryan. Yes, mention my agency. Why don't you add a sentence about the Wayfair's plans to host more concerts next year?"

"Sure."

"Oh, and mention the Sunday brunch the inn will host." He gave the details.

Nathan typed them in. "We're good. Just need a photo."

"You're posting now?"

"On our blog, and then other platforms."

The soft note of appeasement in the drummer's voice made Cat reassess her opinion of him.

She asked Ryan, "Will any of this help us?" The inn was booked solid for Saturday night, but they were still taking reservations for the Sunday brunch.

"You bet. Midnight Boyz has a spectacular following on social media. Their older followers have money to spend on weekend getaways."

With boyish pride, Nathan informed her, "We're nearing a million followers on Twitter."

"Incredible. You're sure doing something right."

"Thanks."

Not to be outdone, Davy pulled out his smartphone. "I'll get the photo." He offered Cat his most solicitous smile. "Move in closer to Ryan, okay? We're making you a star in about two minutes."

"You're posting a photo of us?" Worried, she gave Ryan a meaningful glance.

He slung his arm across her shoulder. "Nothing to worry about. This isn't *USA Today*. We won't reach anyone past the age of thirty."

Davy positioned the smartphone, clicked. "Yeah, but we'll get two thousand retweets. Right, Nathan?"

Nathan flipped the laptop shut. "Three thousand."

In the end, Nathan's prediction was short of the mark. The tweet he sent from the Midnight Boyz account received 3,240 retweets. The photo of Cat and Ryan, featured above the link to the blog post, reached 771,882 people.

Sophomore Gemma Mills of Kent State University was the 400,212th person to read the tweet.

Chapter 13

On the knoll before Merrill Hall, Gemma rubbed her eyes with a yawn.

Skipping a whole night of sleep wasn't her style, not even over a tweet from her favorite band. After roaming the campus until dawn, the initial excitement was gone. Her legs burnt from walking all night. At a respectable hour she'd sent the text before crossing the campus to wait outside Merrill Hall.

Even now, the thought of sleeping didn't appeal. Not until Gemma shared the incredible news.

At nine on a Sunday morning, a serene quiet enveloped the campus. Nothing broke the solitude except the intermittent rumble of cars on East Main and the noise from above. In the yellow birch tree shielding her, black squirrels hopped from limb to limb, their chattering outrage directed at the girl drowsing below.

The scent of Starbucks wafted up the hill. With a groan, Gemma pulled herself upright. Patty Chung, her round face brimming with concern, handed over the vanilla-infused iced coffee. Slender, with a pixie haircut and skin the appealing shade of polished teak, Patty was her all-time best-y.

"What the hell, Gemma?" She dipped her nose into the tendrils of steam rising from her own cup. "Don't ever pull another disappearing act."

"I left a note on my bed."

"You mean the demolition zone on the bunk bed beneath mine? I didn't find the note until midnight. Why didn't you text?"

"Needed to sort myself out first."

"Two words on my cell: *I'm safe.* That's all I'm asking." Patty took a hasty sip of her Starbucks. Then she brought her index finger and thumb to nearly touching. "I was this close to calling your parents and the campus police. What if you'd been abducted?"

"I should've told you I was walking around." As roomies, they'd crafted an agreement to keep each other posted if they went out at night. A college campus offered lots of entertainment—and just as much danger. Before she had stumbled across the tweet by Midnight Boyz, breaking their solemn pact would've been unthinkable. "I needed alone time. I was pretty blown away."

"You walked around all night? Why?"

"I've found Ryan."

The revelation squashed her roommate's temper. "Your half brother? *That* Ryan?"

Gemma pulled out her phone, navigated to the photo taken in the Wayfair's ballroom. "Meet Ryan. Incredible how much we look alike."

Intently her roommate studied the photo of the couple, the man smiling confidently for the camera, the sexy Latina beneath his arm gazing bashfully at him. Patty returned her attention to the man.

She threw Gemma beneath an equally careful inspection. "Talk about a strong resemblance. Only thing different is the hair. Freaky how much you look alike."

"We both take after our father."

"The asshole?" Patty winced. "Sorry."

"It's okay. At least he didn't strap me with a crappy genetic profile. What if he'd looked like a warthog? I wouldn't have landed a boyfriend until I'd clawed my way up the evolutionary scale."

Solemnly Patty nodded. "Good looks count for something."

Although Gemma had inherited her mother's honey-gold mane, her angular features—and her eye color—were a strong match for the short-tempered drifter she remembered from her early childhood. Ryan, with his much-darker hair and strong, masculine face, looked spookily similar to George Hunt.

Patty snatched the phone away. "Who's the babe with your brother? She's gorgeous."

"Cat Mendoza, one of his clients. Also his girlfriend, right?"

"He's sure holding her tight."

"She's in charge of marketing for the Wayfair Inn."

"In Sweet Lake? I've heard of the Wayfair." Patty looked up with puzzlement. "I thought you said Ryan lives in California."

The mistaken assumption was based on the birth certificate tucked in with the photographs that were among Gemma's most cherished possessions. All of the photos were shot in the San Francisco area, leading her to believe Ryan lived in California. It boggled the mind to learn he wasn't a continent away. She'd grown up believing the odds of meeting were negligible, at least until she put together enough cash for a trip to California. Even then, she hadn't been hopeful about finding Ryan Hunt in a city the size of San Francisco.

Of course, there was the additional revelation she'd discovered last night. Somewhere along the line, Ryan Hunt had changed his name to Ryan D'Angelo.

Reading the Midnight Boyz tweet—and recognizing the man in the photo—was incredible enough. Learning her brother lived in the same state fell into the category of major miracles.

"He's right here in Ohio." Snatching back the phone, Gemma navigated quickly. She still felt woozy from lack of sleep, but the relief of sharing her secret provided a much-needed adrenaline boost. Plus she felt vindicated—Patty had never fully bought into the story about her older half brother. Now she seemed totally convinced. "The drummer for Midnight Boyz also posted on his blog. He mentioned Ryan works in Cincinnati, at a place called Adworks. I searched, and found this article. It came out last month."

The *USA Today* feature popped onto the screen. The photos weren't grainy like the one tweeted by the band. Larger, crisper, they depicted a successful businessman with the familiar raven hair and eyes that Gemma's mother described as pine-tree green. The deep, jewel-like color was both remarkable and rare. In all her nineteen years, not once had Gemma found anyone with eyes like those she inherited from her dead-beat dad—until she saw Ryan's photo.

Yet more proof of their undeniable connection.

Patty said, "You have the same mouth."

"Think so?" Gemma studied the photos closely.

"Same nose too. His skin tone looks a little darker. Might be a tan." Patty appeared to reflect on the uncanny resemblance as she sipped her Starbucks. "I don't get the last name. D'Angelo. Why isn't it Hunt?"

After walking the campus all night in deep contemplation, Gemma had settled on a plausible explanation. "Julia must've changed their last name when Ryan was a kid. He *was* born Ryan Hunt. I've got his birth certificate to prove it. She must've done the name switch so George couldn't find them. D'Angelo wasn't her maiden name. It was Brugnet—I have a really old lease from an apartment she rented before she married."

"Slow down. Who's Julia?"

"Ryan's mother—George's ex-wife." From her pocket, Gemma retrieved the timeworn envelope her mother had taken from George's suitcase on the day she and Gemma's stepdad, Simon, had kicked him to the curb. The envelope represented the earliest years of her brother's life, as well as snippets from the years before his birth.

She shuffled through the familiar items like a deck of cards. Beneath a postcard of the Golden Gate Bridge, she produced a photo of a woman with brown hair standing before a jewelry store, the estab-lishment's signage frustratingly out of frame. "Meet Julia. Best guess, she was eight, ten years older than George. I have a photo from their honeymoon—he looks like a young punk, but you can see the tiny lines around her eyes. Julia definitely had some mileage on him." She handed the photo to her roommate.

Patty studied the image for a long moment before setting it aside. "This is all fascinating, but what about your mom and Simon? You're really close. Have you told them you've found your older brother?"

All night long, she'd struggled with the decision on what to do about her parents. "I can't tell them yet. Not until I'm one hundred percent sure I *have* found him."

"What's the problem? There's no missing the genetics. Not when they're shouting this loud."

"What if Ryan doesn't want me in his life?" Uncertainty took a swipe at the confidence she'd spent hours mustering. "His mother went to the trouble of changing their last name, which tells me neither of them want anything to do with George. From Ryan's viewpoint, I'm a reminder of the father we share. Doubt he has any clue George had another kid eleven years after he was born."

Patty considered this. "Ryan may hate George, but that doesn't mean he won't want you around. I'm sure he will."

"Then will you go with me to meet my big brother? Hopefully I'll get up the guts to introduce myself." On her phone, she brought up the blog post drummer Nathan Dukowski had posted on the band's website. "Midnight Boyz play the Wayfair next Saturday night. Big concert on the beach. I can buy our tickets online. I've already found a room on Airbnb. We should book fast before someone else beats us."

"We have midterms soon. My GPA comes before hot boy bands and your wish list."

"We'll curtail our social life all week. Study nonstop."

"I'm broke."

"I'll pay for the whole trip."

"With what? Your good looks and charm? If you sell the bulk of your meal plan to one of the guys on the football team, you're *not* shadowing me in the food court for the rest of the semester. I'm not trading sushi for burgers just because you're itching for a road trip."

Gemma donned the expression her studious friend dubbed the "little orphan Annie" look. For most of her life she'd dreamt of meeting her big brother, but never believed the opportunity would arise. Another chance like this one wouldn't arrive soon.

"I can't do this without my best-y. If you don't come, how will I find the guts to walk up and say hello? The only thing that scares me more than rejection is calculus. Please come with me to Sweet Lake. I won't even ask you to pitch in on gas."

"Nice move," Patty grumbled, "since I'm the one with a set of wheels."

"You'll go?"

Eyes flashing, Patty finished off her Starbucks. "You're a pain, Gemma. In case you didn't know."

⌒◟

Children and adults milled around the green spaces of Sweet Lake Circle.

The commotion caught his interest, and George slowed the car to a crawl. A Sunday bake sale was starting. Men were putting tables into place, end to end on the cobblestone walk. Bright-gold linens snapped down on the tables, which the women filled with home-baked treats. The scent of cinnamon drifted through the air, followed by the rich fragrance of freshly baked bread.

Last night's whiskey still burnt in his belly. George pulled to the curb and got out.

An older woman with thick eyeglasses stood at the last table, the breeze tousling the tufts of white-and-auburn hair around her face. "Are you hungry? Only one dollar a slice. We're taking additional donations if you'd like to help out the high school sports program."

He appraised the pecan pie at her elbow. "Wish I could, ma'am." The scent of the buttery crust made his mouth water. "I'm between jobs."

"Oh, dear. That must be difficult. I hope you find work soon."

"Thanks." He took his time jingling the change in his pocket. "I'm all for good causes, but I'm not sure I should."

The ploy sent pity trembling across her double chins. She took a hasty glance over her shoulder. Assured no one was nearby, she cut a big slice and handed over the paper plate. "My treat. Good luck with the job hunt."

Thanking her, he ambled back to the Mustang. If he'd stuck around for another ten minutes, filling her head with a woeful tale invented on the fly, she would've handed over the whole pie.

Finishing the treat, he drove off toward Highland Avenue. The street where Sweet Lake's wealthiest families lived immediately dulled his mood. It reminded him of how the long, humiliating slide in his life began when Julia up and left with his boy. Her leaving was a foul heap of bad luck he'd never scraped off.

They'd both worked good jobs in San Francisco, his at a Mercedes dealership and hers at Lux Jewels. Julia's apartment was nothing like the roach-infested dives that came after. Back then, he got stoned too much and drank until his temper blazed. She should've been more patient, should've made allowances for the difference in their ages. Every time he beat her, he banged her good afterward, streaming sweat while he pleasured her, holding off his greedy spasm until she finished hers.

He was a man, after all, and knew how to gain forgiveness.

At first, Julia did forgive easily. Not so during their last year together, after he found her holed up in an apartment in Salt Lake City.

The memory of her response still ate at him, the way she'd lain there clawing the sheets. That last year, when their boy was a sullen kid in elementary school, she'd treated George like a stranger. Like he was taking advantage, and not her husband.

Flinging off the memory, George eased his foot from the gas. Three houses down, the white colonial stood like a king's castle on a golf-course green. He brought the Mustang to a stop in leafy shade. Once more he went over the speech, a surefire winner to get Julia's sister to open her purse.

A sharp burst of conversation brought his head up. Silvia Mendoza came out the front door of Frances's house running her mouth. George spit out a curse. Dressed in old slacks and a work shirt, she looked like a woman heading to an afternoon of deep cleaning. Frances came next, her fancy dress making him wonder if she planned to take in her second church service of the day.

Climbing into Frances's Audi, they drove off in the opposite direction.

Burning with frustration, he watched them go.

In the vestibule of Blessed Sacrament Church, Father Thomas chatted with the members of his flock. Ryan, ushering his mother through the stream of parishioners exiting the church, waved in greeting.

The priest's silver brows lifted with mock astonishment. "Speak of the devil," he quipped. "I've been wondering if you'd run away."

"No talk of devils, padre." Ryan chuckled. "We're in a holy place."

"Yes, and one you should visit more often. Say, every Sunday?"

"I'll do better."

"I'm holding you to that promise."

Softening the rebuke, the middle-aged priest gave him a hearty clap on the back. Ryan had always been grateful for his friendship. The pastor of Blessed Sacrament had graced his life since adolescence, when the memory of Twin Falls rendered a traumatized sixteen-year-old nearly incapable of speech. It was Father Thomas who had suggested the angelic surname for the badly abused Julia Hunt and her son. On the day she appeared in court to receive her new name, he'd been there to support their small family.

Father Thomas regarded Julia affectionately. "The Life Teen ministry is looking for volunteers, Julia. You did a fine job raising this one. Would you consider helping at their meetings? They need an expert hand."

"Oh, I'm no expert at parenting." Flustered, she rubbed her thumb across the crystal beads of her rosary. "Easy enough to succeed when God sends you a boy with goodness through and through."

"Will you give it some thought?"

"Not this month. I'm sewing Halloween costumes for some of the children on my street. I help their mothers every year." Slipping her rosary into her purse, she deftly stepped from the spotlight. "Ryan, why don't you look into helping the ministry?"

"A splendid idea!" Father Thomas agreed.

"Sorry, Father. Too busy this year." Ryan splayed his palms in apology. "My boss is having her first child soon, and I've taken on new clients."

"Any news on the personal front?"

At some point today, he'd planned to tell his mother about Cat's offer. The pastor's question, not entirely unexpected, gave Ryan the perfect opening.

"As a matter of fact, I am seeing someone. She's great."

His mother gave a nearly unintelligible gasp of surprise.

Father Thomas beamed. "A serious relationship?"

"Very much so. She's not local. She works for a country inn. Actually, she's invited me and my sidekick to spend the week there."

"How nice. Julia, are you looking forward to the visit?"

Father Thomas leaned closer, eager for the details. An upsetting mix of bewilderment and annoyance stiffened his mother's posture.

Blanching, she turned her chilly regard on Ryan. "Why am I only hearing about this now?" she whispered urgently.

The last of the parishioners entered the vestibule, including a young couple with a baby in a charming sunflower bonnet. The couple paused beside Father Thomas. He seemed glad for the interruption.

With a polite farewell, Julia walked out. Disappointed by her reaction, Ryan followed, wondering how to spin this.

Last night he'd stayed with Cat until night crept across the beach. Midnight Boyz left well before then for the drive back to Cleveland, the four band members bleary eyed after their all-nighter. Nathan was the last to climb into the van, shaking Ryan's hand with admirable maturity and a promise the band would behave once they returned on Thursday. Ryan had capped off the day by enjoying a romantic dinner with Cat in the Sunshine Room, their fingers touching while they sipped wine.

Opening the passenger door of his car, he waited for his mother to climb in. They were nearly home before she broke the frosty silence.

"You're dating a client." She made no effort to hide her censure.

"Cat Mendoza, yes."

"The invitation to stay at the inn . . . what did you tell her?"

"I didn't accept. I'd like to. I told her I needed to run it by you first."

"Why does she want us both to visit?"

A thorny question, but Ryan soldiered on. "I mentioned you've been nervous lately. A vacation will help you relax."

"How nice," she murmured with sarcasm. "Thank you for discussing my emotional state with a stranger."

"A week in the country will do us both good. There's also the issue of the miles I've been piling up since September. It's been hard, making the drive constantly. I have to work the account every day next week."

"You've been piling up miles? You told me you were handling the account from the office." Julia fastened her attention on the road with faint indignation. "I don't appreciate being lied to. Frankly, the behavior is beneath you."

A misstep. Parking in the driveway, he silently chastised himself.

His mother didn't wait for him to help her from the car, rushing up the front steps to let herself inside. The door banged shut behind her.

Mentally Ryan counted to ten before following. There was time to turn this around, but barely. Let her stew too long, and she'd nurse the slight for months to come.

Stacks of fabric were neatly arranged on the coffee table. In the dining room beyond, the sewing machine sat on the table amidst Halloween costumes partially completed in a wild array of colors and designs. Flicking on the machine, Julia reached for a red vest. The spangles covering the fabric sang out as she positioned the garment beneath the needle.

Ryan let the sewing machine whir for a minute before sheepishly taking a seat across the table. An air of injury surrounded her as she kept her attention fixed on the task. It was his well-deserved payment for betraying the trust governing their relationship.

His hand strayed to the scar beneath his eye. "I shouldn't have lied to you." Fending off the nervous tic, he drummed his fingers against the table, stopped. Three weeks of allowing her to believe he left each morning for Adworks wasn't a series of lies told to protect. It was an outright deception. "I should've been more up front about my schedule."

"You haven't been up front at all. We had one chat over drinks weeks ago. You left me with the impression you can't pursue a relationship with a client."

"I changed my mind."

Finishing the seam, she yanked the vest sideways. "That much is obvious." Snapping down the pressure foot, she continued sewing. "I'm stunned you've told me anything at all. When you were younger, there was never any duplicity between us. You've changed. Ever since you—"

At a loss, Ryan searched the remark for validity. "I haven't changed." He wasn't sure why she believed otherwise. "You're blowing this out of proportion."

"I'm not talking about Cat, although I *am* hurt you weren't comfortable sharing your feelings. I'm talking about your discovery last April. Has it been five months? I wish you'd never found them. You've been more brooding since then, less forthcoming."

The impassioned speech increased his confusion. Blinking, Ryan finally deciphered her meaning.

She meant the album with the photos of his father torn out, the one he'd found last spring while cleaning out the garage.

He asked, "Why didn't you throw the photos of George away?" It seemed an oversight to leave them inside the album.

"Lord above, why didn't I? Not once did I consider you might stumble across them."

"You believe I've been acting differently since I found them?" He nearly discarded the theory, but the sickly emotion rushing through him forbade it.

"Son, why don't you ask me?"

For reasons he couldn't analyze, her patience made him defensive. "Ask you what?"

"Stop pretending you don't understand where I'm going with this. Ask me the question you've worked so hard to hide from yourself."

With painful clarity, he understood what she was driving at. Panic crawled across his skin. He felt nauseated, as unmoored as the day in Twin Falls when he'd walked into their apartment to find her bloodied and battered.

At last he formed the despised query. "Am I anything like George Hunt?"

"Because you can see the physical resemblance?" Pain flooded her gaze—and love, the fierce, maternal devotion she'd always given him. "No, Ryan. You're nothing like George Hunt. You're kind, never cruel.

Patient, never volatile. You treat women with the highest respect, and you're unfailingly protective. In my opinion, you take after one of my sisters. You inherited her intellect, not to mention her elegance."

The praise felt like a reprieve. He wanted nothing from his father, certainly none of his traits.

Then her revelation sparked the curiosity he'd spent a lifetime suppressing. "You have more than one sister?"

"I do." She smiled placidly, like a sphinx. "I'll tell you about them someday."

"There's nothing wrong with telling me now."

The statement was poorly timed. Already a grey weariness stained her features, the exhaustion that came with too much remembering. Her past was a minefield he'd never learned to negotiate.

She folded the vest, set it beside the sewing machine. "I'd rather discuss Cat." A note of expectancy shaded the remark. "Why don't you tell me about her?"

"What would you like to know?"

"Are you in love?"

A fierce longing seized him. "Yes."

"Is she aware?"

"It's a safe bet she's catching on."

"Why doesn't she come here for a visit?"

"She will, at some point. The inn's gearing up for a concert next weekend. She's awfully busy." Indecision caught him, and he pressed his palms flat on the table. In a reasonable tone, he added, "Look, if the idea of a minivacay doesn't suit, no worries. I will get home late every day this week, including next weekend. Not a big deal, just letting you know. Don't expect me before nine, ten o'clock. Next Saturday, I'll get in even later. Probably after midnight."

"You're not in the office at all?"

"That's right."

"You're talking about a lot of travel for one week. I hate the thought of you commuting so much. How far away is the inn?"

The question startled him. With no small amount of guilt, he struggled to recall how much he'd shared about Cat and the Wayfair. He grimaced.

Less than he'd realized.

With a nod of satisfaction, she folded her arms. "Exactly." She assessed the remorse rising on his features. "You've shared exactly nada."

"Honestly, I thought I'd told you more."

"You've been trudging in late most nights and going directly to bed. Lately I've engaged in more conversation with the Polish butcher on Meeting Street. Believe me, he's no conversationalist."

"Should I apologize again? How 'bout we take in a double feature at the cinema?"

"No need to bribe me, son. You're a mature adult, under no obligation to share every occurrence in your fascinating life." Pushing the sewing machine away, she regarded him with more understanding than warranted. "Ryan, you're the most devoted son a mother could hope for. I'm not angry because you weren't truthful."

"What *is* bothering you?"

"It's no secret I haven't been myself lately, which is hard on you. I'm not sure I even had the sense to congratulate you on the newspaper feature. I'm so proud of you. It's inexcusable how infrequently I tell you. What *does* bother me? My son has fallen in love. He didn't stop to consider how happy I'd feel for him."

Another unexpected turn in the conversation, and his head snapped up. "Does this mean you'll come with me?"

"On one condition. You won't make a fuss about driving separately. If this little adventure makes me anxious, I'll drive myself home. I'm looking forward to meeting Cat, but I'm no more enthusiastic about a week in the country than you. Let someone else listen to the crickets bringing in the night. We're both better suited for the city."

"I may change my stripes."

Astonishment flashed through her mossy-green eyes. "You're kidding."

"There's a lake by the inn. Blue waters as far as the eye can see. A forest too, which I've visited with minimal panic attacks. Actually walked pretty far in yesterday morning."

"You've told Cat about our past?" She swiped at the moisture gathering in her eyes. "How much have you discussed?"

"Not everything." The horrors were best shared in small doses. "I will at some point, though."

"Did you mention the name change?"

"I wanted to." Pride blocked the attempt. Nothing singled him out as an abuse survivor like the extraordinary means his mother took to stop George from tracking them. Ancient history, now that he was an adult. Still, he didn't want to appear weak in front of Cat. "She was pretty upset when I explained about the scar."

"I can't imagine her opinion of me."

"Mom, she doesn't hold you responsible for what he did to us."

"She sounds like a considerate girl." Dispatching with the sorrow, Julia added, "All right. I'll go. We're leaving tonight?"

"Mind if we take off this afternoon?" Checking his ill-concealed buoyancy, Ryan added, "Tonight's fine, if you'd rather wait, wrap up a few of the costumes."

"I have three weeks to sew. The costumes will be finished long before Halloween." Her attention drifting, she tapped an index finger on the table. "Did I put the suitcases in the garage? I'll take the carry-on. Might as well pack light. Seven days in the country is probably more than I can stand; I'll ask the neighbors to check the houseplants if I'm gone all week." She looked up suddenly. "How long is the drive?"

"An hour and fifteen." Given the infrequency of her trips outside the city, he added, "You've probably never heard of the town."

"Enough with the mystery. Does the town have a name?"

"Yeah, sure." He grinned at the curiosity brightening her features. "Sweet Lake."

The light fled her face. "We're going to the Wayfair Inn? Cat works there?"

"You know it?"

The query hung suspended between them. On unsteady feet, she rose.

The thin cords of muscle in her neck worked as she walked to the kitchen. With confusion he followed, the silence falling down around him in oppressive blasts, like unsettled air moving in ahead of a storm. She went to the stove and stared at the teakettle, her hand finding purchase on the knot of scar tissue beneath her right eye. Then she fled whatever thoughts consumed her and snatched up the kettle.

At the sink, she flinched when he paused a scant foot away.

Stifling his questions, she nodded toward the garage. "Get moving," she said. "We can't go anywhere until you find the luggage."

Chapter 14

Running through the mental checklist, Ryan slammed the trunk of his mother's car.

Their neighbor promised to grab the mail each day, and the timer was set to ensure lights went on and off inside the house at suitable hours. With less enthusiasm than Ryan would've liked, because of his mother's subdued behavior, he'd told Cat to expect them in the early evening. Inside the house, Julia watered the last of the houseplants. The luggage was already stowed in the Beemer's trunk.

With dusk approaching, long shadows painted the driveway. As they crept toward his shoes, the sense of unease returned. Confident his mother was still busy inside, he retrieved the keepsake from his pocket. The gift from Cat was a Siren's token, similar to the headdresses the women wore during their morning ritual on the beach—similar to a memory buried deep inside Ryan and still out of reach.

Which wasn't the most disturbing thought.

His mother was familiar with the Wayfair Inn. While she bustled around the house, he'd tried a series of subtle conversation starters to unearth the specifics. None of his ploys extracted the tiniest fact. To his knowledge, she'd never visited the town.

Yet she knew the inn, and something about the country retreat upset her. She'd done her best to mask her initial reaction, but not before he saw the distress rippling across her face.

She trotted down the front steps with her purse in one hand and a magazine in the other. "Ready?" she asked.

"Just about." He slipped the token back into his pocket.

She held up the magazine. "I also packed a book. If I'm bored, I'll find a quiet spot to read. I don't want to be underfoot while you and Cat are working." She produced her car keys.

"I printed out the directions and put them on your passenger seat." He'd never lose her on the highway, but she'd insisted on the backup plan. "Last chance to take me up on the offer. I'd rather drive together."

She climbed into her car. "No, thank you. If we're in one car, I'd pay a fortune for a taxi if I decided to come home early."

Eager to see Cat, he nodded in assent. "Keep your phone out. If you want to stop and stretch your legs, it's no problem."

"Stop mothering me. I'll manage."

With forced gaiety, she winked. Yet he noted her tight hold on the steering wheel, the muscles in her forearms tensing. Her knuckles locked in an arresting pose. The image brushed against the seedbed of his mind.

Catching his appraisal, she rammed the key into the ignition. "Well, come on. Are we going or not?"

A strange impulse worked through Ryan. Uneasy, he strode to his car. The memory flirted with his consciousness before darting away. It was like trying to catch a playful child intent on evading capture.

When the memory finally broke through, it did so with dismaying clarity: his mother clenching the steering wheel in a white-knuckled grip as she drove them away from Twin Falls on that unspeakable night. Blood clotting on her jaw. The car swerving onto the highway. He recalled how the force of the maneuver whipped his neck sideways, landing his attention on the pouch spilling its contents across the backseat.

The pouch was blue. Ryan inhaled sharply. The bag, made of velvet.

Heeding the whim, he retraced his steps to her car. "I forgot something." His eyes strayed to the house.

"Honestly, Ryan. You've had hours to pack."

"Be right back."

He didn't dare analyze the instinct that sent him sprinting inside. Striding to his mother's bedroom, he caught the memory fully, every bleak, terrifying instant. They'd raced out of the apartment with clothing heaped into garbage bags—and the velvet pouch she'd placed on the backseat of the car.

The bedroom drapes were shut, the bed neatly made. Searching the contents of her dresser was a terrible breach.

He deliberated for only a second before riffling through the drawers. In the third drawer, he found the pouch, blue like sapphires. He dumped out the contents.

Feathers, stones, and tiny shells strung together on various lengths of twine. Most of the items represented a child's handiwork. The technique seemed to improve over time, and he examined a token presumably created in the maker's late adolescence or early adulthood. The royal-blue feathers, and glittery silver paint on the stones and the shells, were similar to the artistry of the keepsake from Cat.

He selected one of the oldest-looking tokens. The feathers were haphazardly painted. The stones were done with primary colors applied with clumsy strokes. But only a fool would miss the similarity to Cat's work.

With care, he returned the rest of the tokens to the pouch.

A disorienting fog carried him back outside. He strode past his mother's car, his mind churning. Swinging around, he pulled out of his musings. She wasn't behind the wheel.

At the end of the driveway, she stood facing the street.

Hearing his footsteps, she turned. Her hands wound together, then unspooled. She looked wounded, like an abandoned child, and just as fearful.

His heart sinking, Ryan guided her back to the house.

Chapter 15

The shriek rocketing from Linnie's old suite went right through Cat's molars. The ear-splitting sound made her mother, scooping up clothes, jerk upright. Tripping on a lacy bra, she flopped into Beefcake Bill.

They went down together in a mass of sprawling legs and inflatable arms.

"Get this ridiculous balloon man off me!"

Tossing Bill aside, Cat checked her for injury, relieved to find none. "You're okay?" She grabbed the dangerous bra, flung it under the dresser.

Another shriek sent her sprinting from the room.

Jada was already halfway down the corridor. Frances was close behind, jogging at an impressive speed for a woman past seventy, the shoulder pads of her dress gyrating toward her ears.

In the center of Linnie's previous digs, Penelope spun in a frantic circle. With a broom in her grip, she made clumsy swipes at the air. Even on a clear day, the heavyset Siren didn't have the best vision. Behind the thick eyeglasses, her myopic gaze rolled toward the ceiling.

"There's a bat!" She took another swing. "Cat, Jada—help me!"

Jada wrested the broom away.

Penelope went into a swoon, and Cat took hold of the hysterical Siren. "Penelope, there's no bat. The workers patched up the eaves in September."

"There's something dive-bombing my head."

"There's nothing flying around."

"There is! Check my hair."

Cat made a cursory examination of the clumps of white hair interspersed with Penelope's wavy auburn locks. "Why don't you touch up the white like my mother does? You have nice hair."

"I can't. I'm allergic to dye."

"Forget dye. There are a million natural products on the market."

"I don't care about natural products." Her double chin wobbling, Penelope felt around her scalp. "I *do* care about creepy-crawlies getting down my blouse. I hate bugs."

"What about ladybugs?" Frances put in. She was perspiring in her delicate way, her lace handkerchief fluttering across her brow. "Bumblebees, the stately praying mantis? You can't love nature and hate insects."

"A bat isn't an insect, Frances. You wouldn't want one tangled in your hair."

"I suppose not."

Silvia appeared. "What's going on?" She flopped against the doorjamb. "The way Penelope's screaming I'd expected to witness a murder."

She lobbed the remark at Cat, her first direct acknowledgment since agreeing to help straighten the south wing. Yesterday's argument on the beach still hung between them. For reasons Cat preferred not to contemplate, the D'Angelos' impending visit only made the situation more strained.

Oblivious to the tension, Penelope tugged at her curls. "Someone check if a spider is crawling on my scalp. I don't want something icky on me!"

Silvia grunted. "There isn't a spider in your hair. Actually, they're good luck."

"I know they're good luck. I just don't want one on my head."

"You're being ridiculous." Something caught Silvia's attention, and she walked past the bed. By the two upholstered chairs near the bay window, she planted her hands on her hips. "Of all the . . . Penelope, you were beating away a moth. You really should have your eyes checked."

Despite Silvia's abrasive personality, her reverence for the natural world was bred to her core. Lowering onto her knees, she tried to catch the moth and set it free. Yellow-tinged wings danced across the carpet, bounding out of reach. Moving in to help, Frances opened the window.

Cool air rushed in, rippling the hem of her dress. "We need a net," she decided.

Jada started for the door. "I'll get a bag."

"No, wait. Silvia, he's right there. Catch him!"

On hands and knees, Silvia growled in the vicinity of Frances's calves, "Why don't you come down here and help?"

"In a dress? I'll snag."

"When Cat asked for help spiffing up the south wing, why did you dress up? We're housecleaning, not visiting royalty."

"Oh, be still."

The moth bobbled under a chair, forcing Silvia to duck lower. "I hope the poor thing's wings aren't broken." Rising back to her knees, she threw Cat a dark glance. "That would be a bad sign."

The moth danced up the wall, blissfully immune to bad omens and Silvia's foul mood. Striding across the room, Cat shooed it out the window.

"Enough with the omens." She guided her mother to her feet. "I appreciate your help getting the south wing ready, but I'm done arguing. If the D'Angelos agree to dinner at your house, I'll give you a call."

Frances, evidently out of the loop, fiddled with her diamond studs. "Aren't we meeting them tonight? I thought we were having drinks in the Sunshine Room."

Silvia wrestled free of Cat's hold. "No, Frances. We're not socializing with the D'Angelos."

"I'm disappointed."

"Sing the blues when you get home. Cat only needs us for grunt work. Why she didn't ask the girls in housekeeping is a mystery for the ages."

"Mami, I told you. There's only a skeleton crew on Sunday," Cat said with forced cheer. The rift she'd created hurt more than anticipated. How to mend their relationship wasn't clear.

Frances asked, "When *are* we meeting the D'Angelos?"

"This week, my house," Silvia informed her. "Assuming they're open to my hospitality."

"Is there any doubt?"

"Ask my daughter."

"Mrs. D'Angelo is very bashful," Cat explained, surprised by Frances's confusion. Rarely did her mother keep important details from her closest friend. Obviously she hadn't mentioned the argument on the beach about Ryan. Silvia was more upset than Cat had realized.

"Mrs. D'Angelo is too bashful to dine at your parents' house? Is that even a thing?"

"I'll convince her to accept." The promise, directed at her mother, didn't alter the cloud of discontent forming around her. Disappointed, Cat looked to Frances for rescue. "I'm sure she'll come with Ryan. I hope you'll be there."

"Whichever day you all get together, count on me. I'm looking forward to meeting Ryan, and I'm sure his mother is a delight."

The polite remark drew a muffled snort from Silvia. Turning away, she regarded Jada and Penelope hovering by the bed. She told them, "One of you needs to help Cat dig out her whirlwind of a bedroom. Find a snow shovel to pick up the clothes. If you can't stuff anything else in her closet, dump the clothing out the window. With luck, none of the inn's guests will notice the debris on the back lawn."

"Mami, you're leaving?"

"I'm going home to your father and a bag of Epsom salts. I need a hot bath."

"Thanks for helping." Cat attempted to place a kiss on her cheek.

Thwarting the gesture, Silvia walked to the door. "You're welcome." She marched out.

In her wake, an awkward silence filled the room. Frances promptly broke it by chuckling.

Cat looked at her questioningly, and she said, "Your mother will grind her teeth all the way to the parking lot. She won't remember I drove until she starts looking for her car."

Penelope, her curls in disarray from so much plucking, lifted her rheumy gaze. "You also drove me. Don't leave me behind." Apparently she still wasn't convinced the south wing was bat-free.

"I'd never leave you, dear. With your night blindness, you're a threat on the road."

"It's after six. I should get home to check my Airbnb account. I spoke to the nicest girl this morning. I hope she's ready to book."

Cat recalled Frances's low opinion of the Sirens renting guest bedrooms for next weekend's concert. Silently she gave her points for holding her tongue. In lieu of lobbing criticism, Frances offered Penelope a benevolent smile.

"Is your houseguest booking for both nights?"

"Saturday night only, with her roommate. They're students at Kent State."

"College students, how lovely."

Penelope beamed at her elegant leader. "I love the idea of hosting college girls. Almost like having daughters under my roof." Ozzie, her only child, was a mail carrier in Sweet Lake.

"Inform your guests you won't tolerate drinking or any other shenanigans."

"Oh, I did. Gemma agreed to the house rules immediately. She's just waiting for her roommate to agree before putting down the deposit. I don't expect any trouble."

"Let's send positive energy to the other Sirens in hopes they fare as well. Norah has already turned down two requests from couples. Ruth may have been correct—the fool has confused Airbnb with a dating site." Dropping the subject, Frances turned back to Cat. Patting her cheek, she said, "Don't let your mother's temper tantrum spoil your evening with the D'Angelos. She isn't truly angry. She's afraid of losing you."

"Will you please talk to her? She won't listen to anyone else. Explain that Ryan would never ask me to leave Sweet Lake. Even if he did, I wouldn't go."

"Never assume what you might do in the future. We all have the ability to surprise ourselves." Softening the warning, she added, "Don't worry about your mother. I'll talk to her." She left with Penelope.

The excitement over Ryan's visit fading, Cat returned to her suite.

Jada followed her inside. "Are you all right?"

Cat picked up Beefcake Bill from where he'd landed on the floor. "No, I'm not," she admitted as she stuffed him inside the groaning closet. "I've spent my whole life dreaming about finding the right guy and falling madly, hopelessly in love. I feel like crying."

"Your wish has been granted. What's the big deal?"

The question seemed bizarre, coming from someone astute like Jada. "Gee, where should I start? Here's one. Explain why my mother is threatening me with bad omens about moths with broken wings. Or why I don't get a few blissful months with Ryan before dealing with his mother. I'm sure she's the sweetest woman this side of the Mississippi, even if she's practically a hermit, but I'm not ready for this. What's the point of falling in love if there's no romance?"

"Stop being impatient. Some relationships have kinks." Jada shrugged. "Work out the kinks."

"Like that's easy."

"You can start by cultivating patience. Your mother is a hothead, but you've got your own faults. I mean, look at this place. You're too self-indulgent to pick up after yourself. There are toddlers with better organizational skills."

Cat winced. She *was* disorganized—inconsiderate too, given the harsh remark about Julia. Because of all the details Ryan had shared, she knew a visit to a country inn was a difficult proposition for his timid mother. A leap of faith too—one made for her son's happiness.

Jada scooped up an armful of clothing, stuffed the garments into drawers.

"Stop beating yourself up. Granted, you're sloppy. Doesn't make you the demon seed."

"I am self-indulgent *and* self-centered." Privately she added *self-loathing*, which trailed her across the room. Reaching for the clean sheets, she began making the bed. "I swore I'd do nothing but practice gratitude. Here I am, complaining about the woman who may become my mother-in-law. I'm pond scum."

"You're not. You want what we all expect when we fall in love. Time alone with your man."

"Won't get any this week."

"We do have a ton of work for the concert. Make sure the events company you hired gets the tables set up on the beach first thing Saturday. Midnight Boyz don't play until seven, but we'll make a bundle serving dinner to the early birds."

Three hundred tickets had already sold online. Sales were still brisk, a genuine success in the making.

Even so, Cat didn't feel like breaking out the party hats. "I took care of it. The tables and the dance floor will be in place no later than ten."

"Linnie showed me the ideas you and Ryan came up with for next spring's ad campaign. Looks great."

"We're still fine-tuning the copy. Penny, the photographer Ryan brought in, will come back on Saturday. We might switch some of the art we've already selected."

"You're doing a good job with the marketing, Cat."

One short month ago, the compliment would've satisfied. Now she felt differently. "Between all the work and entertaining Julia in our spare time, Ryan and I won't get a minute alone."

"Not to fear, grasshopper. I'll run interference." On the opposite side of the bed, Jada pulled the sheet taut. "If Julia passes on dinner with your parents, I'll come up with a plan to keep her occupied."

"Declining the dinner invitation will seem like a major snub. Think Julia will refuse?"

"You need a contingency plan just in case."

"Yeah—one that'll guarantee my mother won't erupt like a volcano. Keep me posted when you conjure up a miracle."

"You might as well face facts. Chances are, Julia will feel totally out of her element in Sweet Lake. You can't insist she have dinner with your parents."

Cat's heart stalled. "I have no idea what I should do about my mother."

"There's nothing you can do." With calm efficiency, Jada pulled up the comforter and smoothed out the wrinkles. "Let her fume."

Becoming a neatnik for the rest of her life struck Cat as an easier task. "She's never been this angry with me." Unexpected tears caught on her lashes. "She blows up at my brother occasionally, and fights with Val all the time. Not with me. Never with me."

"You're such a goof." Nearing, Jada brushed the tears away. "Don't you get it? Your mother keeps you latched to her hip because she nearly lost you when you were a baby. Why do you think she's furious about the thought of you moving to Cincinnati? She has an irrational belief her constant vigilance keeps you healthy."

The observation seemed far fetched. "I *am* healthy. I stopped visiting the pediatrician constantly when we were in junior high. Why would she worry after all this time?"

"Because she's never fully put the fear to rest any more than Ryan's mother has forgotten what his father did to her. Some hurts don't heal.

With luck, they cover over with enough scar tissue to make them bearable. But they don't go away."

"You're comparing apples and oranges."

"Cat, we've never faced anything that's tested our limits. Nothing like nearly losing a child or escaping an abusive spouse. We don't carry those scars. I'm grateful we've been so fortunate." Playfully Jada pinched her cheek. "You see? I'm practicing gratitude. You should too."

Heeding the advice, Cat did her best to pull herself together. Ryan called from the road, saying they'd arrive later than anticipated.

The delay proved convenient. Two members of the kitchen staff were out with head colds, and Linnie was still in her office. The sous chef was scrubbing down counters, her movements spiking the air with an antiseptic scent. At the center island, members of the waitstaff placed the final dessert orders for the Sunshine Room on trays.

Grabbing an apron to protect the conservative pink blouse and grey slacks she'd selected for her first meeting with Julia D'Angelo, Cat got to work on the dirty pots left from the dinner rush.

She'd nearly finished, her face wearing a light sheen of perspiration, when a soft thumping from the windowsill caught her notice.

In the droplets thrown from the sink, a moth, its wings torn, twitched one last time, then grew still.

Chapter 16

Within seconds of making introductions, Cat concluded the description Ryan had given of his mother was wholly inadequate.

Julia D'Angelo wasn't merely scarred by an unfortunate past. She was more ghost than human, a tall, disturbingly thin woman wading through the parking lot's shadows. Her head remained bowed until she reached the soft glow of lights surrounding the inn, and the steps. After she reached the veranda, she turned around without warning. Grinding to a halt at the railing, she made an appraisal of the black sea enveloping the grounds.

"I can't see the lake." Her words were as insubstantial as mist.

Or hear the surf from this distance, Cat realized with a start. Yet Julia moved down the railing with confident steps, zeroing in on the location of Sweet Lake with accuracy. The moon wasn't out; dense clouds crusted the sky. She stood looking toward the lake she couldn't see as if she'd enjoyed its pleasures in the past.

The uncanny performance also gained Ryan's notice. He exchanged an intrigued glance with Cat.

Smoothing away his surprise, he guided his mother toward the lobby. "Would you like to see your room?" Retracing his steps, he grabbed their luggage, a small carry-on and a larger case.

"I would, thank you."

A soft murmur carried from the Sunshine Room as they made their way across the lobby. On the stairwell, Cat said, "I hope you don't mind the south wing, Mrs. D'Angelo. It's not quite as nice as the main portion of the inn, at least not yet. We're refurbishing it later this year."

"Oh, I'll manage."

At a faster clip, Julia went up the stairwell. Cat waited for Ryan, who was thumping the larger case up the stairwell. "Did you pack your entire closet?" she teased him.

"Almost."

"You should learn to travel light."

"While I'm working? Sorry, no can do. Two suits, plus a week's worth of casual clothes—I almost packed a second carry-on."

The light banter didn't ease the tension whirling through Cat. Something was bothering him. Julia seemed equally nervous. Her gait rigid, she moved swiftly, like the bandleader of their small parade. At the end of the corridor, Cat was about to instruct her to turn left to find the narrow, older stairwell leading to the south wing. Once more, Julia surprised her.

Gaining speed, she darted left. She disappeared up the stairwell.

Cat pulled Ryan to a halt. "She's been here before?" she whispered.

"She never leaves the city without me . . . but she's familiar with the inn."

"How? A day trip with women friends, a drive alone in the country?"

"Great theory, except I've already told you—she doesn't have women friends, or travel without me."

"Ryan, she knows the inn like a homing pigeon."

"That's not all. There's another interesting development. I'll explain later." He peered down the corridor then back to Cat. "She almost didn't come. Changed her mind at the last minute. Took me the better part of an hour to bring her around."

"What happened?"

"Beats me. She's been skittish since this afternoon, when I mentioned you work in Sweet Lake. She knew instantly I was talking about the Wayfair." Brows lowering, he canvassed her face. "Hey, whatever *is* bothering her, it has nothing to do with you."

The reassurance didn't allay her doubts. "You're sure?"

"Positive. She's glad for the opportunity to get acquainted. In a day or so, she'll relax. We just need to give her space."

"Will she stay the week? My parents are looking forward to hosting dinner."

"Let's keep our fingers crossed." Uncertainty filtered through the comment. Tempering it with a smile, he motioned to the stairwell where his mother had disappeared. "Lead the way. Mom's gone psychic, but I'm unfamiliar with the south wing. It wasn't on the grand tour."

"I'll add it . . . *after* the place gets a face-lift." She strove for a cheery note to mask her confusion. Even if Julia had visited the Wayfair in the past without Ryan's knowledge, why would returning make her skittish? Her bad case of nerves didn't portend well for the week ahead.

Ryan surveyed the corridor, with its old carpeting and dimly lit wall sconces. "I see what you mean. The south wing definitely needs an upgrade." He swung around. "Where is she?"

In a breezy voice, his mother called out, "Is this one mine? The flowers are beautiful."

Thanks to the ever-thoughtful Jada, a bouquet of fresh daisies sat on the nightstand in Linnie's old digs, to complement the larger bouquet of tea roses Cat had placed on the dresser. The plush apricot throw she snuggled in on wintry nights, freshly laundered, nestled on an upholstered chair.

"You've found the place, Mrs. D'Angelo."

"What a pretty room." She noticed the roses. "Thank you. And please, call me Julia."

"Can I get you anything?" The inn didn't have room service, but Jada was still in the kitchen reviewing the menu for next Sunday's brunch.

"A cup of tea would be nice. Do you have chamomile?"

She sent the text. "Coming right up."

Ryan said, "After you unpack, why don't we meet downstairs? We'll have a drink together."

"The Sunshine Room doesn't close until midnight," Cat chimed in. "Or, if you prefer, we'll sit on the veranda."

Retrieving the carry-on from her son, Julia gave a brave-looking smile. "I'm rather tired. Do you mind if I beg off?" She placed the small suitcase on the bed. "We'll chat more tomorrow."

At the subtle dismissal, Cat led Ryan into her suite, which now belonged to him for the duration of his visit. She'd barely shut the door when he dropped his cool veneer—and his luggage—to steer her into his arms. With an urgent kiss, he backed her into the wall.

Coming up for air, he looked over his shoulder. "News flash. This place has a bed."

"It's my bedroom. What were you expecting?"

He lifted his nose, inhaled. "Your scent is all over the place. Chemical warfare. I like it." Showering kisses on her neck, he teased the skin until she shivered. "If I surrender, will you get into bed?"

"Not tonight."

"Because my mother's down the hall?" He nuzzled her ear, flooding her senses with pleasure. "She's more interested in her book than us."

"Ryan—"

"No sex. Lady's choice. Totally fine." His eyes dilated so quickly, she felt breathless. "What are your thoughts on heavy necking, minus our shirts?"

His reckless hands drifted down to her waist, threatening her resolve. An entire night of lovemaking was a delicious prospect—an idea she shook off with some effort. Angling back, she took his face in her hands.

"On our way upstairs, you said there's another interesting development. What is it?"

The desire ebbed from his features. Setting her away, he scrubbed his palms across his jaw.

"Mind if we talk downstairs? I could use a drink."

"Sure."

The Sunshine Room was nearly empty, the last diners finishing dessert. Toward the back of the restaurant, Linnie huddled with several of the waitstaff, no doubt discussing the week's schedule. The publicity for next Saturday night's concert had worked better than expected, with increased bookings starting well before the weekend. By Wednesday the inn would be sixty percent full, a major achievement for the off-season.

They ordered drinks, Dewar's for Ryan and the house white wine for her. Cat doubted the veranda was free of guests, but the last diners were gone from the patio behind the restaurant. She led Ryan out back.

He chose a table near the end and pulled out her chair. When she'd seated herself, he sat down to nurse his drink in quiet contemplation.

She sipped her wine, aware he didn't know how to begin. Her mother's talk of bad omens and the dying moth she'd seen while washing pots crept into her thoughts.

At last Ryan looked at her. "There's a lot I haven't told you."

An inauspicious opener if ever there was one. "Like what?"

"My name wasn't always D'Angelo."

"You had a different name?"

The question floated between them, unbound. She licked her lips, her shoulders tensing.

"My mother changed it the last time we ran. Soon as we got to Ohio, when I was sixteen. A priest in Cincinnati helped. Father Thomas put her in touch with an attorney, who took care of the details. He also went with her to court. One day I was Ryan Hunt, and the next, Ryan D'Angelo."

George. My father. Not once had he added a last name, and she'd drawn the obvious conclusion. "Julia changed your surname to hide from your father?"

"It was the only way to get rid of him for good. He found us after we were in Salt Lake for a while. They reconciled, and then he went back to his old habits. When it got really bad, we ran again. We moved to Idaho, had some good years before the past caught up with us." He paused, and the stilted account put chips of ice in her blood. "George found us in Twin Falls."

"How did he find you?"

"I didn't crack the mystery until my second year of college, and an all-nighter searching Google. Not like my mother would go into details—we don't discuss the past much. Too hard for us both." Ryan took a gulp of his drink. "The place she worked in San Francisco, Lux Jewels? The owner was born in Twin Falls. I guess it took George Hunt a while to remember that salient fact."

"How long did you live in Twin Falls?"

"I was sixteen when George caught up with us. My parents didn't reconcile, not like in Salt Lake. After what he did to her that day, she finally caught on. She needed to give us a new name, or she wouldn't survive." A muscle in his jaw convulsed. In a steadier voice, he added, "Today, right before we left to come here, I remembered something I'd forgotten."

She struggled to keep up. "A phone number, a name?"

"A memory. The drive out of Twin Falls." Revulsion washed through his eyes, but he contained it. "I didn't remember all the details until we were in the driveway, getting into our cars."

On the stem of the glass, her fingers twitched. "Ryan, you were sixteen when you left Twin Falls."

"I blocked out a lot of what happened. I wasn't aware how much until today. After my father beat my mother, and I came in from school . . . there's a lot I don't remember, never want to remember." His voice faded off, the memories crowding in.

"Tell me what you remembered today." Scooting her chair closer, she took his free hand and placed it protectively in her lap.

The small act of kindness brought a grim smile to his lips. "I have some pretty serious memory gaps." Pride battled the fear in his eyes. "Entire years from childhood I've lost."

"You didn't lose them; you did what you needed to survive. I'm sure there are other adults who've come through abusive childhoods with events they've blocked entirely." A horrible ache drove through her breastbone. He'd endured too much, horrors beyond imagining. Horrors that her comparatively happy life didn't prepare her to under-stand. "What happened in the driveway to make you remember?"

"Mom got into her car. The way she hung on to the steering wheel, like she was hanging on for dear life, kick-started my brain. Like a movie switching on in my head. But I didn't just see her. I saw the vel-vet pouch she'd tossed onto the backseat before we took off for Ohio."

"A jewelry pouch?"

"A large one, big as one of those envelopes for legal documents. Probably meant to hold a jewelry box."

"From the jewelry store in San Francisco?"

"Yeah, that would make sense." He drew back into reflection, his eyes leaping across the darkness engulfing the patio. "Cat, you've got to understand. The last day in Twin Falls, I came home and found my mother practically blinded from the blood running down her face. One of her eyes swelling shut, the bruises purpling on her cheeks—George was passed out on the couch, thank God. I didn't enter the apartment. One look at my mother, and I threw up in the doorway."

He paused again, long enough to finish his scotch. She held his hand fiercely as the past bore down on him.

"I don't remember how she managed to clean me up while I stood there, a sixteen-year-old kid helpless as a baby. Somehow, she managed it. She'd just received the worst beating of her life but she was incredibly calm, reassuring *me*. She told me to stay right there, like she was worried I'd run off. Hell, I was so terrified, I couldn't move. I couldn't do anything but stare at that dumb bastard, snoring loud enough to shake the walls. I hadn't seen George in years, didn't remember him. Another memory I'd suppressed."

Hatred flickered through Ryan's eyes. Instantly he quashed it. Yet the telling of that fateful day was so vivid, panic rattled Cat's pulse. "Your mother told you to wait," she whispered, urging him to finish the story and bring them both relief. "While you waited in the doorway, what did she do?"

"That was another thing I didn't recall until today, how fast she moved. Bloody, bruised—like one of those guys on a bomb squad." Blinking rapidly, Ryan pulled from the nightmare. In a firmer tone, he said, "She went to her bedroom first, got the velvet pouch. She came back out filling it with items I didn't recall until today. She went there before she raced to the kitchen for the garbage bags to stuff our clothes in. She walked right past George snoring on the couch and handed me the pouch, this soft sapphire-blue bag. She told me to keep it safe while she got the rest of our things."

"You didn't remember it until today?"

"Incredible, right? Especially since she didn't let it out of our sight for the entire trip. Kept it right on the backseat. She took it into every diner we stopped at to grab a bite. Must've been her most cherished possession, but I excised it from my brain like I'd reached Ohio equipped with a scalpel."

"You associated the pouch with what you witnessed when you came home from school. That's why you cut it from your memory." Putting the pieces together, Cat inhaled a sharp breath. "This afternoon you found the velvet pouch?"

"I told my mother I'd forgotten something inside the house. I found it buried at the bottom of a drawer in her bedroom."

"What was inside?"

A muscle in his jaw convulsing, he reached into his pocket. The moon drifted out from behind thick clouds to finger the thread of feathers and stones, illuminating the tiny shells strung between them with cold light. Silver and gold pigment, expertly painted on the hair-like barbs of each feather, glimmered in the moonlight. Cat frowned with confusion.

"Ryan, this is the token I gave you."

Grimly he reached back into his pocket. He produced a second, older token. The feathers were broken. The stones were painted in primary colors, bold hues only a child would select.

Cat blinked with amazement.

Chapter 17

Relieved to have found her friends at last, Cat walked into the ballroom. Jada and Linnie crawled across the parquet floor with a yellow tin of wax and rags in their fists. All morning she'd been looking for an opportunity to get them alone.

Approaching, she asked, "What are you doing?"

Linnie rubbed furiously at the floor. "Touching up the scratches your band left in my beautiful ballroom."

"In case you've forgotten, all three of us voted to hire Midnight Boyz." After the depressing conversation with Ryan last night, she'd forgotten about the band's antics in the ballroom. "Do you need help touching up the floor?"

"We're almost finished." Linnie appraised her handiwork with satisfaction. She gave Cat a quick glance. "You look tired."

After bidding Ryan good night, she'd chased shadows across the ceiling for hours. The initial, numbing disbelief at what he'd endured during a tumultuous childhood gave way to anger and, finally, tears. At dawn, she'd fallen into a dreamless sleep.

When she merely shrugged, Linnie asked, "Where's Ryan?"

"He took his mother out for lunch." He'd been quiet all morning, clearly wrung out from the conversation about his father.

"They left the inn? What's wrong with the eats in the Sunshine Room?"

Jada took a last swipe at the floor. "Linnie, consider it a good sign he pried her out of the south wing at all. Julia is a major introvert. Sweet, but jumpy. I feel sorry for her."

"This isn't her first visit to Sweet Lake," Cat said.

Linnie capped the tin of polish. "I thought she rarely leaves Cincinnati."

"She doesn't, not without Ryan. They've never visited Sweet Lake or the Wayfair, which Julia knows well. Last night, when we were bringing in their luggage, she walked right by and found the stairwell to the south wing. Like she'd done it a thousand times before."

Linnie's brows lifted with fascination. "The south wing has been closed to guests for years. If she knows it, she visited the Wayfair ten, twenty years ago. Or longer."

"If you think that's weird, you won't believe this." Cat produced the crude token Ryan had given her for safekeeping. "Julia has a whole series of these. The rest are hidden away in an old jewelry pouch in her bedroom at home."

Nervously, Cat placed the token on the floor between her friends. A soft gasp drifted from Jada. The tin of polish slipped from Linnie's fingers, clattering across the floor.

From the entryway nearest the kitchen, two of the girls from housekeeping came in swinging buckets of sudsy water. They were finishing the tidying up before Mr. Uchida and several of the men on staff brought in the long tables for next Sunday's buffet.

Linnie waved them off. "Daisy, Carol—would you come back in a few minutes? We need the ballroom." After they'd gone, she studied Cat anxiously. "This is a Siren token," she whispered.

"Made by a kid, obviously."

"The Sirens don't hand these out indiscriminately. Ask Julia how she came by one."

"Be realistic. I can't play twenty questions with a woman I've just met."

"Then encourage Ryan to ask. She's more apt to speak freely with him."

The suggestion only managed to increase Cat's agitation. She'd been plagued with a sense of foreboding since Ryan explained about the name change. Julia had gone to extreme lengths to stop George Hunt from ever finding them again. Cat's instincts warned her that the tokens were hidden out of need for self-preservation.

Putting form to her fears, she said, "This will sound like a leap, but I'm sure the tokens are connected to Ryan's father. Julia hid them because of George."

Jada frowned. "That doesn't make sense. What do they have to do with her ex-husband?"

"No clue, but George factors in." She nearly mentioned the name change. Out of respect for Ryan's privacy, she dismissed the impulse. "Maybe she kept them hidden *from* George when they were married."

Linnie picked up the delicate keepsake, turned it slowly in her palm. "Frances says tokens are imbued with feminine power. Didn't she and Silvia begin making them when they established the Sirens?"

"I thought so." Now Cat doubted she did, in fact, know the provenance.

"If they came up with the design, who taught Julia? She has a whole bag of these?"

"A velvet pouch full of them. Ryan saw it right before they drove here."

"We have to assume she made them herself. This looks like the work of a six-year-old."

"Some of the others are more sophisticated. Julia made them in adulthood."

Linnie handed the token back. "Can't Ryan talk to her?"

"He won't. He did some major lobbying just to get her to come here. He's afraid of saying the wrong thing, of giving her an excuse to drive home. He knows how badly I want her to join us for dinner at my parents' house. Plus we want her to experience the benefits of small-town life, in case . . ."

Jada smiled. "There are wedding bells in your future?" Bringing Linnie up to speed, she added, "Ryan is aware Cat won't move to the city."

"We haven't gone into details, but he's open to living in Sweet Lake if everything works out between us," Cat put in. "Assuming his mother agrees."

The optimistic possibility, accenting a troubling conversation, boosted her spirits. If Julia came to enjoy her time in Sweet Lake, everything else would fall in place.

Linnie said, "You should show the token to your mother. She may have an idea of how a child learned to make one."

"I'm not asking her. She's convinced Julia will persuade me to move to Cincinnati. I get how much my mother loves me, but she's going overboard."

"Why does she think Julia's selling you on moving? You've just met."

"Don't waste your time looking for a logical reason. She's being silly. Ryan and I have only discussed the future in a tentative way. It's not like he'll pop the question soon. We've only been a thing for two days."

"Sorry, Cat. She's got reason to worry. I've seen how Ryan looks at you."

"Me too," Jada agreed. "The man's got a bad case of the love bug." She wagged a finger before Cat's nose. "I'm happy for you, but no eloping. Linnie may string Daniel along forever, but we all agree you're more impetuous. If you decide to tie the knot, we're hosting a big reception at the Wayfair. I'll bake a killer cake."

Happy to indulge in the daydream, Cat imagined church pews festooned with bunting, and Ryan eagerly waiting at the altar. Promptly she brushed off the sweet reverie. She *was* impetuous, but not reckless. Considering marriage this early in a relationship was a major no-no.

Linnie, apparently scalded by Jada's comment regarding her perpetually cold feet, narrowed her eyes. "I'm *not* stringing Daniel along. We've only been living together since July."

"And courting for a decade before that," Jada teased her.

"Get your facts straight."

"Face it, Linnie. You're a chickenshit."

"I'm careful—totally *not* the same thing." Ditching the mock anger, she grew thoughtful. "Want me to mention the kiddie tokens to Frances? She might have an idea of how Julia learned to make them."

Cat gave a mock shiver. "Confide in Frances, and we'll put her in hot water with my mother. They're best friends."

"Geez, I hate when Silvia goes on these rampages."

"Like I don't? We leave Frances out of this. She has finely tuned diplomatic skills, which we'll need to get through dinner."

"When are you taking Julia to meet your parents?"

"Wednesday night, if she'll agree." Cat winced. "Assuming Mami cools down enough to extend a second invitation. Julia turned down the Tuesday night invite. Guess she needs time to settle in." She wasn't even sure Ryan would convince her to have dinner with just them tonight in the Sunshine Room.

The suspicion proved disappointingly accurate. At dinnertime, Julia called down to the kitchen for a sandwich and a pot of chamomile tea. Attentive to her comfort, Cat saw no reason to explain about the inn's lack of room service, especially since Jada offered to ferry the simple meal upstairs.

As promised, she also managed to ingratiate herself with their timid guest. Their mingled voices drifted into the corridor as Cat went downstairs to meet Ryan for dinner.

After last night's weighty discussion regarding Twin Falls, they forged an unspoken agreement to keep the conversation on lighter topics, the tasks requiring their attention during the lead-up to next weekend's concert, and the marketing efforts they were wrapping up.

The passion Ryan had exhibited Sunday night was nowhere in evidence as he escorted her back to the south wing.

With a chaste kiss, he deposited her outside the room where she now bunked with Jada and murmured goodnight.

᎙

Frances weighed the wisdom of resorting to swordplay.

At minimum, she'd like to rescue her expensive sun parasol from Silvia. The co-leader of the Sirens had taken complete and utter leave of her senses. Burning a trail across the living room, she whipped the parasol in dangerous arcs to accent her complaints.

After listening to the tirade about Julia D'Angelo for twenty minutes and counting, Frances reached her wit's end. If her comrade refused to shut up, there was no choice but to grab the parasol and pop her on the head.

"Stop pacing, please. You're giving me vertigo." From her virtual captivity on the couch, Frances rubbed her pounding temples. "Ryan's mother declined a dinner invitation. We aren't talking about a major breach of etiquette. Why not suggest tomorrow? I'm sure she'll come."

"She refuses for tonight, so I should invite her again for tomorrow night?"

"Rant all you'd like. Marco will insist on asking. Let's not forget Cat. She'll expect you to extend another invitation. Be a courteous hostess, and do so."

Silvia pointed the parasol like an accusing finger. "Dream on, Frances. Three days now, and I have yet to meet Julia. If the situation were reversed, I would've picked up the phone first thing Monday and introduced myself. The relationship between her son and my daughter is getting serious. Why hasn't she reached out to me?"

"You must have shared a few words when she canceled for tonight."

The comment glazed her comrade with outrage. "You believe the reclusive old bat called to decline?" The parasol whipped through the air. "Julia didn't make the call—Cat did. I have a feeling my daughter may end up with Ryan. I wish someone had checked if I wanted Emily Dickinson for an in-law."

"If your daughter weds, Julia will become her in-law, not yours. As for Emily Dickinson, she suffered from social anxiety disorder. I doubt Julia is in the same league. Didn't Cat mention she's bashful?"

Silvia resumed pacing. "Yes, and why is that the sum of my knowledge? When I spoke to Cat this morning, I asked for background on Ryan's family. You'd think my daughter were the secretary of defense, and I'd demanded a launch code."

"What did she say?"

"'Mami, I can't tell you right now.'"

"A mystery," Frances murmured, intrigued. "How fun."

"This isn't a game. Can't you see I'm upset? This is the first time Cat has kept secrets from me."

"Pardon me for pointing out the obvious, but you're delusional."

"Go on, Frances. Keep laying on the sugar. I ought to string you up by your varicose veins."

"As if I'd let you." She found a patient tone, adding, "Cat is thirty years old, a mature adult. I'm sure she's kept a few secrets from you."

"She hasn't!" Silvia thumped the tip of the parasol on the carpet to emphasize her disgust. "My daughter's involved in a serious romance, but I don't know the first thing about the family. I've only seen Ryan once, when he stumbled out of the woods with my daughter, and his mother stays holed up in the south wing. Is there a father in the picture, or is Julia divorced? Has she been married five times? Maybe she's Elizabeth Taylor, with a man in every port."

"Silvia, you've been kidnapped by your imagination. A woman past middle age doesn't keep a man in every port. She doesn't have the energy."

"Aren't you the least bit curious about her?"

When Frances merely sighed, Silvia veered toward the window. Halting on a dime, she peered out. The parasol flopped to her side.

"There's a girl doing yoga on the hood of her car. Of all the—she's in the street."

The announcement brought Frances to her feet. Highland Avenue didn't see much traffic, but she wasn't keen on adding a 911 call to the day's list of chores.

Wresting the parasol free, she dropped it smartly in the brass umbrella stand.

On the front stoop, she bit back a gasp. Sure enough, a girl sat on the hood of an old Buick in *sukhasana* pose. The Buick was smack-dab in the middle of the road.

"You, there!" In her haste, Frances went diagonally across the lawn at terrible risk to her imitation-snakeskin pumps. There were no cars in either direction, but she couldn't very well leave the meditating girl parked like a bull's-eye. "Hello, miss?"

The breeze spun ribbons of long, honey-gold hair across the girl's high cheekbones. Her thick lashes fluttered. They parted to reveal eyes of an arresting dark green.

Her serenity in the face of danger was perplexing. "You're in the middle of the road," Frances stated flatly.

"No biggie. There's no one around."

"You can't stay there. You might be killed."

"Oh, I have great ears, like a bat." Hopping off the hood, she appraised Frances, who'd lifted a hand to her fluttering heart. "Did I freak you out? I'm sorry."

"Will you please move the car?"

"Sure—I'm out of here." Her keys sang out as she held them up. She yanked open the driver's-side door. "Sorry to have disturbed you."

Curiosity brought Frances closer. She knew every family in Sweet Lake, from the fresh-faced babies to the town's oldest citizens. Yet something about the girl's well-defined features, combined with her deep-green eyes, gave Frances the sensation of homecoming.

"Why were you meditating in the street?" An intoxicating taste of déjà vu made her desperate to prolong the conversation.

"Oh, I meditate in all sorts of places. It's the best way to deal with nerves."

"You're nervous?"

"Yeah, the nerves hit on the drive down here. I need to find my Zen." Slowly she shut the Buick's door. Leaning against the side, she fiddled nervously with her keys. "They must call your street *mansion row*. It's incredible."

Many of the homes on Highland were lovingly restored, ornate Victorians with filigreed porches, and pillared mansions in the Greek Revival style. Frances's white colonial, one of the largest residences in Sweet Lake, drew the girl's appreciative gaze.

"You're here visiting family?"

"Hopefully next weekend, when Midnight Boyz play on the beach. I'll come back down with my roommate. We booked Saturday night on Airbnb."

"You must be staying with one of my friends." Following Ruth's cue, half of the Sirens were listing guest bedrooms on Airbnb.

"I haven't met the woman renting us the room yet. I set up the reservation online. Her name's Penelope."

"Ah, she's mentioned you." Frances recalled their conversation while helping Cat prepare the south wing for the D'Angelos' arrival. "Penelope said she'd rented her guest bedroom to college students. You attend Kent State?"

The query visibly helped put the young woman at ease. "Second year," she volunteered proudly.

"If your family get-together is next weekend, why drive down today?"

"One of those spur-of-the-moment decisions." She toed the ground, apparently unsure how much to reveal. Frances smiled encouragingly, and the student added, "I begged my roommate to let me borrow her wheels, and took off. It was a dipshit move, actually. I wanted to practice."

"Practice what?"

"The meet and greet with a long-lost relative."

The explanation left Frances scrambling for meaning. The loose, beaded top over the young woman's navy yoga pants hinted at sophistication. Yet her expression wore the earnest desire of a child eager to master a difficult task.

Sensing her bafflement, the girl explained in a nervous rush. "I figured there's no harm in coming down early to get the lay of the land. I want to do a little rehearsing on what to say, decide where to make my big move so he doesn't flip out—he knows exactly zip about me. I don't want to give him a major coronary. Never mind. It *was* a stupid idea. One of those dumb impulses you shouldn't follow."

"Were you heeding your heart?"

"Totally."

"Then the impulse wasn't stupid." Following her own wild impulse, Frances motioned toward the house. "Would you like to come inside? I was about to make tea."

"You don't mind?"

Silvia trooped across the lawn. "She doesn't mind." Apparently she'd thrown off her fit of temper to eavesdrop. With keen interest, she gave their visitor the once-over. "Mind telling us who you are?"

"Oh, sorry. I'm Gemma Mills."

Frances and Silvia exchanged a pregnant look. Whatever seemed familiar about the girl had caught Silvia too.

After the car was safely parked in the driveway, they went out back to have the tea at the wrought iron table overlooking Frances's gardens. Autumn was always a difficult time of year for her, when the cooler weather ushered in memories and regrets. Yet she smiled with pleasure when Gemma admired the fire-tipped maples and the many flower beds dotting the grounds. Silvia barely waited for their guest to take her first sip of oolong before launching into questions.

"You're meeting family next weekend for the concert? They live here?"

"I'm not sure where he lives. He's going to the concert." To her merit, Gemma located the inner resources to continue. "He's my older brother. Half brother, actually. He's totally clueless that he has a younger sister."

"How odd."

"Not really." Gemma shrugged, and a gratifying hint of defiance lit her eyes. "Our mothers never met, so we didn't either."

Frances took control of the conversation. "Your half brother, what is his name?" If Silvia grilled the girl relentlessly, she'd scare her off.

"Do you mind if I don't say? I'm feeling awfully superstitious. I don't want to jinx anything."

The wistful comment touched Frances. Broken families were sadly common, and yet Gemma appeared determined to repair hers. "You mentioned your half brother is older. So your mother's relationship with his father came later?" Reaching for the pot, she refilled Gemma's cup.

"Ten years later. My dad was real good looking, even for a guy way older than Mom. They dated on and off for years."

"Your mother never considered marrying him?" Given all the unwed couples today, the question seemed terribly outdated. Even so, Frances couldn't restrain her interest.

A nervous laugh escaped Gemma. "She wasn't that dumb. No, they just messed around whenever he showed back up. I don't really think of him as my dad . . . more like a sperm donor with itchy feet. He moved in and out of Ohio a lot when I was little." She glanced long-ingly at the gingersnaps. Frances pushed the confections closer, and she snatched one up, nibbling thoughtfully on the crisp edge. "He'd already

left Ohio again when Mom got pregnant with me. She moved back in
with Grandma and Gramps—they told her not to list him on my birth
certificate. Gramps is really protective. He helped Mom buy a condo
right after I was born."

"You're certain this . . . sperm donor *is* your father?" From the telling, it seemed a blessing that Gemma's grandparents kept his name off
her birth certificate.

"Mom told me as soon as I was old enough to understand. Guess I
was five or six, used to seeing him float through our lives."

"How did you find out you had an older brother?"

"My dad kept a shoebox with lots of personal stuff inside. The last
time we saw him, Mom snitched my brother's birth certificate, photos
of when he was a toddler, and some other stuff. She figured if I ever
wanted to find him, I should have the tools to get started."

"Your mother is a smart woman."

Finishing the gingersnap, Gemma shyly reached for another. "She's
not the only one. Simon was behind the decision to root through the
shoebox."

The intricacies of an unusual family were becoming difficult for
Frances to digest. "Who's Simon?"

"Doesn't every story with a happy ending have a charming prince
somewhere in the plot?"

"I'm glad this one does," she murmured. Given the girl's precarious
background, she deserved a helping hand.

"Without Simon, Mom never would've had the guts to snatch the
stuff. My dad kept coming around when I was little. He'd move into the
condo for short stays—it really pissed off Gramps, but he mostly kept
his opinions to himself. The guy never paid me much attention. Didn't
treat Mom very nice, though." Gemma reached for another cookie, her
voice strangely animated. Now that she'd begun, she seemed compelled
to finish the story. "Anyway, the last time my dad showed up, Mom was
already dating Simon. They planned the whole charade. Mom let the

loser believe he could move back in. She took the stuff on my brother right before Simon dropped by to kick him to the curb."

Silvia rose from her unprecedented silence. "Please tell us your mother married Simon. He *is* a prince."

"Five months later. Once they were hitched, Simon adopted me." Finishing her tea, Gemma regarded them with ill-concealed relief. She'd needed to share the story. "I have three younger brothers. Well, half brothers."

"And soon you'll meet your fourth brother." Frances patted her hand. "I wish you'd tell us his name. We promise to keep your secret."

"I shouldn't." Gemma sighed, and the possibility of rejection put something poignant in her eyes. "If he tells me to get lost, the fewer people who know about this, the better."

Bobbing between relief and bafflement, Ryan came to a standstill in the Wednesday afternoon light streaming through the lobby. On the over-stuffed couch in the seating area beyond the front desk, Ruth Kenefsky leafed through the ad sketches that had gone missing from Cat's desk.

Cat was still in Linnie's office finishing the first of several radio interviews he'd lined up this week. The purpose of the interviews was twofold—to bring in a last surge of ticket sales for Saturday's concert, while also touting the lodging specials featured on the Wayfair's new website. Thanks to Ryan's gentle nudging, Adworks's tech staff was launching the site weeks ahead of schedule.

"Ruth, I need those sketches. I'm working on the copy."

Why she'd taken them in the first place was a mystery best not explored. Ruth didn't think highly of him. Lowering her opinion further wasn't wise.

Hunched over the coffee table, she shook her head with disapproval. "Ryan, you don't spell worth crap. There's a typo, right there."

He peered at the headline. "The ads are still rough. I would've caught it."

"What sort of an ad man screws up the headline? Cat should dock your pay."

"Take the issue up with her." He reached for the stack. "If you don't mind."

She pushed the sketches out of reach. "I do mind." She looked past Mr. Uchida talking on the phone at the front desk. "Where's your better half?"

"With Linnie."

"That was a trick question, hotshot. I wasn't sure you'd own up to your hankering for Cat, or that she's better than you. Speaks well of your manliness if you have an ounce of humility."

"My manliness isn't in dispute? Good to hear," he remarked dryly. He held his palm out. "Will you give me the stuff you lifted from Cat's desk? Because, you know, it's not yours."

The observation drew an ill-humored grunt. She tripped her attention down his navy suit, coming to rest on his polished shoes. "Take a load off your Ferragamos. We need to talk."

"May I have a rain check?" If she'd brought menacing fruit for the unscheduled tête-à-tête, he was out of here.

"Not happening."

Against his better judgment, he joined her on the couch. "I'm afraid to ask what's on the agenda." With luck she'd make this quick.

"I suppose you're aware Silvia didn't take kindly to your mother thumbing her nose at Tuesday's invitation. This morning she nearly mowed me down in the grocery store with her shopping cart. She was muttering at the canned tomatoes, and she hurled so many insults at a roaster in the meat department, I was sure that chicken would start shouting back. She scared Ozzie Riddle right out of the store when she went rambling down aisle two, screaming for the manager. Doesn't take much for Silvia to ignite the pilot light on her temper. By the way, you missed out on Marco's beef enchiladas."

"We'll be there tonight, I hope. And my mother didn't thumb her nose."

"Whatever." With an angry little gesture, Ruth flipped her white braids from her shoulders. "I'll do what I can to sway Julia. Not making any promises. I will tell you this. If she cancels again, no one is safe in Mill's Groceries."

How could Ruth sway his mother, who'd met only Jada since arriving Sunday night? Julia had even declined Cat's invitation on Monday to come downstairs to meet Linnie.

A more worrisome thought intruded. If the quirky Siren took to rattling her gourd in the south wing, the stab at misdirected friendship would scare his mother witless.

A possible calamity he set aside as Ruth jumped into another topic. "When you do have dinner with Cat's parents, don't let Silvia intimidate you," she advised in an unexpectedly friendly tone. "An April storm has less bluster than Silvia when she's on a roll. It's just her way of looking out for her daughter."

"I have the impression she's very protective."

"Cat's the only one she guards like a she-wolf. Her other kids have more leeway."

The revelation lifted his brows. "Why only Cat?"

"Silvia almost lost her." Ruth's attention drifted back to the artwork, her expression clouding. "Ryan, get your keister back to primary school. There's another typo, right here."

He pushed the sketches away, forcing her beady, intelligent gaze back on him. "What do you mean, she almost lost Cat?" He couldn't imagine losing Cat, now that he'd found her.

Ruth slapped his knee with the delicacy of a lumberjack. "Seems you don't know everything, hotshot."

"Who said I did?"

"Not me, seeing how you can't spell. How's your grammar? If you're writing whole paragraphs for the Wayfair, I should give your composition a look-see."

"Ruth, I'll spend the rest of the afternoon reading the dictionary if you'll fill me in on the secret about Cat."

With a bony finger, she motioned him near. He visualized a bubbling cauldron and a witch cackling madly—a random thought he discarded as she leaned close. He did want a better understanding of Silvia's protective streak, which his unlikely companion was happy to explain.

"Your sweetheart was a preemie, born two months early. Looked like a tiny wisp of baby flesh with nothing but those big brown eyes to latch her on to this world. Mind you, Cat's thirty now. Back then an early baby didn't always leave the hospital in her mama's arms. The doctor wasn't confident of Cat's chances. Marco took the news well enough."

"And Silvia?"

"She keened loud enough to open the gates of heaven. She must've been summoning every last angel to aid in saving her newborn. There's nothing worse than seeing a strong woman fall to pieces while her baby clings to life." A remnant of those dark days swirled around Ruth. "When Silvia and Marco finally brought her home, Cat wasn't much bigger than a newborn pup. Crying every minute, having trouble bringing air into her tiny lungs—that poor baby didn't sleep more than thirty minutes at a stretch. All of the Sirens took turns helping Silvia out."

"Including you?"

"Back then, I was a dispatcher for the PD. I looked after Cat in the early morning, before I went in for my shift."

Nothing in her demeanor spoke to feminine instincts. Yet she possessed the devotion to care for a newborn before heading into work.

"It was kind of you to watch over Cat when she needed you most," he said with husky appreciation.

"Not a kindness done in secret like the Sirens are supposed to do, but a kindness all the same."

"You're a good woman, Ruth."

His sincerity loosened her tongue further. "We weren't Sirens then," she confided. "Truth be told, Cat helped bring us together as a group. Frances too, after she went through her difficult spell. There was a family tragedy, something she wouldn't discuss with anyone but Silvia."

Ryan nodded sympathetically. Contrary to his initial conclusion, more bound the women together than a penchant for craft projects and magical beliefs about feminine power. They sheltered each other through life's most difficult events.

He regarded her with the respect that was her due. "I appreciate the background," he said. "I doubt Cat would've filled me in."

"She was a sickly kid all through elementary school. Got her health straightened away by junior high, and never looked back. Besides, the one with the problem is Silvia. Don't take her moods personally."

The gentle reassurance—coming from the most unusual source—put a lump in Ryan's throat.

Abruptly she got to her feet. "If you'll excuse me. My four o'clock has arrived."

With a stiff nod, she rounded the coffee table and strode into the lobby. Gathering up the sketches, he started back for Cat's office. He caught something out of the corner of his eye.

The sheets fluttered from his hands.

In the lobby, his mother waited in an unfamiliar wide-brimmed hat. A band of silk daisies festooned the rim. Dressed in khakis and her pink gym shoes, she waved timidly at Ruth.

They were nearly out the door before Ryan scooped up the sketches and sprinted to catch up.

"You're going out?" It was a beautiful afternoon, but she'd rarely left her suite since checking in.

"Only for a short while. Ruth offered to take me for a walk on the beach."

"We're not walking on the tourist side of the lake," Ruth clarified. Hitching her fingers in the pockets of her baggy jeans, she seemed aware of his mother's desire to keep a low profile. "We'll drive over to the north side, walk around there."

"Thanks for showing her around," he said, unable to shake off his shock.

"I'll have her back in time to dress for dinner." She regarded his mother. "Silvia's expecting you at seven?"

A stubborn little silence rose between them. Ruth seemed about to add something else, but thought better of it.

Smoothing over the impasse, he said, "Don't worry about dinner." Evidently his mother was still on the fence. "There's lots of time to decide. Enjoy the stroll."

He rocked back on his heels as they trotted across the veranda and disappeared down the steps. They'd reached Ruth's truck when Cat walked up.

The pull of an unusual sight tipped her forward on the toes of her pumps. "Your mother's going out?"

"Walk by the lake. North side, to avoid tourists."

"How did she meet Ruth?"

"Man, would I love to know."

Sorting it out, Cat murmured, "Hear the Siren's call, and give kindness in secret." Mischief glossed her features. "Forget it. You're a guy. You won't understand."

"Guys have brains too." During his conversation with Ruth, he'd wondered at her comment about kindness. "Try me."

"The Sirens are big on practicing virtues. They see it as a way to strengthen their feminine power."

"Giving kindness in secret is one of their sayings?" If so, it was a keeper.

"They prefer to lend help without being obvious. This is Ruth's way of getting Julia past her bashfulness. A kindness done in secret."

"She marched into the south wing and introduced herself? That's an awfully gutsy move. I'm amazed my mother let her into the suite."

"Knowing Ruth, she refused to leave until Julia did. She's not exactly fainthearted."

"No, that's my mother's special talent." Mulling it over, he added, "It's just as plausible Ruth did this to help *your* mother." He skipped an explanation of Silvia scaring people in the grocery store by roaring down the aisles. He didn't like upsetting Cat.

"I'm sure Ruth knows how angry Mami was over last night's cancellation. Intel passes swiftly through the Sirens. By now, they're all looking for ways to get her to swallow a chill pill."

Cat had accepted last night's cancellation with grace, but there'd been no missing her disappointment. Disappointing her again—or her parents—was out of the question.

"Ruth will lobby my mother to make a grand entrance tonight." He grunted. "Personally, I'd consider it a kindness done in secret."

Cat smiled with false cheer. "Let's hope she's successful."

Chapter 18

Cursing, George swerved across the lanes of heavy traffic. A horn blared from behind as he zoomed down the exit for Sweet Lake.

Three days wasted. On Monday, his parole officer had handed over a whole list of garages to check for work. No bites yet, and the boss at each place pushed through the interview like he couldn't wait to throw George out. Pulling a week in the Hamilton County Justice Center for nonpayment of fines didn't make him a criminal.

It was his first stint behind bars—and his last. After he soaked Frances for enough greenbacks, he was leaving Ohio forever.

He never should've come all those years ago looking for Julia, thinking they'd patch things up. When she didn't turn up, he got into the habit of drifting back to Ohio for no good reason, staying in a lousy job until he got fired, dating chicks who weren't half as classy as his ex. Sometimes he'd drink alone late into the night, wondering where she'd gone.

After Twin Falls, she'd disappeared completely.

He no longer cared about her. Years of working dead-end jobs had killed everything he'd once felt for her, the love and the hate. All he wanted now was a payoff to get him a decent place to live and enough cash to buy the drinks until he found a woman to put him up long term.

Enough money to drive back out West, and stop drifting.

Reveling in the dream, he slowed the car on Highland Avenue. He'd find a babe in California, someone fifteen years younger. Let her cover the bills while he slept in late and spent the afternoons at a sports bar until she clocked out for the day.

The fantasy carried him down the wide boulevard. There wasn't anyone in sight. His confidence rising, he pulled to the curb.

⌒᷉

From the first floor, the grandfather clock chimed four o'clock.

Removing a dress from the walk-in closet, Frances laid it on the bed with the others. At this rate, she'd never decide what to wear.

Despite Silvia's negativity about breaking bread with Julia D'Angelo, Frances looked forward to the evening. She was fond of Cat, and hoped her relationship with the young man from Adworks proved enduring.

Sweet Lake wasn't swimming in eligible bachelors. Cat deserved to land with a quality man, someone who'd cherish her *and* earn a respectable income. She'd dated enough dolts in her twenties. Sorting through the dresses, Frances recalled a perpetual student from Cat's inglorious past who never managed to earn a degree but *did* stick her with the check for most of their dates. They'd carried on for months before the optimistic girl wised up.

Her promising romance wasn't the only reason for Frances's good mood. Returning to the closet, she reflected on yesterday's auspicious meeting with the young woman attending Kent State, Gemma Mills. Courage didn't usually develop in one so young. In many people, it never developed at all.

The example of a college student embarking on the noble pursuit of finding her half brother nearly made up for all the young people who squandered time photographing their food when they ought to get involved with good causes.

She was adding another dress to the selections on the bed when the doorbell rang. Displeasure fizzed through her as she hurried down the stairwell. *Anyone but Norah, please.* The Siren was still hopping mad because Silvia hadn't asked her to join them for dinner with the D'Angelos.

Smoothing her hair in place, Frances swung open the door. She stared at her ex-brother-in-law for a full ten seconds before she had the sense to close her mouth.

"Aren't you going to ask me in?"

"Absolutely not."

It was stunning how little he'd aged since their last meeting. He still looked like a man in his forties, still possessed the striking good looks that had once ensnared her sister. A sickening wash of memories drove through Frances. Dizzy, she tried to catch her breath.

"Is this any way to treat kin? I'm coming in, whether you like it or not." George brushed past. He walked to the end of the foyer, retraced his steps. "Are you alone? I've got news you'll want to hear."

"Get out." She gripped the doorknob like a lifeline. "I told you the last time. I'm done helping you."

"Hell, Frances. That's not the way I remember it. Your bitchy friend told me to hit the road. She came at me with a broom even. Silvia isn't here, is she?"

"Get out, or I'm calling the police."

Eyes narrowing, he weighed the weak threat. "No, you're not." Peeling her fingers from the doorknob, he kicked the door shut. "Why don't you sit down before you fall down? This is about your sister."

She listed slightly, not daring to believe. George Hunt had blackened her life for years. He'd appear unexpectedly, needing money, working on her sympathies until she relented. Never did he bring up the sister she'd lost due to him.

This was yet another ploy, his lowest one yet.

"What do you mean?" she asked, despising the tiny thread of hope weaving through the words.

Satisfaction glittered in his eyes. "Take my word for it, Frances. You'll want to sit down for this."

~∂

"There's a crisis?" Eyes fixed on her smartphone, Cat strolled into the Wayfair's kitchen. Sending the text, she looked up. "What's with all the lettuce?"

On the center island, the mountain of romaine rose nearly to Linnie's head. Jada was more visible for the simple fact she kept pacing, her ebony curls bouncing. Her brow puckered with consternation.

"We've got a problem," she said.

Cat eyed the mother lode of fresh produce. "No way did Ellis order this much romaine." Each plastic bag in the pyramid-shaped tower contained two heads of the spring-green lettuce.

"He didn't. Delivery came early. One of the kitchen assistants signed for it."

Cat surveyed the three women and two men lined up near the stove like ducks in a shooting gallery. They scattered beneath her look of disgust.

To Linnie, she said, "Call back the truck, explain there's been a mistake."

"I've already talked to them. The romaine was meant for the Sheraton off Route Fifty, but we shouldn't have signed for it." Linnie strolled down the island, her attention flicking across the other produce that had arrived in more reasonable quantities. "We're too far away for the truck to come back, so they sent another truck from the warehouse to fulfill the Sheraton's order. I agreed to keep the lettuce for a seventy percent discount."

"We'll work it into the menu," Jada put in. "I'll take half for the Sunday buffet, and add Caesar salad to the menu."

Cat poked at a bag. "You need other ideas to use up the rest?"

Jada sent a teasing glance. "Better grab the Magic 8 Ball you hide in your office and check our chances of using up this much lettuce. And, yeah, we need ideas for main entrée salads."

Requesting guidance from a silly children's toy wasn't necessary. "Romaine with mandarin oranges and chicken," Cat suggested.

Linnie picked up a bunch of celery. "We don't have mandarin oranges."

"Then serve meal-sized Caesar salads with grilled chicken or salmon."

Jada waved off the suggestion. "We'll run out of anchovies. I need them for Sunday's buffet."

From the doorway, Ruth said, "Three college-educated women, and not half a brain between you." She tromped forward trailing sand from the hem of her jeans. "Put Cobb salad on the lunch and dinner menus. Ham is always available at the Wayfair. You've got eggs galore. Scratch Ellis's blue-cheese dressing from the regular menu if you're worried about running low on cheese."

Nearly two hours had passed since the gruff Siren left the inn with Ryan's mother. Cat tiptoed toward the corridor in hopes of spotting Julia. Her heart fell. The corridor was empty.

"She went to her room," Ruth told her. "The walk on the beach wore her out."

Cat wanted to ask if Julia was upstairs dressing for dinner. Unfortunately the mountain of green snagged Ruth's attention.

Linnie said, "Cobb salad sounds great, but we don't have avocados. If I ask our supplier to bring them on short notice, I'll pay a fortune."

Jada held up an apple. "Let's put an autumn spin on the salads." She began stacking the fruit in small piles.

Grabbing the opportunity, Cat pulled Ruth aside. "Did Julia say anything about dinner? My parents are expecting us in an hour. I can't bear to disappoint them two days in a row."

The question floated past the diminutive Siren. "You've got enough lettuce here to feed half the town." She licked her lips. "I like romaine."

Cat handed over a bag. "Please, Ruth. Did she say anything about dinner tonight?"

"She's not going."

"She told you directly?"

"On the way back to the inn. Asked me to find you, and explain."

Dismay sank Cat against the counter. The repercussions were too severe to contemplate. Cancelling at the last minute, as her parents put the final touches on dinner. Entering a new ice age with her mother, compliments of the reclusive Julia.

"I tried to play cheerleader, to talk Julia into going. I told her she'd have a nice time meeting your parents. She won't budge." In spite of Ruth's uncommonly brusque nature, the crispy green mountain softened her features with wonder. "Hardest part about living on a fixed income? There's never enough freshness in your diet. If I never see another box of cheapo macaroni and cheese, it'll be too soon."

Her spirits plummeting, Cat handed over three more bags. "What am I supposed to do? No one cancels an hour before dinner." Absently she regarded Ruth, scrabbling to stack the bags neatly in her arms. She tossed a fifth bag on top. "After this insult, my mother won't calm down until Christmas. I'll never hear the end of it."

"Silvia's got her share of good points, but she doesn't take kindly to anyone turning up their nose at her dinner invitations two days in a row. I'm sorry, Cat. You're screwed." Eyeing her hoard of lettuce, Ruth grinned like a pirate. "My work here is done. Good luck." She left.

Linnie came around the counter. "What did we miss?"

Jada took a long look at Cat, then grimly opened a cupboard. She took down the bottle of Jack. "Julia's not going?" She poured two generous fingers.

Cat downed the booze. "She asked Ruth to find me, send her regrets."

"I saw Ruth in the south wing this morning knocking on Julia's door."

"They walked around the north side of the lake together. They just got back."

"Well, that's something. At least Julia's made a friend."

The well-meaning remark melted the last of her composure. "Gosh, I'm so happy," she snapped. "Julia's got a new friend, and I have to call my mother to cancel. Why don't you make the call? I'll spring for the hearing aid. You'll need one after she does a number on your eardrums by screaming."

Linnie swiped the bottle from Jada. She clattered it against Cat's glass while pouring. "Calm down." She held the glass to Cat's lips. "You aren't cancelling—you're showing up with one fewer guest than anticipated. Go with Ryan. He's only met your mother briefly."

"You mean last Saturday, when the other Sirens spotted us coming out of the forest? She hardly looked at Ryan. If we put him in a police lineup, she'd never pick him out."

"They didn't get acquainted?"

Cat shot an incredulous look. "Sure, Linnie. My mother communed with Ryan beneath the trees while they shared their deepest secrets. Then she passed him off to the other Sirens because men love to bare their souls to a bunch of nosy women."

"Geez, you're snippy."

"With good reason. She dragged me off for a private confab on the beach. You know, to accuse me of making whoopee in Freddie's tree house."

A droll grin took Jada's mouth hostage. "You messed around in the tree house? Ryan's a big guy. Was there room to maneuver?"

"We made do." Cat threw back the drink. Firewater burnt a trail down her esophagus, and she flinched. "Don't ask for juicy details—we were only kissing." She wagged the empty glass. Linnie slapped her hand away. Probably a smart move, since the liquor was making her woozy. "If I'd known Mami would accuse me of going too fast, I would've thrown my reservations out the window and seduced Ryan. Why pay the fine without enjoying the crime? Now I'm jonesing for his bod all the time."

Linnie released a dreamy breath. "Life's full of missed opportunities."

"And tonight's one of them. I'm not submitting him to dinner at the Mendoza homestead. Mami's so peeved, she'll leave an extra place setting on the table just to make him uncomfortable."

"Pretend it's Passover, and you're waiting for Elijah."

"Linnie, you're a laugh a minute. After you deal with all the romaine, send your resume to *Saturday Night Live*."

"Oh, come on. I'm trying to cheer you up—and convince you *not* to cancel."

"Forget it. I'm not taking him over."

Linnie angled sideways to look past her. "What say you, brave soldier? Have the courage to dine with your girlfriend's parents?"

Prickly embarrassment froze Cat in place. Heavy footsteps approached. Queasy, she wondered if Ryan had overheard the comment about his bod.

"We're accepting the invitation." Assessing the mortification rendering her mute, he grinned seductively. "You're jonesing for my bod?"

Surrendering the last of her dignity, she covered her face with her hands.

From behind her fingers, she heard Linnie say, "Don't hold it against her. Men get a bad rap for thinking below the waist. Women have their moments too."

"Good to know." The pleasure saturating his voice was one hundred proof.

Cat required no further incentive to snatch the bottle and race past the grinning kitchen staff. *All righty then.* If he insisted on going, she'd muddle through inebriated. Toss a packet of breath mints in her purse to conceal the evidence, and she was golden.

She was twirling the cap off the bottle when Ryan jogged up.

For an awkward moment they tussled over the bottle. Since they'd reached the embarrassingly public space of the lobby, she let him win. He handed off the prize to a befuddled Mr. Uchida at the front desk.

Picking up speed, she darted toward the stairwell. She reached the top before Ryan caught up with her.

"If you don't want to go over to your parents', we'll stay in."

"You want to go? We'll go. There's a slim chance we'll muddle through, but only because my mother's friend is joining us. Thank your lucky stars Frances is willing to attend. No one else can tame the volcano when Mami's out of control—not even my father."

"I would like to meet your father, and get a do over with your mother. Doubtful she came away with a great first impression."

"You catch on fast."

He reached for her to slow her down. She kept moving.

He hurried to catch up. "You're probably tired of the constant apologies."

"About your mother? I get it. She's not ready for the social circuit."

"Not during this visit, apparently." Ryan matched her stride. "Want to wrap up dinner fast, maybe come back here? I've been jonesing for your bod too."

Whether he meant the comment in a serious vein or was nabbing a page from Linnie's comedy playbook, she couldn't decide. A quick glance at his smoldering features solved the puzzle.

He meant every word.

Bad timing, though. Her embarrassment retreating, she pulled him to a stop.

"Don't you get it? My parents understand we're doing more than sharing a few casual dates. They're looking forward to getting to know you and your mother. It's what parents do, Ryan. They're rolling out the welcome mat in case we all become one big happy family. I'm not comfortable telling them why Julia won't come for dinner, or why she's been holed up in her suite since arriving at the Wayfair on Sunday."

The heated explanation curved his shoulders. "What *have* you told them?"

"About your past? Nothing."

"Which means they think my mother's rude."

"I explained she's extremely bashful." Hating the look of defeat in his eyes, she pressed her palm to his cheek with gentle reassurance. "I told you how I've spent most of my life dreaming about finding the right man, and reveling in all those white-wedding fantasies. Until I met you, I didn't fully understand. The superficial stuff? It's not the big draw."

"What is?"

"All the joys that come after. Our families growing close. Building a life together with their love surrounding us. How does any of that begin—how do *we* begin—if we can't encourage your mother to take the first step?"

"Cat, she'll come around."

An unconvincing reply, and tears welled at the back of her eyes. "When?" she asked, grappling to keep her emotions in check. "After she explains her familiarity with the Wayfair? We both watched her walk to the south wing like she'd memorized the route. Or will she become more outgoing after she explains how she learned to make Siren tokens?"

Regret shuttled across Ryan's face. He seemed prepared to give another apology she didn't want.

"Ryan, I'm not upset with you." She brushed a kiss across his lips, needing to repair the damage from her outburst. The heaviness in her chest increased. "There are all these holes in your past, things Julia has kept from you—it isn't fair. What George Hunt put her through doesn't give her the right to keep the past hidden. It's your past too." She paused to steady her voice. "Listen, I get that she's scared of your father. That doesn't give her the right to cut you off from your family. Nothing does."

A stubborn little light crossed through his eyes. "She has her reasons."

"No, she doesn't." A bitter laugh escaped Cat's throat. "Julia is buried beneath so many secrets, can you honestly say you know her at all?"

Chapter 19

Frances tugged the comforter, and the lap blanket heaped on top, all the way to her chin. The movement sent another dress sliding to the floor. Teeth chattering, she listened to the back door slam.

"Where are you, and what's the emergency? Damn it, Frances—I've got a chicken coming out of the oven soon!"

Impatient strides reached the stairwell. Frances pulled herself up against the headboard. Another dress slithered off the comforter as she tucked the lap blanket around her chilled shoulders.

"I'm in my bedroom."

Silvia came through the doorway. "Are you dying?" Her temper vanished.

"I hope not."

"You look like death." She came around the bed. "Let me check your eyes. Are you having a stroke?" Pivoting, she peered toward the master bath. "I'll fetch the baby aspirin. You might need several."

"I'm not having a stroke." Frances hugged her frozen hands beneath her armpits. "The situation is more dire."

"What's worse than a stroke?"

"George was here." She clenched her teeth to slow the chattering. "If you're curious, he's still driving the Mustang with the hopped-up engine."

The fury returned to Silvia's face. "He was here? No."

"Yes."

"Did you call the police?"

"After he barged inside? There really wasn't time." Rubbing her jaw, Frances halted the fearsome clacking of her molars. "He left twenty minutes ago."

"You let him in the house? For the love of all that is holy, *why?*" Silvia gripped her skull, which was tightly layered in curlers. Apparently she had been dressing for dinner when the SOS came in. "We're not going through this again. How many times have you bailed him out? He's been playing on your misguided, softhearted impulses for years. Enough!"

The tirade sent a shudder down Frances's spine. "Stop shouting, and listen. He's seen her."

Silvia's mouth twitched. She pressed her lips together.

"Last week, in Cincinnati," Frances said, "quite by accident. She came into the garage where he works."

"No."

"She brought her car in for an oil change."

"You believe him? Please."

"Not at first, but the way he described her, and their curt exchange . . . she paid for the service and stormed off. She called the garage two days later, and agreed to meet for coffee." Inwardly Frances cringed. The story *did* sound far fetched. But she rushed on, adding, "They aren't getting back together, not after all this time. She only agreed to see him because Ryan misses his father."

Her expression darkening, Silvia perched on the edge of the bed. "Frances." She pressed her hand onto the mountain of covers, glanced worriedly at the trembling coming from beneath. "Look at this logically. It's unlikely Ryan Hunt remembers his father, let alone misses him. As for your sister, you last talked to her in your fifties. That awful call from Salt Lake, when she told you goodbye? If she left Utah at some point, she's back in California. Not San Francisco—she'd never risk bumping into George on their old stomping grounds."

"She may have come home."

"She hated Ohio. It's ironic how George is the one who's been coming and going from here for longer than I care to remember. She's in LA, or San Diego. Somewhere near the ocean."

"She loved the ocean," Frances quietly agreed. The sad reality didn't extinguish the hope clinging to her. Hope was a treacherous emotion, the way it made your heart vulnerable to more despair, and scarring disappointment. "He was so believable, the way he described her walking into the garage. People *do* come back to their roots. It's not uncommon."

The curlers bobbing on her head, Silvia crawled in beneath the comforter. No doubt they looked ridiculous, two women roosting beneath the blankets on a clear autumn day. The afternoon light flickered across the dresses crumpled on the floor.

"We're not doing this again." Silvia cradled her close. "Remember the trip to Hilton Head with Archie and Marco when you were in one of your worst phases? It was only a few years after they disappeared."

"Of course I remember." She meant the poor woman playing with her son in the surf at the resort where they had stayed.

"Frances, you prowled around that woman and her son for nearly an hour. You followed them into the hotel, bellowed for them to stop. You scared her half to death. I'm sure she thought you were a stalker, not a heartbroken woman convinced some stranger was kidnapping her lost nephew. And what about the weekend in Columbus? Remember jumping into the elevator to get a better look at that woman? You pounced on her. *Pounced.* She thought you were a lunatic. I thought you'd completely lost your mind."

Softening the harshness of the unvarnished facts, her stalwart comrade brushed the thinning hair from Frances's brow.

When she'd finished smoothing every hair into place, Silvia couched her words in tenderness. "They're gone, dearest heart. They aren't coming back."

"Ever?"

"Not ever."

"How do I bury my hope? Every time I do, George reappears to exhume it."

"We'll see about that." Fire licked through the comment. "Now, promise I won't lose you again to this madness."

"You won't."

Throwing off the covers, Silvia rose. "How did you leave it with George?" she asked.

"I told him I wasn't sure I believed his story."

"He wants money for her address?" An awkward silence, and Silvia crossed her arms. "When's he coming back?"

"He didn't say. Later this week, I suppose. He'll give me time to decide."

A curler at her nape came loose, and Silvia yanked it out. "Don't answer the door unless you're sure who is on the other side." From the floor she picked up a rumpled dress, held it out. "Want help dressing, or should I call Penelope? If you're not joining us tonight, I don't want you alone."

❧

The questions festered between them after they finished dressing for dinner and left the inn. On the short drive to her parents' house, Ryan caressed her thigh through the thin material of the dress she'd chosen in defiance of her dismal mood, a boldly patterned silk. Tension wove through Cat as the BMW turned into the driveway. Ryan, more relaxed by yards, threw the car into park and came around the hood.

Opening her door, he caught her wrist before she could sweep past. "Want to check the odds before we go in?" he asked.

Ducking his head into the backseat, he produced the Magic 8 Ball she kept in her office. Gratitude tightened her throat. Despite the harsh questions she'd posed this afternoon, he seemed determined to brighten her mood.

"You snuck into my office while I dressed?"

"You'll feel better if you check the odds." The mischief faded from his mouth. "I *am* sorry about my mother skipping out on us."

"It's not your fault. I'm the one who should apologize for giving you a hard time. No reason to blame the Jack Daniel's. I get too emotional at the worst moments. Don't hold it against me."

"Not a chance." Lightly he kissed her forehead. "Did the coffee help?"

Jada had appeared with a steaming cup while Cat dressed. An unnecessary precaution—anticipating tonight's dinner was sobering enough. "A little." On a deserved twinge of guilt, she asked, "Did you check in on your mother before we left?"

"Right after I went downstairs and grabbed your Magic 8 Ball. She's fine, enjoyed the stroll with Ruth, and is now planning to read until bedtime. She sends her apologies, and hopes you aren't too disappointed by her behavior. Those were her words, by the way."

"I'll bring her breakfast tomorrow. I don't want to leave the impression I'm upset." Her attention strayed to the house. If they stood outside much longer, her parents would spot them.

"Cat, hold on." Ryan stepped back, as though coming to a decision. Then he plunged forward quickly. "What you said this afternoon about everything you want—your dreams aren't far fetched. You deserve every one of them. Why wouldn't you want a mother-in-law who's approachable? I want the same things, including a good relationship with your parents. I've never had much in the way of family, not like you have. I want to make you happy—and our kids, whenever we decide to have them. No child of ours will grow up without the love of an extended family."

"Our kids?" Angling her neck, she regarded him teasingly. "Moving awfully fast, aren't you?"

He met her eyes with breathtaking confidence. "I'm speaking hypothetically." He rocked back on his heels. "Essentially."

She laughed. "Now you're scaring me."

"Definitely not my intention." He dropped the Magic 8 Ball into her hands. "Go on. Check our chances for tonight. We're not going inside until you do."

She gave the ball a vigorous shake. "Will Mami and Papa like Ryan?"

It is certain.

From over her shoulder, Ryan gleaned the answer. "There, you see? Everything is fine." He returned the toy to the car.

The succulent fragrance of roasting chicken provided a savory greeting. The music from her father's favorite easy-listening station lent the house an air of tranquility. He came out of the kitchen with the tufts of his salt-and-pepper hair dancing as he walked.

"Ryan! I've been looking forward to meeting you." Beaming goodwill, Marco clasped Ryan's hand. Winking at Cat, he added, "I hope my daughter didn't promise one of my Mexican specialties. Silvia got it in her head to make chicken and mashed potatoes in case your mother doesn't like spicy foods."

Ryan's poise nearly fled. "Mr. Mendoza, I'm sorry to inform you—"

"Relax, son. Ruth filled us in twenty minutes before Cat did. I'm looking forward to meeting Julia whenever she's available."

The gracious response knocked Ryan back a step. Appreciation eased across his features. "Thank you, sir."

"Sir. What sir? Call me Marco." Drawing them into an affectionate circle, he lowered his voice. "It's just the four of us tonight. Frances planned to join us, but she changed her mind. Your mother came back from her house furious—you know how they get."

Ryan appeared stricken. "They were arguing over my mother?"

"Son, they're still arguing over Frances's dead cat. There's no telling what's got my wife lit like a Roman candle. If she and Frances couldn't find areas of difference, they'd invent them. I have no idea what type of glue keeps their friendship together. I can tell you this. It's flammable."

The subject was quickly dismissed. Silvia came into the foyer in an uncharacteristically subdued beige dress, her ebony locks swept into a chignon. The quintessential hostess, she hid whatever emotions churned inside behind carefully composed features.

Her hand lifted to accept Ryan's in greeting. Unaccountably she paused before their fingers touched.

Her attention leapt to his face. With a nearly impolite thoroughness, she scrutinized every inch, from his forehead to his chin. Throwing off the reaction, she shook his hand.

Cat inhaled a sharp breath. Thankfully the bewildering response went unnoticed by the men. They all shared a few words before Marco led Ryan off to the living room.

She followed her mother back to the kitchen. "What's with the strange look you gave Ryan?" The timer dinged, and she went to the stove. "I'll get it."

She lifted the heavy pan from the oven. Behind her, Silvia fiddled with the chunky gold necklace at her throat.

Cat snatched up potholders, then removed the roaster's lid. "Where's Frances?" Without the Sirens' most gracious member, the night ahead was sure to contain more awkward exchanges. "You aren't fighting with her, are you?"

"Not today."

"What did you do wrong to upset her? She was looking forward to dinner with us."

"Wrong? What wrong? I went over to pull her back together."

At the strain in her mother's voice, Cat paused in her search for tongs to lift the chicken out. "Papa said you were furious when you got back."

"I'm still mad." Disgust thinned her mouth. Smoothing away the reaction, she added, "A headache from Frances's past is back again. Don't ask for details."

"Fine, I won't." Cat found the tongs hidden under a cookbook. Concentrating on the task, she set the chicken on the cutting board. "Will you at least explain the weird look you gave Ryan? He didn't catch it, but I sure felt stupid. You were gaping at him."

"He has beautiful eyes."

"They're unusual—not a fleck of gold, or brown."

"Rare to meet anyone with pure-green eyes."

"I guess." A peculiar sensation rippled down her spine. Turning, she discovered her mother slumped in a chair. "What's wrong?"

"Today I met a girl with eyes the same color."

The conversation's odd turn was perplexing. She'd arrived for dinner expecting an argument about their missing guest, conducted in lowered voices with Ryan safely out of earshot—not her mother acting dazed. "Who is she?"

"A student at Kent State. She drove down to get the lay of the land. Believe it or not, she parked in the middle of the street to practice yoga on the hood of her car."

"You're kidding. Where?"

"In front of Frances's house."

"You're telling me this girl has eyes like Ryan's?"

"And honey-gold hair. Her features are a lot like Ryan's."

"Weird."

"Frances asked her in for tea. Her name is Gemma Mills." Slowly Silvia shook her head as if waking from a long nap. "Talk about a strange day. Two odd visits in a matter of hours—I don't like the feeling I can't prepare for whatever is coming next."

"There's nothing coming, aside from a concert that'll fill the town with tourists." She didn't like where this was headed, didn't like her mother's vacant expression. "What are you trying to tell me?"

The air between them thickened. Cat felt the pressure on her shoulders. Then the burden, an uncomfortable weight, found her heart.

"Do you want to know why Gemma was in Sweet Lake today?" her mother asked.

"I'm not sure."

"She needed to practice."

"For what?"

"A first meeting. On Saturday, when your Cleveland band performs on the beach, she's coming back to find her older brother. Her half brother—he doesn't know he has a sister. They have the same father."

The implication was too outlandish for serious consideration. With jerky movements, Cat transferred the chicken to the waiting platter. The potatoes, already mashed, sat beneath plastic wrap on the counter. Tearing off the plastic, she put the bowl in the microwave.

Her mother's fingers came to rest on her shoulder. Slipping out from beneath the gentle touch, she began carving the chicken in large, unattractive chunks.

"*Mi florecita*, you must listen."

At the softly issued plea, Cat set the platter aside. In turmoil, she leaned heavily against the counter.

"I didn't understand why this girl seemed familiar. Why would I? When you and Ryan traipsed out of the forest last weekend, I saw him only briefly." She took Cat's hands firmly, steadied her with the power of her affection. "And then I understood when he walked in tonight."

"Understood what?"

"Remember what you told me? 'Don't ask about Ryan's family.' There's something broken in his life. You don't wish for your Mami to examine the pieces. You don't want her to see what has shattered, though you're willing to walk across this brokenness as if your feet are bare and your eyes closed. Don't you see the risk of injury to yourself?"

"I don't want to be hurt." She hesitated. "I don't want Ryan hurt either."

"To fully love him, you must accept everything he is, not simply the pieces of his heart he's willing to show you. You must love the whole man."

"He's not broken."

"Stop evading me, child. There's something wrong here. Tell me what it is."

Vacillating, Cat perked her ears. The mingling of masculine voices in the living room were far removed from the harsh secrets bearing down on the kitchen.

"His mother is the one who's broken," she said in a rush. "She cut her family off years ago—Ryan's not even sure when his grandparents died. He has no idea where they lived, doesn't have the smallest details about his extended family. He was a toddler the last time his mother saw anyone in her family."

"Why would Julia D'Angelo cut her son off from his entire family?" Contempt iced the query. "If a mother severs those ties, she uproots her child. She destroys the connections that allow him to flourish in his world."

Silvia's reaction spoke to the unwavering devotion that guided her life. There was nothing more important than family, a lesson that had always blanketed Cat in love. The conviction also spoke to Cat's private reservations: How was she supposed to build a solid foundation with Ryan, given all the questions surrounding his past?

In whispered breaths, she gave a short account of his abusive childhood, and the beatings Julia had suffered at the hands of her husband. Cat nearly added a mention of the tokens Ryan found in the velvet pouch, a discovery she'd shared only with Linnie and Jada.

The idea was dismissed as Silvia listed sideways.

"Mami, are you all right?" She clasped her mother's shoulders. The revelations were clearly too much for her, especially the mention of physical abuse. "Let me help you sit down." She started toward the table.

Her father came into the kitchen. "Ladies, can you catch up on gossip later? The men are hungry." Marco appraised his wife. "Silvia, what is it? You don't look right."

Remarkably she spiced her voice with mock impatience. "Just a little indigestion." Brushing Cat aside, she finished carving the chicken. "I'll take an antacid before we eat."

Satisfied with the explanation, Marco said, "You two have made up?"

Cat pinched his cheek. "Yes, Papa. We have."

"If your mother is mending fences, have her call Frances after dinner. Whatever she's done, make her apologize."

Silvia nudged him toward the door. "Pour the wine. Dinner is in ten."

"Hurry up. No one likes cold mashed potatoes."

The moment he left, Silvia drew her back to the stove. Lowering her voice, she said, "You must take the upper hand in this matter." She smoothed the hair from Cat's brow. "The band you hired, they arrive tomorrow?"

"They're coming in early for two days of practice in the ballroom. They were awfully rowdy last weekend. I'll spend most of tomorrow and Friday keeping an eye on them." A distinct inconvenience, given the other prep work for the concert.

"Have Ryan handle your adolescent musicians. Ruth mentioned she plans to take Julia for another walk tomorrow."

"They've struck up a real friendship."

Her mother grew thoughtful. "Frances and I were wondering why, of all the Sirens, Ruth chose to give kindness in secret. Did you fill her in about Ryan's violent father?"

"Of course not."

"Doesn't matter. Ruth has an instinct about these things. Before she took the dispatcher post with our PD, she worked at a facility in Columbus for battered women. She taught lessons in self-defense, helped with counseling—she became a perfect marksman during her stint at the facility. To this day, she can hit a bull's-eye from quite a distance. I've seen her do it."

"Ruth worked in Columbus?" She'd been a fixture in Sweet Lake since Cat's childhood. Imagining her living anywhere else was nearly impossible. "I assumed she grew up in Sweet Lake."

"She's originally from Columbus. She took the job at the women's shelter when she was barely in her twenties. She signed up for the marksmanship class less than a year after taking the job. One of the abusive husbands tracked his wife to the facility and stormed inside. It took five women to restrain him, including Ruth. She lost a tooth during the scuffle. Bought her first pistol the following week."

The explanation sent a shiver through Cat. It took five women to restrain one man?

From the dining room, her father shouted, "Wine's poured!"

Her mother shouted a reply.

Drawing Cat near, she said, "I pity Julia for everything she's suffered, but this is about Ryan. After she gets back from her walk with Ruth, talk to her. It's unconscionable how she's kept Ryan hidden from his family. If young Gemma Mills from Kent State *is* his sister, they deserve to have a relationship." Eyes blazing, she added, "Don't leave Julia until you get answers."

For the first time since August, the inn was free of the racket from pneumatic nail guns and the whirring of table saws.

At noon on Thursday, Linnie had sent the construction workers away in anticipation of the busy weekend. Everyone on staff was putting in long hours, from the kitchen staff preparing to serve triple the usual number of guests, to the housekeeping staff hurrying from one room to the next, readying the inn for full occupancy. Like Jada and Linnie, Cat split her time between normal management duties and helping the staff wherever needed.

With the inn at high gear, finding an opportunity to speak with Julia alone was gratifyingly easy. In the early afternoon, Ruth escorted her back to the inn after their stroll on the beach. Ryan was in Linnie's office discussing options for upcoming concerts next spring. After he finished, he planned to watch Midnight Boyz practice in the ballroom.

Steeling herself for a difficult conversation, Cat went upstairs balancing a tray of Earl Grey tea and a plate of Jada's delectable brownies. She rapped lightly on the door.

Ryan's mother surveyed the silver tray. "This is a surprise. I wasn't expecting to see you until tonight."

"I thought you might like an afternoon snack."

"I am rather hungry. Ruth took me on a long walk. We covered two miles of the north shore." Frowning, she noticed the second cup. Clearly she wasn't expecting Cat to join her.

Two upholstered chairs were grouped before the bay window. Cat placed the tray on the round table nestled between them. "Mind if we talk?" Boldly she sat down.

Confusion tripped across Julia's face. "You seem upset." She remained rooted by the door, clearly unwilling to join Cat.

"I suppose I am. Not about last night; my parents hope to meet you soon. If not during this visit, maybe the next time you're in Sweet Lake."

"Please thank them for their understanding. Perhaps they'll come with you to visit us in Cincinnati." She hesitated. "What *is* bothering you?"

Cat's bravado nearly fled. "I need some answers about your life," she managed.

"About my past?"

She grappled for a reasonable tone. "I wouldn't ask if it weren't important."

"Hasn't my son told you the basics? I don't like to discuss those years."

The tightly issued remark, meant to close down the conversation, sent Cat's thoughts to Ryan. He'd been deprived of his family. The love she felt, and the strong, irrepressible desire to fight for him, made her press on.

"What you do or don't like to discuss no longer matters," she replied impatiently. "Yesterday a young woman from Kent State came to Sweet Lake for what's essentially a practice run. Gemma Mills is driving back down on Saturday to look for her half brother. They've never met."

"I don't see what this has to do with me."

"They have the same father. I don't have all the specifics. My mother met Gemma." Cat paused for a perilous beat. "She's convinced Ryan is Gemma's brother."

The pronouncement chilled the air between them. Then a derisive laugh escaped Julia. "Your mother is making quite a leap, isn't she?"

"Those unusual green eyes helped her make that leap."

The disclosure battered Julia's thinly held composure. "She has eyes like Ryan's?"

"An exact match."

The revelation punctured her resistance. "George's eyes," she murmured. "I'm sure my son has mentioned how much he takes after his father. Practically twins."

"After your divorce, did your ex-husband take up with another woman?"

"I have no idea."

"Gemma was raised here in Ohio. She's nineteen—eleven years younger than Ryan."

"Then she was born the year after I left George in Salt Lake. It's certainly possible he had a relationship with another woman." Troubled, Julia studied the floor. "Have you mentioned this to Ryan?"

"It seemed wise to speak with you first." There was something tragic about the sense of capitulation bowing Julia's spine. "You keep a lot hidden, maybe out of a need to protect him. Maybe you have other reasons for hiding so much. Whatever the reasons, I do need answers."

"About what, exactly?" She came across the room and sat.

She appeared incapable of withstanding a journey into the past. Yet remarkedly she found a reserve of composure. With stiff movements, she took a cup of tea.

With growing anxiety, Cat took her own mug. Since there was no simple way to begin, a direct course seemed best. "When you arrived Sunday night, you seemed familiar with the inn. You walked straight to the south wing's stairwell like you'd memorized the route. Guests never come up here. The stairwell is practically hidden."

"I *am* familiar with the Wayfair. I came quite often before Ryan was born. Twice when he was a baby. He doesn't remember."

The admission snatched the breath from Cat's lips. She'd expected a flurry of denials, with every one of her claims challenged. What she hadn't anticipated was this ready confession. She was still scrambling for a response when Julia spoke again.

"My son sees me as a victim. I imagine you have the same impression." Self-disgust strengthened her voice. "The truth is more complicated."

"You didn't deserve what happened to you. The day when George injured you and Ryan near the forest, or Twin Falls—"

With a dismissive hand, Julia cut short the defense. "Ryan deserved love and safety, not a home wrecked by violence. No child should live in the sort of world we made for him."

With weary acceptance, Julia stared into her tea. "Ryan is the victim—not me. I got exactly what I bargained for in a husband."

Chapter 20

A shudder went through Julia at the confession's brutal honesty.

"I was so different from my family," she said, drawing deeper into her story. "Their priorities were always in the right place. They were loyal to each other, proud of our roots in the Buckeye State. None of them could imagine living anywhere but here—not my parents or my sisters."

Cat hung on to every word. "You were raised in Ohio?" she asked, greedy for information sure to benefit Ryan. He didn't know where his extended family lived, or where his grandparents were buried. She'd keep Julia's darkest secrets, but not this. "Your sisters still live here?"

"All four of them, yes."

"How were you different?"

"I craved adventure. I can't even tell you why. I had loving parents, and all the advantages of wealth. It was never enough."

"You wanted more?" Of what, she couldn't imagine.

"I wasted hours dreaming about a new life away from the family that gave me so much. I wanted adventure, no matter the cost. Or perhaps I hoped the cost would be high—high enough to puncture the cocoon of privilege I'd always known." Julia pressed her hand to the scar beneath her eye. Blood fled the site. "Why are some people fascinated by danger?"

"I'm not sure. I'm not one of them."

"You're fortunate. When I left Ohio, my family was distraught. I loved California—the liberal thinking and the lively art scene. So I moved to San Francisco, nearly put an ocean between my future and the happy past." Julia returned the teacup to the platter so her shaking hands wouldn't spill the entire steaming cup. "That was one of my favorite sayings growing up: even an ocean between us won't make me completely free. It made my older sister furious when I talked that way."

"She didn't want you to leave?"

"Heavens, no. Not that she could refute my success, how I made a new life on the rim of the Pacific. All of my sisters married, settled down—but I was content to design jewelry and work my way up the career ladder at Lux Jewels."

A shadow crossed her eyes, bringing with it untold memories. In her lap, her fingers curled into the folds of her loose sundress. "I'd lived in San Francisco for many years before George came along. He was uneducated, utterly gorgeous, more than ten years younger. I let passion blind me." She grimaced. "Willingly."

Cat struggled to understand. "You knew about his temper before you married?" Surely he didn't reveal the worst parts of his nature until after they wed.

"I wasn't stupid. There were enough warning signs to ward off a sensible woman. If I was stupid about anything, it was my reproductive chances. Much as I wanted a child, I didn't expect to get pregnant at forty-one. I knew what kind of life I'd bring our child into."

"Why did you ignore the warning signs about Ryan's father?"

Bitterness swirled around Julia. "The sex was enough to sway me. More than enough—it was everything. I'd never met a man so capable of giving me pleasure. I'm telling you this in confidence," she added. "I'm relying on you not to share the worst aspects of my past with my son."

"I won't tell him."

"Thank you. It's best to leave Ryan with his illusions. I've destroyed enough relationships for one lifetime."

"You mean with your family?" Cat whispered, astonished by her curiosity. The revelations were shocking. Beatings accepted in trade for passion, and a marriage descending into violence. The urge to shut down the conversation nearly brought her to her feet.

The impulse didn't escape Julia. "Do you believe in coincidence?" She posed the question lightly, as if they were playing a game.

"I don't." The firm reply brought to mind the circle of women who met on the beach in dawn's purplish light, and other meetings Cat had glimpsed through the years when the moon rode high in the star-flecked sky. "My mother is part of a women's group. They believe every moment of our lives carries purpose. Not like predestination; we make our own choices. Each decision opens up new opportunities that wouldn't exist if we'd made a different choice."

"You're referring to the Sirens. Ruth mentioned them on our walks. I do agree. Our lives are twined with surprising opportunities." Regret punctuated the comment as she added, "When my son explained he'd fallen in love, he didn't mention immediately where you live. When he did, I was frightened. Confronted with the worst sort of synchronicity, and the best. I'm still not sure if all of this is a blessing or a curse. I've done nothing to warrant the chance to heal the relationships I've destroyed. Certainly not the most important one."

Cat's mind sprinted ahead. "When did you break off contact with your family?"

"I don't recall the exact date."

"In September?"

Julia stared at her blankly. She swallowed a gulp of air. "Why, yes. It was September. I called her from Salt Lake—"

The words choked off, leaving behind a painful silence.

Cat used the moment to weave the threads into meaning. She latched on to Julia's words, the ones spoken in jest to her older sister.

Even an ocean between us won't make me completely free.

The taunt brought to mind the feathers used by the Sirens for the most significant tokens. The talismans were meant to impart courage, or guide a woman forced onto a treacherous path. They were meant to provide spiritual protection during the most pivotal moments of a woman's life.

The feathers used for those most significant tokens were always blue, like the ocean.

Breathless, Cat produced the token retrieved from the velvet pouch. "Does your older sister live in Sweet Lake?"

The question met with a small cry of anguish. "Where did you get this? Did Ryan find the token? It's not possible. He doesn't have any idea—"

"He remembered the velvet pouch," Cat broke in.

Julia rose, as if to distance herself from the facts.

Cat withdrew the second token, the one she'd made for him. "I gave this to Ryan a few weeks ago. My mother taught me how to make tokens." She paused long enough for Julia to draw in a ragged breath. "Did your older sister teach you?"

"We've dredged up enough bad memories for one day." Julia went to the window. She shut her eyes against the stark, revealing sunlight. "I thought I had the courage to fix things. I don't. We've been dead to her for years. She's old now, too old for the shock my reappearance will bring."

"You're wrong. I'm sure she'll be overjoyed to have you back in her life."

"No, Cat. I took Ryan and disappeared. I dread imagining how my parents reacted to the news once they realized we were gone. How does anyone mourn a child and a grandchild at the same time? I'm sure they were devastated. My older sister watched over them, the dutiful daughter. She buried them with the knowledge I'd stolen all the joy from their waning years. She has every reason to despise me."

Hot tears blurred Cat's vision. Of all the errors made in her life, the foolish choices and rash decisions, none were so black as to destroy the family that grounded her. She pitied Julia for all she'd willingly thrown away.

Cat struggled to her feet. Julia's back quaked, but she seemed determined not to give voice to her ravaged emotions. Her mute weeping was an awful sight. She curled into herself like an injured sparrow.

The desire to offer comfort grew strong. But instinct warned that Julia would view the gesture as an imposition.

Leaving her where she stood, Cat scooped up the tokens and stepped back.

Julia's hollow gaze latched on to her. "What will you tell my son?"

Nothing.

Everything.

Caught in the maelstrom of secrets, Cat brushed her wet eyes. "I'm not sure."

~♾️~

"Gemma, go back to sleep." On the top bunk in their dorm room, Patty struggled onto an elbow to stare drowsily at her smartphone. "It's not even six. We don't have class for another three hours."

"Sorry—I didn't mean to wake you." The statement wasn't entirely true, but Gemma dimmed the backlight on her laptop anyway as she sat at her desk. With the trip to Sweet Lake one day away, she'd chased dreams in unsatisfying snatches before giving up. She wished Patty would give up too. "Midnight Boyz put a new post on their blog. Want to see?"

"I can't read with my eyes closed."

"They checked into the Wayfair." Scrolling down the post, she paused at her favorite photograph. "There's a new pic of Ryan with Cat and the Midnight Boyz in the Wayfair's ballroom."

"I still don't care." From her perch, Patty flung down a pillow.

Giggling, Gemma leapt out of range. "Liar. Your online stalking puts mine to shame." Yesterday her roommate had found Ryan and Cat on Facebook, and Cat's Instagram. "You're totally invested in my family reunion. You said my big brother is hot."

"Damn straight."

"Stick to dreaming, pal. He's taken. Plus he looks great with Cat. She's a beauty queen."

"Miss Ohio. I'd give her a big, fat crown, and a cool scepter with rubies and pearls."

"Is Mendoza a Mexican name?"

"I'll answer useless trivia if you stick to questions about Seoul or Beijing."

Gemma held up the laptop like bait. "Come on, my little wonton noodle. You know you want to look."

Her curiosity getting the better of her, Patty grudgingly climbed down. Wresting the laptop away, she skimmed the blog post, pausing at the photo of Ryan and Cat. "Have you figured out your game plan? We can check into Mrs. Riddle's house tomorrow afternoon, then go right over to the inn. I still vote for finding Ryan before the concert. Wait until nightfall, and we'll have trouble spotting him in the crowd. You agree?"

Gemma trudged to her unmade bed. "Still not sure." She flopped face down.

When to approach Ryan, or how, remained the biggest dilemma.

Chapter 21

On the street of solidly middle-class homes, the Riddle house stood out like the party girl in a group of wallflowers.

Easing off the gas pedal, Cat surveyed the dwelling with its lavender paint and spring-green shutters. A variety of dragonfly and butterfly wind chimes hung across the cozy front porch, sending bright music down the sleeping street. Dawn hadn't yet arrived, and garden gnomes in a variety of sizes smiled from the shadows. They sat beside black-eyed Susans still in bloom and late-blooming roses offering up their last buds.

From the backseat, Linnie gave a bleary appraisal. "Why are we at Penelope's house?"

Jada, who'd received a tad more information after Cat shook her awake, pushed open the passenger door. "Stop bitching. Like we told you, Cat has to check something out."

"With Penelope?"

"It's about the conversation with Ryan's mother. Cat isn't comfortable telling Ryan anything until she gets some facts."

"I'd like to remind you both that the Wayfair will officially reach full occupancy as of noon today. We should be getting ready for work, not embarking on a scavenger hunt. Besides, I thought you said we're driving out to the cemetery to check on something."

Cat opened Linnie's door. "The cemetery is up next. Now, get the lead out. I have to see Penelope."

"She's expecting us?"

"This early? No."

"Great move. You should've called ahead."

"The next time I show up before daybreak, I will." Since the disturbing conversation yesterday with Julia, Cat had been too upset to arrange her thoughts in an orderly fashion. With every layer of secrets Julia had peeled back, new and distressing questions had come to light. Needing answers, Cat pulled Linnie from the car. "I'm sure she's awake—Ozzie heads to the post office early." Penelope never let her mail-carrier son leave in the morning without making him a breakfast fit for a king.

Sure enough, the scent of searing ham greeted them as Penelope opened the door. Her robe, like her home, was Siren inspired: tiny silver stars winked on the purple fabric. She pulled the robe tightly across her stout frame and gave them a quizzical look.

Adjusting her glasses, she released a gasp. "Oh no. Has something happened?"

Linnie shoved past. "No one's dead, but I *am* premeditating the murder of my friends." She followed her nose to the kitchen, undoubtedly to snag a cup of coffee and a bite of Ozzie's meal.

Cat gave the befuddled Siren a quick hug. "Everything's fine. We aren't here with bad news."

"Thank goodness!"

Jada said, "We're sorry about bothering you at the crack of dawn."

"Oh, it's fine. I have to get ready soon. I'm on patrol this morning at Frances's house. Tilda and Yume are helping me."

Patrol? A Siren thing, clearly, but there wasn't time to sit through an explanation. "Penelope, I have a favor to ask," Cat said. "May I see your Airbnb correspondence with the girl from Kent State? I need to verify a hunch about Gemma Mills."

A more suspicious soul would inquire why Cat was curious about a girl she'd never met. The trusting Penelope merely gave a brisk nod. She trotted out of the foyer.

Jada leaned in, her voice lowering. "What's she doing?"

Cat, whose familiarity with the Sirens went leagues past Jada's or Linnie's, gladly explained. "She's getting her computer."

"You show up unannounced, and she lets you into her Airbnb account without an explanation?"

"Yep."

"What if you'd asked for a peek at her bank accounts?"

"Same thing."

"You really are an honorary Siren."

"This is one of the perks."

Laptop in hand, Penelope led them into the kitchen. Ozzie was already gone; Linnie dragged a slice of toast through the egg he'd left behind.

Between mouthfuls, she asked, "Is there coffee?"

Penelope ushered Cat into a chair. From over her shoulder, she typed in the Airbnb password.

KindWorld4ever. Cat chuckled. Count on the softhearted Siren to create an idealistic password.

Penelope dropped a ham steak on a plate, slid it before Linnie "How do you take your coffee?"

"Lots of cream and sugar. Thanks."

As Linnie drank happily from the jumbo mug, Cat found the correspondence on Airbnb. The photo of Gemma was grainy, taken in dim lighting.

She looked up at Penelope. "You didn't happen to 'friend' Gemma on Facebook, did you?" she asked. Like many of the Sirens, Penelope was happily addicted to Facebook.

Penelope gave an energetic nod. "Of course I did. She posts the cutest photos of her family. They live in Shaker Heights. We had such a nice chat when Gemma booked the room last weekend. She'll arrive tomorrow with her roommate sometime in the morning . . ."

The lively explanation barely reached Cat. Navigating quickly, she found Gemma's Facebook page. As she peered at the large professionally shot profile picture, her heart thumped wildly. Gemma's high school graduation portrait, she guessed.

Jada, standing behind her in a state of fevered curiosity, whooshed out a breath. "Wow."

Shoving a wedge of ham into her mouth, Linnie garbled, "What? What did you find?"

"Cat's right," Jada told her. "Our mysterious Gemma Mills must be Ryan's sister. A lot younger, but she looks just like him. She's blonde, but her features are the same."

"Wait. Ryan has a sister? Since when?"

Shutting the laptop, Cat dropped a kiss on Penelope's cheek. "Thanks for your help." She started off, hesitated. "Don't tell my mother I stopped by. In fact, don't tell any of the Sirens. I need to get to the bottom of this first."

"You have my word."

Linnie took a last slurp of her coffee. "I'm totally lost." She scrambled to her feet. "Isn't Ryan an only child?"

Cat pushed her toward the door. "We'll explain in the car."

On the twenty-minute drive to Walnut Grove Memorial Gardens, Cat shared the cryptic details she'd gleaned from Julia. Wrapping up, she pulled into the wide, paved circle marking the entryway to the cemetery. Parking near the grass, she cut the engine.

Jada asked, "What's the plan?"

A maple tree spread its generous arms over the wrought iron fence. *Perfect.* Cat got out of the car with the intention of climbing over. It was still dark, but if she took care, she'd make it over the fence without a problem.

Fighting off a yawn, Linnie caught her intent. "You've got to be kidding me." She hung her head out the window. "Tell me we're not climbing over."

"You won't fall." Jada unhooked her seatbelt. "We'll go first."

"I'm going first." Grabbing on to a low branch, Cat swung herself up. She'd reached the second branch when she noticed Linnie still in the car. "Oh, come on. We'll help you over."

"Didn't Silvia and Frances pull this stunt with a ladder? Where's our ladder?"

"I didn't bring one, all right? I was occupied with waking Jada and sneaking out of the south wing without disturbing Ryan or his mother."

"This is stupid. Let's wait until visiting hours. We'll drive through the gate like normal human beings."

Reaching the third branch, Cat sent a look of exasperation. "We're checking this out before Ryan notices I've left the inn. I can't tell him what I discussed with his mother until I'm sure of what I'm dealing with. I have exactly *no* idea how to tell him about his kid sister."

Linnie nodded sympathetically. "Sheesh, the news will blow him away."

"So, will you get the lead out? We have to get back before the Wayfair turns into a madhouse. As of today we're at full occupancy, remember?"

Taking care not to lose her footing, Cat fixed her attention on the sharp finials decorating the fence. Gingerly she stepped over, finding purchase on a sturdy limb on the opposite side. Frowning, she assessed her options. A halo of light spread from the horizon to finger the tops of Walnut Grove's undulating hills. Ten feet below, a sea of shadow rippled on the ground. Jump from this height, and she might sprain an ankle.

She was still working it out when Jada gave a soft growl. She hoisted herself into the tree.

Nearing the trunk, Linnie flapped her arms. "All right, Cat. I'll risk serious injury if you'll explain why we're checking the mementos Frances left for her dead cat. So she fills a tin with trinkets to memorialize the critter. Who cares? She's old. She's entitled to her eccentricities. If you want to know what she puts inside, let's drive over and ask."

"We will talk to her—later. But only if my suspicions are correct."

"*What* suspicions?"

Clamping her thighs around a limb, Jada lowered a hand. "Linnie, if you don't zip it, I'm coming back down with the biggest branch I can tear free and beating you senseless. Now, come on!"

Linnie was on her way up when Cat spotted a thick, low-hanging limb in the muddy light. Ducking beneath a curtain of leaves, she grabbed hold and leapt down to the grass. Following her cue, Jada descended with ease. Linnie was last, scooting into their waiting arms.

Cat sprinted off to the central hill. In the rising daylight, the large tombstone, with cherubs carved into the pink-veined marble, carried an eerie, phosphorescent glow.

A mason jar of roses sat before the headstone. Kneeling on the sod, Cat searched for the tin.

Jada reached her. "Found it?" she asked.

"Not yet."

Scanning the inscription carved into the stone, Jada cleared her throat. "Good morning, Mr. Dufour. I hope you don't mind if we ransack your grave. It's for a good cause."

Cat arched a brow at her friend. "I'm sure he understands." She hesitated, glanced at the marble, and made the sign of the cross. "We appreciate this, Mr. Dufour."

Having concluded the social niceties, she resumed searching for the tin.

"Frances makes a small memorial out of stones for her cat," Linnie told her. "Find the stones. The tin will be nearby."

"What do you think I'm doing?"

Jada dropped onto all fours to pat her hands across the grass. The sun, rising behind the headstone, sent blinding shafts of light into their faces.

Cat squinted through the glare. "Damn it, Linnie. Are you going to help, or not?"

"I'm helping!" Obediently she began crawling across the grave. "What does the tin look like?"

Crawling forward, Cat winced as her knee landed on a sharp stone. "It's a small rectangular tin for keeping embroidery thread. Frances uses a different one each year." Retrieving the stone, she inspected the smooth, heart-shaped surface. "We have a problem. The groundskeepers have mown over the stones Frances puts out for kitty's grave."

Jada shoved the nest of tight curls from her eyes. "Now what?"

Often in the past, Cat accompanied Frances to the grave. Usually she came with her mother and whichever of the Sirens was available that day. Frances knew the mowing schedule kept by the groundskeepers. She followed their schedule like clockwork, bringing the largest bouquets for her late husband's grave on days after they'd finished their work.

"Frances brought the tin out here in September," she said aloud. "The cemetery has been mown at least twice since then. She would've made sure the groundskeepers didn't run over the tin."

Linnie dropped onto her butt. "Okay, Sherlock. Where'd she hide it?"

Giddy excitement sent Cat to where the thick green sod met the base of the headstone. Driving her fingers between the damp soil and the cool marble, she moved down the crevice, breaking a nail and clotting her fingertips with dirt. At the corner of the headstone, her knuckles bumped against a hard, metal lip hidden beneath the sod.

"Found it!" Carefully she withdrew the tin from its hiding place.

On the opposite side of the headstone, golden light caught the dew on the grass like a scattering of diamonds. Squinting against the brightness, she wedged the lid off. Jada and Linnie hemmed her in as she set the lid aside.

The first items to catch her notice were the beautiful feathers, shells, and stones expertly laced together with simple twine. Frances's work, clearly, with every item painted in vibrant shades of blue.

Reciting Julia's words, she murmured, "Even an ocean between us won't make me completely free." Looking up at her puzzled friends, she added, "It was something Julia used to say to her older sister as a joke."

Linnie took the keepsake, ran her fingers across the feathers. "She wanted an ocean between them? That's not funny. It's more in the category of hurtful remarks."

"She *did* move to the West Coast, and nearly put an ocean between herself and Ohio." Cat recalled Julia's heartbreaking words. "Between her future and a happy past."

"This is all fascinating conjecture. It doesn't prove Ryan's mother is related to Frances. Maybe Frances's cat liked the color blue."

"Aren't cats color-blind?"

"I'm not sure." Linnie rubbed her chin. "What exactly do we have here? The love tokens Frances brings every September aren't for her cat—which is what everyone in town assumes—but to memorialize the sister she lost?"

"Bingo."

"Did Julia come out and say she has a sister in Sweet Lake?"

"She didn't deny it."

Jada, sold on theory, said, "Linnie, you're being obtuse."

"Yeah? The next time you goofballs send a crack-of-dawn text, bring caffeine for the road trip. I should've asked Penelope for a thermos."

Jada glared at her. "Forget the java and listen. Julia must've broken off communication with Frances in September, then took Ryan and disappeared. If you or Cat disappeared, I'd be devastated not knowing where you'd gone, or if you were safe." A tear wended down her cheek. "If I were in Frances's shoes, I'd let everyone think I was mourning over a silly cat. It's a better alternative than having to discuss the most painful event of her life."

Linnie shrunk into herself. "Okay, okay. Geez, you're touchy. I'll keep an open mind."

"You'd better. If Cat's right about this, we're on the brink of reuniting sisters who haven't seen each other in decades."

"And introducing Ryan to the aunt he doesn't remember, and the sister he's never met," Cat put in. "Let's not forget about Gemma."

"I get it! Ryan meets Frances and his kid sister, the music swells, and Julie Andrews rolls into Sweet Lake belting out the song about the hills—" At the thunder in Jada's eyes, Linnie ditched the jokes. She nudged the tin in Cat's lap. "What else is inside the little box of wonders?"

Cat withdrew a second token, similar to one from the velvet pouch. Sensing victory, she held it aloft. "Made by Frances and Julia when they were children?"

Linnie nodded. "Guess your mother didn't come up with the original design with her faithful co-leader when they founded the Sirens. Frances has been making tokens since she was a kid." She peered into tin. "Look under the lace handkerchief. There's something else."

Trembling with anticipation, Cat rolled the handkerchief back.

An old photograph lay beneath. The thick white border brought to mind a sweet memory of the old-school camera her grandfather had toted around when she was young. In the photo, five young girls wore matching shorts with frilly ankle socks folded neatly above their saddle shoes. They stood with their shoulders pressed together, at a carnival or an amusement park. The two youngest girls, toddlers, really, were caught on film dunking their noses into large cones of cotton candy. The middle girl, still plump with baby fat, stared gleefully at the camera.

The two oldest girls, lean legged amidst childhood's first growth spurt, regarded each other with mischievous grins.

Jada pointed to them. "Frances and Julia?"

Intuition told Cat the assessment was correct. "Must be, right?"

"Hard to tell. They're so young. Third and fourth grade?"

"Or second and third." She ran her finger around the blurred faces. Best guess, the photo was more than sixty years old. "I'm sure it's them."

"Incredible that Frances has four younger sisters."

"Mami's gone with her to visit two of them. They both live outside Cincinnati, on the north side of the city. She also has a sister outside Cleveland or Akron."

"Sad to think Julia lived near them all this time, but never got in touch."

"She had good reason for staying hidden."

Jada brushed away the tear lingering on her cheek. "She never really escaped her ex-husband's abuse. After he found her and Ryan in Idaho, I can't blame her for the choices she made."

Cat's heart shifted. "Yeah, but she moved back to Ohio anyway. Julia left her family on bad terms, but she must have wanted to reach out to her sisters at some point—especially Frances." She thought of something else. "Ryan's half sister is from Ohio, which implies George came here looking for Julia. Why else would he have come? I wonder how long he was with Gemma's mother."

"For Gemma's sake, I hope it wasn't long."

Linnie, impatient beneath their theories, took possession of the tin. She withdrew a small bundle of dried herbs. The lavender sprigs included in the bunch sent out a pungent scent. "Hold on, ladies." Reverently, she placed Frances's handkerchief on the grass. "There's more." She handed the tin to Cat.

Inside lay a second photograph.

With wonder, Cat withdrew it from the tin.

Chapter 22

If the photograph of the five girls refused to supply definitive proof of the connection between Frances and Julia, the image now in Cat's possession put even Linnie's doubts to rest.

There was no mistaking the identity of the small boy with the raven hair and the strong jawline seated on his mother's lap. The image provided a more startling shock as Cat studied the man standing behind them in a chambray shirt and chinos, his defiant, arrogant gaze steadied on the camera. The family shot was taken in a studio against a multicolored background that resembled confetti.

Jada made a small noise of unease. "Julia looks miserable. Cat, when do you think this was taken?"

"Not too long before she left George the first time. Ryan's about four years old, I'd guess."

"Check out his father. Ryan looks just like him."

Her stomach knotting, Cat studied the image closely. It was unnerving, how much Ryan took after his father. How such an uncanny resemblance molded two men who were nothing alike.

Appearing to sense her distress, Linnie plucked the image from her fingers and dropped it back into the tin. "Now what? Cat, you have to talk to Ryan."

"Not until I speak to Julia."

"Hold on. Didn't she say she doesn't have the courage to patch things up with her sister? Granted, you've figured out whom she was talking about. Doesn't mean she'll change her mind because you've become a super sleuth."

"I can't divulge her secrets without running it by her first. She had good reasons for dropping out of sight. We know George *did* come to Ohio looking for her—Gemma is also his child, right? He was probably stalking everyone in Julia's family for years, hoping she'd turn up. In between, he was messing around with other women—including Gemma's mother. I can't ignore the genuine fear that's kept Julia hiding all this time."

"What about Ryan and Frances? They deserve to find out about each other."

Cat pressed the lid firmly on the tin. "Julia carries a lot of guilt about Frances. Her older sister, the one who cared for their parents after she disappeared. How do you comfort your parents after that sort of loss?" She appraised the morning light spreading across the hills, her emotions in flux. "This isn't just a matter of bringing a family back together. According to Ryan, Julia can get very depressed. She's off the meds now, but she's gone through periods when she needs them. It's been tough on them both."

"I have a cousin with serious depression," Jada confided. "He doesn't take big changes well. Good or bad, they're hard on him. Cat, make sure you handle all of this with Julia carefully."

"I will."

Linnie asked, "What about Gemma? Will you at least tell Ryan about his sister?"

"Gemma has gone to the trouble of finding him. She'll talk to him at the concert whether I give him a heads-up or not. It might be easier on Ryan to get his family secrets in small doses." All the revelations heading his way were sure to floor him. "I'll look for Gemma before the concert, talk to her. If she's nervous about approaching him, I'll offer encouragement."

Linnie brushed the grass from her slacks. "I totally get the issue with Julia's depression. All the same, I hope you convince her to get in touch with Frances. For Ryan's sake."

Jada took the tin and returned it to its hiding place at the base of the headstone. "If she's not on board, it'll be awkward telling Ryan he has an aunt living right here in Sweet Lake—especially if bringing all of this puts his mother back on antidepressants."

Doubt flooded Cat's heart. "What if I can't get Julia on board?"

The question dogged her throughout the morning. For once, she welcomed the harried pace of her workday. People checking in clogged the lobby, and the staff dealt with a series of small disasters. In three rooms, guests called down complaining about missing bath towels. Small arguments broke out in the kitchen as the staff worked without a break, preparing breakfast orders until past ten o'clock, then serving the first lunch patrons, who appeared in the Sunshine Room promptly at eleven o'clock.

Cat didn't share more than a passing word with Ryan. It was an odd relief. Penny Higbee from Adworks had decided to come in a day early. They were roaming the grounds together, photographing the inn and the lake.

Throughout the day, Cat found her tangled thoughts repeatedly drawn back to Julia. The desire to stride up to the south wing, and lay out all the discoveries she'd made, was strong. Caution stopped her. With the Wayfair a bees' nest of activity, waiting until after the busy weekend to confront Julia seemed the kindest choice.

He'd given Frances long enough to decide.

Certain of the payoff awaiting him, George turned onto Highland Avenue, humming a tune. He cruised past a postal truck slowing before a brick mansion. The driver's plump arm popped out of the truck's window to pull open the mailbox. Across the street, an old gent in a plaid robe was stooping on his front lawn, retrieving the newspaper. He shuffled back inside, leaving the street once again empty.

George pulled into Frances's driveway. This early on a Friday, odds were good that she was making her first cup of coffee.

He'd barely lowered his feet to the pavement when the strangest woman came around the side of the house. A tentlike yellow robe covered in black sparkles flowed to her ankles. That, combined with the crown on her head of whatnots bobbing on lengths of wire, made her look like a ginormous bumblebee. From the small bag she carried, she sprinkled something pungent on the asphalt. Cloves?

On closer inspection, he cursed his bad luck. It was the do-gooder who'd given him the free slice of pie last weekend.

Halfway down the driveway, she noticed him gaping at her. She shrieked.

The ear-numbing sound brought a slender Japanese woman out from behind the house. She was followed by a pretty gal with cinnamon-colored hair, who scrambled for something in her purse.

George dropped his keys.

He was searching the pavement as the Japanese woman began pelting him with small, foul-smelling wax balls. A chunk of something putrid got past his lips. Gagging, he spit it out. Then he dropped onto his hands and knees to reach frantically beneath the Mustang for his keys.

They were scraping across the pavement when Miss Bumblebee stopped shrieking so quickly that George paused a heartbeat, certain his skull was still vibrating. He was shielding his face from another barrage of wax balls when she whirled toward the postal truck.

"Ozzie—save us!"

Four houses up, the truck screeched to a standstill. The door swung wide, shooting envelopes across the curb. With a growl, a pudgy youth leapt out.

"Mama, I'm coming!"

For a kid so out of shape, he was damn fast. Two houses away he vaulted over a hedge, the mail bursting from his hands to shower across the grass. George lunged for his car. He'd brought the engine to life when the pretty chick with the cinnamon-colored hair withdrew a pink tube from her purse that sure as hell wasn't lipstick. She came at him like an angry wasp, spraying Mace in an arc.

Eyes burning, he backed out in a hurry. Swerving around the enraged postal carrier, George shot down the street.

"I've got great news and interesting news. Which would you like first?"

Closing the door, Ryan managed to reduce the noise level only slightly. In the corridor outside Cat's office, a mostly good-natured crowd waited for tables to open up in the busy Sunshine Room. At this rate, lunch service would merge directly into the dinner rush.

Cat looked up from the computer. "Great news first. I need the boost. I've done everything from checking people in at the front desk to waiting tables in the Sunshine Room. I should join Linnie in the basement and help scare up more towels."

"Guests are still calling down?" He'd heard about the complaints.

"A new hire in housekeeping missed some of the rooms. Bringing her in at the start of an incredibly busy week wasn't our smartest decision."

"With the inn at full occupancy, you didn't have much choice."

"We should've hired her in September. Learning the ropes during this much chaos isn't easy." Cat rested her head on the back of her chair. "Hit me with the great news. I'm feeling more than a little frazzled."

The explanation dovetailed with his observations. For reasons he couldn't identify, Cat was preoccupied about some matter. Whatever the problem, she preferred not to discuss it.

This morning she'd left the south wing early without explanation. The long workday showed in the faint patches of exhaustion beneath her eyes. He made a silent pledge that once the busy weekend finished, he'd suggest they sneak away for a short vacation. They'd use the time to solidify their relationship, and catch up on much-needed sleep.

Returning to the issue at hand, he said, "Cleveland's *Plain Dealer* is sending a reporter next week. They're putting together a feature on the best Ohio getaways for autumn."

"They're including the Wayfair?"

"Sadly you won't get center billing. You're sharing the limelight with seven other small hotels and B and Bs, some of them very high end."

"I'm glad we made the grade at all." She eyed him knowingly. "Should I thank you?"

"I called in a favor. Part of the job."

"Then thank you." Slowly she swiveled the chair from side to side. "What's the interesting news?"

"Midnight Boyz has invited the public to watch their final practice session tonight in the ballroom." She began to object, and he hurriedly added, "I've already run it by Linnie. She's fine with it. A good thing, since our favorite drummer posted on the group's blog and Twitter."

"Nathan sent out an invite without checking with you first?"

Ryan chuckled. "Three hours before we talked." For a twenty-year-old, Nathan had chops.

His amusement proved contagious, and Cat smiled. "I can't decide what Nathan likes better, chatting with his fans on social media, or clearing the kitchen of porterhouse steaks. You know he's had a steak with every meal since he's arrived?"

"He's too young to give heart disease a second thought."

"Apparently." She brought the chair to a stop. "When's the practice session?"

"Seven o'clock tonight."

The news put alarm on her face. "It's already past four. How many people are we expecting?"

"At least a hundred. Linnie sent someone on staff out to buy hot-dogs and buns."

"They should add Cobb salads to the impromptu menu, use up some of the extra romaine."

"Linnie added Cobb salad. Mr. Uchida is printing up the menu now."

"We should pull tables out of storage, get them into the ballroom."

"Already done. She also called two of the bartenders in early for their shifts."

"Whoever she sent shopping should also pick up paper plates. If people are wandering in and out of the ballroom—"

"It's on the list," he cut in, approaching. Tracing a soothing path across her jawline, he assessed the fatigue beneath her eyes. "What's going on, Cat? Trouble sleeping last night?"

"Like I said—I'm frazzled."

The subtle evasion nudged the small seed of worry lodging inside him, lending it the impetus to grow. The promotions they'd devised together were bearing fruit, this week especially. But the past days had brought an equal number of personal disappointments in the form of canceled dinners and hard feelings, all thanks to his mother's refusal to break out of her shell.

For the briefest instant, he considered the odds of losing Cat if the situation didn't improve.

Pushing aside the troubling thought, he pulled her up into his arms.

She rested her head on his shoulder. "Where's Penny?" she asked.

"Still photographing the beach. She's looking for a pristine shot to use on the website's landing page. At this rate, you'll have enough photos for a year's worth of Instagram posts."

Mention of the beach lifted Cat's head. "Did Julia go for another walk with Ruth? I haven't seen either of them today."

With a pang of guilt, he realized he'd only given his mother a passing thought all day. "I'm not sure if she went out or not." They'd only shared a few words before he left the south wing to start his workday. "I haven't seen Ruth."

"How *is* Julia today?"

"She seemed fine when I left the south wing earlier. Why?"

Cat drifted out of his arms. "You haven't talked to her since then?" When he lifted his brows in a light admission of guilt, she added, "Check on her."

He pulled out his phone and called. After the fifth ring, he said, "She's not answering. If she's walking the beach, she may have left her phone in the suite."

"Ryan, go upstairs and see if she's all right. If Ruth didn't stop by, she's been alone for hours."

"Sure," he said slowly, still trying to get a fix on the problem. His unease increased. Cat seemed incapable of regarding him directly. "Come with me?"

"I should stay here. Lots to do." She began straightening papers on her desk.

The refusal took him off guard. "It'll only take five minutes."

At last she regarded him, the doubt in her eyes impossible to miss. "All right."

The door to his mother's suite was ajar, the bed made. He spotted the note on the dresser.

He read quickly. "She's gone back to Cincinnati."

Cat threaded her fingers together, turned away.

"I'll call the house in an hour," he added. A sense of helplessness washed over him. So much rode on his mother's reaction to Sweet Lake.

She'd failed every test. Predictably she'd fallen back on the habit of running. Only this time, she was running from a future he wanted desperately to build. Even though he had every reason to stay in Sweet Lake, the bad habits she'd cultivated for years took precedence.

"Cat, I'll fix this. We'll encourage her to come back during a less hectic week. She'll meet your parents. Once she's comfortable, I'll tell her that we're moving here."

"Shouldn't you call her now?" She left his other statement unaddressed.

It was an upsetting development, but he shrugged off the impasse. This was only one week. In time, he'd impress upon his mother that changes *were* coming. He wasn't giving up Cat.

"She won't pick up on the road," he explained. "In her opinion, cell phones cause more accidents than drunk drivers."

"Should you drive home, make sure she's all right?"

"Cat, I am home." Erasing the distance between them, he clasped her shoulders. When he finally captured her flittering gaze, he added, "This doesn't change anything. I love you. My home is with you. I need a few months to get everything in order, but I am moving here. We're moving here—I'll get my mother on board. I'm not losing you. Do you understand?"

"I do." Cat blinked back tears. "I love you too."

"You do?" In wonderment, he held her at arm's length. Her pledge washed a dizzy sort of delight through him.

"Yes, Ryan. With all my heart." On tiptoes, she brushed her nose affectionately against his. Her smile fading, she glanced around the room. "Your mother leaving . . . I feel like I'm at fault."

"Don't be ridiculous. She needs time, that's all."

Cat rested her forehead against his chin. "I know. We'll make this work."

A shudder went through her, dulling her promise. It was enough to puncture his heady delight. With the returning worry, a question shuttled through him, one he despised. Would he get the chance to build a future with Cat?

The answer stalled his heart. He wouldn't, if his mother continued to stand in the way.

Chapter 23

Redneck types crowded the bar in Nowhere, Ohio.

His eyes still burning from the Mace, George pushed through the throng. In the hours since the she-devils had come at him, he'd done nothing but drive aimlessly. His fury rising, he still couldn't believe Frances's meddling friends had thwarted him.

There was nothing waiting for him back in Cincinnati but a night at a men's shelter, and another slew of useless job interviews come Monday. A whole weekend ahead of him—days he'd expected to use for the drive to California. Now he had no choice but to drive back to Sweet Lake tomorrow and figure out another way to get to Frances.

Once he did, he'd break parole and leave the state. With all the real criminals clogging up the justice system, Ohio law enforcement wouldn't canvass the whole US of A for a guy who'd done a few days on a misdemeanor charge.

Jarring rock music thumped through the tavern. The scent of burgers grilling drew him to the long counter in back. He waved down a girl covered in tattoos.

"Got a menu?"

She slapped one down. "What are you drinking?"

He nearly ordered a whiskey, hesitated. Between gas and meals, he'd used up most of the cash he'd taken from the lonely heart he'd met in Cincinnati the day he got out of jail. A hundred dollars and change—he'd lifted the bills from her purse on his way out of her apartment at five o'clock the next morning.

"I'll have a beer."

"Give him something stronger."

A chick with peroxide-blonde hair flowing down her back slid onto the next bar stool. Cheap silver earrings jingled to her shoulders. Young, thin, with a rhinestone pierced through one brow, she gave off a low-burning rage. She was one shade from ugly, but he smiled.

"I'll take a shot of whiskey," he said, "and a burger and fries."

"I'll also take a shot," she told the bartender. When Tattoo Girl moved off, she held out a hand covered in rings. "Stevie."

"George. Nice to meet you."

"Bad day? Looks like you've been crying."

"I got hit with Mace." He saw no reason to lie. Stevie wasn't like the lonely career-types he usually targeted.

Sure enough, the comment sparked interest in her pale-grey eyes. "Got on your wife's wrong side?"

"Friends of my sister-in-law. She's giving me a loan, and they don't like it."

"Why do they care?"

Two shot glasses thudded down on the counter. He swept one up. "No reason, except they're assholes."

"Here's to bitches sticking their noses where they don't belong."

Stevie downed her shot, motioned for another round. When the drinks arrived, she threw an elbow on the counter. She opened her thighs like a man getting comfortable and made no effort to hide her pleasure as she coasted her eyes down his body.

"Your sister-in-law, how much is she loaning you?"

"Originally? Five hundred. After the crap from her friends, I'm thinking about asking for more."

"She can afford to give you more?"

"She's rich. If I ask for ten grand, she'll never miss it."

"Go for it, man. You've got a rich relative, you ought to take advantage."

She ordered them both another round, and he asked, "How come you're flush?"

"Just lucky." The bartender brought his meal, which George ignored. She nodded at his plate. "What are you waiting for?"

"You to let me in on the secret." He pressed his palm to her thigh, slid a slow caress up to her crotch. "You can trust me."

"All right." She pressed her spine to the back of her bar stool, giving him access to roam. "A guy on my crew went in. As of today, I'm taking over."

Drugs. The cocky chick wasn't older than twenty-five, but she sure had means.

They stayed at the bar downing shots until her speech became slurred. By the time George suggested leaving together, the music had taken most of his hearing. Given the liquor she'd downed, he practically carried Stevie out. The night air bit at his cheeks as he helped her into the passenger seat of the Mustang and got directions to her place.

The mobile home was a rat hole of the first order. Dishes green with mold were heaped in the sink. The thick scent of weed blanketed the miniscule living room. A plastic milk bottle filled with change sat on a crate beside a bed that stank of sweat.

Low as he'd sunk in his life, George wasn't sure he could do a chick like this. He sure as hell didn't want to get into a bed filthier than a men's restroom. Giggling, Stevie flopped down on the mess, her arms splayed wide.

Turning on his heel, he strode back to the living room.

"Where are you going, baby? Help me undress!"

In the built-in cupboard beneath the couch, he found the booze stash. Three bottles of cheap wine. He kept searching. Relief coasting through him, he pulled out a bottle of vodka. It wouldn't take much for Stevie to pass out, allowing him to skip the sex.

But fortune's unpredictable wheel was already turning his way. Returning to the bedroom, he found Stevie passed out cold.

She'd dropped her oversize cloth purse on the floor. Grabbing it, George hurried back out. Five twenties inside the wallet, a ten note, and a wad of singles. Stuffing the cash into his pocket, he was tossing the purse aside when the glint of metal deep in the bag caught his eye.

A pearl-handled pistol.

For a split second, he hesitated. Then he slipped the gun into his pocket and went out.

Chapter 24

Morning light glinted off the cars on the highway.

At the last fast-food joint before the Sweet Lake exit, George sped away from the drive-through window.

He was still nursing the dregs of his coffee when he reached the town. Spending the night in his car had left him in a foul mood, impatient to finish up his business and clear out. After parking behind one of the shuttered buildings on Sweet Lake Circle, he ambled onto the green.

Choosing a table far at one end, he sat down to work out his dilemma. Break into Frances's house, and confront her? Wait until she went out, and approach her in public? However he managed to pull this off, he sure didn't want another run-in with her friends. He needed money, not a stint in jail for battery.

A woman came into the center green with her dog. He was glad she didn't notice him, deep in the shade at the opposite end. Finishing his coffee, he crumpled the cup and tossed it away. Irritation burnt across his skin. He still wasn't sure how to get at Frances.

Deep in thought, he gave a second woman a cursory glance as she strolled into the park and struck up a conversation with the first woman.

"What a sweet face! What breed is your dog?"

"Susie is a Bedlington terrier."

"She's gorgeous. Do you mind if I get a shot of you both? We're working on ad concepts for the Wayfair."

"Where would you like us to stand?"

"Hold on." The second woman, taller than the first, bent down to pet the dog. A camera swinging from her neck, she glanced over her shoulder. "Ryan, do you have the release forms?"

A business type in a navy suit joined the women. Recognition poured ice through George's veins. For a disorienting moment, he stared aghast at a more successful version of himself outfitted in a thousand-dollar suit and a red silk tie.

Ryan.

Dumbfounded, he scrambled from the bench and shot behind a tree.

The last time he'd seen his boy up close, he was a moody kid latched to his mother's hip like a barnacle. Seeing him now put knots in George's gut. Looking at Ryan was like seeing a mirror image. Only a more powerful version: with smooth authority, Ryan withdrew the document from his briefcase and explained the details to the woman with the dog. The commanding air surrounding him, the self-confidence, kindled the hatred George thought he'd put to bed long ago.

He waited, hidden and seething, until they finished clicking photos. They got into a slick BMW and drove off. The dog barked, straining against the leash. The woman was pulling a Frisbee from her bag when George strolled up.

"Excuse me, ma'am. The man who was just here—was that Ryan Hunt?"

She struggled with the leash, finally got her mutt to sit. "You mean Ryan D'Angelo?"

Disbelief punched him in the gut. "D'Angelo, right," he said, the tumblers in his mind clicking into place. No wonder he'd never found Julia. The bitch had either remarried or taken a fake name. He wasn't sure which possibility enraged him more. Thinking fast, he added,

"Right—his mother's maiden name was Hunt. We went to high school together. Great gal. I was hoping to say hello to Ryan, ask how she's doing."

The woman tapped the Frisbee against her thigh, clearly happy to help. "Go on up to the inn," she suggested. "I heard Ryan brought his mother with him this week . . ."

Shock lanced through George. He steadied his feet. Julia, here in Sweet Lake? All the time wasted this week—all the time wasted searching for her over the years—and she was right here, under his nose.

"Ryan is doing such a great job for the Wayfair," the woman was saying. "Everyone in town is excited. We're sure looking forward to those tourist dollars."

"I'm sure they'll help the town."

"Are you going to the concert tonight? My husband isn't crazy about rock and roll, but I'm making him take me. I enjoy Midnight Boyz."

"Tonight's concert?" he said, and his heart fell into a dark place. "I wouldn't miss it."

"We're staying in a purple house?" Patty maneuvered her ancient Buick to the curb. "Looks like something out of *Grimm's Fairy Tales*."

"It's lavender, not purple." Hopping out, Gemma grabbed their luggage from the backseat. "The garden gnomes are a nice touch." She counted eight fat porcelain men scattered in the flower beds.

Throughout the drive from Kent State, she'd subdued the nerves jumbling inside her with moderate success. Now that they'd arrived, she felt nervous enough to jog from one end of the picturesque town to the other.

Eying her, Patty ducked into the backseat. "Don't forget this. You definitely need it." She slung Gemma's yoga mat beneath her arm.

They were barely up the steps when Penelope Riddle appeared on the small front porch. Thick eyeglasses, double chin—she looked exactly like her Airbnb profile pic, with the additional curiosity of a crown of feathers stuck on her head and a flowing black caftan sprinkled with silver stars covering her stout frame.

"Girls, hello!" She practically shoved Patty inside without a second glance. Her smile deepening to benevolent, she cornered Gemma in the tiny foyer. "How are you, dear? The drive wasn't too tiring?"

Gemma wasn't sure what to make of her solicitous tone or her strange outfit. "We didn't hit too much traffic."

"Oh, good. I sent positive vibes to aid you on your journey." She followed the enigmatic remark with a look of concern. "Are you ready for tonight? So exciting!"

"Um, yeah. I love Midnight Boyz."

"Ah, I'd nearly forgotten about the concert. You aren't too anxious, are you?"

Catching the subtext, Gemma said, "I'm cool. A little nervous, but I'm handling it."

From behind their merry hostess, Patty leaned sideways to mouth the question, *What's with her?*

Gemma lifted her shoulders a nearly imperceptible degree.

Oblivious to the exchange, Penelope clapped her hands together. "Well, let's get you settled. Right this way, girls."

If the exterior of the house brought to mind a fairytale, the guest bedroom added marvelously to the effect. From the canopy above the four-poster bed, tiny silver stars, similar to those decorating Penelope's flowing caftan, spun aimlessly on shimmery golden threads. The walls, painted midnight blue, showed off celestial paintings of the heavens in heavy, burnished-gold frames. On the floor, a cream-colored rug shaped like a rainbow nestled against gleaming oak floorboards.

Gemma turned in a slow, appreciative circle. "I could live here for the rest of my life." She chuckled at the look of wonder on her roommate's face. They were equally awestruck by the beauty of their surroundings.

"You like it?" Behind her glasses, Penelope's filmy gaze registered delight. "When I redid my guest bedroom, I asked the other women for advice. I took their best inspirations and came up with this."

"The photo you put on Airbnb is nice, but the room is much prettier in real life."

"If I rent out my guest room again, I'll make sure to upload a photograph taken in daylight." She plodded to the center of the room, caught her reflection in the mirror above the dresser. Giggling like a child, she plucked at the delicate stones and shells arranged beneath the feathers of her headdress. "Good grief—I forgot I'd already changed into my outfit. I suppose you're both wondering why I'm dressed like this."

She giggled once more with an utter lack of artifice. Gemma decided she liked their unusual hostess very much. "You're celebrating Halloween early?" she guessed.

"No, no—this has nothing to do with Halloween. I'm a member of a special women's group. We're meeting in Sweet Lake Circle this evening to gather positive vibrations for the Wayfair." Penelope's face lost its gaiety by degrees. "We're also performing a special ritual for one of our valiant leaders. She has a vermin problem."

"Mice in her house?"

"No, she has a rat. We'll combine our energy to send him away."

"You're not going to the concert?" A major tragedy, in Gemma's opinion.

"Heavens, no. At my age, rock and roll sets my teeth on edge. Besides, this is such an important weekend for the inn. They need all the good vibes we can muster. After our ceremony, we'll toast the Wayfair's success with Silvia's mojitos. She always brings the libations for our meetings."

Eager as she was for clarification on how a bunch of women conjured positive vibes—or how a fancy headdress figured in—Gemma's interest clung to another aspect of the explanation. "Are you talking about Silvia Mendoza?" She'd already deduced that Silvia was the mother of Ryan's girlfriend. "I met her the other day."

The admission brought Penelope near. "Look for Silvia's daughter at the concert," she whispered urgently, leaving Gemma with the suspicion she'd been waiting for the opportunity to steer the conversation in this particular direction. "I'm sure Cat will help you find success in your pursuit. Would you like a photograph of her so you know who you're looking for?"

"I know who she is."

"Perfect. Look for her near the band. She's overseeing the event. Now, don't be shy. Walk right up and introduce yourself." A hint of merriment returned to Penelope's features. She patted Gemma's cheek. "Good luck tonight."

With that, she hurried out. The door clicked shut behind her.

Patty stared after her with ill-concealed confusion. "Man, I have no idea what's going on. Why was she coddling you? And what's with the advice to find Ryan's babe? Gemma, did you tell her why we're here?"

"No, but someone sure did. Not Silvia or Frances—I didn't give them Ryan's name. I'm sure they don't know I made the road trip for him."

"Penelope may have figured it out on her own. You and Ryan *do* look like brother and sister." Flinging her suitcase on the bed, Patty chewed this around. "So? Will you follow her advice?"

"About looking Cat up first?" Actually it wasn't a bad idea. "She *is* Ryan's girlfriend. It'll be easier to avoid throwing up on my shoes from nerves if I talk to her first."

Patty wrinkled her nose. "No puking. And definitely no dinner. Skip the munchies until after you've dropped the bomb on your brother's head."

Gemma nodded in agreement. She hadn't eaten so much as a lettuce leaf all day.

She was too anxious about meeting her brother.

~♥~

A river of people streamed in and out of the golden sandstone mansion.

Parking at the back of the lot, George congratulated himself on his good luck. With so many people at the inn on this bright Saturday afternoon, there wasn't much chance of anyone noticing his resemblance to the man from Adworks. Still, for safety's sake, he grabbed a ball cap from the trunk of his Mustang and slid it low on his forehead.

Wherever his son was inside the grand structure, Julia was surely nearby. After the concert began tonight, finding her in the crowd would be a simple enough task. How, exactly, to drag her off without causing a stir was a conundrum George planned to solve this afternoon.

Let Frances and her band of she-devils thwart him all they liked. He'd find another way out of this godforsaken state. He'd get out, one way or another—*after* he settled his score with Julia permanently.

He walked down the sloping lawn, which spilled out into a flat area of green. The chatter of three youths carried on the breeze, their lean arms moving quickly to unwind a roll of orange fencing. Past them, where the grass met the sand, two older men heaved a ticket booth into place. Avoiding them, George trotted along the hedgerow that muffled the murmur of the surf. He ducked unseen into the woods.

Safe in the shadows, he pulled out his smartphone and flipped back to the inn's website. The concert would begin at seven o'clock.

There was also a buffet scheduled to begin within the hour; he lifted his nose, caught the scent of grilling dogs. Following the savory aroma, he trudged through the forest, taking care to remain parallel to the lake.

Through the trees, he spied a black woman with a killer body directing the people setting up long tables for a buffet line. A ruddy-cheeked cook stood before a large grill. Apparently he was feeding the employees before they took their stations. The sizzle coming off the grill made George's mouth water. After he mapped out how to grab his ex-wife tonight, he needed to find somewhere to eat and lie low until darkness fell.

Checking his watch, he concluded the trek through the forest took less than three minutes. Add another sixty seconds to drag Julia up the hill to his car, and he'd make off with her in about the time it took Midnight Boyz to finish one tune and lead into the next.

Satisfied with the plan, he retraced his steps to his car. Pulling out of the lot, he thumbed through his phone in search of a restaurant. Nothing came up but the Sunshine Room at the Wayfair. His belly growled in complaint.

Muttering a curse, he searched again, this time for a grocery store.

"Doesn't this thing ever give the right answer?" Disenchanted with the Magic 8 Ball's results, Linnie tossed the toy into Cat's waiting hands.

Usually Linnie didn't subscribe to superstition. Jada didn't either, but she'd also tried her luck in the hopes of lifting the collective mood. They'd all been in the doldrums since finding the tin hidden at Archibald Dufour's grave.

Tugging off her heels, Cat swung her feet onto Linnie's desk. They'd decided to meet in her office for a brief respite before parting ways to change into jeans for the concert.

Cat rubbed the soreness from her shoulders. "Ryan's already out on the beach with the videographer and the photographer. I still haven't told him anything."

Jada slumped in the other chair. "How's Julia?"

"Happy as a lark back in the city. She's finishing Halloween costumes for the kiddies."

"Have you spoken with her?"

"Only a few words, when Ryan checked in with her this afternoon."

Placing her elbows on the desk, Linnie glumly lowered her chin onto her palms. "Cat, you have to tell Ryan he has family living right here in Sweet Lake."

"Not tonight. I've had a weird feeling all day, like bad karma has been stalking my heels since the moment I got out of bed. It's enough to make me hold off."

"Hold off for how long?"

"Until tomorrow. After the Sunday buffet winds down, I'll offer to go back with Ryan to Cincinnati. He's been hinting about taking a few days off together."

Jada grunted. "Doubtful he meant a few days off with his mother in the next room."

"Jada, I know what he meant." As much as a romantic getaway appealed, Cat pushed the notion aside. A precious slice of Ryan's personal history lay in her possession. Until she shared it with him, a vacation alone wasn't worth contemplating. "If I'm with Julia on her home turf, there's a better chance of reasoning with her. In retrospect, I shouldn't have confronted her while she was camped out in the south wing. She has lots of troubling memories associated with Sweet Lake, and Frances. I wish I'd known before I talked to her."

"And if she flat-out refuses to come around?" Linnie made no effort to hide her doubt. "Listen, I don't want you to feel responsible if all of this brings on her depression, but you have to do something."

Cat dreaded the prospect of triggering Julia's depression. "I'll tell her I'm no longer comfortable leaving Ryan in the dark. This *is* his life too. Once I put him in contact with Frances, Frances will get right in her car and drive to Julia's house to mend their relationship. Julia has a thousand regrets, none of which will matter. Frances *will* forgive her. Hopefully that'll be enough to stop Julia from getting too low."

Jada brought up another troubling point. "Once she is back in touch with Frances, she'll forfeit her anonymity. George Hunt will be able to track her down. The name change, the years of lying low—all the precautions won't matter."

It was another issue she'd fretted over for hours. "If George turns up at some point, I have to believe Ryan can handle him. It's been a long time . . . Ryan believes he's out West somewhere, too far away to ever hurt Julia again. Let's hope it's true."

Her friends regarded her worriedly as she rose, bringing the conversation to a close. Outside, in the raucous crowd converging on the beach, a college student was searching for the brother she'd never met. Cat was determined to do everything in her power to ensure Gemma made Ryan's acquaintance tonight.

After she changed into jeans, she went outside. A carnival-like atmosphere surrounded the beach, with people ordering burgers and dogs, and others milling around the dais where Midnight Boyz would perform. The crew from the events company she'd hired was arranging the last row of chairs before the dais, and setting up the dance floor nearby. Following her instructions, they left the outer perimeter free of seating. Couples were already marking out spots and laying down blankets to watch the band play. By sunset, as the floodlights surrounding the dais blinked on, she'd walked through the crowd repeatedly without finding a girl with honey-blonde hair who bore a strong resemblance to Ryan.

The harvest moon came out, fat and golden in a sky glittering with stars. She checked in near the dais with Ryan and his colleagues from

Adworks. They were busy filming and photographing the event. He pulled her into his arms for a deep kiss before turning his attentions back to the work at hand. His high spirits gave her the impetus to keep looking for Gemma. No doubt his younger sister was somewhere in the throng, nervously mustering the courage to approach him.

Walking away from the dais, Cat scanned the sea of faces. Where was she?

Chapter 25

Safely hidden near the people by the grill, George kept his eyes trained on his son. A greedy anticipation filled him as he waited for Julia to appear. When she did, she was sure to meet up with their boy.

From the crowd, the familiar Latina beauty materialized. It beat all that Ryan was hot for Silvia Mendoza's daughter. Not that the photos of Cat on the inn's website did her justice. In real life, she was stunning with her long hair and sultry beauty.

After she finished chatting with Ryan, she dove back into the crowd. Then she paused for a heartbeat, her dark, fluid gaze returning to linger on Ryan like a slow caress. Bitterness filled George's mouth.

Ducking behind the buffet line, he matched her strides. With purpose she moved toward the entrance to the beach. With night descending, the blue waters of the lake faded into the gloom. Shadows pooled on the beach as Cat swiveled around in search of someone in the crowd. Her preoccupation gave George an inspired solution to his dilemma.

To hell with waiting for Julia. There was an easier way.

He'd let Cat bring his quarry to him.

The pearl-handled gun, a reassuring weight in his pocket, promised to bring the revenge he'd been waiting for since Twin Falls. He'd drag Julia out of here and find an open field.

The only problem with the airtight plan was a minor one.

Under no circumstances was he leaving behind a witness to inform the authorities. He'd done a week in lockup, a bitter experience he planned to never repeat.

Like his ex-wife, Cat wouldn't live to see the dawn.

Chapter 26

On each picnic table in Sweet Lake Circle, votive candles pricked the darkness with flickering light.

As the women surrounding her chanted softly, Frances let her eyes drift open to appreciate the moment. In lawn chairs they'd each brought from home, twenty-eight of her comrades sat clasping hands. Love for them brimmed inside her for the care they'd given her all week long. Whenever George turned back up—and she doubted he'd given up—she needn't face him alone. The efficient Silvia had drawn up a calendar clear into November, with a different Siren staying at Frances's house every night. As for the fracas yesterday—well, she felt bad about Tilda wielding Mace and Ozzie Riddle spraining an ankle. At least they'd driven George off.

Setting her personal travails out of mind, Frances sent positive energy toward the inn high upon the hill above the town. All day long cars had streamed toward the Wayfair, the undeniable proof that Cat's efforts were a success. According to Silvia, her daughter's work advertising the concert had brought in four hundred attendees. The final tally wildly exceeded Cat's expectations.

The ceremony ended. When Silvia rose, Frances followed her to the closest picnic table. Together they handed out plastic cups filled with Silvia's tasty mojitos.

Penelope hoisted her glass toward the star-studded night. "To your successful journey," she whispered.

"Are you toasting Gemma Mills?" Frances asked. When her comrade nodded, she added, "I was hoping to see her today. I asked her to stop by if she had time before the concert. Did she seem nervous this afternoon? She's looking for her brother tonight."

"Oh, I know." Excitement laced Penelope's voice. "I promised not to say anything, but I know who he is. I can't wait to hear the details after they meet."

The announcement brought more of the Sirens near. Tilda asked, "Who is he? You can't pique our interest then keep the secret to yourself. Coming to Sweet Lake, finding a long-lost brother—I love happy endings!"

"I'm sorry, Tilda. I promised not to breathe a word."

Ruth elbowed Norah out of the way to nab a mojito. "If you're supposed to keep your trap shut, then do it," she advised Penelope. "The girl has a right to her privacy. If she meets her brother tonight, we'll all get the details soon enough." She grinned devilishly. "I'd rather hear about Norah's tragedy on Airbnb."

Norah bristled. "I've already told you about Mr. O'Grady."

"You told me, and no one else. Tell the story again. Listening to your failures is the great joy of my life."

Norah appeared ready to give her petite nemesis a thrashing. Recalling their last tiff in her living room, Frances wisely intervened. "Do tell us, Norah. What is Mr. O'Grady like?"

"The seventy-year-old hippie roosting in my guest bedroom? He's awful. The man has more lewd one-liners than a drunken fraternity."

Ruth snickered. "What were you expecting? Anyone booking a room this weekend came for the concert. Including the old guys."

"I was hoping for a suave Cary Grant, not a blast from the psychedelic past."

"Next time you're looking for a man, use a real dating site."

Wishing to steer the conversation to lighter topics, Frances said, "Ruth, how is Julia? Did you take her for another walk today?"

Ruth tapped the side of her glass. After Silvia gave her a refill, she told Frances, "She went back to Cincinnati."

"Already? I thought she planned to stay until tomorrow."

"She left Friday afternoon awfully upset. Understandable, really. The woman's seen enough tragedy for ten lifetimes."

Frances shared a meaningful look with Silvia. Whatever secrets Julia D'Angelo kept, the only woman in town with a clue to their contents was Ruth.

"She's been through a lot?" Frances prodded.

"With her ex-husband. The man abused her something terrible."

"Oh, that's heartbreaking."

"Yeah, and don't ask for the particulars. Like I told Penelope, it's important to keep a confidence. I'm not breaking mine with Julia."

Silvia removed her feathered headdress and tossed it on a nearby table. "This is different," she snapped. "Julia's well-being affects her son, and my daughter. In case you haven't noticed, Cat and Ryan are head over heels for each other. I won't be surprised if they're engaged by Christmas. His family will become *my* family. Reason enough for you to fill me in."

Evidently Ruth wasn't aware of how quickly the relationship between Cat and Ryan was progressing. She'd always had a soft spot for Cat—they all did. Her features worked as she weighed her affection against her distaste at breaking a confidence.

She was still deciding when Silvia threw her hands into the air. "I'm not asking you to air her dirty laundry. Give me the basics, and leave it at that. From where I'm standing, she's unconscionably rude."

At the blast of temper, Ruth lowered her brows. "Fine, Silvia. I'll give you the basics." She took her time removing her headdress and setting it aside.

"Well? I'm waiting."

"Julia told me only bits and pieces during our walks." Setting her drink aside, she crossed her arms. Clearly she viewed sharing the story an unpleasant task. "She ran out on her ex-husband because the man used to beat her, and bad. I feel sorry for her, what with the constant reminder. According to Julia, Ryan looks just like his father. His spitting image."

Now it was Norah's turn to register surprise. "This afternoon, I stopped into the grocery store. There was a man by the deli I swore was Ryan. When I got close, I realized my mistake. Still, there was no missing the resemblance."

Ruth's head snapped up. "You saw George Hunt? Here in Sweet Lake?"

The blood left Frances's head. "Julia D'Angelo's ex-husband . . . his name is George Hunt?"

Ruth nodded. "She took another name to steer clear of him." She peered closely at Frances. "What's the matter? You don't look right."

Frances's knees began to buckle. Silvia rushed forward. Norah helped her lower Frances to the bench.

Shock and heartbreak threatened to close Frances's throat. "Ruth, my ex-brother-in-law, the one who's been coming around—his name is George Hunt. He's a danger to Ryan." She looked wildly to the others. "Someone call the police."

All of the Sirens scrambled for their purses. Tilda whimpered at her oversize bag, dumped the contents on the grass. Penelope, overcome by the bad vibes descending upon the Sirens, wept madly as she fumbled with the zipper on her purse. Several of the Sirens dashed off to nearby tables, where they'd left their bags.

Ruth's mouth thinned to a harsh line. She stalked toward the street.

Silvia spun on her heel. "Where are you going?" she barked.

Ruth climbed into her truck. The engine's roar announced her departure.

"Crazy fool. What is she doing?" Brushing off her strange behavior, Silvia wrapped an arm around Frances. She frowned at the others. "For Pete's sake—will one of you find your cell phone and call the police?"

❧

Before the inn, every parking space in the lot was taken. "You'll have to park by the road," Gemma told her roommate. "We'll never find a space up here."

"We would've found somewhere decent to park if we'd come earlier." Patty threw the car in reverse, then slowly drove out of the lot. "I'll tell you what, Gemma. For someone who was looking forward to this weekend, you sure wasted a lot of time stalling."

"Don't get on my case, okay? I'm nervous."

"Fine. I'm not getting on your case."

On the road near the inn, they squeezed in behind another car. Slamming shut the passenger door, Gemma caught the guitar licks of her favorite tune by Midnight Boyz, "Don't Let Go." She latched on to the lyrics to drown out the erratic thump of her pulse. Much as she longed to meet her brother, she wasn't prepared for this much anxiety.

Trudging up the hill, Patty huffed out small breaths. "Want to start by looking for Cat? She'll take you to Ryan."

"Yeah, Cat first. I'm still not sure what to say to my brother."

"Start with *hello*. The perfect icebreaker."

The inn blazed with light. Pausing midway across the parking lot, Gemma surveyed the brightly lit veranda. All of the wicker chairs were vacant. In the lobby, two employees stood chatting behind the front desk.

"I'll check inside first, to see if Cat's there." Gemma squared her shoulders.

"Should I go with you?"

"Go on to the concert. If Cat isn't inside, I'll head down to the beach." With misgiving, she read the dismay on her roommate's face. "I'll be okay. I need to do this alone."

"Send me a text when you're finished. I'll let you know where I'm at."

"Got it."

Patty disappeared into the darkness. Mustering her courage, Gemma started toward the inn.

❧

For the third time, Cat circled through the crowd.

With the band now five tunes into their first set, squeezing through the crush of people became nearly impossible. Every seat before the dais was now filled, and countless blankets surrounded the perimeter, with couples lounging as they listened to the loud wails of electric guitars and the heart-thumping beat of drums. Beyond the area set aside for blankets, an outer rim of people stood shoulder to shoulder. On the dance floor, others managed to squeeze out elbow room to get their groove on.

Veering toward the surf—the only area free of people—Cat wended her way to the ticket booth. The last stragglers were entering.

Gemma wasn't among them.

With frustration she pivoted away, resigned to continuing the search. She stopped, sighed, and glanced at the hill that swept ever higher to the inn. A sheet of darkness accosted her. None of the beach lighting managed to illuminate the area.

Even with all the details checked and rechecked, she'd obviously missed an important one. After Midnight Boyz finished playing at ten o'clock, how would the concertgoers reach their cars? If she didn't come up with a solution, and fast, she'd have people stumbling around in the dark—and the inn facing a potential lawsuit if anyone were injured.

The only option? Find every flashlight stowed in the Wayfair. It would be easy enough to post the staff at intervals on the hill to guide people back to their cars. Cat only hoped Mr. Uchida wasn't too busy to help her dig up every flashlight they could get their hands on.

"Why the sad face?"

Pulling from her musings, she found Ryan at her side. She explained about the unlit hill, adding, "How did I miss something this obvious?"

"This is the first time you've organized a concert. You were bound to miss something."

"Why wasn't it something less critical?"

He nodded toward the inn. "Should I go with you?"

"And miss all the fun?" She kissed him briefly. "Thanks, but I can handle this solo."

"I don't mind helping you hunt for flashlights."

Grinning, she pushed him gently. "Mr. Uchida will help. Enjoy the concert."

She let him go, wondering if she'd return shortly to the happy news that Gemma, wherever she was, had made a nervous introduction. And if not? After she unearthed every flashlight in the Wayfair and organized the staff, she'd find Ryan's sister.

The harvest moon painted the sloping area closest to the inn with a silvery glow. In contrast, the area of the hill closest to the parking lot was draped in shadow. She trekked into the darkest reaches, near the forest's edge, to map out where to station employees.

Goose bumps sprouted on her arms. An uneasy sensation followed.

Someone was watching her.

Sensing danger, she quickened her pace. She jogged up the steep incline, taking the hill in big strides. From the beach, applause rose to a hearty pitch as Midnight Boyz finished another number.

The applause was dying down when the man came at her from behind.

Forcibly he caught her by the arm, nearly lifting her feet from the ground. "Make a sound, and I'll put a bullet in your head."

The deep timbre of his voice—so similar to Ryan's—wicked the moisture from her mouth. He dragged her into a sliver of moonlight. With dread, Cat met his eyes.

They were large, a deep forest green, set in a cruel, weathered face. Disoriented, she froze.

Assessing her confusion, George laughed. "I'm Ryan's father, Miss Mendoza. Nice to meet you." He tightened his hold. Pain bolted through her blood-starved arm. With horror, she watched him lift the gun with his free hand to prove he wasn't bluffing. "I'm looking for Julia. Where is she?"

Cold, animal panic seized her. "I'm not sure," she bluffed.

"She's inside the inn? Which room?" His grip was a vise, and she clenched her teeth against the pain. He dragged her another step forward. "Tell her to meet you in the parking lot."

"No." She struggled vainly against his overpowering strength.

He pushed her back and took aim. "Get your phone out, or I *will* put a bullet in you."

The threat started a ringing in her ears. He lowered the gun an inch, zeroing in on her chest. In her mouth, the metallic taste of fear glazed her tongue.

Refuse, and he'd kill her.

Complying, she scrabbled for her phone. She lifted it high. "What will you do to Julia?" she asked, stalling for time.

With a growl, he dragged her forward. They reached the gravel perimeter of the parking lot. Helplessly she scanned row after row of cars. Terror iced her blood. There was no one nearby, no one to save her.

Bucking against the fear, she dug deep into her gut for courage. "Answer me," she demanded. "What will you do to Julia?"

"Like you haven't figured it out." Something inhuman inked his gaze.

A fierce defiance flamed inside Cat. She was already dead. One look in his eyes confirmed he'd never let her go. The only chance for survival? Making a run for it.

George blocked her path. "You're a smart one, aren't you?" he sneered, guessing her intention.

"More than you know." For proof, she heaved the smartphone away in a fast, furious arc. End over end, it spun into the darkness.

"You stinking bitch! I ought to take you out right here."

He threw her forward, slamming her into a car. She took the impact on the side of her body. Agony rocketed through her chest.

He was coming at her again when a girl leapt out from between cars. Coming full throttle, she clipped him on the side. He was a big man, but the impact spun him around. The gun in his fist glinted in the moonlight.

"Leave her alone!"

Her vision blurring, Cat made out the long blonde hair whirling across the girl's face as she rushed forward again. *Gemma.* She cried out in warning—too late.

Finding his balance, George caught his daughter by the collar of her shirt. He rammed her against the car. She crumpled to the ground.

Cat, still dazed, dropped down beside her. When George approached with fists clenched, she slid him a look of pure venom. "Don't touch her."

He towered above them. "Get her on her feet."

Cat did, slowly.

A trickle of blood streamed from Gemma's lips. Brushing it away, Cat whispered, "Don't provoke him." Gemma gave a tearstained nod of understanding. Bringing her upright, Cat stepped protectively in front of her.

With the pistol, George waved them forward. He yanked open the passenger door of a Mustang. "Get her inside."

Cat helped the whimpering Gemma climb in.

"Now, call up to Julia's room." He slapped his phone into Cat's palm. "Tell her to get down here." He leaned in menacingly. "Do it."

Cat left the door ajar, making it patently clear she wouldn't let him lock Gemma inside. "You can't escape with three of us," she said, unable to mask the terror in her voice. Julia wasn't inside the inn, and she feared his reaction once he learned the truth. Yet she found the emotional reserves to reason with him. "What are you going to do? Kill us all? George, think about what you're doing."

He shoved the barrel of the gun beneath her jaw, forcing her head to a painful angle. "How 'bout I take care of you first, seeing as you don't know when to shut up. You'll call up to Julia now, or I'll—"

Past the thump of music drifting from the beach, a wail of sirens pierced the night. They weren't coming from the beach. Tilting her head slightly, Cat peered toward the town far below them.

What happened next seemed out of a nightmare. George stumbled back. He pivoted toward the white and blue lights strobing across the night sky. Taking another step away, he lowered the gun in confusion.

Ryan burst out of the darkness and sped up the hill.

But he didn't approach silently. Rage erupted from his throat. It was all the warning George needed.

Honing in on the danger, George took aim. He got a round off, and Cat screamed against the deafening blast. Shadows fell across the spot where she'd just spotted Ryan.

Alarmed, she turned back toward his father. Bewilderment fell across George's features. He spun to his right. Cat followed his widening stare with confusion, unsure of what had caught his attention. Then she heard the crunch of gravel beneath swift strides.

Halfway down the row of cars, Ruth planted her feet. Eyes narrowed, she swung her pistol to chest height in a two-handed grip.

A second blast of gunfire cracked the night.

Chapter 27

"The offer still stands. If you'd like a trip to the ER, one of my officers will take you." Police Chief Rand McCluskey nodded toward the officers milling around the kitchen, sipping the coffee the kitchen staff had brewed and snacking on the cheese and crackers they'd put out. "It's not a bad idea to have your ribs x-rayed."

"I'm fine," Cat assured him. "Just bruised, and a little shaken up from the ordeal."

In the last ninety minutes, the inn had filled with state troopers and virtually every member of the Sweet Lake PD. Ryan was still out on the veranda finishing his statement and helping Linnie prepare for the concert's end. Some of the troopers were already on the hill with flashlights, preparing to escort concertgoers safely to their cars.

Another disorienting wave of relief bolted through Cat. It was sheer luck that Ryan hadn't been hit by the round his father had fired off.

George wasn't as lucky. Thanks to Ruth's quick thinking and unerring aim, he had been pronounced DOA at Park Center Hospital.

Ruth was also at the hospital. After much debate, Chief McCluskey had convinced her to let a doctor look her over as a precaution. The former police dispatcher had suffered from heart trouble in the past, and the chief had felt it only reasonable that she go in. Frances had already sent word from the hospital that Ruth was fine.

Cat looked to the chief. "Do you need anything else?"

"We're done here. I'll let you know if I have any other questions."

With a soft groan, she rose. Her ribs *were* tender. "Where's Gemma?" she asked. In the chaotic aftermath of the shooting, she'd lost track of Ryan's sister.

"In Linnie's office. Jada promised to stay with her until her parents arrive."

"When should we expect them?"

"Close to midnight. They're driving down from Cleveland."

"Does Gemma know?"

The chief nodded. "Jada told her."

On the couch in Linnie's office, the rattled girl and her roommate from KSU were wrapped together in a blanket. They shared a plate of Jada's delectable brownies and tall glasses of cold milk.

"How are you doing, Gemma?" Cat attempted to drag a chair near, winced, and let Jada do the honors. When she was seated, she managed a grin. "Nice to meet you, by the way."

"You were crazy brave out there." Gemma pulled the blanket tighter across her shoulders. "Weren't you scared?"

"Terrified."

"Thanks for protecting me."

"It's what big sisters do." The comment slipped out of its own accord.

There wasn't time to backpedal, as Gemma's roommate spoke up. "We were pretty sure you and Ryan were a thing, but we weren't sure if your relationship was big time. We've been stalking you on social media." From beneath the blanket, she produced her hand. "I'm Patty."

"Nice to meet you, Patty."

The girl darted a glance at Gemma, looked back to Cat. "Did they . . . take his body away?"

"A short time ago."

The pronouncement sank the room into silence, but only for a moment. Setting down her glass of milk, Gemma pulled her knees to her chest. "I'm not sure how to feel," she admitted. "I'm not happy George is dead, but I'm not sad either. This is weird. He never really was a part of my life. I haven't seen him since I was a kid."

"You're still a kid," Jada remarked, smiling. She fussed with Cat's tangled hair, frowned. "Wait until your mother sees this. You're getting a line of bruises down the side of your face."

"She won't see them anytime soon. She's with Frances at the hospital."

"How's Ruth?"

"Still bitching at the doctors, last I heard." Catching herself, Cat sent a look of apology to the girls. "Sorry."

"No problem," Gemma said, and her amusement put a trace of color in her cheeks. "About my brother . . ."

She left the words hanging, which was all the incentive Cat required. "Are you ready to meet Ryan? If you'd rather wait until your parents get here, that's fine."

"I'd rather go now." Gemma flung off the blanket.

"Hold on. We're doing this blind. Is that all right? Ryan doesn't know you're his sister."

"No one has told him?" The inconvenient fact put worry in Gemma's eyes.

"Gemma, the police are preoccupied, and I was giving my statement."

Jada helped the girl up. "I'll stay here with Patty," she said. "You go on with Cat."

The lobby brimmed with the drone of mingled voices. The first guests were returning from the beach with looks of alarm at the law enforcement streaming through the Wayfair. Easing her way past the clutch of state troopers rimming the front desk, Cat waggled her fingers behind her back.

Gemma latched on like a nervous child.

In the crowd milling on the veranda, Ryan handed out flashlights to anyone willing to man a station on the hill. He shouted something to Linnie, who was trotting down the steps. She gave him the thumbs-up before disappearing through the parking lot.

Cat waved to catch his attention. Over the top of Mr. Uchida's head, he noticed her.

"Hey." He took her face in his hands, gingerly kissed her forehead. "I meant to check on you thirty minutes ago. With the concert ending, I got sidetracked. Do you forgive me?"

"Forgive you? I'm grateful. I wasn't up to managing my duties."

He noticed the bruises, but not the girl behind Cat. "Are you all right? Should I take you to the hospital?"

"I don't need a doctor, but you may need a chair."

"What for? I'm cool." He swiped at the hair brushing his brow. "Honestly, I don't know how to feel about this . . . about him, I mean. I'm not happy, but I'm not sad either."

"Interesting. That's not the first time I've heard that tonight." She paused for a delicious moment. "I have something to tell you."

"Yeah?" He caught the excitement in her voice. "If you've got happy news, hit me. I could use some about now."

He leaned in to kiss her. Thwarting him, she stepped aside to reveal Gemma standing behind her back in silent anticipation. Less than two hours ago, he'd glimpsed her only for a moment in the unlit parking lot. Evidently he'd forgotten about Gemma during the intervening minutes.

Now, looking at her fully, his eyes widened with shock.

When he listed slightly, Cat slid a steadying arm around his waist. "This," she said, "you're going to love."

Chapter 28

Of all the treasures in her home, he adored the family portraits.

Countless paintings graced the house, but the large grouping on the second floor of his aunt's colonial was remarkable. In the wide hallway, portraits of the illustrious Brugnets dating back generations hung in orderly groupings on the walls.

With George Hunt dead for nearly two weeks now, Ryan would never learn about his father's side of the family. Those lost details didn't bother him in the least. Listening to Frances explain the successes and rare foibles of the ancestors on his maternal side gave Ryan all the answers he required.

In her gentle, educated voice, Frances wove together the personal history he'd craved all his life.

She drew him to the end of the long hallway, away from the low hum of voices and the soft thumping of footfalls as the men from the moving company neared the stairwell. "Last but not least, this is Philippe Brugnet. I believe he was in his early twenties when he sat for this portrait." At the top of the stairwell, two of the men appeared with a large dresser. Frances gave them barely a glance, her fingers trailing across the shadowbox frame. "Philippe was born in Dieppe, France. He's the first Brugnet in our family to reach the New World. He landed in Boston in 1702."

"Also a banker, like your father?" Ryan studied the intelligent face of a man with a trim beard and a neat mustache.

"No, Philippe was a trader. His son became a merchant. Our family didn't enter banking until your great-grandfather moved from Philadelphia to the Cincinnati area."

Balancing the dresser between them, the men plodded down the hallway to the last bedroom. Next Ruth tromped up the stairwell. She carried a large box in her arms.

She gave them a disapproving frown. "Haven't you left for Walnut Grove yet?"

"We'll leave in thirty minutes," Frances told her.

"Are Cat and Gemma going with you?"

"They'll meet us here. We'll all drive out together."

From his mother's bedroom, Ryan caught the impatience in Silvia's voice as the movers brought in the dresser. Excusing himself, he said, "Let me check if they need help." He started down the hallway with Frances and Ruth trailing behind.

In the center of the spacious room, Silvia stood with her hands on her hips. The men mopped their brows as she tapped her foot, evidently caught in indecision.

She looked up with relief. "Ryan, should the dresser go on the wall near the door, or the one by the closet?" She cast a pitying glance at his mother in the rocking chair by the window. "Julia doesn't seem willing to lend an opinion."

Ryan crouched beside the chair. "Mom? Do you care how they arrange your room?" He rested his hand on her knee, tucked snugly beneath the lap blanket. A whisper of light glimmered in her vacant gaze. "We need to get your dresser situated so the movers can bring in the rest of your things."

"I'm not sure where to put it." Consternation furrowed her brow. "What does Ruth think?"

The low, childlike query brought her stalwart companion forward.

Ruth joined him beside the rocking chair, and his heart filled with gratitude. He owed the eccentric Siren his life.

"Julia, let's have the men put the dresser near the door," she said. At the decision, the movers heaved the dresser into place. When they'd finished, Ruth settled her hand on Julia's shoulder. "It looks good there." She waved off the men. "Go on, now. Fetch the rest of her things."

The men left. Frances said, "Ryan, why don't we go downstairs? There are a few items I'd like to go over with you. Ruth and Silvia will stay until we're back from the cemetery."

"That's right." Ruth nodded toward the door. "Finish your business with Frances. We'll take care of your mother."

"Thanks." Impulsively he kissed Ruth on the cheek. "For everything."

The affection startled her. For a split second her beady gaze flashed. Then she swatted him away, but not before he caught the pleasure on her face.

"Save your gratitude," she said gruffly. "Come the holiday season, you're paying up."

He wasn't sure what she meant. "Hankering for a special Christmas gift? I'm open to hints."

"I mean the holiday food drive." She hitched her thumbs in the pockets of her roomy jeans. She didn't quite achieve a pose of irritation, given the smile on her lips. "Plan on being my number-one volunteer. Start practicing your sales pitch, hotshot. I'll have you knocking on doors across Sweet Lake until your knuckles are sore."

Ryan nodded. "You can count on me."

"I will."

He followed his aunt downstairs to the paneled library. "She's no better today," he said of his mother. He wandered down the long shelves, trailing his fingers across the spines of leather-bound books. "I'm not sure what to do."

"There's nothing you can do. Julia has agreed to see a therapist. I'll begin taking her next week. The therapy will help."

"The antidepressants are too strong. She's practically out of it all the time."

"Ryan, we both want your mother back to full health. She's been through a terrible shock. Hiding you both from George for years, then learning he almost murdered someone at the inn—frankly, she's handling this relatively well." Seating herself behind the desk, Frances pressed a hand to her heart. "I suggest you focus on the positive aspects of the situation. If my sister hadn't found the courage to bring Ruth into her confidence before George made his appearance, we might have lost Cat and Gemma—and you."

"Strange how things work out. My mother picked the surname D'Angelo with the belief angels would guard us. Turns out divine intervention *did* come—in the unlikely form of Ruth Kenefsky."

"Ruth *is* an angel. Now that she's saved my nephew, I feel obligated to keep her in Häagen-Dazs for the rest of her life."

Ryan chuckled. "She likes ice cream?"

"She has an insatiable lust."

"Then count me in. I'll foot the bill for her Häagen-Dazs from now until eternity." He'd do much more, in fact. From what he'd learned, Ruth didn't have children.

Didn't everyone deserve angelic intervention now and again? From here on out, he'd do his bit by protecting Ruth.

"Actually, you *can* keep her in Häagen-Dazs, easily," Frances said. He took a seat before the desk, and Frances opened a drawer. With ceremony, she placed a bank check in front of him. "This is for you."

The check was drawn on an account at Liberty Trust. Intrigued, Ryan read swiftly.

With disbelief, he set the check aside.

When he couldn't find his voice, Frances laughed. "Don't spend it all in one place." A hint of devilry lit her hazel eyes. "There's a stunning brick mansion at the other end of Highland you might wish to investigate. The Dolans have wanted to sell for years. Both of their children are grown, and they'd like to downsize. Cat will never tell you as much, but the Dolan mansion is one of her favorite homes in Sweet Lake. I suspect she'd rather move in there than her old bedroom at her parents' house. You haven't forgotten that she and Jada are moving out of the south wing soon, have you?"

From the front of the house, Cat's voice sang out. "Hello? Where is everyone?"

"Well. Off we go." Frances pushed out of the chair.

Ryan found the presence of mind to point at the check. "Now, hold on. We're not going anywhere until you explain."

"About the check? Why, it's from your grandparents. When you and my sister disappeared, I was left in charge of your inheritance. I invested the money in quality stocks—Fortune 500 companies, mostly, but tech stocks too. Last week, I closed the accounts and cashed out."

"Frances, this is just shy of one million dollars."

She shimmied her fashionably clad shoulders. "I did rather well, didn't I? Not that I'll take all the credit—my late husband taught me a thing or two about the stock market. Lucky for you, I was a good student." She came around the desk, pinched his cheek. "You know, there's a sweet little house that's just come on the market—Tilda has the listing. A two-bedroom bungalow down the street from Jada's parents. It's darling." She gave him a meaningful look. "I doubt anyone's mentioned Ruth's place to you. It's a wonder the roof hasn't come down on her head."

The chance to help Ruth brought him out of his stupor. "I'll call Tilda ASAP."

"Will you also look at the Dolan place?"

He nodded. "Sure thing."

The devilry in her eyes increased. "Do you need the name of a good jeweler? Oh, and please don't hire a wedding planner. Let me and Silvia do the honors."

"I haven't asked Cat any life-altering questions—not that I wouldn't like to. I'm waiting for the right moment." He got to his feet. "Besides, her father says the glue binding your friendship with Silvia is flammable. Does your offer to plan the wedding come with a fire extinguisher?"

"I suppose so." She picked up the check, waved it before his nose. She nodded with satisfaction when he slipped it into his wallet.

Cat strolled in with Gemma.

"Hey, bro," Gemma said.

"Hey, little sister." In less than two weeks, they'd slipped into the easy camaraderie of siblings. "How's school?"

"I'm flunking calculus."

"Don't ask me for help. I barely scraped by."

Cat slipped her hand into Ryan's. "Ryan, you look like someone hit you with a two-by-four," she said. "What were you and Frances talking about?"

❧

Near the northern end of Walnut Grove Memorial Gardens, the simple granite stone, flush with the grass, marked the grave of George Hunt.

Ryan and Gemma, each with their separate reasons, hung back. Leaving them where they stood in the dappled light, Cat approached the grave. When she reached George's resting place, she laid the small bouquet of daisies she'd purchased this morning beside the stone.

She glanced back at Frances appreciatively. "I still can't believe you took care of this."

An air of melancholy followed the elderly Siren as she slipped off her pumps and came slowly across the grass. "I can't excuse his behavior, but he *was* Ryan's father—and Gemma's. I did this for their sakes more than anything else."

"Will you tell Julia?"

"Someday, perhaps. Not soon. At the moment, I'm more interested in helping my sister come through her bout of depression."

"If you hadn't offered, what would the authorities have done with him?"

Frances withdrew a handkerchief from her purse, patted her brow. "I'm sure I don't want to know."

On further consideration, Cat didn't either. In the aftermath of the terrifying events at the inn, while the police interviewed everyone involved over a series of days and news of the attack by a drifter blared on news stations across Ohio, Frances had quietly petitioned a local judge for release of the body and made funeral arrangements. Although she owed George Hunt nothing but her contempt, she'd provided for a graveside service. The only other people in attendance had been Cat's parents.

Cat nodded at the stone. "Ryan and Gemma aren't the only ones who have mixed feelings about him. I do too." The admission put a lump in her throat.

"Because he *is* Ryan's father?" Frances asked. "Ryan wouldn't exist without him. A diamond wrought from a common element."

"Julia swears Ryan takes after you. I agree. He's certainly gentle like you. And elegant."

Frances swatted away the compliment, which clearly pleased her. "You haven't seen my sister at her best. Not yet. It's a fair assessment that the bulk of Ryan's decency comes from her."

At last Ryan and Gemma approached. They both seemed determined not to look at the grave. "Speaking of sisters," Ryan said to his aunt, "you never did tell us the origin of the tokens."

"You have your Grandmother Brugnet to thank for them. She was a self-taught naturalist, always dragging her flock of daughters into the woods. When Julia and I were barely school age, she taught us how to make necklaces out of acorns, tiny stones—we incorporated the shells later, after a family trip to the Bahamas."

"And the feathers?"

Frances toyed with the pearl earring dangling from her ear. "That was all me. I've always loved birds. There's something magical about a creature living in defiance of gravity. Instructive too. One of the most difficult lessons we learn is how to soar—above our doubts and perceived failings, beyond the abilities we believe limit us."

She broke off suddenly to canvass the three sets of eyes trained on her, all of which were damp. "Listen to me, prattling on like I'm deep into my second sherry. Why don't we say a prayer for the wretched soul lying here, and be on our way?"

Chapter 29

Leaving a trail of crumbs in her wake, Linnie dropped into the chair by the window. "Call Goodwill, ASAP," she quipped. "For your sake, I hope they make house calls."

Cat reached into the closet. "In lieu of eating cookies, you could help me pack." She pulled out a handful of dresses, hangers and all.

"No thanks. It's more fun watching you fill garbage bags with a decade's worth of fashion. Should I call Silvia, warn her that she'll need to make room in the garage? There's no way she's expecting you to haul this much crap into your childhood bedroom."

"I'll make everything fit. It's not like I'm staying with my parents forever."

"You ought to follow Ryan's lead, and move into Frances's place. She has enough extra rooms to compete with the Wayfair."

The idea was tempting, if unrealistic. With November approaching, Frances was busier than ever. Twice a week, she drove Julia to a therapist forty minutes outside Sweet Lake. She'd also rearranged her beautiful library, bringing in an extra desk and filing cabinets for Ryan's use. For the last three weeks, he'd been splitting his time between his house in Cincinnati, which was now on the market, and Frances's home.

What he planned long term, Cat wasn't sure. An apartment in Sweet Lake? A place big enough for them both? She would've begun dropping hints about living together if not for the other pressures dominating his time. Between helping Frances care for his mother, catching up at Adworks, and showing his house, Ryan's days were full.

Jada came in. "You're still packing? I finished an hour ago." She noticed Linnie, busy cramming the last bits of evidence into her mouth. "Damn it, Linnie—I don't have time to make another batch of raisin-oatmeal cookies. Do I need to banish you from the kitchen, or what?"

"I only took one," Linnie muttered. Jada regarded her with disbelief, and she added, "Okay, I took three."

"It's official. You're banished." Having issued a declaration they all knew was unenforceable, Jada stalked to the closet. Impatiently she pulled out three dresses. "Here's the rule, Cat. If you haven't worn a dress in the last year, donate it. How many glam outfits do you have in here? If you're too cheap to hand clothes off to Goodwill, you're just plain pathetic."

"Take that back. I'm not cheap!"

"You have a shopping addiction. Seek help." Jada plunged into the closet. She came back out with the striped steel-blue-and-cream dress Cat had purchased nearly eight years ago, the same week she opened her events company on Sweet Lake Circle. "Man, does this bring back memories. Cat channeling a businesswoman motif. This frock is ug-lee."

Cat snatched the dress, tossed it on the bed. "I was such a dope back then. Opening a business before I was ready—"

"—closing shop early most days to date whatever hot body came along." The laughter Jada attempted to hold in rippled across her shoulders. She mimed a serious expression. "It's okay. You were young. We forgive you."

Linnie flicked crumbs to the floor. "But only because you've found Ryan. Why don't you get down on bended knee and tell him you'd like to make the relationship permanent?"

"Gosh, let me ponder that one. Because it's too soon?"

"It's only too soon if you're not ready."

"Like you should give her advice," Jada said tartly.

"My situation with Daniel is different."

"Says you."

They were perilously close to bickering. Cutting in, Cat said, "I *am* ready."

The pronouncement silenced her friends. Ditching the mirth, Jada neared. "Honest?"

"If Ryan asked tomorrow, I'd say yes. I'm the first one to admit I spend too much time doubting myself, wondering if I can succeed in my job, wondering if I'm too much of a lightweight or gullible or stupidly optimistic—but I am sure. That night, with his father . . . I keep replaying it over in my head. How frightened I was, and George taking aim at Ryan. What if I'd lost Ryan? What if . . . ?"

"Hey, you didn't lose him. Everything worked out fine."

"Not everything," Cat replied, her voice catching. "Julia's worse now than ever. It's hard for Ryan. Me too."

Linnie joined them. "Depression is manageable. Julia will get better. Just give it time."

From the doorway, someone cleared her throat.

Apparently sensing the gloomy atmosphere, Gemma sent a fleeting glance toward the hallway. "Did I drop by at a bad time?"

"Of course not," Cat assured her. She prayed Gemma hadn't overheard the discussion. Since George's death, she was no more inclined to discuss the events of that night than Ryan.

They weren't ready, not yet.

Jada, who'd become as protective of the college student as Cat and Linnie, arched a brow. "Gemma, how does one just stop by when she lives, oh, four hours away?"

"Keep dropping in unannounced, and I'll put you to work," Linnie added.

Gemma perked up. "Will you? Hire me, I mean."

"Um, I was joking."

"Sure. Not like I can work for you right now, with school and all. What about next summer? Frances says I can stay at her house whenever I like."

The eager reply boosted Cat's spirits. *Family is about the people we choose to hold close in our lives.* It mattered little to Frances that Ryan's half sister wasn't her relation. She considered her family now.

Linnie smiled. "Send me your resume," she told Gemma, and rattled off her e-mail address.

Together the women finished packing the suite by late afternoon. They went out to the veranda to sip mugs of hot chocolate and enjoy the fall colors. After living at the Wayfair for the better part of a decade, Cat knew that she and Jada were not eager to leave for their respective parents' homes. Soon the renovations would begin, bringing to a close the era when three friends shared the south wing—and the audacious hope they could save the Wayfair from going under.

Not audacious, she mused. They were well on their way.

The sun was sinking behind the trees when Ryan pulled into the parking lot. Cat set her mug aside and met him by his car.

"I thought you were staying in Cincinnati tonight," she said. "This is a nice surprise."

"Changed my mind at the last minute. Frances is making goulash for dinner. Want to join us?"

"Sure."

He swung his briefcase from hand to hand in an apparent case of nerves. She was about to ask if he'd encountered a problem at work today when he noticed his sister on the veranda.

"Gemma, what are you doing here? Keep goofing off, and you *will* flunk calculus."

She came down the steps. "I'll head back to school soon."

"Aren't you taking advantage of your roommate?" He leaned in, gave her a peck on the cheek. "I hate to ask. How many miles are you putting on her car?"

The light criticism sent Gemma's gaze to her feet. "The truth? Too many. I *am* saving for my own wheels. If I nail down a job for Christmas break, I'll have close to three thou saved."

"I'll make you a deal. Bank three grand by January, and I'll match it." He reconsidered. "Scratch that. Come up with three, and I'll pitch in seven. Doubtful we'll find you a safe car for under ten thou."

"Ryan, I can't take your money."

"I'm your brother, and you can. And don't ask your parents to pitch in—they've done enough bankrolling your KSU tuition."

Immediately Cat caught his drift. "You have three younger brothers, kiddo. One day sooner than you realize, your parents will need to get them through school too."

Ryan gave Cat a soulful look, dragged his hand through his raven locks. "So." He glanced toward the Beemer, then back at her. "What do you say we go for a drive?"

"Anywhere in particular?"

"How about the other end of Frances's street? I want to see the Dolan place. My aunt says it's a beaut."

He *was* nervous. Happy to play along, Cat sprinted to the veranda for her purse. A drive meant time alone to discuss important topics. Like moving in together?

They were halfway around Sweet Lake Circle when Ryan pulled the car to the curb. Scanning the empty picnic tables in the center green, he began drumming his hands on the steering wheel.

"We aren't driving down Highland?" Absently Cat watched a Ford pickup cruise by.

"In a sec." He stopped drumming, slid her a quick glance. "The other day, in Frances's library—I didn't tell you what we discussed."

"I assumed you were discussing your mother's care."

"No, Frances filled me in on my inheritance."

This got Cat's full attention. "Frances gave you an inheritance?"

"It's from my grandparents. She's been managing the funds. The money got me thinking."

"About us?"

"Yes."

Cat's heart leapt into her throat. "Yes," she replied eagerly.

Blinking, Ryan looked at her fully. "What?"

Her heart promptly fell to stomach. "Oops." She cringed. "Ryan, I'm a total idiot. I thought you were about to . . ."

Humiliated, she sank into herself as he cut the engine. The driver's-side door swung open. Ryan moved quickly around the hood, opened her door, and guided her out. The moment she was on her feet, he sank to one knee.

Without thinking, she followed his descent, until they were both on their knees. Was this a panic attack? She reached for him, to pull him up and lead him to a picnic table.

The expression on his face stopped her. "Cat," he remarked soberly, but his eyes sparkled, "there are lots of reasons why I love you, but your goofiness may top the list. Are you going to let me do this or not?"

The husky promise in his voice evaporated the humiliation scalding her skin. Elation followed. "Are you . . . ?"

"Yes."

"Then my answer still stands."

For proof she flung herself into his arms. Then she flinched as a car whizzed past.

Steering her up, Ryan chuckled. "We're in the street. This will make an interesting story for our children." He led her to the curb.

"Our children? You *are* moving fast."

"Don't you want any?"

"Sure I do." She moved into his arms, hungry for a kiss. "May I have a wedding first?"

"Oh, yeah. The perfect wedding of your dreams." He hesitated. "And a house."

302

"You don't mean the Dolan place? Ryan, it's huge. We can't afford—"

"Yes, we can," he said, cutting her off. In his eyes, she glimpsed their bright future. "I hear they're ready to sell. Looking forward to downsizing."

She opened her mouth only to discover her voice was gone.

Which didn't seem to bother Ryan in the least as he kissed her.

Acknowledgments

WITH HEARTFELT THANKS

To my wonderful editor, Kelli Martin, for believing in the Sweet Lake concept from the outset.

To my agent, Pamela Harty, for her generous advice.

To my developmental editor, Krista Stroever, for all her brilliant suggestions; my copyeditor, Irene Billings, my production editor, Sara Addicott, and my proofreader, Kirsten Colton, for both their patience and their careful edit; my author relations manager, Gabriella Dumpit, for guiding me through the publication process; and the talented Rachel Adam, for her lovely cover art for the books in the Sweet Lake series.

To Alan Rapoport, for answering legal questions in a pinch, and my author assistant, Marlie Ahola, for handling far too many tasks each time I ducked into the writing cave.

To Loreen Potvin, Linda Weber, Erin Finigan, Gail Demaree, and Joy A. Lorton for offering suggestions and catching errors during the manuscript's early stages of development.

To Barry, for reading every review throughout the years and believing even when I entertained doubts. I love you, always.

ABOUT THE AUTHOR

Photo © 2016 Melissa Miley Photography

Award-winning author Christine Nolfi writes heartwarming and inspiring fiction. She is the author of *Treasure Me*, a Next Generation Indie Awards finalist; the Liberty Series novels; and *Sweet Lake*, her first book in the Sweet Lake series. A native Ohioan, Christine currently resides in South Carolina with her husband and four adopted children. For the latest information about her releases and future books, visit www.christinenolfi.com. Chat with her on Twitter @christinenolfi.